P9-CMK-707
RICHMOND HILL
PUBLIC LIBRARY
FEB 2 6 2014
CENTRAL LIBRARY
905-884-9288

PILLAR TO THE SKY

Book by William R. Forstchen from Tom Doherty Associates

We Look Like Men of War

One Second After

Pillar to the Sky

RICHMOND HILL
PUBLIC LIBRARY

CENTRAL
BOOK

PILLAR TO THE SKY

William R. Forstchen

BOOK SOLD
NO LONGER R.H.P.L.
PROPERTY

A TOM DOHERTY ASSOCIATES BOOK
NEW YORK

This is a work of fiction. All of the characters, organizations, and events portrayed in this novel are either products of the author's imagination or are used fictitiously.

PILLAR TO THE SKY

Copyright © 2014 by William Forstchen

All rights reserved.

Mention of "Novus Magnificat: Through the Stargate" and "Sanctum Sanctorum" by permission of Constance Demby. Find her online at www.constancedemby.com.

A Tor Book
Published by Tom Doherty Associates, LLC
175 Fifth Avenue
New York, NY 10010

www.tor-forge.com

Tor® is a registered trademark of Tom Doherty Associates, LLC.

Library of Congress Cataloging-in-Publication Data

Forstchen, William R.
Pillar to the sky / William R. Forstchen. — First Edition.
p. cm.
ISBN 978-0-7653-3438-1 (hardcover)
ISBN 978-1-4668-1077-8 (e-book)
I. Title.
PS3556.O7418P55 2014
813'.54—dc23

2013025945

Tor books may be purchased for educational, business, or promotional use. For information on bulk purchases, please contact Macmillan Corporate and Premium Sales Department at 1-800-221-7945, extension 5442, or write specialmarkets@macmillan.com.

First Edition: February 2014

Printed in the United States of America

0 9 8 7 6 5 4 3 2 1

There are so many I wish I could dedicate this work to and the choosing has been hard. The first is to my mentors, such an interesting concept, that of a mentor, thinking of that ancient bit of wisdom that when a teacher is needed one will be found. And thus this dedication to Betty Keller, librarian at Hightstown High School, and Russ Beaulieu, history teacher who shaped my life at such a crucial and sensitive time. And, of course, Gunther Rothenberg of Purdue University, what a blessing it was on the day you came into my life.

A dedication must go out as well to all those who inspired the dreams of my youth, the team at NASA who shaped a belief in my young heart that the greatest adventures were still ahead of us.

ACKNOWLEDGMENTS

It has become almost pro forma that when I think of who to acknowledge when a book is done, the thought always forms that for any author, we build our dream castles on the works of those who have gone before us, and those who help and shape what I work on now as a writer.

Up front is the team at Tor/Forge. A long time ago, in a galaxy far, far away, I was a new author with my first paperback book, the new kid on the block invited to a publishers party at a legendary Boscon. (For those not sure what that was, Boscon was a sci-fi convention in Boston.) It was there that I first met Tom Doherty and left that party with a desire if ever there was a publisher I hoped to some day work with it was Tom and his team. My expectations were one day fulfilled and far exceeded. Tom has shaped this business for over fifty years, and I am honored to say I am a member of "his house." Part of that Doherty team are editors like Bob Gleason, with special thanks to the patience of Whitney Ross, Linda Quinton, and so many others. The mechanics of creating a book far exceed what you, good reader, find on the shelf; it is a team effort and without such people like Tom and those with him, you would not be reading this. (But I must add, you are certainly dedicated if you are reading this acknowledgments rather than just digging straight into the book.) If the book works for you, know that the Tor/Forge folks made it happen, and I will take the heat if it does not work!

When Bob Gleason called me with what I thought was an off-the-wall idea, "Would you be interested in working in cooperation with NASA," I actually thought he was joking. NASA? My heroes want me to work with them? It was like asking a kid if he wanted a free pass to Disney World, and the results have been such a wonderful adventure. So thanks, Bob, for that call.

And then to my agent, Eleanor Wood. We've been together for over twenty-five years. I am blessed that Eleanor is not just an agent but a friend I can always count on for guidance. Thanks as well to Josh Morris of Content House and to Joanne McLaughlin, for all the times when people have overlooked the good you have done, where credit never came, know you have made a difference.

The fear with writing acknowledgments is missing someone important, while at the same time worrying about dragging it out into a half dozen pages like the ramblings of some Hollywood type on Academy Awards night. Bill Butterworth, who some know as W. E. B. Griffin IV, was my editor long ago when I was writing short stories for *Boys' Life,* that realm where heroes such as Heinlein, Bradbury, and others first ignited my dreams of space exploration. A tough editor and always a darn good guide and to this day always a good friend. I must mention as well other guides such as Professors Gordon Mork and Dave Flory of Purdue, Tom Seay of Kutztown University, and my ever-patient administrators at Montreat College, where I have been blessed to teach in what is now my twentieth year. My comrades in flying, Don Barber, Danny McMullen, and Brandon NeSmith, who taught me how to handle my beloved Aeronca L3, should be mentioned as well. I think in reading the book you'll see that flying is definitely in my blood. And, of course, Jeff Ethell. If St. Pete hands out P-51 Mustangs when you cross through the pearly gates rather than wings, I am certain you received one, Jeff. Our last flight together still haunts my dreams. A warm mention as well of heartfelt gratitude to Robin Shoemaker, who already offers so much inspiration and hope.

This book was the fruition of an idea first hatched by Tom Doherty and some NASA personnel long years ago to again merge those of us in science fiction with the team that does the real stuff and to try to tell their story. The days spent at Goddard when first kicking around the idea for this book were a whirlwind of conversations, "what ifs," a coming together of dreamers such as me in the realm of both novels and also my background as an historian, teaming up with the men and women who actually crunch the numbers and by the thousands worked in the background to put us on the moon and most recently a high-tech rover on Mars. Others might sail the ships of the future, but without the team at Goddard and our other NASA facilities, we never would have gotten off the ground. I believe our future renewal as a vibrant force for good and the protecting of our environment for future generations really does rest in their hands, hearts, and brilliant minds.

Regarding what some will see as a leap of faith, that a space elevator is already within the realm of hard science, I hope this book just might serve as a booster to their hard efforts. Granted it is fiction, but it is fiction based on reality. This historian, who specialized in the history of technology, learned that so many of the dreamers of the past such as Hypatia of Alexandria, Galileo, and Newton, engineers like Brunel and the Roeblings faced mocking criticism only to be hailed later as the guides to the future. The legendary Arthur C. Clarke, mentor for a whole generation of young emerging authors, in his seminal work *The Fountains of Paradise* first presented to me the idea of a "space tower," a "Pillar to the Sky." Even that visionary believed in the 1970s that the technology to build one was two hundred years away. Sir Arthur, you were right in so many other dreams, but technological innovation has compressed that timeline from two hundred years to just thirty years since you finished your work. Though I've written a novel, I drew my research on the here and now and fervently pray that some, after reading this book, will say, "We can do this now!" And in so doing truly open up space while also addressing so many problems confronting us here on Earth. A space elevator might very well be The answer to the problems confronting us in this second decade of the twenty-first century. What a dream for this author if *Pillar to the Sky* helps to ignite interest in the subject and inspire brave new innovators who will see it happen not a hundred years hence but within the next decade or two.

The best days can indeed still be ahead of us and thus in closing an acknowledgment to my wonderful daughter, Meghan, who has shown such patience across the years when her father promises something but then has to say, "Just let me finish this chapter first." This book is for her because if it actually serves to shape her world for the better, to lay in its grave once and for all that dystrophic tome *The Limits to Growth*, and helps in some small way to fire the dream that a better future is ahead, I will most certainly be content.

So in closing, yes, it is a novel. But it is also a dream that can become a reality, for to paraphrase the legendary Goddard, the dreams of today can indeed become the realities of tomorrow.

It is difficult to say what is impossible, for the dream of yesterday is the hope of today and the reality of tomorrow.

—Dr. Robert H. Goddard

The progressive development of man is vitally dependent on invention.

—Nikola Tesla

I believe that we are children picking up pebbles on the shore of the boundless sea.

—John Stevens, engineer, Panama Canal

PILLAR TO THE SKY

PROLOGUE

"Dr. Morgan, and Dr. Petrenko, with all due respect to your academic credentials, your proposal for this space tower—or Pillar, as some call it—is absurd."

Senator Proxley, head of the Senate committee that had oversight of NASA's budget, looked to his left and right for support from the other senators present. Nearly half the chairs were empty, and of those present most just looked off as if bored and waiting for the meeting to come to its inevitable end so that they could rush off to what they felt were far more important affairs, either of state or personal.

"In these times of economic stress, of towering deficits and public demand for budget cutbacks"—he paused for effect—"pipe-dream schemes that are a waste of taxpayers' money are utterly absurd and, frankly, a waste of *my* time as a senator who believes in fiscal responsibility."

He cast a sidelong glance at one of his staffers who was recording his comments for later distribution, since even C-SPAN had decided not to cover this hearing. He cleared his throat and continued.

"I find it disturbing that such a proposal even reached this level and was not terminated by the proper administrators in your program, and believe me, I shall question them about that after this hearing. We are facing the worse deficit crisis in our nation's history. If I approved continued research funding for this sci-fi fantasy, let alone the insanity to actually go ahead and build it, I can only imagine the howls of protest from my constituents and every other taxpayer. I agree NASA should continue as a government entity, but let it set realistic goals and not allow this type of idea to worm its way up through the budget proposal. I know it has been popular with some to praise the recent mission to Mars, but even with that I ask: Why do we spend more than a billion to go explore a lifeless rock when that same billion could be better spent here on earth, solving a multitude of problems rather than being wasted out there?"

Dr. Gary Morgan threw a quick look at his wife, Evgeniya Petrenko Morgan. It was an attempt to warn her not to lose her temper now. She could be tough as nails when angered and at such moments would often slip into her native Ukrainian, which—given the current cold feelings between America and Russia—would only make matters worse, since few knew the difference between the two languages.

They both knew beforehand what they would be facing here at this hearing, which was not even a remote chance of success. They were the "sacrificial goat of the day" receiving a dressing-down at the hands of one of the country's fiercest opponents of any expansion of space exploration beyond the bare minimum to keep the program alive. There had been some hope of increased research budgets after the stunning success of the Mars *Curiosity* touchdown and its continuing mission, which he had just pointedly denigrated. But that enthusiasm, which so many supporters had hoped would renew support for the space program, had proven to be short-lived with yet another oil crisis pushing the price of the precious black gold up over $150 a barrel, the threat of yet another war in the Middle East, and all the other issues that had plagued and continued to plague humanity.

It was an inside joke that if only NASA could figure out how to use corn and milk to fuel its spacecraft, they'd have Proxley's vote, as he was from a midwestern state that did not have a single NASA facility and thus could target it with impunity.

Gary's wife caught his gaze, took a deep breath, and nodded for him to go ahead.

"Senator Proxley . . ." Gary looked down at his notepad and fumbled for a moment. He had never been much of a public speaker, except when debating with the "inner circle" of teammates at NASA's Goddard Space Flight Center. In that environment he could hold forth for hours on this "special project" that he and his wife had worked on for over two decades, scraping by each year on a minimal budget buried inside another budget for "advanced research and development." Their dream was a space tower, or "elevator," that would reach from the equator to geosynchronous orbit, 23,000 miles above the earth. At first glance it did indeed seem like a mad scheme, but the science was there to prove it had long ago migrated from the realm of science fiction to that of scientific possibility in the same way that other dreams—to reach the moon, to cross the Atlantic by plane, even to just fly or move a ship without oars or sails—had long ago started out as dreams.

However, this year Proxley had singled out their particular dream for this one-hour grilling, bestowing on it his infamous "Golden Fleece Award," which he announced each month as some example of absurd government extravagance (usually money spent on building projects like "bridges to nowhere" or museums for teapots, or why some people are left-handed), and at least a couple times a year he aimed his sarcasm at NASA.

Thus the absolute shock of several weeks earlier when one of the top administrators at Goddard called them into her office and, with genuine sympathy, informed them that their budget would be "zeroed" at the end of the fiscal year—which is to say, at the end of the month—and then handed them notice that they were to appear before a Senate hearing on the subject of NASA's budget. The subtext: for the "good of the service" they could defend their program, but there was no chance it would be defended by anyone higher up the "food chain."

It was heartbreaking, but both Gary and Evgeniya understood. They were loyal to NASA, which had quietly nursed along their dream—had even helped to arrange some grants nearly a decade ago to test possible propulsion systems for "tower climbers"—but in the larger struggle to stay alive, they would have to be "let go." There were even some tears as Evgeniya and the administrator—old friends with daughters the same age and attending the same high school—chatted over tea after the hard news had been delivered.

Gary paused, looking at Proxley. He was the classic example of the bureaucrat, forever the opponent of the inventor. One was an idealist, a believer, a "doer" of dreams, transforming them into realities that could change a world . . . the other was a naysayer, holder of the public purse strings, forever drawing them tighter unless the loosening of them would directly benefit him. NASA, of course, had no professional lobbyist whispering into Proxley's ear, with fat campaign contributions promised for the right kind of vote. The great industrial powerhouses that first made America the aviation innovator of the world, then the preeminent explorer of space—those once enterprising firms were barely hanging on in these economic times and in turn had to devote their efforts to more immediately profitable and less ambitious projects; for them, the prospect of a space tower was not on the table.

Gary knew they should just fold their cards, yield the rest of the time allotted to their reply, and leave. But he could not let it go. After twenty years of effort, he felt they had the right to make a final statement.

Gary shuffled his papers, nervously brushed back the strands of slightly graying hair from his forehead, then looked straight at Senator Proxley. As he gazed at this man, he felt his frustration and anger rising.

"Senator," he began. "Ten years after its completion, this project has the potential of transforming the global economy and in so doing give our country a preeminent economic position for the rest of this century in much the same way as Apollo, by putting Americans on the moon, also triggered a technological revolution right here on earth, fueled our economic growth for the next thirty years. That cell phone in your pocket has more computing power in it than the computer that guided Armstrong and Aldrin to the moon. Sir, where do you think much of the initial research and development came from for that in the first place? It started in the 1960s when NASA said it needed compact computers to get us to the moon. No one then was thinking of cell phones, the GPS in your car, the myriad of medical tools that we take for granted today, but they had a start, and that start was with NASA. Just the research for a space tower can open fields of endeavor that will revolutionize our technology base yet again with innovations not yet dreamed of.

"This project . . ." He paused, faltering, but his wife gently nudged him under the table to press on. "This project is not some ill-conceived flight of fantasy like those we see in far too many government proposals, which either deservedly get filed away and forgotten or become public embarrassments after they are attempted, when they fall flat, with cost overruns in the tens of billions of dollars."

He was tempted to cite a few examples of programs that Proxley had supported in the past but knew better than to do so. To try to embarrass his opponent would serve no purpose now.

"The project to build what some call a space elevator and our team calls a 'Pillar to the Sky' has undergone rigorous review, not just within NASA, but outside our community as well. Try to imagine an America in 1880 without a transcontinental railroad, an America of the 1920s without Henry Ford or Charles Lindbergh, an America of today without the Internet linking the world via communications satellites put up there by who else but NASA in the first place. This will have the same impact."

He felt he had gained his stride after being knocked off-balance by Proxley's scathing comments, and there was a touch of anger in his voice now. He held up the economic impact report supporting the building of a space tower, then looked around the room and saw that of all those facing him, only one had a copy on her desk: Mary Dennison of Maine, who subtly pointed to her copy of the report and, with a sad smile, just nodded an acknowledgment. Taking the gesture to be encouragement, he pressed on.

He took a deep breath, his nervousness gone.

"This project, within ten years after completion, will make the deficit our country now struggles with a thing of the past. It offers a future of limitless growth, Senator, by truly opening up space and all that it can offer us—not the dead end we are approaching now. If we can thus boost our economic growth by but a few additional percentage points a year, within that decade the deficit that terrifies us now will become manageable again and in two decades seem almost trivial. We faced an equally staggering debt at the end of World War II when compared to our total national production, but the economic boom that came in the decade after—because of all the new technologies we had developed to save the world from tyranny—wiped that debt clean. This could do the same, sir.

"Instead, at this moment we are still drilling for oil, the cost of which is becoming more prohibitive each day; we are scrambling for ever dwindling resources, ignoring the fact that as the rest of the world—especially China and India—strive to achieve our economic level, they are also triggering a global economic and environmental crisis. We must face that reality, sir. We are plunging headlong toward a dead end—a dead end economically, certainly, but an environmental dead end on a global scale as well. This project offers an answer far better than what we now do: plunder food crops covering entire states just to produce a trickle of fuel in an effort to stave off the inevitable. We are trading food production for fuel in order to keep the wheels turning just a little bit longer. How long can we do continue to do that in practice? And with an ever expanding global population, how long can we continue to do that *morally*?"

Gary's ally Dennison shook her head at that comment, but since he already knew they were defeated, he didn't really care. Proxley, from a farm state, of course heavily supported subsidies for such food to fuel projects running into the billions. He wanted to add that if Proxley would at least allow them to limp along with just a few million more for research and development, afterward he'd work on a way to try to turn corn into rocket fuel. For that matter, even milk could be turned into alcohol if you allowed it to sour, then drew off the whey and fermented it, then distilled it into burnable fuel. The only drawback to that scheme was that the hundreds of millions of gallons of curdled milk would not be pleasant to work with.

He knew that would bring the house down—become the quote line of the day if anyone in the media ever bothered to even cover this other than Proxley's assistant, who had pointedly turned his camera off while Gary replied; but he had too many friends still with NASA who might suffer an even greater backlash, so he fell silent but remained defiant as he stared at Proxley.

"Your pie-in-the-sky figures, like everything else in this report . . ." Proxley said, grimacing with disdain as he held up the five-hundred-page general report on the construction of a "space tower." His assistant had switched his camera back on in time to record the senator dismissively tossing the document aside so that it slid off the table and crashed to the floor. This symbolic act made Evgeniya and Gary wince with surprise at such rudeness.

"To be frank, sir"—Proxley's tone became harsh—"I have far more pressing matters than to remain here listening to yet another unrealistic proposal. This is a waste of my time and taxpayers' money, sir. I see no reason whatsoever to amend the budget for NASA as currently presented."

He offered an ironic smile.

"I was willing to convene this committee to at least hear by what logic your program was allowed to survive as long as it did. Now I am absolutely convinced we are doing the right thing by sending the budget proposal back on to the floor, with programs such as yours deleted. Therefore, with the approval of my esteemed colleagues, I excuse myself from these proceedings to attend to more important matters."

Without further comment, Proxley stood and headed for the door, his aides scrambling to pick up the piles of paperwork, stuffing them into briefcases, and falling in behind him.

As Proxley made his way down the aisle toward the exit, Gary Morgan, Ph.D. in astrophysics and engineering, and Evgeniya Petrenko Morgan, Ph.D. in aerospace engineering, remained seated, their eyes fixed on the retreating form.

The dream was over and they had lost.

"What would you have said to Columbus?" someone shouted.

Gary and his wife, called "Eva" by her friends and colleagues, recognized the voice and looked to the back of the room, Eva broke into a smile but Gary just froze; he did not even know that their sixteen-year-old daughter, Victoria, who was on her feet, had somehow managed to slip into the hearing room. Savvy with regard to all things computerized, she had most likely forged some sort of pass and ID to get in—typical of her, Gary thought, with a touch of pride, but he feared what his fiery young daughter might now say in righteous wrath at her parents being treated in such a manner. Victoria was gangly and tall at almost six foot, like both her parents, and pushed a lock of blond hair back from over her eyeglasses as she stepped out into the aisle to block the senator.

Gary actually started to stand up and call to her to stop, but Eva reached out, grabbing his arm and smiling.

"That's our girl; let her have her say," she said.

"She definitely has your temper," he whispered.

"Damn right she does," Eva replied in Ukrainian.

Proxley slowed.

"Are you talking to me, young lady?" He said it with a bit of a threatening edge, reminding Gary of a famous line from an old movie.

Gary could not help but smile. The senator might be used to the game of intimidation, but he had never tangled with this young lady when her blood was up.

"Yes, I am talking to you!" She hesitated just long enough to sound ironic when she added one more word: "Sir."

She pressed forward, not budging an inch to get out of Proxley's way.

"Senator Proxley, what would you have said to Columbus and Magellan?"

There was no mainstream media covering this hearing; for all practical purposes, like a tree falling unheard in a forest, it didn't exist, except for a few pro-space Internet bloggers who were holding up iPads to catch the exchange. Proxley looked at them from the corners of his eyes. Such things could go viral and without doubt he was thinking that beating up on a skinny teenage girl who had just witnessed the taking down of her parents might not be good press.

He forced an indulgent smile.

"If history serves me right," Proxley replied, "Columbus was convinced he had reached China, his so-called discovery an accident which then resulted in the deaths of millions of Native Americans. And as for Magellan, nine out of ten who sailed with him died."

"But still they opened up an entire world and changed the stagnant economy of Europe to centuries of growth," Victoria fired back. "The tragedy of the native population of this land I concur with, sir, but the factor of disease was unknown in the sixteenth century. As for space sir, we do not face that moral problem."

"And at what price this progress?" Proxley said coldly. "The mess the entire world is in today, perhaps?"

Gary realized Proxley was maneuvering the argument into one of colonialism, of guilt over the past hobbling the limitless potential of the future that he was utterly incapable of seeing along with the technophobia that was so ironic from those who denounced technology even as their lives depended on it. It was like trying to argue with a man stranded in the desert who was futilely digging in the sand for water, refusing to see or believe that just beyond the next ridge was a flowing river of plenty, which was indeed awaiting humanity just above the atmosphere.

"We are not debating the tragedies of colonialism, sir," Victoria replied sharply. "This meeting was about space exploration, which you are killing—a tragedy not just for our country but the entire world. You are ignoring the potential of opening up the universe for all humanity and the finding of resources to transform our world while bringing no harm to others."

Victoria's voice rose and squeaked a bit as she spoke, for after all, at sixteen she was tackling a United States senator of more than twenty years' experience, and he knew his game well.

"I admire your zeal for defending your parents, young lady," he said condescendingly. "I admire idealism in youth, even if misdirected and impolite at times. As for history, I think I do know a bit more than you; after all, I did major in it as an undergraduate. Might I urge you study that a bit more when you go to college"—he paused—"and perhaps a course on showing manners to your elders and elected representatives as well." There was a cutting edge of dismissal to his voice as he moved to step around her.

Victoria would not be diverted even as Proxley tried to move around her, a staffer having opened the door out of the hearing room while one oversize aide, more bodyguard than assistant, tried to move between the senator and Victoria, but she refused to budge. Gary was now on his feet, and there would have been an explosion on his part if the aide had touched his proud, defiant daughter.

"Now if you will excuse—"

She cut him off.

"No, I will not excuse you yet, sir," Victoria retorted. "As an American citizen I have a right to this conversation. I recall that the First Amendment states that I have a right to petition my government for redress and, sir, you have an obligation to listen. In fact, according to your own schedule and that of this committee, you should still be here for another hour."

Before he could reply, she fired the next question off.

"If you want to talk about history, Senator, what about the Roeblings, father and son, or Stevens and Goethals?"

Proxley hesitated. Gary grinned. She had caught him on that! He had no idea who she was referring to.

"Engineers, Senator. The Roeblings built the Brooklyn Bridge while Stevens and Goethals engineered the Panama Canal. They were told it was impossible but built them anyhow in spite of people like you. If men and women like them had listened to people like you, where would we be today? History is plagued by those like you, sir. *Plagued* by you."

Gary did wince a bit at that. Calling a senator a plague might not be the best of politics. As a NASA employee, he, of course, could never say it; but if called on the carpet about it in his exit interview, he could only shrug his shoulders and say, "Hey, I have a strong-willed daughter," and chances were there would be subtle smiles of agreement.

Proxley glared at her coldly.

He looked at Victoria's mother.

"May I suggest, madam, that in the future this young lady's education include some basic manners and proper etiquette."

And now Gary's wife, Eva, spoke. It was doubtful Proxley understood Ukrainian. Since everything was recorded, Proxley would without doubt get the translation later.

"Oh, yes," Proxley sniffed, "your Russian mother."

Gary looked at both his wife and daughter with an expression that urged them not to respond to that insult. No one ever called a Ukrainian a Russian, and he knew it was deliberate. "Given the current state of foreign affairs, I do find it curious you even have access to our facilities."

A brawl in front of a Senate committee hearing was definitely a bad career ender, so he put a restraining hand on Eva's arm and shot another restraining glance at his daughter, for she knew Ukrainian as well.

One of Proxley's aides, the one who opened the door, had a hand on the senator's shoulder to guide him—or perhaps drag him—out of the room, then looked back at Gary. Was there a glimpse of a smile, a subtle nod of agreement? The door closed with Proxley on the far side, leaving Victoria sputtering with ill-concealed rage.

Senator Dennison sighed and looked to her left and right at the empty chairs as the other senators—some nodding politely to Gary, others ignoring him—began to file out as well.

"Since we no longer have a quorum with the absence of Senator Proxley," she announced, "I must adjourn this meeting without a vote. I therefore declare this hearing to be closed."

Gary had failed. But that had been a foregone conclusion before they even walked into the room; his effort was no different from arranging deck chairs on the *Titanic* as it sank, and he knew that. At least his daughter had added a certain zest to it all at the very end.

Senator Dennison stood up, came around from behind her desk, and put a gentle, calming hand on Gary's shoulder.

"I'm sorry, I tried every way possible to get a quorum here to support you. I am so sorry for the three of you." As she spoke she flashed a warm smile at Victoria as if to say, *Masterful, young lady. Bravo!*

She looked around the room as the last of the few spectators left. A blogger took a moment to get a few comments from Victoria, before shutting down his iPad and leaving the room. They were alone.

"May I suggest you head back to Goddard? You have an old friend waiting for you there, and who knows"—she actually did seem to take on a mysterious air—"perhaps some new ones as well."

Though Dennison's home state of Maine did not benefit much from what little funding NASA still received, she was a woman with vision and held the belief that no matter how insurmountable the cascading series of crises facing America—diminishing energy supplies; valid environmental concerns about climate change due to worldwide pollution; the ever rising cries that America was tottering toward collapse—she believed that American know-how would, in the end, come through, and had placed her political chips on NASA. For years she had worked behind the scenes to ensure that at least some marginal funding for the agency was designated for what seemed like the dreams of today but could be the breakthroughs of tomorrow. In fact, only a tiny part of the agency's budget—less than a hundreth of a percentage point—went to Gary and Eva Morgan and the NASA Innovative Advanced Concepts division (NIAC).

Gary and Eva first met Senator Dennison a decade and a half earlier when they had been sent to Dennison's office, at the senator's request, to discuss their ideas and request funding for further research. That meeting had stretched longer than an hour and turned into an invitation to dinner at Dennison's modest apartment just a few blocks from Capitol Hill. The Morgans came prepared for some tough questioning, and "dinner" went on until one in the morning, and a bond had been formed.

Dennison had been an easy audience to reach. She had started out as a high school teacher of math, but—frustrated with the restraints of the education bureaucracy—she went on to do graduate work in engineering. Rather than return to the classroom, she came to the fundamental conclusion that if there was one thing Congress lacked, it was some members with a knowledge of the hard sciences. So she set out on a political career path with single-minded determination, first by getting elected to Congress and then moving on to a seat in the Senate. She played a critical role in preparing and protecting the nation's electronic infrastructure against the destructive potential of solar storms; pushed through support for the first maglev trains (the bill disappeared in another committee); and was at times all but a lone voice in the Senate to keep an ever-dwindling NASA alive as the nation struggled to somehow rein in its crippling debt load.

After hours of reviewing the Morgans' plans that night, she sat back and exclaimed, "Good heavens, I think your mad scheme will actually work.

I'll see that you at least get some money for continued research; not much, but enough to keep you two—soon to be three—alive."

Naively he had assumed that all was a done deal, and within the year work—real work—on building a tower would actually begin.

That was sixteen and a half years ago. Over those years the clock had ticked on and the climate continued to shift; whether due to man-made causes, a natural cycle, or a combination of both, the impacts were becoming more catastrophic. The debt had taken the nation to near bankruptcy. Conflict had escalated in the Middle East as energy production peaked, then began to dwindle as the world went to ever greater lengths to squeeze out an extra barrel amid escalating costs. A malaise seemed to be setting in as Americans began to feel that the days of their greatness had passed and would not come again.

And today Gary and Eva's plan for addressing these problems had come to an end.

"How is he doing by the way?"

Gary looked at Eva and they both smiled.

"Professor Rothenberg?" Gary paused. "Still going strong at ninety-two, but . . . he is ninety-two."

"That old character will outlast us all," Mary said with an understanding smile.

"And who knows?" she added, lowering her voice as if imparting a secret, "There might still be a surprise in the wings. He's famous for that, you know. My first visit to Goddard as a member of Congress . . ."

She sighed.

"We were still flying the Shuttle back then." She shook her head. "He was the one who showed me around. The old guy had me absolutely charmed even then. He's not one to give up, even now."

"What do you mean 'a surprise in the wings'?" Eva asked.

Mary shrugged, looking around as if to be certain no one was hiding in a corner of the room. Years of experience had taught her well that one never knew where an eavesdropper might lurk, recorder or just an iPhone in hand to catch every whispered word.

"Well, one never knows, and besides, even if I did not—and I am not saying I do—it is way outside my control now."

"Outside of your control . . . ?" Eva asked.

"Oh, call it classified for the moment," Mary replied. "And just know that, even though it looks like you lost the war today, there is no denying what happened here."

She looked back disdainfully at the empty chairs of the committee.

"NASA is still in for some hard times, and you two dear friends are out of work with that beloved agency in a few more weeks, your project tossed aside like so many other opportunities we've tossed aside in recent decades. But I predict it ain't over yet by a long shot. Just know that I'll be behind the scenes, even though your program has been cut."

"Thank you, Senator," Gary said.

"Come on, we're out of formal session: it's Mary."

She squeezed his shoulder and then looked at him with concern.

"How is your health?"

"Just fine, no problems."

She said nothing in reply, then looked around and smiled.

"That daughter of yours, she's a fighter. I like that."

He looked back to where his daughter waited patiently by the doorway.

"It's her world I want to help shape," he said. "We've pretty well had our game and not done so well by it."

"We can still try, so go out and do it."

"With what?"

"We'll see, and God be with you." She kissed Eva on the cheek and at the door stopped to pause for a momentary chat with Victoria, shaking her hand and then hugging her with a compliment about her fighting spirit and congratulations on her early acceptance to college. Then she left the room.

"Proud of you, Victoria," Gary said with a grin. It was obvious that after her confrontation with Senator Proxley, Victoria was a bit shaken, afraid that she had gone too far. Mary's warm compliment had reassured her and she had looked at her parents for approval.

"At least you didn't kick him in the shins," Gary said, sweeping his girl into an embrace.

"I wanted to."

"So did I, and a lot more," Eva said in Ukrainian with a smile.

"Come on you two fighters. Let's go to Goddard and break the news."

For Gary, clearing the security gate at the Goddard Space Flight Center lifted a weight from his weary shoulders. It was like coming home: he always had a flashback of the happiest summer of his life, an internship that set out the paths not just of his career but his personal happiness as well. It was here that he and Eva both came under the spell of Erich Rothenberg.

He and Eva had, of course, missed the high glory days of the 1960s—that was half a century ago now—but at least they had been in the space program when there was still talk of returning to the moon—plans for Mars, even—and, of course, all the other less glorious but just as important research paths. Many of the old veterans of those times still walked the corridors, and Erich was one of them. But cutback after cutback had left Goddard something of a ghost town, remembering past glories, still hoping that the day would come when society again believed in positive dreams for the future and was willing to throw its backing behind it. It was like a monastery preserving dreams and knowledge in the hope of a renewed renaissance.

There was no problem finding a parking space, and their old mentor, Erich Rothenberg, was at the door of the small office complex that housed his once burgeoning domain, as if waiting for them. He came out and, in classic European fashion, took Eva's hand and kissed it lightly, then grasped Gary's hand, looking straight into his eyes.

"How the hell are you?"

"How am I?" Gary sighed. "I think you know how I am."

"Yeah, I was listening to it on the Internet. That Proxley really cut our throats."

When Erich got angry, his German accent really came through. He was perhaps the last of the legendary breed of famed German scientists who had shaped America's space program back in the fifties and sixties. In his office hung fading photos of him with Wernher von Braun himself, the two posing alongside an early model of a lunar landing module. But there was one big difference: Erich had been on the opposite side from Von Braun during the war that had bred the legendary team of German scientists who had led America to the moon.

Erich was on the other side in that conflict because he was Jewish.

His family had managed to get out when the Nazis took power in 1933. Erich's father saw the future clearly enough, packed what they could take, and fled with his family to friends in Holland. Erich was a university student in physics in Amsterdam when the war came crashing into Holland. His father, a highly decorated officer of the First World War, still had friends and old comrades in the German Army, who pulled up to their home in Amsterdam, shouting that the SS was right behind them with arrest orders, and helped smuggle them down to the Spanish border once France surrendered. Some months later he was in Palestine, eagerly recruited by the British Army as a commando, given that he could speak perfect Berliner German.

It was indeed a strange mix when, in the mid-1950s, Rothenberg came to the States and was tossed in with Von Braun and all the others. The bond of a dream of reaching to space transcended any past differences, which in reality were few, the German scientists were as appalled as the rest of the world when the full truth of the dark psychotic madness behind Hitler and his followers was finally revealed to the world. Together, they believed in the future of space, and that America must lead the way.

Now Erich was the last of them. Amazingly the old man still stood sharply erect, as if a British drill sergeant just might be lurking around a corner, ready to pounce. Holding an emeritus chair in aerospace engineering, he still came in to the office at Goddard every day to check up on his "ladies and lads," as he called them, with decidedly dated Old World charm. In a field dominated by men, it had been Eva who refused to be addressed as one of "Erich's lads," and he had finally broken under her determined will.

The affection between them was genuine, as he offered and she accepted the traditional kiss on both cheeks and Victoria smiled as she received the same courtesy.

Erich patted Victoria affectionately on the shoulder then hugged her.

"You nailed him right between the eyes, young lady!" he cried, grinning like a proud grandfather at his newest prodigy. "I might have added a few more choice words in Yiddish and let him try to figure it out later, but, of course, that would have been improper."

"Oh, I had a lot more to say," Victoria responded, her features reddening because this old man, who was indeed like a beloved grandfather, had praised her.

Erich laughed.

"Remind me to teach you a few," he said with a grin.

"She knows too many such words in Ukrainian as is," Gary replied, and Erich, laughing, nodded.

"I knew you were coming. I already have tea made, and for you, Gary, I think you need something a bit stronger."

The corridor was all but empty as Erich led them past office doors that were closed, with no light coming from within: empty. He once held sway over an entire suite with a staff of fifty or more, but now? At least the powers that be still graced the old man with the dignity of an emeritus position and, out of respect for nearly sixty years' service, kept him on as a reminder of the glory days. His office was small and cramped, the bookshelves sagging in the middle, piled high with bound and unbound papers, yellowed at the edges. His desk was still the same: not government issue, an indulgence to his eccentricities; the heavy oak table was still kept clean except for two pictures, one of his departed wife. The other picture was of him in British commando uniform, Sten submachine gun in hand. His unit had been dropped in to occupy what was left of the German labs at Peenemünde at the end of the war, a secret mission sent in the day before the Russians overran the facility to snatch up anything that could help England's postwar missile program. The hangar behind him had several V-2 rockets. Everyone knew he deliberately kept that portrait very visible to needle his German friends.

It was at that place where Erich's future had been decided. Gazing in wonder at just how dangerously ahead the Germans were in 1945, after accompanying crate loads of plans for what was being called the "New York Rocket," he was discharged from service. He went back to university to study not aeronautical engineering but something new called aerospace engineering, a field that he had helped to define with his dissertation on what would be necessary to actually get to the moon and establish a base there.

Gary smiled at the sight of the photo of Erich in uniform while Eva and Victoria graciously accepted the offer of tea. What happened next was strictly against all regulations as Erich pulled his favorite Scotch, hidden in a filing cabinet, and poured a larger one for himself and for Gary.

"Well, do we drink a toast against all those like Proxley," he asked, "or our traditional one instead?"

"The traditional one," Eva replied softly, and there was actually a catch in her voice.

"To our journey to the stars," Erich whispered, choking up a bit as well.

"To the stars," Gary whispered, and as he took a sip, tears were in his eyes, too, because being there, at what seemed to be the end of his dream, only served to remind him of the day that dream had first begun to form . . .

1

Eighteen Years Earlier
Goddard Space Flight Center

"Dr. Rothenberg?"

Erich Rothenberg, director of the division of advanced propulsion designs, and who oversaw interns assigned to the NASA Institute for Advanced Concepts, looked up over the top of his wire-framed glasses. There was no welcoming smile, just a cool gaze as Gary Morgan stood nervously in the doorway.

"So you are one of my new interns for the summer?" Erich asked. "I already told them there is no need for interns here—at least, those who want a solid future. May I suggest you just go back to the personnel office and ask for a different assignment."

Gary didn't move. He had been warned by "veterans" who had served as interns with Dr. Rothenberg that this was his typical greeting, the first winnowing-out process in which more than one graduate student had taken him at his word and fled.

He stood his ground.

"I volunteered for this division, sir. It is why I came to Goddard for the summer and asked to be assigned to you."

"Oh? Pray tell why." Still there was no welcoming gesture to take a seat.

"I've read most of your papers, sir, at least the unclassified ones: your prediction that Apollo would turn into a political dead end after the first landing, objections to the space station rather than an effort on advance propulsion systems and setting Mars as the next goal . . ."

"I sail against the wind," Erich said gruffly. "Not a good path for career advancement."

Gary didn't move.

"Oh, damn it, come on in and sit down," Erich sighed. Gary was smart enough not to show any emotion; he had at least passed the first test. He was, at least, literally through the door and into the office. Very few ever made it that far.

Leaning back in his chair, Erich pulled out a battered Zippo lighter adorned with the faded insignia of his old commando unit and puffed his pipe back to life. It was now a violation of the new no-smoking rule for the facility, but like all such rules, Erich had a few choice words in reply, either in High German or Yiddish, depending on who he was addressing—though he did compromise by keeping the door closed and a noisy air purifier running.

"Let us skip the sentimental formalities of greetings," Erich announced. Gary had yet to learn it, but beneath the tough exterior of a German disciplined in war with nearly six years of service with the British Army, he was a sentimentalist at heart. His forty years of marriage to his recently departed wife had never produced children, and thus the ebb and flow of young interns and wide-eyed graduates had become his extended family. The honor of admission to this special club, "Erich's Dreamers"—or, as some called them behind his back, the "Warp Factor Club"—meant guidance, late-night sessions at his modest home just outside the gate, and dreams of what was and what should be.

The mainstream of work at Goddard now was on the beginnings of the international space station and post-Challenger recovery, and start-up on work for a second-generation shuttle design. There were even teams waiting for the word to develop a return to the moon and some talk that the president might even ask for funding of preliminary plans for Mars. But as for Erich's team, they were off in a far corner, their work buried deep in the yearly budget. They had been written off as dreamers . . .

Some wag, as a prank, had pinned a picture of Yoda on the door with the name "Erich" printed across it. Rather than tear it down, Rothenberg laughed softly and let it stay. It was now faded but still there.

"Erich's Dreamers." In their cramped quarters and with their marginal budget, they kept alive visions of ion drive; of solar sails that would actually use the minute pressure of sunlight and that theoretically could accelerate a payload up to a sizable fraction of light speed; of hypersonic and ramjet engines mounted on first-stage airplane-like "carriers" that would lift rockets to the edge of space and launch from there . . . They even had plans—seriously worked on back in the 1950s and now at times tweaked a bit—to use nuclear power microburst engines that could cut the transit time to Mars from months to just weeks.

This had become Erich's domain after Apollo slipped away with barely a whimper.

For any ambitious graduate intern, when offered a variety of choices, the advice was to stay away from this collection of fantasists who read too much sci-fi and had seen too much *Star Trek* and could lip-synch every episode. Better to stick with the programs that had a real future, such as the next generation of the Space Shuttle, if they wanted to advance.

For Gary (who would not admit he could lip-synch every episode of the original *Star Trek* series), that was a challenge, not a warning, and he had specifically requested the assignment. Of the fifty-five graduate student internship applicants that summer, only two had been advised on how Erich would greet them. Before making the long trek to this office in a small out-of-the-way office complex, he knew that Erich had at least approved the interview, along with the only other intern's, the first exchange intern from the Ukraine, now a former member of the collapsed Soviet Union. That had caused a bit of a stir, and during his placement interview earlier in the day someone sitting in on his interview (who never identified herself) casually suggested that if he noticed anything unusual with this other intern to let security know.

Erich pointed to a chair, took Gary's dossier, thumbed through his transcripts for several minutes without comment, then started into his typical Germanic grilling.

"Why in hell do you want to get into aerospace engineering when thousands of my old coworkers have been laid off and are trying to land jobs as high school teachers, and the rest are just praying to make it to retirement?"

Before Gary could even form an answer, Erich fired off the next question.

"Why are you even here in this office? Bright young man like you should try for the Jet Propulsion Lab out in California, or one of the private contractors like Boeing or Lockheed, and angle for a job once you graduate."

"Your work intrigues me, sir," Gary finally replied, a bit nervously.

Erich sat back and shook his head, and laughed softly as he continued to thumb through Gary's file.

"Why?"

"Because I believe a day will come when humanity realizes space is the only answer left to us if we are going to make it to the twenty-second century."

"Why care about the twenty-second century? You plan to live that long?" Erich laughed softly. "I sure as hell don't. I've seen enough in this century to fill half a dozen lifetimes."

"No, sir, but maybe my children will. My great grandparents came to America eighty years ago. Before my grandfather died, he said they came here because of me."

Gary fell silent with that. He knew it sounded sentimental, and he had yet to realize how sentimental Erich truly was. But it was true. Three of Gary's four ancestors had come through Ellis Island and all spoke of the dream that brought them there: it was always about a better world for their children and grandchildren and how he should dream the same. Though only twenty-two and with all four of his grandparents gone—along with both his parents, lost in a small plane crash two years back—he knew that his reply to Erich's question would have been theirs as well.

His father had been a navy aviator who even tried for the astronaut corps in the mid-1960s—and almost made it—and this had encouraged Gary's fascination with flight. He actually should have been with his parents on the day they died, but a chronic sinus infection kept him home. His dad promised they'd go up together the following week, but there was no following week. An idiotic accident—a pilot pulled out onto the active runway just as they were touching down—had taken both his parents. As usual with such things, the fool who caused it walked away with barely a scratch.

Perhaps that was why he had tried to learn to fly—although, on the advice of his instructor, he had given it up. He didn't have the "instinctive" feel his father had, and frankly he was always on edge when aloft: that could be dangerous. Though grounded in a literal sense, his dreams were still "up there."

Gary's paternal grandfather—his beloved "Tappy"—had taken over as parent until he slipped away just the year before his internship interview, truly leaving Gary alone, at least in a physical sense. Yet all of his grandparents had instilled in him "the dream." Tall, gangly, rather uncoordinated—branded a nerd by many when that term was not the compliment it would become in the Internet age—Gary lived in a world of devouring works on aviation and space history, and at least found a few friends in the realm of fantasy gaming. Girls? That was something that left him tongue-tied and self-conscious; his friends even joked that maybe he should join a monastery, since that was the way he seemed destined to live. A favorite novel of his, Walter L. Miller Jr.'s *A Canticle for Leibowitz*, did involve a religious order devoted to science, and he actually thought at times that if such an order existed, he would just give up on the rest of the world and join it.

Erich Rothenberg, who was five foot seven, wiry, and at best 145 pounds soaking wet, also had something of the nerd look as he continued to gaze at Gary over the rims of his glasses. But then there was the other, legendary side of the man, a commando who had survived five years of combat, been wounded three times, and had been awarded the Victoria Cross—all before gaining his reputation as a brilliant space science engineer. No one would ever dare to apply the term "nerd" to him and expect to leave the office in one piece.

"So Mr. Morgan, you are here because you want to save the world, is that it?" Erich asked, but there was no mockery in his voice.

Gary did not answer for several seconds, then replied, "Maybe I can help in some way, sir."

"Then go over to the design team for the shuttle replacement."

"That's the past, sir."

"What do you mean? I helped with some of the design, you know."

"And I read where you howled all the way, from the day they shifted the original plan from a two-stage liquid fuel launch that would take off like a plane—and continued to voice your concerns right up to the day *Challenger* lifted off—that putting men and women on top of solid boosters would one day end in a tragedy. And it happened."

They were both silent for a moment. *Challenger*, for everyone at NASA, was still an open wound. Gary still could not look at the footage without getting a lump in his throat when Houston radioed, "*Challenger*, you are go at throttle up . . ."

"That is the past," Erich said, breaking eye contact and gazing off as if to some painful memory.

Gary leaned forward. He could sense that Dr. Rothenberg was showing some interest with this brief breaking down into an emotional response.

"Chemical rockets are to space travel what steam trains are to magnetic levitation or even diesel electric locomotives."

"Go on." Erich took his Zippo out again, relit his pipe, and leaned back in his chair, unflinching gaze again fixed on Gary.

"Well, sir, we all know Newton's law about thrust and opposite reaction. Even the most efficient chemical rockets have a maximum velocity, which we are already approaching. And the fuel-weight-to-energy-produced ratio forever limits just how much we can loft up. Apollo burned millions of pounds of fuel to get less than 20,000 pounds of spacecraft into a lunar trajectory. To save weight they even shaved off a few ounces of metal on the steps leading down to the lunar surface and back. The steps were calculated to be able to hold the load at one-sixth gravity but would collapse if used on earth. To go to Mars in any reasonable amount of time—it is a dead end, sir. Every day added because of lower velocity means that much more water, food, and other supplies for the astronauts, which means yet more weight of fuel to put it up there . . . It is a dead end."

Erich nodded sagely then smiled.

"I was the one who suggested shaving down the steps on the module to save those few ounces."

"It's like building a 747 to fly three people across the Atlantic," Gary continued, "then junking the plane after landing."

"You took that line from me, Mr. Morgan," Erich said, with just the hint of a smile.

Gary nodded, acknowledging his appropriation of what was now a much-quoted line.

"So tell me, Mr. Morgan"—Erich looked at the file—"Mr. Gary Morgan: What wisdom do you bring to me, along with your youthful idealism, to solve this dilemma?"

Gary hesitated.

"I don't know, sir," he replied truthfully. "But I do sense we are at the limits of what we can do to get into space. It is so damn frustrating, because out there limitless resources await, but we are stuck in a deep well—the gravity well of the earth—and it costs tens of thousands of dollars per pound just to crawl out of that well. I don't have the answer that fits within our realm of aerospace engineering, and that is why I volunteered to be on your team—because maybe you do have the answer."

Erich chuckled.

"Right answer. If you had said one word about folding space or wormholes—a bunch of rubbish—you'd be back at Personnel. And outside this office, if you say 'warp' even once, you are fired. I am barely hanging on to a budget as it is without some intern bubbling over in front of a jaundiced member of Congress, like one of our critics who just the other day was asking why couldn't NASA make fuel out of corn from his state and then he'd support us."

Erich stared up at the ceiling, still puffing on his pipe, motioning for Gary to close the door so that there would not be any complaints while he reached back over his shoulder to open the window to air the room out.

"You are right. We're at an ultimate dead end. The ratios of required fuel to cost to get a given number of pounds into space, combined with the risks of chemical rockets, is a paradigm that has been with us ever since my old friend Von Braun was told to start shooting V-2 rockets at London. Even he admitted that he knew the folly of it all: one rocket to deliver one ton of explosives just two hundred miles cost far more than the planes America and England were building and pounding Germany with in a thousand-plane raid every night. It was a dead end, but in Von Braun's case he was praying that his employer would get what he deserved and end the madness, but the rockets would become the foundation for the American victors to get into space. But the math of launching a rocket in 1944 is still the same nearly fifty years later, whether it is two hundred miles or to a translunar or trans-Mars trajectory.

"So they throw a fraction of the budget, less than a tenth of one percent of the budget that finally comes to NASA, to the NIAC and a few other teams like us at JPL, White Sands, telling us to try something different—and, of course, to come in under budget. As for you as an intern, your college gives you a small stipend so your work to us is for free, other than helping you a bit with nearby housing. But from small acorns there have been times when a mighty chestnut has grown, Mr. Morgan."

He finally made direct eye contact with Gary and smiled.

"You report at 0730 every morning. I do not like these new coffee shop chains with their French names for what even we Brit soldiers called 'joe.' There's a diner just down the road south of the main gate. Tell them you are my new assistant; they know what I want. Get copies of *The New York Times* and *The Washington Post* as well while you're there. You need coffee, get some for yourself; they'll put it on my tab."

"Thank you, sir."

"You'll need it," Erich said with a sardonic smile, and then pointed to one of the bookshelves sagging in the middle from the heavy weight of volumes and papers.

"Start with that book in the upper left corner; it will take you back to the beginning of all things. A good aerospace engineer is also a good historian. An old friend of mine, L. Sprague de Camp, wrote that first book up there about ancient engineering. You will read how the Romans built roads, how Prince Henry of Portugal designed ships that could sail round the world . . . Ever hear of him?"

Gary could only shake his head.

"Well, start with the book by de Camp. A book a day, young man."

Gary all but gulped openly as he looked at the rows of books. He was there for ten weeks, not ten years, and besides, though he could devour math in any form, his parents had been told he had some sort of learning disability called dyslexia and reading of regular texts came very slowly.

"I want you to start with that, the history of it all, even before Von Braun in Germany and Goddard here in the States began their work. I want you to get inside the minds of the inventors, the engineers, the dreamers."

He chuckled.

"Yes, the dreamers. I want you to learn what they went through and find out if you have the stomach to face what they faced.

"Ever hear of Brunel?"

"No, sir."

"What in hell are they teaching you at Purdue?"

"Engineering, sir."

"Well, they should throw in a history class or two. Isambard Brunel. In the 1850s he built an iron ship nearly as big as *Titanic*, but he was fifty years ahead of his time. There were no docks big enough in the world to handle his dream, no market big enough to fill the hull for a profitable journey, including the amount of fuel it would need to cross the Atlantic—though they finally found a use for it when it was used to lay the transatlantic cable.

It is said the mockery about 'Brunel's Folly,' as they called it, is what killed him. Fifty years later he was hailed as a visionary. I want you to learn that now."

"Is that what keeps you going, sir?" Gary ventured.

Erich looked at him crossly and did not reply.

"By the end of the week I want you up to speed on through Brunel; Eads; Ericsson; the Roeblings; Herman Haupt, a railroad engineer as important to the Union cause as Grant or Sherman; the private entrepreneur Hill, who built a transcontinental railroad on his own, the Great Northern, without a dime of government money only twenty-five years after the first transcontinental, which proved to be one of the great boondoggles of its time—names few know but you will know. Then we'll start talking about space."

Gary was a bit surprised. He had come here to learn what was the cutting edge, not some darn boring history lessons.

Erich smiled.

"In time you will see why I make you learn the past, then learn how to shape the future and have the strength to do it.

"So, I expect to see a book a day off that shelf. Don't forget the book by de Camp on your way out. Have it read by tomorrow."

"Yes, sir."

Erich looked down at the paper he had been reading and for several minutes focused on it, ignoring Gary, so that he wondered if he had been dismissed. Erich had a red pencil out and began scratching some notes along the margins, then folded it over.

"This was given to me by the other new intern." He looked up at the old-style clock hanging on the wall. "And in another minute that person will be late."

There was a knock on the door with thirty seconds to spare.

"Enter."

Gary could not help but gaze in admiration. He had noticed her in the group orientation for new interns the day before. Blond; tall, at least for Gary, at about five feet ten inches; startling green eyes; and classic Slavic high cheekbones. She was tastefully dressed in a modest skirt and blouse—actually, rather formal for the facility, where "dressing down" to jeans and T-shirts had become the norm with the younger staff over the last few years, though the "old-timers" still wore white shirts and neckties.

"Am I interrupting?" she asked politely. The accent revealed by those three words told Gary she was the Ukrainian exchange intern.

"Not at all, young lady," and Old World charm took hold of Erich as he stood, nodded slightly, and pointed to a chair next to Gary. Erich made a polite offer of tea, which she gracefully accepted. Gary, a bit flustered, because he hated tea, accepted a cup as well but was a bit chagrined that Erich had not offered him tea or coffee when he came in.

Erich made the introductions, and Gary stood to shake Evgeniya Petrenko's hand, unable to avoid those green eyes, which seemed to bore into him. He sensed that she was the type who on a daily basis brushed off the attention of fellow male grad students and perhaps many a professor as well. Then he nervously sat down again, self-consciously pushing his own glasses, which had slid down a bit, back up on his nose.

"Your translation of this paper," Erich said, holding up the printout. "May I ask, is it accurate?"

Evgeniya seemed to bristle slightly at this question about her English ability.

"I assure you, sir, it is accurate."

"I've not seen it before, though I've, of course, heard of the theory. Some years back Arthur C. Clarke even wrote a novel about the idea. But even he said when he wrote it he thought it would be two hundred years or more from now before we had the technology to do it."

"The paper was published in, of all places, a popular journal in Moscow in 1960. I am surprised your CIA did not grab it and rush it here."

Shadows of the Cold War still lingered in the way she had said "CIA."

"Perhaps the KGB blocked it," Gary said softly.

She looked at him crossly.

"It was in a popular magazine like your *Scientific American*, which I should add we read every month within a day or two of its release."

"Free flow of information," Gary could not help but reply.

She seemed ready to snap back, and Erich extended a hand in a calming gesture.

"The Cold War is over, you two," he said with a smile. "And I am glad to see a Russian intern on my staff."

Though he had been in this man's presence for less than an hour, Gary sensed something of a line, but the response by Eva caught him off guard.

"I am not Russian, sir," she replied, with a hint of irritation. "I am

Ukrainian. It just so happens that to pursue my field no such schools exist in my country, so I had to go to Moscow to study."

Erich was a bit taken aback but then smiled.

"My apologies, Miss Petrenko. I know the history of the persecution your people suffered by both Hitler and Stalin. I am surprised they would let a Ukrainian study aerospace engineering."

"My grandfather was a hero of the Great Patriotic War, and received our highest decoration Hero of the Soviet Union. I was first in my class, and friends and admirers of my grandfather helped me to gain admission and now this assignment."

"And your plans after your summer here?"

"To return to Moscow, of course."

"I see."

"Dr. Rothenberg. Your government and mine have already signed accords and understandings about building the space station. Would it not be helpful for me to work for that once I return home?"

Erich nodded in agreement even as he poured her another cup of tea.

"Then if that is the case, Miss Petrenko, why did you feel it necessary to give me this paper?" He nodded to the document on his desk.

She smiled.

"Because the space station is just a beginning. Perhaps even a dead end. I came here to learn about what is beyond that. And to bring along this suggestion as well."

"Bringing this to me might cause problems for you."

She laughed softly.

"Sir, it was published, as I told Mr. Morgan here"—she shot him a look of disdain—"in a popular magazine. Not classified, if anyone here had bothered to take the time to look. No harm in sharing it."

"And may I guess that this is what you wish to research further?"

"I plan to write my dissertation on it. But I will need access to computers here that are not yet available in Moscow to run some algorithms to test out some theories. That is what I hope you will give me the freedom to do."

Erich gave a mischievous smile and tossed the paper over to Gary.

"Regarding access to our Cray, I'll have to ask security about that, but I think we can arrange it under proper supervision."

She beamed with delight.

"But"—again that smile—"since this is, as you say, public information in your country, I will ask this young man to take a look at your paper. Perhaps he can help, as his transcript shows some unique skills in programming."

She looked over at Gary with an icy gaze.

"Sir, I hardly think—"

"Miss Petrenko, we work as a team here. I am intrigued with this idea—very intrigued. Mr. Morgan tells me he has a visionary soul and is looking for some sort of 'dream' while here this summer. Maybe what you present openly to us here is it. So, Mr. Morgan, after you read de Camp, I want you to read this paper, because it is so visionary it borders on the absurd, then pick up coffee for three . . ."

He looked at Evgeniya.

"Do you like your coffee with or without cream?"

"I prefer tea, sir," she said, with another cold glance at Gary.

"Fine, then. I doubt if my friend George down at the diner even knows what tea is, so I'll just boil some water here. I'll brew your cup of tea and see both of you at 0730 tomorrow. Coffee for two, then, Gary. You may go now."

As Gary walked out the door, clutching the dusty book by Erich's old friend and the dozen-page printout, he could almost sense daggers from Evgeniya's eyes going into his back.

He muttered a curse to himself. He already had a crush on her—and had from the moment their eyes met.

2

Eighteen Years Earlier

Ten minutes ahead of schedule, Gary arrived at Rothenberg's office, balancing two cups of coffee, a battered satchel containing de Camp's book and the report Eva had lent to Erich, and his fourteen-pound Tandy 1400 laptop. Just one day in and he was already exhausted. He was a very slow reader and it had taken him till midnight to finish de Camp's book—which he actually found to be fascinating—then another three hours of reading and rereading Eva's article, taking notes and loading them onto a three-and-a-half-inch floppy disk before finally turning in for a two-hour nap. But such a routine was normal in graduate school, especially in the final weeks leading up to exams, and today somehow felt like an exam: he had to either place at the top of the "class" or face the suggestion he try another department at Goddard. He knew that, with a man like Erich, fulfilling the entire assignment on day one was exactly like a final exam, except in this case it was either pass or get out.

Setting down the cup of coffee, Erich took a sip, grunted approval, took the *Times* and *Post*, opened the former to Tuesday's science section, then looked around the edge of the paper at Gary, who was unfolding the half screen for the Tandy and starting to boot up the writing software.

"What in hell is that?" Erich asked.

"It's a laptop, sir."

"Wouldn't a pencil and paper be a bit easier to haul around than that monstrosity?"

On many a winter day hiking across the Purdue campus, facing a windy blast as he struggled the half mile from the parking garage to the lab, he would have readily agreed. But his handwriting was so atrocious, and the ability to take notes quickly such a blessing with this machine, it was worth the weight. One of his friends had even written a program that allowed the punching in of calculus formulas—a bit cumbersome, but it worked well in combination with his Texas Instruments handheld.

He waited as the machine booted up over several minutes, sipping his coffee and glancing at the clock. At exactly 07:29:30 the door opened and Eva came in. She was dressed in Goddard "casual": modest slacks, a blue men's-style long-sleeved shirt, but typical of her culture it was obvious she had spent plenty of time making sure her hair and makeup were perfect. Gary half stood and offered his hand, wishing her a good morning, which she politely returned as she settled into the seat next to him, opening her briefcase to draw out a notepad. She glanced at his laptop but made no comment.

Erich already had the teakettle heated and offered to fill her cup, which she accepted with a polite nod.

"So, Mr. Morgan, you read the report she loaned to us? I am curious as to your reaction."

Gary immediately felt trapped. He had read it, reread it, and wished he had access to a library at three in the morning to look up other sources, but, of course, did not. And yet, looking at her, he felt his heart skip over as she brushed a wisp of blond hair back off her cheek.

He did not reply, just continued to look at her.

Erich actually chuckled softly and put down his newspaper, leaned back, and puffed his pipe back to life.

"Mr. Morgan?"

"Sir?"

"I asked your opinion about the report Miss Petrenko loaned to us." There was a bit of a sly grin on Erich's face: mentoring graduate students for years, he had seen this more than once.

"I gave the report to *you*, sir," she replied primly, and then fell silent, the veiled rebuke obvious.

"Miss Petrenko, if it is not classified, it is open information in this facility. No interns have access to classified information; that was, may I remind you, part of the understanding when you arrived here as an exchange student for the summer. Whatever information you decide to share is open to all."

He paused and smiled.

"Or is the Cold War still on?"

She blushed and shook her head.

"No, sir, of course not, sir."

"Fine, then. Now, Mr. Morgan . . . ?"

Gary took a deep breath, unsure of himself.

"Go on, Mr. Morgan, I'm curious."

Gary looked over at Eva, but she was ignoring him, instead gazing into her cup of tea as she sipped it.

Oh, well, he figured, what was more important, the tenuous prospect of trying to impress Evgeniya favorably, or the reason that he had come to Goddard?

"It will never work," he said softly, staring straight at Erich, and there was a flicker of a smile from the old man in response. Did Erich know the dilemma he had just put him in?

Eva did not slam the cup down, but she certainly set it down heavily so that a few drops spilled over the rim, and as she turned, her green eyes all but flashing, he felt his heart skip a beat.

If only her expression was that of a warm smile, the way some of the undergrad females at Purdue would look at him at the corner pub—a bit wide-eyed when he told them what he was majoring in, and they'd exclaim, "Oh, you're one of the guys studying to be an astronaut?"

Absurd, of course, with his thick glasses, but at times he would play along, hoping for a date, though most of the humanities majors would burn him off as yet another "science geek," some even lecturing him on how it was technology that had messed up the world, that man should return to his natural state; then they would go looking for better hunting, like one of the ballplayers or even a history major. But at this moment, if looks could kill, he'd already be buried and forgotten.

"Let the debate begin," Erich said with a smile, relighting his pipe and sitting back, opening his window, and gesturing for Gary to close the door. "You first, Mr. Morgan." He extended a hand in a calming gesture to Eva, indicating that her turn would come.

Later, Gary would learn this was exactly how his mentor worked. He would take young interns coming out of top universities with some cutting-edge ideas, throw them into what his team called the "gladiator pit" to fight it out, and perhaps just perhaps a synthesis might emerge—though at times a blood feud could result when a cherished idea, especially a dissertation topic, was cut into bloody tatters. More than one intern had staggered out of the gladiator pit in tears, tossed their dissertations, and switched majors. It was heartless in a way, but also compassionate: better to lose it here as an intern rather than a few years down the road with the realization their theses were dead ends.

Gary cleared his throat nervously and took a long, deep sip of the still-hot coffee. The battle was on.

"Your article, ahhh, Miss Petrenko . . ." He trailed off, not sure of how to pronounce her last name.

"Eva is fine," she said coldly.

"Ahh, yes, 'Miss Eva' would be easier for both of us," Erich chuckled. "With your permission, of course."

She nodded, saying nothing.

"Well, Mr. Morgan, she proposes this thing called a 'space elevator.' "

"A tower—a space tower," Eva cut in. "The idea was invented in Russia nearly a century ago, and some of our people take it seriously."

"I regret to say it is the stuff of science fiction here," Gary replied. "I did read Arthur C. Clarke's novel *Fountains of Paradise*. Have you?"

"No, but I have heard of his work."

"He postulated it would be two hundred years or more before the technology would be available."

" 'Science fiction,' you call it," she retorted. "In the Ukraine we call it 'fantastic science.' "

"Well, this is 'fantastic science,' then," Gary replied, figuring he had won a point.

"So, Mr. Morgan," Erich prompted. "Go ahead. Take it apart, tell me why this is so 'fantastic'?"

Gary nodded, the glare in Eva's eyes now giving him some strength. Any hope of winning a date with her was obviously dead, so what the hell?

He scanned the notes on his small computer screen for a moment, then stood up and went over to the whiteboard on the wall to the left of Erich's desk.

"May I, sir?"

Erich nodded.

At the bottom Gary drew a curving line, wrote "earth" under the line, then near the top of the board sketched a curved dotted line.

"Geosynch orbit is the high ground," Gary began. "That's 22,236 miles above mean sea level. You understand miles versus kilometers?"

He looked back at Eva.

"The scientific community prefers metric," she sniffed. "Someday the West, with its miles, or statute miles, or nautical miles, or whatever, will get a mission in trouble."

Erich chuckled.

"Point to her," he announced.

"Fine, then it's . . ." He hesitated for a second, running the numbers through his head. "Geosynch orbit is 35,786 kilometers above mean sea level. Your article proposes the building of a tower with a height of over 35,000 kilometers? Then another 20,000 kilometers beyond that to provide a counterweight? Good heavens, the tallest building in the world is . . ."

"At this moment, a radio tower in Moscow at half a kilometer tall."

Gary hated metric; to him it always made things sound bigger or faster than they really were.

"Just over sixteen hundred feet," he retorted, "a little more than a quarter mile."

"So?" Eva replied.

"You are proposing a tower that is something on the order of nearly a hundred thousand times taller?"

"Yes."

Gary drew another line extending from the curving line representing the earth at the bottom of the board, up to the dotted line of geosynch at the top, and then put a question mark next to it.

Erich held up his hand.

"Perhaps I started this backward," he announced. "Let us start with a positive rather than a negative. Eva"—he paused—"may I call you that?"

She gave him a winning smile and nodded.

"Of course, sir."

"Explain to our doubting Thomas here the thesis."

"Gladly, sir," and she stood up, taking the blue marker from Gary, the flicker of a grin on her features as if saying, *Now I will cut you apart with this!*

"The proposal—as I assume you know, Mr. Morgan, from reading the article—was first suggested by the Russian scientist Tsiolkovsky shortly after he worked out the orbital dynamics of placing a satellite into orbit. At that time, in 1905, rocket fuel of sufficient thrust to fit his dream of space flight had yet to be tested, let alone developed. That would not happen for another thirty years.

"From this evolved the idea of building a tower at the equator, clear out to what you call the high ground, geosynchronous orbit, that place above the earth where an orbiting satellite will take exactly one day to complete one revolution or orbit, and thus appear to remain stationary. It is indeed the 'high ground,' unlike low earth orbits, where a satellite passes swiftly overhead and requires dozens of ground tracking stations, and even at five hundred kilometers up, there is still enough atmospheric drag to eventually slow it down, causing it to plunge back to earth."

There was no argument on that point, and Gary simply nodded in agreement.

"Tsiolkovsky realized that the higher the tower, several things begin to happen. The first, that gravity begins to drop off the farther you are from the center of the earth—that there is an inverse ratio between gravity and distance from the center of the earth's core. Too many people foolishly assume that everything is weightless in space. Of course, it is not. The only thing that makes it appear that way is that in low-earth orbit you are traveling at nearly ten kilometers a second; you are actually falling around the curve of the earth.

"But the farther out one travels if ascending a tower, the lower apparent gravity will become, until at geosynch orbit the gravitational pull will appear to be near zero. Granted, the gravitation effect is there—again, at an inverse ratio to distance, which is why the moon stays in orbit and in turn its gravitational pull affects our tides."

As she spoke, she started to write out the formula defining this on the whiteboard, forgetting her audience for a moment and making the notations in Russian.

"Second major point," she continued as if delivering a classroom lecture, and she was so involved in what she was saying that she did not even look back to see if there were any questions. In spite of her antipathy for him, Gary could not help but feel admiration for her obvious brilliance as she jotted down various equations.

"The second point is the centrifugal force of the earth's rotation: attaching the tower to the earth at the equator will help it to remain rigid, imparting at geosynch an orbital velocity as well that will appear to negate gravitation effect. Thus it will at least feel and act like zero gravity, as most mistakenly call that effect for any object in orbit.

"The tower would not actually end at geosynch but continue on for nearly another 20,000 kilometers, and would be anchored at the far end by a mass, depending upon the weight of the actual tower. So . . ."

To his amazement and Erich's bemused chuckle she reached into the pocket of her slacks and pulled out a string; at one end was attached, of all things, what looked like a lipstick tube. Eva started to turn around, twirling the string, then holding it up over her head, letting it spin in circles, and then to her utter embarrassment, the lipstick container broke free and went flying across the room, nearly hitting Gary.

"Rather proves your third point, which I assume is angular momentum," Erich said, laughing.

For the first time Eva's icy exterior melted, her little demonstration of centrifugal force having gone awry, and she actually blushed, which softened Gary's increasingly defensive response to this young woman with such a dynamic presence.

"Well, uh, sir, that is getting a bit ahead," she said.

Erich smiled indulgently for her to continue.

"With the base of the tower attached to the surface of the earth at the equator and extending out past geosynch orbit, the rotation of the earth itself will provide centrifugal force to keep the tower rigid and erect, unlike a tower only half a kilometer high, which must rely solely on its foundation and massive steel frame to hold it up.

"And, yes, you just saw the third part—the beautiful part, in my eyes." There was a growing enthusiasm in her voice. "The tower can also act as a catapult. How much fuel was required by your *Apollo* and *Saturn V* rockets to break free of the earth's orbit and reach TLT, translunar trajectory?"

"Nearly eight million pounds of fuel burning at over 50,000 pounds of fuel a second."

"The tower," she continued, even more enthusiastically, "gives it to us for free, using the earth's rotation as the source of energy. We could haul any size payload up to the top of the tower and, once released, the angular momentum atop the tower will be just like a catapult of old throwing a rock. The released object will then head off to wherever we desire, guided by the precise timing of when to release it and a small amount of fuel, a fraction of the amount currently needed to accelerate out of the earth's gravitational field. This tower could send to the moon the equivalent of a hundred *Apollo* payloads if we desire, at a fraction of the cost. Using advance drive systems such as Plasma Ion, we could go to Mars in weeks rather than months or years at a cost of hundreds of billions. The cost of one trip to Mars as NASA is now thinking about, if invested into building this tower instead, would give us the path to Mars, with a true transportation system from earth to space thrown in for under the same cost."

She paused.

"Or even beyond Mars. It will open space to limitless exploration, even colonization, of whatever we desire, at a fraction of the cost in energy."

"How much would the energy cost to get the object from the ground station, attach it to the tower, and have it climb up to this magical release point?" Erich asked quietly.

Eva nodded and wrote down another formula.

"Even using an old-fashioned climber, with wheels attached to the tower or using a magnetic levitation rail, the energy cost will average out to about thirty rubles a kilo."

"English, please," Erich said. "And besides, the ruble is collapsing."

She was a bit taken aback for a second, then answered, "About seven dollars per one of your pounds to geosynch."

Gary could not help but snort in derision at that one.

"It currently costs somewhere around $100,000 a pound to loft an object by rocket to geosynch, and you are telling us this tower thing will cut that cost by over 99.99 percent."

She nodded again, not thrown by his question or tone.

"The elevator car or capsule that hauls up the material to geosynch, as it descends, will actually generate electricity, its wheels now acting like a dynamo as gravity pulls it back toward the earth, accelerating as it gets closer. It can thus generate over 90 percent of the electricity it used while climbing up—even more if well designed."

She put her whiteboard marker down.

"Besides moving large objects to geosynch either to place in orbit or catapult to the moon, Mars"—she paused—"or beyond, it would mean that the cost for the average person to go to geosynch, either to work, visit, or even live there permanently, would cost only a little more than a flight from Moscow to New York. It would open space for everyone, not just a select few cosmonauts."

For the briefest of moments Gary did feel hooked in by it all; after all, that had been his childhood dream until the age of seven, when it was found that he had a rare form of astigmatism, which meant he could never become a pilot and venture toward the stars; years later, he would be unable to earn a license to fly even a Cessna or Piper a hundred miles solo.

"Think of what that could mean for millions: the elderly who gravity has bound to wheelchairs; paraplegics and others who would benefit from low-gravity environments while recovering from illnesses . . . It would not be a high-stress three- to five-g ride atop a dangerous rocket; it would be the same as taking an elevator—a very long elevator ride of several days, the cab designed for comfort, almost like a cruise ship. Think of their lives when free of the bonds of earth."

She hesitated for a second; when she resumed speaking, there was emotion in her voice.

"My grandfather," she paused, "lost both legs and a hand at Stalingrad. He was a Stormovik pilot."

She paused again.

"He flew nearly two hundred missions, most of them dangerous ground support, before he was shot down. Think of what living in low or zero gravity would have meant for him. He was the one who inspired me to go into this field of study."

That hit a nerve with Erich, a veteran of that war, and he nodded.

"Convey my respect and honor to him," he said softly. "We were on the same side in that war, and I see him as a true and gallant comrade."

"He died in a veterans' hospital five years ago," she whispered, voice filled with emotion, and Gary could see the subject was a sensitive one for her. "I would go with my grandmother every week to visit him. He used to say he looked forward to the day he would die and then could run again in heaven, and perhaps God would give him wings so he could fly again as well."

She lowered her head for a moment, eyes damp, obviously struggling to control her emotions. Gary was silent; Erich looked up at her, his gaze distant, as if remembering his own sorrows from that time.

"I use to promise him that when I grew up," she finally continued, voice a bit husky, "I'd find a way for him to run and fly again. A little girl's promise. He'd hug me, laugh, I still remember the feel of his whiskers on my cheeks when he hugged me and how the nurses at the hospital treated him with such respect. He always wore his medals on his hospital bathrobe and . . ."

She cleared her throat, coughing a bit nervously, her eyes bright with emotion, and then she looked back at the whiteboard, filled now with her diagrams and formulas.

Neither of the men spoke, Erich just looking at her with a knowing smile, Gary averting his eyes and then noticing the framed Victoria Cross on the bookcase behind his mentor. Hero of the Soviet Union, Victoria Cross, both the equivalent to the Medal of Honor in America . . . He felt humbled.

"It will make the rocket propulsion system obsolete," she announced, swiftly but not too adroitly changing topics, "as obsolete as steam power for trains or piston engines for long-distance flight."

"In other words, your proposal would put a lot of people working at Kennedy Space Center and Houston out of business," Erich said dryly, and Gary could see that the old man had been touched by her personal moment and was glad they had shifted back to this proposal. "I still do have a few friends working there."

She did not reply for a moment.

"Should we have stuck with steam-powered trains, sir?" she finally replied.

He chuckled and shook his head no, then looked over at Gary. It was time for the "gladiator games" to begin again.

"Now, Mr. Morgan, I'll give you the first shot at the questions."

Gary hesitated, still touched by the comment about her grandfather. His own grandfather had flown B-17s during the war, and he had gone to many an air show and several reunions as a boy. It had triggered his own fascination with aviation and that of his father as well. A father who had been a naval aviator, flown in the early days of the Vietnam War, then died in a senseless civilian aviation accident. No heroic medals—as was true for so many in that war and the one his grandfather had been in—for men who fought with utmost bravery, in conflicts where heroism was commonplace. Growing up, Gary and his father would go along with Granddad to air shows. The old man would always puff up with pride whenever he was near a B-17, and anyone within hearing distance, especially a fellow vet, would know he had flown one through twenty-five missions. On the other hand, there were at times long silences, and sometimes Gary heard him waking up in the middle of the night, crying out for a comrade to bail out, bail out . . .

Gary wondered for a moment what had compelled Eva to go into aerospace engineering besides the memory of her grandfather. But then again, what had compelled him as well? Perhaps it really was the wonder of it all, the idea that a frontier still awaited.

"Mr. Morgan, any comments, or are you so captivated by Miss Eva's arguments that you fully agree and believe we should start construction tomorrow after I put in the hundred-billion-dollar budget proposal, which, of course, will pass without comment?"

Gary looked over at her, made eye contact, and tried to smile, then saw that she was still a bit off-balance from a public recollection of what were obviously very private memories.

"What are you proposing it be built out of?" Gary asked, going straight to the core problem.

"We don't have the material yet," she answered openly, obviously having been hit by this question before, "but . . ."

Erich chuckled as he tapped the ashes out of his pipe, refilled it, and lit it. Both looked at him.

"We all know there is a ratio between compression strength, tensile strength, and width of the foundation. Cathedrals are a good example. As they strove for height, the width of the foundation had to become bigger. They solved it, at least to the limits of their ability, with the flying buttress support, but even then the practical limit for stone buildings was only several hundred feet before the foundation became cumbersome to the point of absurdity.

"If you want an interesting example go, take a look at the highest stone tower in England, at Salisbury, at over four hundred feet high. The support beams inside the cathedral bulge outward more than a meter from the stress. A sharp eye by a full-time structural engineer assigned to that wonder, and high-tech lasers monitoring the bulges in the support columns, keep constant watch on it, because someday the stress overload will cause it to collapse. The same is true with any tower: the more weight compressing downward due to gravity, the wider the foundation. If we tried to build this tower with tungsten steel, for example, the foundation would be scores of miles in diameter, clearly an absurd proposition.

"So, Miss Eva, your answer?"

She nodded in agreement.

"Steel gave us the skyscraper," Erich continued, "but above a few thousand meters, you start to run into the same problem, though you could just keep expanding the support base and make the building wider—but then, that adds more weight and more foundation.

"You could build this tower of steel, even a Tower of Babel of bricks, but the foundation?"

She smiled, sensing he was playing with her a bit, but Gary did know this point was true. You could build anything you wanted to any height if you kept broadening the foundation to bear the tremendous weight, but that, of course, did not take in a number of other factors that would tear a steel tower apart long before they even got a fraction of the height desired.

"Even if you built it of diamonds," Gary interjected, "I doubt if it would met all the stress demands."

"There's promising research in carbon fibers," she replied. "It is already revolutionizing aviation design, and the Japanese apparently are doing a lot of behind-the-scenes research on this."

Erich nodded.

"To what percent of usability?" he asked.

"I'm not sure, sir. That's classified by them, and that fact alone should tell us they are onto something big. But the published literature is saying it's moving along a lot further than anyone predicted five years ago."

Erich stood up and sighed as he stretched. For the first time Gary saw him walking and noticed a slight limp—a memento, he'd learn later, of a commando attempt to capture Rommel and the source of the Victoria Cross.

The old man opened up his briefcase and, of all things, pulled out a pack of paper soda straws, then opened it up, drawing out several. Limping over to the whiteboard, he took the blue marker from Eva and drew three arrows alongside the line representing the tower.

"Whatever it is built with has to be able to withstand three stresses. The first is compression, the weight of the object itself, which increases, of course, the higher up you go. You could actually build this tower out of soda straws, but at some point the weight of the straws above will cause the bottom ones to buckle unless you add more and more to the base until they cover half the planet."

To make his point, he held up a straw, then put a finger atop it and pressed down until it buckled.

He tossed the broken straw aside and now held up three straws and did the same, but this time they were bundled together in his hand and did not buckle.

"So tie three straws together but then you have to do perhaps two straws for the next ones atop the first three, and so on."

He took two more straws, positioning them atop the three.

"We could play around with building a tower ten feet high now with these," he said as he used a bit of tape to secure the three straws into a bundle, then did the same to the two atop the first three, and then the one atop the two. He set it on his desk and pressed down on the top straw with a finger until finally the structure collapsed.

It was obvious Erich had thought this little demonstration out the day before, and Gary inwardly smiled. It was more befitting of a high school science class, but it definitely illustrated the points he was making.

"Now, if my budget allowed for additional straws, I'd bundle six straws together, then put five on top of them, then four, and so on, and maybe we could build a tower fifty feet high of straws, but in the end it will collapse.

"Which definitely tells us we cannot build this tower of soda straws"—there was a bit of a playful smile—"unless we build a base inside the entire beltway around Washington and cover over the entire city."

He paused.

"Actually, not a bad idea," he muttered.

"So," and he wrote a C next to the downward arrow, "first there is compression, which can be defeated only by expanding the base to an utterly absurd width."

He then put a finger next to the arrow pointing up.

"So now we have our second problem, and that is vertical tensile strength. Not much of a problem for an earthbound tower a few miles high. But go out 23,000 miles?"

He shook his head.

"The centrifugal force imparted by the rotation of the earth will actually be trying to fling that tower up and away once you get out past . . ." He paused.

"Around 18,000 kilometers up," Eva interjected, "but, yes, sir, that upper part will be imparting a tensile or extension pressure. But to a certain extent that relieves the compression. Also—and this is crucial—gravity decreasing at an inverse ratio becomes significant even when just a thousand kilometers up. This is where the entire formula gets very complex. The higher you go, the less the compression weight created by gravity and then eventually the tensile effect of it trying to pull itself apart from above. In part, this does cancel out the issue of compression once above a certain height."

Erich smiled, as if pleased with an exceptional student, even as he fished a few more straws out of the pack and put all but one aside.

He held up the remaining straw, held one end, then pulled on the other, and it quickly stretched out and became distorted.

"So, even if you have something that can withstand the compression weight, it still has to hold up to the force that will try to stretch it out until it breaks and the upper part just goes flying off into space because of the momentum imparted by the earth's rotation. That is one tough formula to play with, Miss Eva."

She nodded without replying. It was obvious the old man had already prepared these responses and was a step ahead of any intern.

"Now, finally, the third force, which is lateral stress."

This time he held up one straw and pushed at the midpoint: it buckled over.

"The difference in angular momentum the higher up you go and lower down within the atmosphere can be impacted even by terrestrial weather. You ever been up a tall building, like the World Trade Center towers in New York, during a storm? Those buildings are designed to sway as much as six feet, and they are only a thousand feet tall. Some people have to quit their jobs there because they keep getting motion sickness. In fact, NASA has helped more than one building designer with wind-tunnel testing.

"You figure out the square footage of a side of the tower: it gets hit by a hurricane all the way up through and beyond the stratosphere, and the lateral stress loads are enormous. Out in space you even have, of all things, the solar wind, minute but impacting during a major solar event. Along over 20,000 or more miles of structure, it would be noticeable, especially if there is a major solar storm or coronal mass ejection storm.

"Now let's add in the fact that there are slight but noticeable anomalies in gravity, depending upon where you are above the earth's surface. That really threw us off-balance when the first satellites were going up and their orbits seemed a bit odd because of that difference in gravity over different locations because the earth is not a perfect sphere. And then let's add in the influence of the moon's gravity, even the sun's gravity. It all adds up to one heck of a calculation."

He looked at the broken straws on his desk, sighed, and sat back down.

"What about meteors, space debris, and satellite impacts?" Gary now threw in, and he almost regretted asking the question, because it was obvious that Eva, who was looking at the straws, was more than a little crestfallen at the moment.

Erich nodded in agreement.

"There are something like 10,000-plus objects in orbit as we speak, ranging from fingernail-size fragments, to an astronaut's glove, a rather expensive camera someone let float away, and satellites weighing several tons. All of them cross the equatorial plane twice in each orbit around the earth. On any given day, chances are one will come very close indeed to the tower. I'd guess that at least a few times a year, though we've yet to model it on a computer, a tower even a few centimeters wide would suffer an impact. And as Gary mentioned, meteor impacts are an unknown quantity but have to be anticipated, from something the size of a grain of sand to a darn big boulder tumbling along."

Eva sighed and finally said softly, "So you think it is impossible, sir."

Erich was silent for a moment, picked up one of the straws, twirled it around, then inserted a second one into it, then a third, and let the end drop into his empty coffee cup so the small tower leaned up and out at a drunken angle.

"No, I don't think it impossible at all. If I believed in that word, Apollo never would have gone further than that whiteboard"—he smiled—"and you would not be my intern this summer.

"You just told me your research project for the summer. And amongst other things some Cray time to try to model how many impacts per year striking a one-centimeter-wide tower would give us a solid number beyond mere guesswork for now."

She looked at him in surprise, a delighted grin creasing her features, green eyes sparkling.

"I'm running a lot of different things here, most of them crackpot, and I'm already late for my next group. We'll meet here same time every morning to talk things over, and once a week I'll want a written report from both of you as to the progress you've made. First things first: the latest data—declassified, of course—on carbon nanotube development, which will most likely be the only material that could withstand the forces involved."

"'We,' sir?" Gary asked, a bit confused.

Erich gave him a smile and he wondered, just wondered, if the old man was enjoying himself a bit too much at this moment.

"That's right, Mr. Morgan. You and Miss Eva are teamed for the summer and this is now your project as well."

"Sir?" Eva asked, looking at Erich with open surprise, but there was now a flash of anger in her eyes. "Do I not have the right to decide who I am going to work with on this idea?"

"Not here," Erich said with a tight-lipped smile. "Remember, Miss Petrenko, you are here as an exchange guest, and there are more than a few of the old Cold War crowd that would prefer if you were not here at all. I was already informed that you were to be paired with an American intern for whatever project you were assigned to, with access only to declassified information."

"You mean he is my KGB handler," she muttered softly.

His features changed in an instant in a flash of anger.

"No," he said coldly.

She lowered her head.

"My apologies."

"Nor will there be FBI, NSA, CIA, or"—he paused, eyebrows knitted—"Gestapo following you around. This is America of the 1990s, Miss Eva. So drop that line of thinking while you are our guest.

"We are scientists working on shared dreams. But doing research in conjunction with American interns is part of your package, and I've just selected who you work with, and that is final."

"Yes, sir."

Gary looked from Erich to Eva and suddenly wondered if he should ask for a transfer after all. Any fantasies he harbored that perhaps he could work his way toward a date with Eva had just been dashed by Erich.

"Uh, sir, I am of the opinion that this idea is sci-fi at best. It will never work."

Erich glanced at Gary and nodded.

"And that is why I am teaming you together. Sometimes the best science of all comes out of debate between those who say it is impossible and those who dream it is not. The one reaches up while the other keeps their feet on the ground."

He smiled again.

"And maybe, just maybe, the pragmatist learns to float a bit as well and believe in dreams. In the early days of Apollo, there were damn near duels using slide rules as swords."

"Slide rules?" Gary asked.

"Ancient instruments of calculation not requiring batteries," Erich said and now there was a smile again.

"Now, you two get to work, and no dueling!"

3

Today

"I feel as if the last eighteen years have been a waste," Gary sighed, gazing morosely into the teacup that Erich had filled with several ounces of Scotch.

He looked up at Erich, who was silent, the old man's gaze steady. Erich was not the type of person to pour out a line of self-pity to. He recalled that the first time he had done so, Erich had shut him off with an angry wave of his hand and asked him if he had ever been shot, been left behind by his comrades, had a friend press a pistol into his hand with the obvious message that he would have to finish himself off, because an SS unit was sweeping the field, looking for survivors of the recent fight. The SS did not take prisoners when it came to commandos, though they did entertain themselves by extracting what information they could before finishing their prisoners off. A Yugoslav resistance fighter found him first, and it was a five-mile hike to a safe haven, where a doctor finally took the bullet out of his chest, with only a single shot of morphine to deaden the pain—a bit. For years he kept the bullet pulled out of him and that pistol in his desk—empty, of course—until firm rules were sent out that any firearm was forbidden at the center. He said that when any adversity beset him, the pistol and bullet were a reminder that he had gone through worse.

After that brief story, Gary never went for self-pity again.

Eva sat by his side, sipping her tea without comment, while Victoria, sensing the three wanted to be alone and talk freely, had taken her iPad and was sitting outside. Gary could see her outside the office window, sitting against a tree, iPad set to one side, just staring off in the distance. He felt a swelling of pride and love just looking at her. At sixteen, she was far beyond her years in maturity, already focused on following her parents, and had already been accepted at the end of her junior year in high school to Purdue, to pursue a degree in aerospace engineering as well. She was almost up to the same level as they were on the engineering that would go into a space elevator. While other girls her age had posters of the latest rock phenomenon plastered around their rooms, she had photos up from *Curiosity*, a mission that absolutely enthralled her, and the classic old photo of a wild-haired Einstein. For her birthday, they had given her a somewhat beat-up old Subaru, but what made her grin was that her parking place in their driveway had a sign with "Genius Parking Only" and a picture of Einstein on it.

"The next step," Erich grumbled, interrupting his thoughts.

"What next step?" Gary asked, attention focused back on his mentor.

"There is always a next step," Erich replied.

Gary did not reply. After the grilling and humiliation of this morning, he felt all their dreams had been permanently dashed.

"You have any plans for the next week?" the old man asked.

"Well, if my wife and daughter would let me, I think I'd just go home and get drunk, sir. It is the end of the road. Our positions are cut, as you know. Eva can find a teaching position, but me? You know I was never the one to stand in front of a class of freshmen and give a lecture. Write a book and try to sell the public that way? Doubt if that would work; you need a storyteller for that, not someone who juggles calculus problems in their head."

He instantly regretted saying that. He and many others had been pestering Erich for years to write his autobiography, to which the old man growled he was not ready for that final act of retirement before fading into the night.

Again the icy stare, but this time Gary, filled with frustration, returned the gaze.

"Why do you ask if we are free this next week?" Eva interjected, putting a calming hand on Gary's shoulder. She had caught on, whereas Gary had not, that Erich must have something up his sleeve.

Erich smiled. Almost from their first day together she had Erich wrapped around her finger, the way a father would feel toward a special daughter.

"Actually, I am thinking about young Victoria out there. Her schedule?"

"She doesn't start college for a month," Eva replied.

"Excellent. There is room on the flight for her as well."

"Sir, I'm not sure I follow you on this," Gary said.

"Go home, pack your bags." He paused to look at his old-fashioned wristwatch. "You've got four hours to get to BWI Airport. A friend of ours will have his corporate jet waiting for you."

Gary stirred from his morose mood.

"Who?"

"A friend of ours who has taken great interest in the events of today. He expected this debacle. The moment the hearings closed and it was clear that NASA would be forced to entirely drop this line of research, he was already in flight from Seattle."

"Seattle?" Gary said, and there was now a touch of recognition.

"A friend who thinks it is time he stepped into this mad scheme of ours."

"Who, may I ask?" Gary whispered.

Erich smiled and pointed behind his desk, where an old battered suitcase was on the floor.

"Go home, pack bags for all three of you for a week, then come back here to pick me up."

"And do you mind if I tag along?" he added as he broke into a rather uncharacteristic grin.

Eighteen Years Earlier

"You are utterly impossible to work with," Eva snapped, getting up so swiftly from her chair on the other side of the table that she knocked it over.

"I need some fresh air," she announced, and stalked out of the room.

Gary yet again wondered if Dr. Rothenberg had teamed them together out of some perverted sense of humor, but as he watched her leave the room, he could not help himself. Intellectually he could barely stand to be with her for more than a few minutes, especially when forced to sit by the hour going over every tidbit of information they could dig out of the center's archives or, worse yet, down at the Library of Congress, pulling up obscure Russian aerospace journals, which she read out loud to him on their drive back to Goddard. Her nationalistic pride demanded she first translate into Ukrainian, then into English, and often it would be so confusing, he could barely understand what she was saying.

And yet, his attraction to her was evident to anyone watching the nuances of their interactions. Dates had been far and few between, and when he did get a date, either he was bored silly or within an hour it was obvious the girl could not wait for the evening to be over. Was there not a young woman out there who might enjoy sitting up late over cups of coffee, talking about dreams of space?

It was still a time when, in spite of the rise of feminism, it was felt that "women just don't go into math or the sciences." What absolute idiocy: he'd die to meet such a young lady, and at both a professional and personal level wished the gender ratio were the same. As a grad student he had taught freshman-level math classes, the usual three-credit prerequisite course for all students no matter what their majors were. When he had a female student who was obviously gifted in the subject, he would appeal to her to continue in that field, but for whatever reasons few rarely did. It was a brain drain of those who could potentially be the best in the field, and it saddened him.

Granted, he did have several female friends—"fellow nerds," they called each other—but there was never a sense of attraction like the one Eva triggered.

He got up, followed Eva out the door, stopped in the snack room to get a diet soda, then stepped outside into the boiling humid heat of a D.C. summer. To the northwest, dark clouds were gathering and there was a distant rumble, perhaps offering the momentary relief of a cooling rain, which an hour later would turn back into humid heat again.

She had sat down against a tree and just stared at nothing. He approached and held out the soda as a peace gesture.

"Thank you," she sighed in Ukrainian, popping the lid and taking a sip.

"Why are you so damn obstinate?" she asked, looking at him, but at least without the anger of five minutes ago.

"It's our job to ask for the hard facts," he replied. "Your whole premise for building this tower of yours is based on a what-if."

"It will come far sooner than nearly anyone realizes."

"Eva, you just assume that this talk about Japanese research on nanotube carbon fibers is going to surge forward and in another decade we will have something with the strength to build the tower. A snap of the fingers and the magic material that can withstand all the forces that can rip a tower apart will appear. But they are not even halfway to the tensile and compression strength you dream of, and our job here this summer is hard science."

"Give it ten years," she said coldly. "We will move ahead with all the other problems to be solved, then have them cleared and be ready to go the day the material is at last available to build with."

"All right. Let's say for the sake of argument your dream happens and ten years from now this miracle of C-60 carbon nanotubes appears. Then what?"

She was about to snap at him again, but somehow the peace gesture of the soda stilled her frustration. She took a big gulp and offered the can back to him and he took a sip.

"Go on. I'll listen," she offered.

He was about to add, *You mean, listen until you disagree, then tear my head off.* But he held back on that.

"You postulate your theory on building a tower on a what-if: the expectation that someone will figure out a way to manipulate carbon atoms and build molecules—what some are calling 'buckyball' molecules—into nanotubes hundreds of times stronger than tungsten steel. And then, not just strands a few millimeters in length in a laboratory, but hundreds of thousands of miles of the stuff, turned out by factories that are then capable of spinning them into cables thousands of kilometers long the way they used to make cables for suspension bridges."

"Your American history," she retorted. "When the first suspension bridges were built a hundred and fifty years ago, they didn't trust steel and used iron, even though it was brittle. So they overbuilt the cables to handle the stress. Fifty years later it was all steel and no one would even think of using something as ancient as iron. But they built the bridges with what they had, and that is my point.

"Can't you dream just a little?" she continued. "Back when the people in that building we work in, Dr. Rothenberg included, were dreaming up something called Apollo, they came up against a brick wall. The lunar lander needed an onboard computer. In the final minutes of landing, they could not rely on just an onboard radar system to send the data back to earth and then send the flight corrections back. That would take several seconds at a time when the astronauts needed split-second decisions. They needed a computer on board that could do it instantly. Only problem was, the computers of 1962 were bigger than the entire landing module. Six years later they had one the size of a suitcase that could handle the job. Rather than stop the program until the computer was built, they surged ahead and fit the computer in when it was ready."

"Barely," Gary replied. "Remember, *Apollo 11*'s computer froze up. The famous 1201 and 1202 alarms. I've listened to the tapes. It was a near run thing. There was too much data overload for its forty kilobytes to handle. If not for Armstrong and Aldrin being the best pilots in the world—or should I say the moon—and keeping their cool, they would have crashed."

"I'll acknowledge that," she said. "But Alexei Leonov could have pulled it off even without the computer."

He could not help but smile at her nod to Russia's most famous cosmonaut, the first man to "walk" in space back in the 1960s—a hero who she was proud to boast had actually come to the veterans' hospital her grandfather was in, sat by his side, and saluted him before leaving.

"Listen, Eva. My point is that you are postulating this entire tower on a carbon fiber that does not yet even exist except in theory and mathematical models. At least the guys who built bridges like Roebling and Eads did in the nineteenth century knew the strength of the iron they were using at that time. Your carbon nanotubes are still the stuff of science fiction. And now you are talking about building this tower the moment we think we have material strong enough. NASA does not get or give funding to manned missions with barely a safety factor."

"They did with *Apollo 11*. I read where the experts figured there was a fifty-fifty chance Armstrong and Aldrin would not return."

He was silent for a moment. There had been a lot of speculation about that long after the mission. Yes, the odds had been there; what happened with *Apollo 13* showed that. But times were different then. Real or not, there was a so-called race on to get to the moon first. That was no longer the case.

"At the time," he finally offered, "*Apollo 11* was thought to be way beyond 100 percent capable. Believe me, there was a lot of scrambling to upgrade a lot of components on board before they let *Apollo 12* take off four months later.

"You are saying ten years from now someone will develop a material strong enough, just at 100 percent, to handle the stress loads of a tower that will be 23,000 miles tall. Actually around 40,000 when the counterweight is added in."

"Talk in kilometers please," she said haughtily.

He could not help but smile.

"OK, 40,000 kilometers just out to geosynch."

"So?"

"No mission is going to get funding into the tens of billions of dollars based upon a zero-safety factor. No one will even begin to entertain the idea until there is a 200—better yet, a 300—percent safety factor. And even then, it will seem so sci-fi and high-risk, you'd be laughed out of the first funding hearing."

She shook her head angrily.

"If we wait that long, you and I will be gone and dead fifty years. There was a time, damn it, when people took risks because the payoff was worth it."

"Sell that to Congress. You wouldn't last ten minutes in a hearing, let alone in front of a doctoral dissertation committee."

"If we don't pick a point in the process where we at least make a trial attempt at building the tower, it will never happen."

"Not at only a zero-safety factor," Gary replied. "Get us up to 200 to 300 percent, but then you are back into pure science fiction, and that is not the mission of this place."

As he spoke he nodded at the Goddard campus around them.

She took the can of soda back from him and drained the rest.

And now, for the first time in the weeks they had been working together, she actually did manage a smile.

"Could I ask you for some more soda, please? It's hot, I'm tired, and if you want to continue this argument, I would appreciate something more to drink."

He knew he was being conned by a warm smile, and he was happy to go along with it. He returned a minute later with another can, which was already dripping with moisture in the humid air. In the distance the rolling peals of thunder were beginning to increase.

"Take that storm for example," he said while opening the soda and handing it to her.

"Yes?"

"The tower has to be built on the equator.

"One could build it off the centerline of the equator, but that starts to increase stress loads; so, yes, a given for a first attempt. Build it on the equator.

"So let's say Brazil or Indonesia. You get storms like that almost every day, towering giants 50,000 feet"—he paused to calculate—"fifteen kilometers high. Wind shear that NASA will not even send a plane through to try to measure. Hail the size of baseballs blowing around at a few hundred kilometers per hour. Take the surface area of the tower, measure out the total stress loads, and you are way past the snapping point the first time a storm like that hits."

She sighed, nodded, staring at the dark clouds.

"We build a buffering shield around it."

"A what?"

"First of all, the weather on the equator, contrary to what some think, is not at all violent. Hurricanes never happen there because the earth's rotation imparts a spin effect either clockwise south of the equator or counterclockwise north of the equator. So weather is not such a dynamic feature. Then picture the tower as a pencil. Now slide a cardboard tube over the pencil made of the same material for the first fifteen kilometers up. It can absorb the blows of a storm like that, even be broken in places, but the inner section, the tower itself, is protected."

"Oh, great. And how much more weight does that add on?"

She looked away.

"I haven't calculated that yet."

He pictured her description of a tower that, at points of potential high stress or impacts, had a shield around it, even just a mesh web the way an eighteen-wheeler truck exhaust pipe would have a protective baffle around it. It could absorb impacts of solid objects and break up lateral stress. But then, what to anchor that to? Anchor it straight to the tower and the problem would be worse with added surface area. But still, some sort of shock absorbers at the anchor points? He heard her laugh softly and looked back at her.

"Gary, you have been sitting there in silence for the last five minutes."

A bit embarrassed, he realized she was right; the problem had drawn him in and he was now trying to visualize an answer.

He nodded, took the can of soda back for another sip. He could have purchased two cans, but he liked the idea of sharing one with her.

"So let's buy the idea of a baffle down in the atmosphere; what about in low- to mid-earth orbit?"

"Go on."

"At this moment there are something like eight to ten thousand objects orbiting the earth, and it looks like we won't get the Cray computer time this year to run the calculations as to probability of impacts. Hundreds of them are valuable satellites—for example, your *Mir* or the *Hubble*, which weighs several dozen tons. They cross the equator twice in every orbit. Most are just junk: burned-out boosters, fragments from rockets that have blown, even junk just tossed out the window by manned missions or that floated off by accident. You add them up, do a cross section of the tower, and odds are . . ." Again he paused, running the numbers in his mind of a stationary object two hundred miles up and at least half a dozen feet across. "I'd guess on an average every six to eight months or so something will hit, and hit damn hard, moving at five miles"—another few seconds' pause—"at least eight kilometers a second. Even if it was just a stray bolt or an old camera or an astronaut's outer glove, that is a helluva lot of kinetic energy."

"Already thought of that," she replied with a knowing smile. "We'd have mounted lasers capable of vaporizing or shattering the smaller fragments. Functional satellites once the tower goes up, they just have small thrusters mounted on them, and if on a collision course just a few pounds of thrust can move them a couple of hundred meters to one side or the other out of harm's way."

He shook his head.

"After it goes up? As if everyone would cooperate. I can picture a few nations out there that would get a big laugh out of saying, 'Gee, sorry we hit your tower and broke it. Our apologies.'"

"Gary, I think anyone capable of orbiting a satellite would want to co-operate."

"And suppose they don't."

She was silent about that one.

He wanted to mutter again that she was dreaming, but things were going cordially at the moment: they were working together without passionate arguments.

"And that does not even factor in sats already in orbit."

She hesitated.

"We'll figure something out," she said.

" 'We'?"

"You're in on this too."

"To poke holes in it, Miss Eva. And frankly, a one-ton satellite would poke a very big hole, even if the tower was made of your miracle fiber."

The storm was drawing closer, and now the first heavy drops of rain began to fall, bringing with them the refreshing scent of a summer rain after a day of stifling heat.

She startled him by actually reaching over and patting his arm.

"That's our job this summer. To figure it out. Now let's get back to work."

4

Today

Following Erich's rather confusing directions, they at last found the terminal for private aircraft at Baltimore-Washington International Thurgood Marshall Airport.

They had packed so hastily, and Erich was being so mysterious about the reason for this trip now, that Gary was absolutely disoriented. Victoria had snatched his GPS for her car and he forgot to bring it along for this run to the airport, and though Erich could navigate the stars, getting from Goddard to the private terminal at BWI did throw him a bit.

Six hours earlier Gary was being torn apart at a Senate hearing, and now here he was? For what? He had flown in private jets a few times before, and inwardly admitted he was excited by the prospect, whatever it was, given Erich's insistence that they were going to the private rather than public terminal. At least, it sure beat what commercial flying had become of late. Victoria was beside herself with excitement, and Erich, while occasionally offering vague directions, entertained her with stories about the "old days" and all the famous astronauts and cosmonauts he had known.

Pulling into a parking space, Gary was surprised when several attendants descended upon their vehicle and helped them to off-load their bags. Years of commercial flying on a NASA budget had conditioned him to lugging his own baggage around and praying it would arrive at the other end. They didn't even stop inside the terminal other than an offer for a "pit stop" and a soda for Victoria, who took bottled water instead, before heading out on to the tarmac.

The pilot was at the base stairs to a Gulfstream jet and extended his hand, introducing himself as Danny McMullen. Then Gary looked up and saw who was standing at the top of the stairs, waiting to welcome them, and he suddenly understood why there was so much fuss and attention being paid to them.

Erich grinned and went up the steps first, and in spite of his ninety-plus years he almost had a spring to his walk, extending his hand to the man who was waiting for them. When he turned and looked back, Gary could not conceal that he was more than a bit surprised.

"Drs. Gary and Eva Petrenko Morgan," Erich announced formally, "it is my pleasure to introduce Franklin Smith."

Franklin Smith? Gary wondered. What in hell was going on here?

Smith was definitely a legend in the dot-com world. African-American, he had grown up in the South when segregation was still a reality. If fate had played out just a bit differently, he most likely would have been trapped in the world of his parents and grandparents. But the winds of change were stirring even in a remote corner of southeast Virginia. A friendly local electronics store owner, a refugee from Soviet-occupied Hungary, took an interest in him after catching him one day prowling around the Dumpster behind his shop, fishing out broken and discarded parts of televisions. When questioned, he said his family couldn't afford a televison, so he figured he would just build one himself. He soon had a part-time job at the store that quickly went from sweeping floors to working on repairs in the back room, and at night he trudged home with various castoffs to tinker with. From such simple gestures of interest, friendship, and love . . .

An African-American tech nerd in the South in the 1960s? The school guidance counselor in the typical once-a-year fifteen-minute interview suggested he go into television repair once he graduated or go into the army, but his friend at the store told him to reach much higher and believe in his dreams.

At seventeen Smith built his first computer. The school librarian, Betty Keller, sat there in wonder when he lugged the thirty-pound contraption into school; it could actually do some rather complex formulas, when it wasn't shorting out. Three months later, thanks to the love, guidance, long-distance phone calls, and help with applications by Miss Keller—a teacher every student should find at least once in their lives—Franklin was admitted with a full scholarship to MIT. But he never quite finished that degree when it was discovered he had hacked into the university's supposedly impenetrable computers to change grades for friends . . . an indication of his entrepreneurial skills at twenty-five bucks a pop. Even as he was being expelled, the dean said he had a bright future, given that the MIT registrar's office database system had been designed by MIT grads, only to be cracked by a third-year undergrad. On his way out the door, Franklin was paid a rather handsome sum—behind the scenes, of course—to close the door on the registrar's computers before leaving the campus.

If someone had been savvy enough to give him five thousand bucks as start-up money back then that benefactor would be worth hundreds of millions today. As for the high school teacher, Betty Keller, and his friend at the electronics store, they were enjoying retirement with beachfront homes in Maui, with scholarship funds set up for the store owner's multitude of grandchildren and an endowment fund for Miss Keller to do with as she pleased. There had been no hoopla and publicity about such gestures; it was simply that Franklin always remembered his friends, especially those who helped launch his career. Even MIT received a major donation every year, scholarships for kids from third world countries—something of an inside joke, given that it came from a student they had expelled!

Franklin Smith, losing out on the edge of the first "home computers" in the early 1980s, had built a firm specializing in scaled-down hard drives for the first so-called laptops when everyone else was looking for bigger, with the ability to put in a few more megs of storage. Few were thinking that smaller meant fitting them into the fifteen-pound laptops even if they had less than half the storage capacity. He had stayed one skip ahead of that market, selling off a few patents to the big players, but with a royalty fee adroitly added in for each unit sold. He then pulled out of that to go into the "dot-com" field with this new thing called the "Internet." And then, yet again, he pulled his investments out just before the big collapse, reinvesting in cell phone technology at a time when only the rich could afford such "toys" but foreseeing a day when even kids would be doing something called "texting."

He was always one step ahead of the game. Gary had met him several times at conferences, along with hundreds of others who had queued up to shake his hand. He was surprised to see Franklin sitting in the back of the audience when he and Eva delivered a paper on the use of space elevator technology that would eliminate the need for thousands of cell phone towers on the ground. After their talk, which was greeted with polite smiles and nothing more, they were surprised when Franklin presented his card and asked if he could receive autographed copies of their dissertations and any other research that NASA had in the public domain regarding this insane concept. They had not heard from him since that day.

Franklin was nearly twenty years older than they were but seemed ten years younger, his dark features framed by a neatly trimmed gray beard and gray hair. He stood tall and erect, features alight with a welcoming grin. He extended his hand to grasp Eva's and then Gary's, all but pulling them into his plane.

"Are you really Franklin Smith?"

Gary turned to see his daughter looking up at Smith's towering frame, wide-eyed, as if gazing at some film star.

"Last time I looked in the mirror, young lady, I was," he said with a chuckle.

"This is so cool!" she cried, and Franklin grinned with delight.

Gary could feel himself swelling with pride as his daughter, now blushing over her outburst, took Franklin's welcoming hand. She truly was a "nerd" and he adored her for it.

"I just read your article on disruptive technologies and marketplace investing as affected by that thesis," she said. "It was dead-on, sir."

"I think I sense an internship here," Franklin said, smiling. "Maybe next summer, young lady. I understand you start at Purdue, the same as your dad, in a few weeks."

Now she was truly blushing and could only nod.

"Consider it a firm offer, Victoria. We'll set it up for you."

She was speechless for once.

"If your parents are going to be helping me with a little idea I've been kicking around, it is the least I can do for them and you as a thank-you. Besides, I see something of me when I was sixteen in you as well.

"And might I add my compliments in standing up to that bully of a senator, always have wanted to see him put in his place."

"You saw that?" Victoria asked, a bit embarrassed.

Franklin chuckled.

"The blogger that filmed it, let's just say he works with me," Franklin grinned.

He gestured for the four to board the plane, pointing out where they were to sit and buckle in.

"Time for a little fun," he announced. "Once we clear D.C. airspace, I love flying this bird of mine. Five hours to Seattle—plenty of time for us to talk, if you don't mind hanging around the cockpit while I copilot. Captain McMullen there won't let me take his seat, though. I'm still working on my hours to qualify for the left seat of this plane."

He nodded to the captain of the plane, who grinned and shook his head.

"Sorry, sir, that's my job, or do you want to take it from me?" Danny had a decidedly Georgia accent and a warm, friendly grin. "Anyhow, the FAA would have my hide if I ever let you take the left seat."

The copilot didn't say a word, just looked up at Franklin with a nervous smile, obviously not pleased that he wasn't logging the seat time.

"Well, at least the copilot can go sleep while I have some fun. And I promise I won't try any rolls or loops this time.

McMullen looked at him sharply and Gary wondered if this remarkable man had actually tried to pull such a stunt. He felt it was better not to ask.

Minutes later they were safely buckled in, Victoria about ready to explode with excitement, Franklin punching in a loudspeaker switch so she could monitor air traffic control and hear that they were number one for takeoff, the sixteen-year-old exclaiming how, once at Purdue, parents' objections or not, she was getting her pilot's license.

As they climbed out of D.C. airspace, Gary sat back, looking out the window, the city disappearing beneath a shroud of low-hanging clouds. Smith got up to act as host. Erich, half curled up on the wide seat aft, which could be converted into a bed, was fast asleep. Eva gratefully accepted a glass of wine, Gary ignored her sharp look when he accepted a Scotch, which Franklin mixed with plenty of soda, and Victoria dived into the offering of sandwiches, a soda, and munchies. Franklin poured a sparkling water for himself and maneuvered two of the seats to face aft, where Eva and Victoria were sitting, motioning for Gary to sit beside him, folding down a table, and pulling out iPads for each of them from a storage cabin.

"I've taken the liberty of loading some things into the iPads," Franklin announced. Victoria began to open her carry-on bag to get hers out but Franklin shook his head.

"This is the latest model with a few extras added in by friends with that company," he said, and Victoria's eyes went wide as she hit settings and saw the extra gigs of power and features.

"Take it with you when you start at Purdue," he added. "It will blow everyone there away."

"You mean you're giving this to me?" she asked, gaping at him.

Franklin chuckled and Gary immediately started to feel a deep bond with this man. The laugh was rich, deep, taking delight in their tech-head daughter. He was obviously a man who enjoyed such things for the pleasure they brought to others, and not to show off his wealth, or as some subtle bribe upon opening their conversation. He spent a few minutes more chatting with Victoria, explaining the new flash drive chips that quadrupled the power of the device over the current commercial model, and then, in a serious tone, he cautioned her, for heaven's sake, not to lose it or let it be stolen, because the machine she held was still a year away from public release, and more than one competitor would pay a bundle to get their hands on it and take it apart.

"Perhaps we should leave it at home when you go to school, dear," Eva offered, and Victoria reluctantly began to nod in agreement as Franklin laughed again.

"If I didn't trust her, I wouldn't have given it to her," he said, and then winked. "And besides, it has a built-in destruct: if you get your password wrong three times in a row, the insides will cook off."

He settled back in his seat, and Gary looked at his iPad a bit nervously, noticing that one of the app icons was titled "Pillar to the Sky." He touched it and then sat in silent wonder as a video without narration began to play. Franklin touched the same button on his pad and a screen on the bulkhead flashed to life and began to play the same high-res video, in which computer-generated people boarded what looked like a high-speed train car, similar to the new French five-hundred-kilometer-per-hour rail coaches, and began securing their four-point belts and shoulder straps. The view shifted for a moment back to outside as the car began to accelerate like a maglev, switching onto a track that began to curve upward, ever upward. Then there was a view out the forward window of the car as it whisked through a terminal-like building that looked hauntingly like a Gothic cathedral. The angle of the car tilted higher and higher until it burst through an opening in the roof, and Gary could not help but gasp with delight.

The image shifted and swayed a bit, as if the car were transferring from one track to another, and then the view went straight up a wide pillar several dozen meters across, while to their right a car was coming down a parallel track, silently decelerated as it passed, then disappeared into the terminal, which was now half a kilometer or so behind the ascending car. The view shifted forward again. They were climbing straight up, clouds above, climbing on the side of the "pillar" that cut arrow-like through the billowing cumuli above. A few seconds later they were into the clouds, all going gray for several seconds, a dramatic flash of lightning off to their left, and then bursting through the clouds. It was twilight, the sun setting to the left, the landscape to either side and the tops of clouds brilliant with reflected light, while straight above, the sky was shifting to blue and then dark indigo.

It was a computer-generated vision of his dreams. He looked over at Eva and saw tears glistening in her eyes. Victoria had laid down her pad and sat in silence, watching the large video screen. The view shifted as if a passenger were looking out the window and the curvature of the earth was now noticeable, the glow of the atmosphere on the horizon giving way to a deeper indigo. The view shifted forward again, and then the screen was filled with a sea of stars beyond that pillar, which continued on straight up, ever upward, with no end in sight.

The heavens above, a sea of stars, a full moon off to the right. But it was the stars that held Gary's vision and dreams, and he, too, had tears in his eyes as if he were actually aboard that "car," riding his dream to the heavens.

The video suddenly came to an end.

"With your help we are going to build that," Franklin said, and his voice was actually touched with emotion. Gary turned away from the video screen and saw that Franklin was indeed filled with emotion. He chuckled a bit self-consciously.

"Some of my IT guys put that together for me—promotion video when the time is right. A lot still to be added. Stopping at what they call 'Five Hundred Mile Station,' a tourist destination. Some really cool views from five hundred miles up that only astronauts had before. Then a stop at what they are calling 'Geriatric One,' at the 12,000-mile mark. Some interesting thoughts there about medical benefits of low gravity for the mobility impaired. Then on up to the top at geosynch orbit. They promise it will go viral when we use it for selling the program."

He looked to Eva, then Gary, and again gave that infectious laugh.

"If it wouldn't embarrass you later, I wish I had this cabin rigged for taking video. Your expressions right now are priceless."

He paused.

"Well, actually I do have it rigged, but that is rather against the law if folks are filmed unaware . . . No, there are no hidden audio and such. I know some others in my position and in government who do that, but I hope you trust me on that."

"Trust him."

It was Erich, who apparently had woken up at some point.

"I hate take offs," Erich grumbled. "Bad memories of the time we wound up ditching in the North Sea. Then again, lucky we did: the Krauts were waiting for us where we were supposed to drop, and the other two teams were wiped out."

He shrugged, forcing a smile: it was a story that Gary had never heard about his war experiences, which he would try to prod out of him some day.

"Ah, my friend, the usual?" Franklin asked, and Erich nodded, coming up to sit across the aisle from them, refusing Victoria's offer of her seat and accepting the double Scotch handed to him by Franklin.

Franklin sat back down, pausing to look at the video image, the sea of stars bisected by the tower that rose into infinity.

"How do we do that?" Gary asked, staring at the screen filled with stars. "You saw the massacre we endured today at the Senate hearings. It is over with, at least in our lifetimes."

"That? Just a speed bump. NASA though a government agency—and dare I say the best of them all, along with our military who keep us free—does have friends in the private sector. Patriots, though that word sounds old-fashioned to some, who believe in dreams bigger than the narrow minds of a few who get elected for a few terms and then disappear without a trace in our history books. I have friends in a dozen different companies who kept projects alive when government funding was not there because they believed it was best for our country to keep those projects alive. So, my friends, just say I am one of those who still believe."

"And you are suggesting . . . ?" Eva asked.

"If the government won't start building it, we will, and then there will be a day when Congress catches on to the idea and NASA gets the funding it truly deserves. Then together we finish it."

He paused.

"Actually it was obvious years ago, in spite of the touch of optimism when they did some testing on lift vehicles out at White Sands. You might not have noticed me then, but I was there to observe the testing. But I knew a space elevator seemed so far-fetched to too many, and that is when I became, shall we say, very interested. Early on, I learned to look into ideas that others thought impossible."

"Like cracking MIT's computers to change grades?" Erich asked with a chuckle.

"Only illegal thing I've ever done," Franklin replied with a smile. "At least, so far.

"And thus our conversation now as to the next step we can take together."

He said it so matter-of-factly, as if it was already an assumed reality, that Gary just sat there, silent and wide-eyed. Six hours ago he had been calculating how much he and Eva would get in pensions, and at least, thank God, Victoria was on a scholarship. But now this?

"Sir, I do find this a bit unbelievable," Eva interjected, always the pragmatist. "You are saying you want to build the Tower. How?"

"Oh, the usual way," Franklin replied. "Draw up the plans, get the money, hire somewhere around 20,000 workers, and start laying bricks."

"Bricks?" Victoria blurted. "We need nanotube carbon, by the thousands of miles."

He laughed his infectious laugh.

"When I was a boy and the preacher first read the Tower of Babel story to us in Sunday school, I was actually rather ticked off. I told him it was lousy engineering, and after it collapsed, someone doing the investigation as to what went wrong got paid off to blame God."

He smiled at his own joke.

"I got spanked by my father for being disrespectful to the preacher over that one. Though later I remember the preacher over at our house and overhearing him talking with my parents to encourage me to question and do something unheard-of in my world at that time: go to college.

"When I was growing up, we didn't have Erector sets or stuff like that for us to play around with, even in school. So as a child I used to act out Bible stories in our yard, building hanging gardens, pyramids, and, yup, a few towers out of mud and cast-off bits of bricks."

"You didn't even have Legos in school at least?" Victoria asked innocently.

Franklin smiled but didn't say anything.

"You grew up in the South, didn't you, sir?" Gary asked.

"From now on it's 'Franklin,' though I prefer 'Frank' with my friends," he replied. "And I hope 'Gary' is OK with you."

"Victoria," Eva said, looking at her daughter, "Mr. Smith grew up when schools were segregated."

Victoria looked at him and blushed a bit.

"I'm sorry, sir."

"Sorry I grew up in a segregated world?" he asked.

"Well, I meant about how stupid my question was."

"There is never a stupid question, young lady, when it comes from a heart that wants to learn. As to my school, I didn't know any different; you don't when everyone is just like you and you don't see how the other half lives. But I was blessed with teachers who loved us; a school librarian who urged me to study math; a preacher who encouraged me but also taught me that I was part of a far bigger world and had a responsibility to that world; a kindly old man, a refugee to America, who would fish through his bins of discarded electronic parts at his store, explain what they were, their function and how I could put them together into something useful . . . I actually built a television for my family when I was in tenth grade—first one we had."

He sighed as if looking off to a distant memory.

"And now? Well, let's just say I was blessed with loving parents, same as you, and a country where I could fulfill my dreams after all. So there is nothing to be sorry about."

He reached over and patted her reassuringly on the shoulder.

"Anytime you want to learn more about what it was like growing up then, you just ask. I am proud of where I came from . . . and where we are going."

"You've said 'we' several times now," Eva interjected.

"Oh, we'll get to contracts and all that at some point."

"Ask for a million apiece for starters plus some royalties—gross, not net profits," Erich grumbled. "Hell, he can afford it!"

"Are you their agent?" Franklin asked in mock horror. "God save me from patent lawyers and agents."

"Better than that: I'm their mentor."

Eva smiled at that, and reached across the aisle to squeeze Erich's hand.

"I will not discuss what my retainer in all of this is," he said with a smile.

"I am certain we'll come to a satisfactory arrangement before we finish this leg of the journey," Franklin replied, nonplussed by Erich. "So, let's talk a little business first, then I'm up to the cockpit to do some flying, if I can drag the copilot out of his seat. Victoria, there is a jump seat up forward. I suspect you'd get a kick out of giving me a hand."

She grinned with delight, nodding eagerly. Gary said nothing, and Eva just looked straight ahead. In spite of their dreams of where they hoped to one day go—the riskiest venture in the history of aviation and space exploration—both were less than enthusiastic about their daughter's obsession with learning to fly. Several years back, the young son of one of their friends had "augered in" while still a student pilot, trying to show off over his girlfriend's house by attempting an aileron roll.

"While we're up front having fun, you two will find the usual contracts, nondisclosure forms, W-4s, incorporation papers; it's several hundred pages' worth on your iPads," Franklin continued. "You can go over them at your leisure. If you should desire, you can be referred to several lawyers in Seattle who are contract experts to go over the paperwork, though I hope that, as is, it meets with your satisfaction. We got plenty of time later to talk details, and, yes, I know Erich will act as your agent."

"Without charging them the usual agency fee, I might add," Erich muttered, drifting back into sleep as the double Scotch took effect.

"But for now, let me give you what we used to call in ancient times 'the CliffsNotes version.'"

Gary laughed at that, though Victoria and even Eva seemed a bit confused.

"Back in the old days," Gary explained to them, "when we used to listen to music from black disks that spun around on what was called a turntable and televisions came with rabbit ears sticking out of them, the way to get around your English and history course readings was to buy something called CliffsNotes. All the works of Shakespeare explained in thirty pages. Plato and all those other Greek guys in thirty pages. Stuff like that. Problem was, the professors read them as well."

"You mean, like Wikipedia today?" Victoria asked.

"Sorta like that."

"Got it."

"That is infamous that you did that, Gary. I never knew that," Eva exclaimed, genuinely upset. "I read every word of Pushkin and Tolstoy assigned to me, even if they were Russian and not Ukrainian."

Gary shrugged, a bit embarrassed.

"Franklin, maybe you better dig in and give us the straight line now, to save me from my wife's wrath."

Franklin got up and poured himself a soda water, no Scotch. He motioned to Gary's glass—which Gary put a hand over as a refusal after a sharp glance from Eva and Victoria—then sat down again.

"I am proposing that we build the Pillar."

No one else spoke; the only sound in the plane other than the engines and the occasional brief chatter on the radio channel, which was still open, was that of Erich's gentle snoring.

"I have followed your work ever since your dissertations. I met Erich"—he paused to look affectionately at the old man, fast asleep in his seat on the other side of the aisle—"when I first visited Goddard years ago to discuss some computer hardware designs for one of the Mars orbiters which my company was bidding for.

"Not many people realize that Goddard does the hard research, has people like you two working, dreaming, but then it is people like me who take those dreams and build them and make them work. Erich fired me up on my old childhood dream of the Tower of Babel; that was when he first mentioned that he had two young assistants working on the concept. You could say it seemed so insane that I could not help but be captivated by it.

"So, years back, I quietly created a corporation within my corporations tasked with seeing on our own if the idea was feasible and, if so, how we would do it.

"I assumed all along, political currents being what they were, that ultimately you would face the heartbreak of rejection you endured today."

Eva muttered something in Ukrainian that Gary and Victoria understood, but Franklin did not, and Gary was glad he did not.

"I felt morally bound to sit back to see what the government would do. You who labor at Goddard, Langley, Houston, and elsewhere under the NASA umbrella are like monks at times. You labor, intent on your dreams of a better future for all humanity. Your work is, as is said in the business, public domain, meaning it is free to anyone around the world to learn of and, dare I say, seize hold of and even build with the appropriate rights of patent attached to them. It might seem mercenary to some, but all benefit in the long run. Look at all the spin-offs of Apollo that private companies seized upon to enrich our lives."

He looked at the three staring at him and, a bit nervously, cleared his throat.

"My company within a company used material you two first pioneered, along with that of others, such as the NASA team at White Sands, who actually ran tests using laser-beamed energy to power an 'elevator climber.' Nice try, but I felt not feasible.

"That being said, I will have Mr. McMullen up front turn the plane around, we'll go back to D.C., I'll go with you to the patent office, and you can see where my company has quietly, and without any fanfare, filed scores of patents which originated in research you two have done—which, as you were government employees of our nation, was research free and open for any to use."

"Somehow what you said seems troubling to me," Eva replied.

"It is the beauty of our system in this country. NASA has created thousands of wonders that impact all our lives, from that iPad you have in front of you to some hospital tonight using imaging systems to save a child who needs surgery to clear out blood clots in their veins because of a birth defect that forty years ago would have been fatal. Without companies like mine to build on your research and make it viable, scientific progress would be at a crawl. It is what made America preeminent in the twentieth century, and my hope is to see it continue in that position in the twenty-first based upon ideas hatched at NASA that people like me then pick up and run with. That has always frustrated me more than anything else: how few in our country realize how much NASA has made their lives better and, in the case of millions now, saved their lives.

"Without companies like mine to take that basic research, which opened a door first cracked open by NASA, how different our world would be today, and how much poorer our quality of life."

Gary nodded in agreement. "Regarding the Pillar," he said, "I think we should focus on why we are on board this flight with you this evening and save the philosophical side for later."

Franklin smiled and cleared his throat.

"I have the plans in place to build it," he said, as if this were just a matter of simple fact that should not surprise them in the slightest. "The Japanese are years ahead of us in carbon nanotube technology research, but . . ."

And he grinned.

". . . I put quite a few billion into becoming the major stockholder of that company. We've developed, in secret, the technology to spin out not just a few millimeters of carbon-60 nanotubes. We have in place the ability to produce threads, continuous threads of whatever length you desire."

"Forty thousand kilometers' worth?" Eva asked with incredulous delight.

"Two hundred years ago, what was then called 'spring steel' could only be made by specialists, a few pounds at most in a pour. Fifty years later someone named Bessemer was making it by the thousands of tons. So, yes, Eva, I can give you—can give us—any length we want. And my goal was to be able to mesh together threads 40,000 kilometers in length, a means of fusing them together in a vacuum and low- or zero-gravity environment."

"My God," Eva whispered in Ukrainian.

"It is all in your pad computers. Now, to cut to the chase, as they used to say. I want to incorporate with you. This started out as your dream. It is now time to translate that into reality. You two"—he smiled, nodding to Victoria—"and when she is eighteen, your daughter as well, will be partners in this venture. To be blunt, since you were working for Goddard with nearly all your research, your efforts are public domain. I think my team, in secret, as is common in this business, such as the legendary 'skunk works' of the 1950s and '60s, has improved on the practical aspects and patented many of your initial efforts."

"If so, why do you need us?" Eva asked, and after her initial enthusiasm, with a touch of cynicism now.

"I know this sounds like a line but I believe in honesty and fair play," Franklin replied. "You two thought up most of this, though others had a role as well. If you want me to sound pragmatic and not sentimental, there is a lot more to be done to transfer this from theory to practice, and at this moment I feel you are the two most valuable people on this planet to make my dream come true, and thus I want you on my side."

"With that said," Erich muttered, obviously not fully asleep, "to hell with a million dollars: ask for ten million a year."

"I thought you were asleep," Franklin said, looking over at the old man half curled up on the double-wide seat.

"Old habit from the war: always sleep with one eye and ear open," Erich whispered.

They could not help but laugh.

"I think we need each other, my friends," Franklin said, nodding toward Erich as well. "You are the brilliant minds who dreamed of this. I am asking for you to partner with me to build that dream, because I have the resources to do it."

Gary, Eva, and Victoria, who together had felt so defeated less than a dozen hours ago, just looked at him in stunned disbelief.

"Tell them what you are willing to put into this," Erich muttered.

Franklin was silent for a moment.

"I think it was Andrew Carnegie, reflecting on his accomplishments, who said that the pleasure of life was, in the first half to build his empire, and in the second half to give nearly all his earnings away . . . that he who died rich, ultimately died poor."

"How much?" Erich grumbled.

Franklin's features were now fixed with intensity.

"I'm putting up everything I own. At last count it was something like fifty billion dollars."

Eva actually gasped. Victoria looked at him wide-eyed. Only Gary could respond.

"Not enough," he sighed, "regardless of what the dreamers—of which I am one—would say. It will be a hundred billion or more to have a fully operational tower viable not just for exploration but commercial use as well."

"What is fifty billion more or less?" Franklin said, and there was a look of complete earnestness in his eyes. "I'll find the money; it is out there from my generation who created the computer revolution. Men and women like Branson, Rutan, and others, when they see we are dead serious about this, will be knocking on our door. And that is where you, my friends, come in. With your names attached to this, they will come. You might have led a somewhat cloistered life at Goddard, but believe me, your work is known where it matters and thus another reason I want you on my team. You carry the respect of more than you know with you.

"Together, we will build it. We will create a new American dream for the twenty-first century, and though some shortsighted types in our government lag behind, the work of NASA will shine forth again as it did with Apollo and *Curiosity*, which still roams the plains of Mars. Believe me, they will come and we will build our Pillar to the Heavens."

As he spoke, it was as if Franklin were standing before an assembly of others like him, making his pitch. The force of his personality was such that none could ever disagree.

And Gary could not help but believe.

"This flight is only the first leg of our journey. Three days from now I look forward to showing you something that will prove my point. But, for now, look through the contracts on your computers. I am certain, of course, dear Dr. Rothenberg will want certain addendums to your contracts, and I'll be frank. There was an old Western movie I loved where the main character said, more than once, 'Make a deal that is fair to the buyer and fair to us.' Feel free to tell me any concerns."

"Three days from now?" Eva asked. "I thought we were just going to Seattle."

Franklin smiled.

"For starters. I want you to meet our team first. I regret this, but my darn lawyers will hang me if I don't say this now: you will have to sign the nondisclosure forms before you decide to work with me. After that, then on to someplace else once we get the paperwork taken care of."

As he spoke he stood up and stretched, the somewhat narrow cabin of the Gulfstream confining his towering six-and-a-half-foot frame.

"But for right now, I feel like I need a few hours of log time copiloting this bird. Miss Victoria, would you care to copilot for this copilot?"

She leapt up with a grin.

"Can we try a loop?" she cried.

He laughed softly.

"I think the FAA and the pilot would not approve, but we'll still try a few tricks—all legal, of course, young lady."

Minutes later, after Victoria had announced over the intercom that all passengers should expect some turbulence and to secure their seat belts, the jet was weaving and banking. The now replaced copilot was sprawled out in the aft bed, fast asleep; Erich was stirring and muttering that the turbulence felt like the damn flak while going in for a drop; Eva was complaining that this man up at the controls was not the best example for their daughter; and Gary was silently reading through the pages of data in his computer in all but absolute disbelief.

The dream could indeed be real.

5

Eighteen Years Earlier

The two stood at Erich's door, both nervous. They had sent up their joint report to him the day before and now it was time for the final meeting of their internship. Eva was flying out from Dulles at the end of the day, and Gary would drive back to West Lafayette, Indiana, after dropping her off at the airport.

The door opened and both stiffened slightly. It was the assistant director of Goddard, saying something over his shoulder to Erich about him coming over for dinner soon. He paused and looked at the two interns.

"So you two are his imaginative geniuses," he said, extending his hand first to Eva and then Gary.

"Now, the real act of genius," he chuckled, "would be convincing the higher-ups to try to work just fifty billion or so more into the budget. If you could pull that miracle off, I'd hire you on the spot right now!"

Neither of them spoke and he smiled.

"Of course, your luggage must be checked, Miss Petrenko, before you depart our company today."

She reddened, and Gary, standing behind the administrator, started to wave his hand to urge her not to explode.

The assistant director laughed and extended his hand for a fatherly pat on her shoulder.

"The Cold War is over, Miss Petrenko. Just joking, there will be no luggage check. Please convey to Professor Rakolvski, who I assume you are working with, my warmest regards. Years ago we agreed that most of this rivalry was foolishness and it is time to work together."

The icy glare changed to a warm smile.

"He is my mentor."

The assistant director winked at her.

"I know; that is why we agreed you'd be our first exchange intern. My old friend Basil and I had a long talk about you before you were even aware of our plot. Safe travels home."

He held out a small box.

"Not sure if this will get through your customs, but Basil claimed a great weakness for my wife's pecan pie. Please convey it to him with our warmest wishes."

Eva actually curtsied slightly as she took the box, definitely still an Old World custom and clear indication this meeting was no accident: the assistant director had been waiting to meet her and bid her a fond farewell.

He shook her hand again and left. Erich, as usual behind his desk, had tea already poured for Eva and coffee for Gary. He waved them into his office, motioning for Gary to close the door.

"So you met the assistant to my boss," he said. "I think he was hanging around to meet you two."

"Why would that be, sir? There are fifty interns checking out today."

"Besides his friendship with your Basil Rakolvski, whom I hold in high regard as well, I daresay it is because I passed your report on to him last night. He e-mailed back to me." Erich gestured at his computer. "Actually, I hate those things; everyone says they will make life easier for us, but I think we'll wind up spending half our days just answering the darn mail. Anyhow, I think he said something to the effect of I was bloody crazy for letting you two work on this and nothing else for the summer. That it was a sci-fi fantasy dream. If a Senator Proxley got wind of the fact that even interns were working on it, especially one from Russia . . ."

He paused.

"Excuse me: especially if one from the newly independent Ukraine was involved, he'd be screaming about security. And after saying that, he said he wants the two of you back next summer to continue your research, this time with a stipend and expenses covered by us as well."

The two could not contain their grins. In the last few weeks Gary had taken to bringing along an extra bologna sandwich and a bag of chips when he noticed how Victoria would beg off going to the café for lunch.

"So, you two finally reached some sort of agreement?" Erich asked.

"We met in the middle," Eva said. "Actually, about 90 percent my way."

She looked over at Gary and smiled.

Erich picked up the 155-page printout that they had written together over the last two weeks. It admitted to one predication outside the realm of current science: that research in carbon-60 nanotube technology would accelerate and reach the strength required for the tower within fifteen to twenty years. After that assumption, everything else followed.

Erich made the gesture of thumbing through the report.

"I like the idea of it being a ribbon rather than a thread but, given costs and the complexity of manufacturing a ribbon when we have yet to even create sufficient material beyond a few millimeters in length, that the first attempt should be a single wire—good thinking—and that from that single wire, we later haul up material for a ribbon at a fraction of the cost of sending it up via rockets."

He paused.

"But regarding collision avoidance with the wire by deliberately triggering a harmonic wave to swing the tower out of the way, I think you are a bit overoptimistic about the ability to dampen that."

"I know, sir, the whole 'Galloping Gertie' nightmare," Gary replied, "but it is the only alternative we could come up with for collision avoidance."

"Exactly."

Both he and Eva had pulled up videotapes of the infamous "Galloping Gertie" bridge disaster of 1940 and even watched the original 16-millimeter films of the incident in the National Archives, at times pausing frame by frame. "Galloping Gertie" was the tragic, sarcastic nickname for an elegant, slender suspension bridge built over the Tacoma Narrows in Washington State in the late thirties. Too elegant and too slender. The design engineers had run all the usual calculations about the impact of wind and weather but had let slip by wind of a particular velocity from a particular direction. It had set the bridge to swaying, which like all suspension bridges it was designed for. But a harmonic wave had set in, like a vibration on a violin string, running up and down the string; just as the wave reached a particular point, the impact of the wind increased the vibration, building on it, doubling its intensity with each wave running up and down the length of the bridge.

It was a remarkable film to watch. A car abandoned by a panicked driver in the middle of the bridge was soon being tossed up in the air like a child's toy as the waves of the harmonic vibration raced back and forth along the length of the bridge. Torque began to set in, the bridge floor twisting and swaying . . . and then it simply ripped itself apart.

It was fascinating and it was horrifying.

"So you propose that eventually there will be thrusters not just to bend the ribbon out of the way of any debris or satellite but also to dampen out any harmonics."

They nodded.

"A tricky game when you think of 'Gertie.'"

"Sir, the computer technology to work in advance of that and fire at precisely the right intervals will handle it," Eva replied. "If we can get some time on that Cray computer next year, we might be able to work out a variety of simulations."

"We have no other alternative," Gary said.

"No, obviously not. Just, at times it is healthy to think worse-case scenario. You are coming into your landing site, your computer is overloading, spitting out a 1201 alarm, where you were programmed to land on close inspection is a boulder field. You spot what might be a good landing spot a couple of miles away and Mission Control is telling you that you've only got a minute's worth of fuel left."

Of course he was referring to the famed piloting of Armstrong and Aldrin with *Apollo 11*. If they had not abandoned the programmed landing site, they would have crashed. If they had panicked even for a second and been indecisive or decided it was time to argue about where they should land, they'd have crashed.

"I only trust silicon so far when it comes to decisions. Suppose there is a full power failure along the entire system while the mother of all storms is blowing out a coronal mass ejection from the sun, and an ascent or descent car has jammed up on its track."

The two were silent.

Erich shook his head but then smiled.

"My job is to encourage, but then to poke holes in the dreams of interns and freshly minted Ph.D.'s. Neither of you have factored in two or more potentially disastrous events hitting at the same time. Thank God for *Apollo 13* they still had the lunar lander attached when the command module had its blowout and power was lost. No one had ever thought up that one for the simulators, or using the lunar lander engine as a booster to get them home quicker before they ran out of power and breathable air."

The two were silent.

He closed the report.

"A good start, you two. Brilliant, actually. Just poking you a bit to start thinking about the next step, the numerous steps to come. I'll send you my analysis and the holes I see after you get back to your universities. I can tell you right now that the weight to send what you call a 'ribbon' aloft would be staggering, so start smaller, lighter, then build from there as you suggest. It's brilliant.

"You are both invited back next summer to continue your research—together."

He gave them a conspiratorial smile. Eva did not react. Gary did blush a bit as he looked sidelong at Eva. After ten weeks he was absolutely smitten with her, but she had indicated no interest beyond an occasional sister-like peck on the cheek when he had shown some courtesy. He knew that darn near every male intern and for that matter every single male staffer, some well into their forties, had tried hitting on her this summer, and the result was that she was referred to as the "ice princess," along with a few other less than complimentary nicknames. The few times she had really opened up about her personal life, it was always about her parents, younger brother, and sisters, who she adored, reverence for her heroic grandfather, but never a word about at least a boyfriend back home. She was absolutely focused on one thing, her dream of this tower. And he had allowed her to pull him into that dream, not in order to try to win her favor, but because he found that he actually could believe.

There was another change in Eva that had become apparent over the summer. She had even grudgingly admitted in roundabout ways that she tended to look upon the idea of a tower almost as a work of art, a spiritual act, and when she did "loosen up," it was about the beauty of it, the societal impact, the dreams of humanity to reach for the stars and how, once that doorway was open, the world could be transformed. In contrast, he saw it from the more analytical perspective of a born engineer and at times sent her crashing back down to the hard earth of mathematical realities.

"When's your flight?" Erich asked, looking at Eva.

"Leaves at 5:15, direct to Moscow."

"Who'd have thought it ten years ago. Direct flights daily, Dulles to Moscow, but God protect you if it's Aeroflot," Erich said softly. "Anyhow, that leaves you two enough time to get over there and say your good-byes."

He made a show of looking at his old-fashioned wristwatch, the same one he had worn in the war.

"One final question. Your academic plans for the forthcoming year?"

"Well, sir, I have my dissertation, of course. Professor Rakolvski has already approved the topic."

"Very good, I look forward to seeing the drafts next summer."

He had just put the pressure on her. When it came to dissertations in aerospace engineering, two to three years was the norm.

"And you, Gary?"

"I'll submit my dissertation proposal next week, once I'm back at Purdue."

"Subject?"

He took a deep gulp.

"Space elevators," he said, his voice a bit strangled.

"*What?*"

Eva turned in her chair, and if looks could kill . . .

"We can both work on the same subject," he said hurriedly. "No one else has taken it to a dissertation level yet."

"I had the idea first."

"It's not copyrighted," Gary said defensively.

"So all summer long you were just acting polite so you could pump me for everything I know and run out and publish it first."

"Like hell," Gary snapped, surprised that anger had taken hold of him. Beyond their work together, he had all oh-so-cautiously tried to truly earn her trust and maybe even some emotional response. Her malevolent gaze told him that had just been vaporized.

"Eva. You hooked me on the idea. What else could I possibly do?" he offered hastily.

Erich, sitting across from them, just relit his pipe and smiled good-naturedly without saying a word.

"Don't you dare publish first," she said bitterly.

"Both of you, wait a minute . . ." Erich began, but it was like trying to wade in between two wildcats that had finally cut loose. They ignored him; the building tension of the entire summer had been unleashed, with accusation and counter-accusation being shouted back and forth. That he was a thief plundering her ideas; that she was arrogant, stuck-up, and it was not her idea to start with, that Tsiolkovsky had thought it up first a hundred years ago and anyone could work on it from there.

"Both of you, shut up!" Erich finally shouted, using his German-turned-British officer commando's voice.

The two fell silent.

"There is room for a dozen dissertations—fifty dissertations—on this. You two are the start. Follow the ethics. No collaboration while drafting; pursue your own research. You'll both be published 6,000 miles apart, and someday, someone doing your biographies will wonder about it all. Now get out of my office without another cross word between you two!"

It was not a suggestion, it was a command, and they were indeed silent, gazing at him.

"And, damn it, no arguing as you head to the airport. You can both contact me via this e-mail thing whenever you need information or advice. I'll keep your files separate out of ethical consideration, since you are both working on the same topic, and will offer no advice without providing the same to the other. Fair enough?"

Eva, breathing heavily, simply nodded while again glaring daggers at Gary.

"I think a year from now, when both of you"—he place an emphasis on the word "both"—"have your drafts done, you'll enrich the field by having different perspectives."

"But . . ." Eva started to retort, but an icy glance stilled her protest.

"Save it for next year," he said, and there was an ever-so-faint smile.

"I think you two will have come to some understanding by then. OK, get going or you'll miss your flights."

Standing outside, Eva announced she'd prefer to take a taxi, which Gary ignored, muttering that it was absurd: it would cost fifty bucks, which she didn't have, and she'd miss her plane.

The drive to Dulles, on the far side of the Beltway, was in total silence. He had thought that there would be time to pull into short-term parking, help her get her luggage in, even spend a few minutes together before she headed for her gate. Instead she just gestured to the ramp where passengers off-loaded and drivers went on their way.

Opening the trunk, she pulled her own bags out before he could offer a hand, and then she slowed, stopped, and looked back at him, and he could see there were tears in her eyes.

"I came to trust you," she said, her voice breaking.

"And you still can. Dr. Rothenberg was right. I would never use anything you created this summer, Eva. I swear to it. Most of our time was looking at what others wrote and trying to calculate if it was viable or not. You had the idea of the mesh and ribbon first; I'll never mention it. I really swear to you I won't."

She nodded, started to turn, and looked back at him.

"I'll try to believe you," she said.

"I'll prove to you that you can trust me."

She finally let go of one of her bags and extended her hand.

"Good-bye, Gary, I hope to see you next summer."

He took her hand and then ventured to do something he had thought about for weeks. He drew her in closer and kissed her gently on the lips . . . and she returned the kiss.

"Eva. I love you."

Her eyes widened in surprise.

"Really?"

"Yes, really."

She leaned forward and kissed him again, then stepped back.

"Then I publish first."

"How about on the same day?"

"Moscow time is seven hours ahead of Washington time," and now she stepped closer to him, smiling, offering another light kiss.

"I'll agree to seven hours, then," she whispered.

The doctoral dissertations of Gary Morgan, Ph.D., and Eva Petrenko Morgan, Ph.D., were published two years later, on the first anniversary of their wedding, which took place at the end of their second summer interning together at Goddard. Erich Rothenberg stood in as "father" to give the bride away. Three days after their marriage, Eva returned to Moscow to finish her dissertation and defend it. Upon receiving her degree, she flew back to the States to be with Gary permanently. Victoria was born a year and a half later, her parents working side by side at Goddard for the next sixteen years.

Eva did beat Gary to publication by seven hours, and never let him forget it. She had never bothered to point out that seven hours could also mean a one-day difference as well. Therefore, in all academic and scientific journals henceforth, she would be listed first when it came to credit, as her work had been published seven hours plus one day ahead of Gary's. It was a technicality that never bothered him, since she had given him Victoria and a spiritual vision of the tower that she had eased into the soul of an engineer.

6

Aranuka Island, Republic of Kiribati

The helicopter touched down gently, and Gary smiled sympathetically at Victoria, who looked decidedly green. The poor kid's enthusiasm had dampened significantly in the last hour and a half. On the flight from D.C. to Seattle she had stayed up the entire way, glued to the jump seat in the cockpit, then sleeping most of the day while her parents toured what was basically an ordinary-looking office building before taking off that evening on the next leg of their journey out to Honolulu. Victoria was again glued to the jump seat up front, chatting with the pilot and Franklin while Gary and Eva luxuriated in actual real pull-down beds aft.

Erich had been left behind in Seattle; though offered a seat, the elderly gentleman begged off, and Gary felt it a wise move. Jumping halfway around the world, even for someone half his age, would take its toll; and after the fiasco of the hearing with Proxley, he was asked to come back to pour oil on the troubled waters, since the senator was now making noises about entirely wiping out NASA's advanced research division.

After refueling in Honolulu, it was on to one of the most remote island nations in the world, Kiribati, once known as the Gilberts, approximately halfway between Hawaii and New Zealand, its more than seventy tiny coral atolls neatly bisected by the equator.

When they came in to touch down at the main airport for the Republic of Kiribati, Gary fell silent as the plane turned for the final run in to the airport, which ran the length of the island of Tarawa. Tarawa was a name branded in his family's memory. His grandfather's kid brother had died there in 1943, his remains never recovered. He recalled the day he asked his grandmother about "Uncle Gary," whom he was named after; she had produced an old yellowed album, pages brittle, with photographs of the family in the 1920s and '30s. Among them was a photo of his namesake, looking so young and proud, a marine corporal at eighteen. And then the faded telegram: "missing in action and presumed dead." There were two certificates on the next page, for the Purple Heart and Navy Cross, and a final photograph taken years later of his name on the memorial to the missing at the national cemetery on Oahu. Gary would never forget the aged, wrinkled hands of his grandmother brushing across the telegram and how she began to cry on recalling how, when the Western Union boy arrived, at first she did not know if it was news of her young husband flying missions over Germany or her brother-in-law, and the guilt she felt because she was relieved that at least her husband was still alive.

As they touched down on the short runway, plumes of coral dust kicking up, he wondered if the dust of his namesake swirled about them.

"This is where your Uncle Gary died?" Eva whispered, squeezing his hand in understanding. He could only nod.

"Who was Uncle Gary?" Victoria asked, looking over at her father, concerned that he was visibly upset. He realized he had never spoken of him to his daughter.

"He was your father's great-uncle," Eva said softly, "There was a battle fought here during the war and he died here. Your father is named after him."

Victoria was silent. Her mother had often told her about her own grandfather, a hero of Stalingrad, but she had never heard her father speak of his family's loss.

Franklin overheard the conversation, and as they disembarked the plane, he put a hand on Gary's shoulder.

"Our dropping in here is somewhat unannounced," he said softly. "I want you to see some things first. On the way back, after we've had a chance to rest and wash up, we'll have to go through the diplomatic niceties of meeting with the president of Kiribati, do some politics. After that, I am sure, if you wish, he will be more than glad to provide a guide to explore the battlefield here, perhaps even lend assistance to try to find where your great-uncle died, if that would be of comfort. The citizens here know more than most how much they owe to the United States Marines."

A helicopter was already waiting and Franklin hurried them to it.

"Word will get out fast that I am here," he said, his tone serious, "and these folks take hospitality seriously. I did call the president to let him know we're coming—it would be rude of me not to—and besides, he is one person I must keep very happy. But I wanted you to see something first before all the ritual greetings and such take up the rest of the day."

Once hustled aboard the helicopter, burdened down only with overnight bags, they lifted off.

The day was scorching hot and humid, and within a minute after liftoff the turbulence began to hit.

Franklin reached into his pocket and pulled out a small medicine bottle. "Forgive me, I should have thought of these before. Ginger root. Forget all that medicine that knocks you out. Saw it on that show about busting myths, and it really does work. Even some of the astronauts swear by it."

He popped two into his mouth, passed the bottle around, but ten minutes into the flight it was too late for Victoria as the helicopter bumped and swayed through the turbulent air.

She was utterly embarrassed and in tears of shame, the pilot then going for higher altitude to reach smoother air, where it was at least cooler.

"It's only forty miles to where we are going; we'll be there in another fifteen minutes, young missie," he said.

"Not soon enough," Victoria gasped in despair.

The helicopter, up at over 5,000 feet, dipped over slightly and raced toward its destination. Franklin, unable to contain himself, pointed to an atoll straight ahead.

"There it is!" he cried, voice filled with excitement. "Aranuka."

To a tourist, it most likely would have looked like paradise: a low palm-studded island, sand that was blindingly white under the morning sun, an outer reef, the water between the reef and island a brilliant turquoise, the ocean beyond a near indigo blue. As they drew closer it actually looked like three islands linked together by sandbars.

But at this moment, after two straight days of travel, Gary was exhausted, something that he noticed was hitting him more of late if he did not get regular sleep; and in spite of the ventilation, the scent in the cabin was less than pleasant, a mixture of K1 turbo fuel and Victoria's unpleasant misery. He just gazed at the island without comment, though Franklin was grinning as they were coming in to land.

As they drew closer, details became clear after passing through a low-hanging tropical cloud that caused the chopper to bounce and Victoria to moan in distress. There was a small landing strip at the north end of the island that looked to be at most 3,000 feet long. But on a long northwest-to-southeast axis, heavy construction equipment was at work, the outline of a runway extending most of the length of the island being laid out, some of it disappearing into water, where it looked as if a couple of dredging ships were dumping fill. Half a dozen ships were anchored in the lagoon, one of them a rather large vessel several hundred feet in length that reminded him of ships used for exploratory drilling. From the air he could see a large hole had been cut through the coral atoll, with breakwaters built to either side. He wondered if this country had an Environmental Protection Agency: the thought of blowing holes through coral reefs was anathema now back in the States and most islands of the Caribbean, not to mention filling in a fair part of the lagoon for what looked like a runway nearly two miles long. Dozens of Quonset huts arrayed in neat rows filled the south end of the island, and on the northwest-to-southwest axis of the island.

As the helicopter swooped down low, it was obvious that Franklin in his excitement wanted to give them an aerial tour, but out of concern for Victoria he told the pilot to touch down in the middle of the runway and taxi into the open shed hangar.

There was a gasp of relief from Victoria as the helicopter gently settled down, and once the pilot announced it was safe to get out, Victoria all but sprang from her seat and lost it again within seconds after her feet touched the ground. Eva, in motherly fashion, put a supportive arm around her daughter's shoulders.

Several men were coming over; to Gary's amusement, one of them was wearing an old-fashioned pith helmet, the others the standard yellow or orange construction helmets. The man leading the group and wearing the cork pith helmet was dark-skinned, obviously a native of the area. He grinned, hand extended.

"Frank, how in hell are you!"

"George, damn good to see you."

The two embraced, patting each other on the shoulders. Quick introductions were made. Franklin explained that George, a civil engineer and a graduate of Stanford, was his chief of construction on the island. George paused, eyes filled with pity for Victoria, and went to her side.

"Come along with me, little lady. Our doctor has a magic cure; then a dip in the ocean to cool off and you'll feel just fine. You're not the first or the last to have a touch of the sickness of the air flying here. We have just the thing for you."

She was grateful to be led away. Eva wanted to follow. The pilot had obviously radioed ahead, and a heavyset woman, who George explained was his wife, and one of the doctors for the crew, was already running up to Victoria, giving her a warm embrace in spite of the state she was in, chattering away about how Victoria was the same size as their daughter and they'd get her some fresh clothes and even a bathing suit so she could swim after a quick shot to fix up her tummy.

"Do you think of everything?" Eva asked, looking back gratefully at Franklin.

He smiled.

"I try. I puked my guts out a couple of flights back. I'm sorry I forgot to have you all take some ginger pills before we even landed at Tarawa. Where we are standing now is just several miles from the equator. It gets damn hot, turbulent at midday, and as for the work crews, we have to keep a sharp watch for heat exhaustion. Sarah, George's wife, is our doctor and a favorite on this island, something of a supermom with six children of their own."

He paused, looked around at the construction crew, and pointed out a young man driving a grader leveling the new runway. "That's their oldest, home from Stanford for the summer. I swear, half the crew feigns sickness on a regular basis just to get some motherly attention from her."

He motioned them over to a jeep and they piled in, George driving, and headed off on what started as a paved road, but halfway down the length of the small island became a rutted track, swinging around the road crew, which in spite of the hundred-degree heat were hard at work grading and laying down hot asphalt. Franklin pointed to the right, where the dredging ships were at work, explaining that the plan was to have a 6,000-foot airstrip operational in six months, and within two years an 11,000-foot runway that could handle anything short of an Airbus 380.

They passed the rows of Quonset huts, most of them empty except for the dining hall serving out a late-morning brunch, and crews at work to the east side, putting up yet more huts to house additional workers, and then came to a stop at the southern tip of the island.

Franklin got out and, with a touch of a showman, proudly pointed out to sea.

"Nine hundred and forty-two feet out that way is the equator."

Gary and Eva stared out to sea and then both of them laughed, Eva commenting that somehow she half expected to see some sort of line out there marking that it was indeed the equator.

"I'd take you out there, but if you take one step beyond, both of you will have to endure the ancient ritual of the sea, meeting King Neptune, and graduating from being polliwogs. We'll save that for another time when Victoria can join in the fun. My friends here put me through hell with that one, but it will be toned down a bit with ladies present.

"So I flew the three of you all this way to see this," Franklin said, and he gestured to the huts, the ships anchored in the lagoon, what definitely looked like an oil rig out just beyond the barrier reef . . . and that was it.

It was all a bit anticlimactic, Gary thought for a moment. And inwardly he was calculating the expense of just flying them here on a private jet for this view.

"This, my friends, is where we are going to build our pillar."

Neither spoke for a moment. There was no joyful jumping up and down, shaking of hands, or backslapping. The two, more than anything else, were beyond exhausted, and only three days ago had sat in a Senate hearing room, being humiliated and believing their dreams had been crushed.

"I don't understand something," Gary finally said.

"Go on."

"How in hell did you get away with even doing what you are doing now? I keep track of every scrap of news about elevator development, and there has never been a whisper about what you are doing here. There was a bit of a flurry of news some years back when a Japanese consortium purchased an option to build what they claimed was a space port here, because—like the French are doing in Africa—the closer you get to the equator to launch, the more momentum you get from the earth's rotation and thus cheaper on fuel. I thought it was a cover story, that they were going for a Pillar and would preempt us."

"That all fell through years ago when their economy flatlined," Franklin said, nodding in agreement as he pointed to the horizon. "They had an option on the next island over. You can just barely see it because of the haze, but I now have that option as well and have several hundred working there already."

He smiled.

"A Singapore company quietly picked it up a year ago, and except for the workers out there, no one has really noticed. Nor have they noticed what is going on here. The cover story is that I have gone crazy and think this will be some sort of super resort."

"And let me guess: you have controlling interest in that Singapore company," Gary conjectured.

"So how did you keep all of this quiet?" Eva asked.

"Ohhh, what you are looking at is the transformation of an island into a twenty-first-century tourist destination. I just never explained to the media and those who got a bit too nosy as to what kind of tourism I am really thinking about. Besides, investments are spread out between half a dozen companies around the world.

"The only ones on the inside, so to speak, are some of my friends working here, investors, the president of Kiribati, a team working at another location we'll talk about later, and that is pretty well it. Though I doubt the cover will last much longer with you two on my team and some others coming aboard as well."

"So essentially you just purchased this island and are now carving it up?" Eva asked.

Franklin nodded.

Sweat was trickling down Gary's face as he shaded his eyes and looked out to the sea. Could this be possible? Or were they in the hands of a madman?

The question of where to build their dream had always been a troubling point. South America, Africa, Indonesia, or out in the Pacific? The first three were repeatedly rejected. Political history always pointed to the question of a major investment of the hundreds of billions of dollars suddenly falling into the hands of an unstable government, one motivated by greed or hostility. Howland Island was in fact still American territory and only half a degree off the equator. But here, in what had once been the Gilberts, was never raised as a possible site for a Pillar. But as he stood there looking about, it struck him. This would indeed be the ideal place, politically, socially, even in terms of protecting it from terrorists—which, after 9/11, had become a major objection to the idea of a tower as well.

"Let's get out of this heat," Franklin announced, and he gestured to a nearby Quonset hut. Opening the door for them, Gary breathed a sigh of relief: the air-conditioning was on full blast. George went to a fridge and pulled out cans of beer and bottles of water. Franklin went for the beer as did Gary and George, while Eva gratefully took a bottle of water and rubbed it against her forehead for a moment before opening it.

Franklin sat down in a straight-backed chair and sighed.

"Let's start this from the beginning," he said. "Let me ask: Do you believe in global warming?"

Gary and Eva looked at each other and smiled.

"No," Eva said. "A multibillion-dollar scam. There are natural cycles to weather and climate, including the fact that energy from the sun—from all stars—has a slight variable. In the end it all averages out. But my husband here . . ."

Gary looked at her and shrugged.

"Work for NASA, see some of the hard data from their climatology people, see the models of CO_2 output from industrializing China and India, even Africa twenty years from now. Yes, I believe in it."

"George, you tell them," Franklin said, nodding to his friend and construction foreman.

"If global warming is true? We here believe it is," George replied, sipping from his cold can of beer. "There is not a spot in our entire nation of Kiribati that is more than twenty-five feet above sea level. Nearly all our people live where it is below ten feet. If we lived anywhere but in the equatorial region where typhoons occur, this nation would be uninhabitable; also if it was in an earthquake zone with threats of tsunamis. The one that hit Indonesia some years ago or Japan more recently would have annihilated us. So climate- and geology-wise, we are one of the safest places in the world."

He smiled and nodded to Franklin.

"Thus my friend's wisdom in coming to us with his mad scheme."

Franklin chuckled and raised his beer in salute.

"But there is another factor in his wisdom, and that is global warming and thus why our president and those of us who know the true purpose embraced his plan. If global warming is real—if the oceans rise as NASA predicts—our nation will be the first on this planet to disappear, or forced into crowded retreat to a scant few square miles above the high-tide line. Several years back our government signed treaties with New Zealand and Fiji for refugee status. Meaning our entire country will cease to exist and we go in exile to a foreign land. So we do take it seriously."

Franklin nodded his thanks to George, motioning for him to sit down, enjoy the air-conditioning and the cold beer, and relax, which he was more than happy to do.

"Kiribati," Franklin continued, "at least according to the United Nations, is ranked as one of the poorest nations in the world, though my friend George would debate that vigorously. It might be poor in terms of dollars or yen, but in terms of their lives it is very rich."

George nodded.

"Anyone who would trade living here for being in Washington is insane. Tell me, Dr. Morgan, where would you rather be, here or stuck in Beltway traffic?"

Gary looked back out the window at the view of the tropical beach and had to nod in agreement. There was some sense to that, and besides, he'd be free of Washington politics and a climate that made him wonder if the Founding Fathers had been more than a bit insane to choose such a spot as their capital. Perhaps the old joke was true that they did so because staying there would be so miserable, sessions of government would be kept as short as possible so they could get the hell out of town and thus do little damage by passing more laws. Someone had even written a paper arguing that the invention of air conditioning enabled the creation of "big government."

"When this project goes forward, Kiribati will, I believe, become the center of the global economy. It will be the Dubai and Singapore of the twenty-first century. Certainly there will be some social dislocation. More than a thousand people currently live on this island; the vast majority of the adults are working on building the infrastructure before we go to the main task, and they are earning Western-level wages. I know, because I am funding it."

He looked out the window.

George did not comment, but Gary could see that the man respected Franklin as someone he trusted and not just as his boss.

"Next consideration: security. Given the current state of world affairs, an investment of this magnitude would sooner or later draw attack. We are thousands of miles from any potential source of threat. I do not feel comfortable speculating yet about how such security will be arranged, but given what happened on September 11, 2001, we will and must be vigilant. I would like to think that ultimately, given the international effort that will go into this project, there will be accord to help with that security. But given the current threat zones of this world, Kiribati is about as remote as you can get.

"Tied to security, meaning another potential threat, is weather. We've done the analysis on major storms and typhoons out here. You need the rotation of the earth, the Coriolis effect, to help spawn them. It's interesting how they are counterclockwise once north of the equator, and clockwise south of the equator. At the equator they are nonexistent. Earthquakes—that instantly rules out Indonesia along with Ecuador. Therefore, this is one of the best low-risk weather and geological locations on the planet.

"And now to the fourth consideration: economics. I could go into some long-winded statement on this: I got a young history intern specializing in nineteenth- and early-twentieth-century industrialization to write that stuff for me. I got another who writes about what is called 'disruptive technologies' and is a darn good adviser when it comes to economic impacts and potential political threats that will emerge from that."

Eva nodded.

"You will have a fierce critique from a professor where Victoria is going to school who writes about that topic as well."

Franklin smiled.

"Exactly why I hired away one of her graduate students to work for me.

"Then you understand my reference. This project will rival, even exceed, the building of the transcontinental railroads in America and Russia. The Hoover Dam or the great dam that just went up in China. It will transform economic structures. I think our world will come out the winner, but there will be many of far shorter vision or pure self-interest who will see it for the threat that it is and do whatever is in their power to stop it. That is why I chose Kiribati, beyond the fact that it is so remote, no one has even noticed yet what is going on here. Imagine if I were trying to pull this off on Catalina Island . . ."

He chuckled.

"My God, the lawyers would be coming in on landing craft to file injunctions that, if stacked atop each other, would be a true Tower of Babel. I remember some political candidate pointing out that America has become so mired in paperwork and rulings, it took twenty years just to get one new runway built at the Atlanta airport, where everyone darn well knew it was desperately needed. Hoover Dam today? Impossible; just imagine someone even suggesting it."

He shook his head.

"Ironic in that I am far more pro-environment than nearly anyone even remotely realizes, but America as a place to build the great mega-projects that turned us into the greatest economic power in history? Those days are done, at least for now."

He finished his beer, tossing the empty into a bucket clearly marked "recycle." Getting another one out of the fridge, he motioned to George, who accepted it, but Gary, still nursing the first one, refused. Gary realized that it was typical of Franklin, who continued to pace the room, filled with nervous energy.

"The hundred thousand good people of this country, once this enterprise is made public, will see they could be the true gateway into the twenty-first century, and I pray that, as an independent nation, they will support it. That is what matters most, politically. From other sources around the world, I fully expect there will be howls of protest about interfering with space traffic, environmental impacts, economic disruptions, especially from oil-producing countries, but this nation, I am certain, will rally behind it and others will follow."

Franklin paused for a moment to look out the window at a heavy truck—much bigger than anything legal on an American road—hauling what looked like steel beams down toward the beach on the south end of the island.

What little Gary had seen so far had left him awed. Before even the bare beginnings of a tower had been started on, this man must be spending hundreds of thousands of dollars a day on the ground infrastructure. This, perhaps more than anything, convinced him that Franklin was dead-on serious.

"You mean America and NASA," Gary asked.

"Precisely," Franklin said forcefully. "NASA was the place of America's dream in the 1960s; of any government agency, it ranked number one in public esteem. It will do so again. But we need to get something for the American public to grab hold of first and then demand that NASA again take the lead. Something that will override the naysayers in Congress and even in the White House, that the public demands that the project goes forward. That was the tragedy of Apollo. Once *Apollo 11* landed, then what? The attitude quickly became 'Been there, done that,' and with the waning in public support the dream of building a base on the moon, the logical extension of Apollo, and from there going on to Mars—not just to visit and collect a few rocks but to actually colonize—died with it."

Franklin went to the door, opened it, and stepped outside.

"I want you to look out there and picture it ten years from now. This island from end to end will be transformed into the terminal hub. I don't want any aircraft except those first landing at Tarawa for a rigorous security inspection coming within fifty miles of it; memories of past tragedy and the need for security mean that once the tower is up and functional, no aircraft will be allowed within fifty miles of it. The airfield on this island now is for bringing in the equipment needed to build the infrastructure and support construction, but once completed, except in rare highly secured situations, it will be shut down and converted to other use. Back at Tarawa we'll have the main international airport hub, then connect it to here via maglev trains."

"My God, that alone will cost billions," Gary whispered.

"Yup."

He gestured around him.

"This island will be the main terminal. Passengers and freight will offload at Tarawa and be transferred by maglev trains from there to here or to the ocean port to be built at the north end of the island. The main terminal to the tower will be here. I always liked Gothic cathedrals; I'll show you some concept ideas on the flight back home. Upbound vehicles and cargo pods will start just about where we are standing, ascend an arcing track, then connect to the pillar and go straight up for the three-day journey to geosynch orbit. And from there we can go wherever we want to go. The moon and Mars, where eventually we'll build towers at a fraction of the cost of this one. And then?"

He laughed softly.

"Eventually the stars."

He pointed out to sea.

"Can you imagine the pillar—our pillar—out there, less than a mile from where we now stand? Imagine it going straight up, aimed at the noonday sun overhead, and after an hour's ascent you are in space with a sky full of stars.

"But there is something else to it," Franklin said, "something not even the two of you have thought of, so focused were you on going up rather than on what would be coming back down."

"And that is?" Gary asked, feeling a touch defensive with this comment.

"It was the selling point to the president of this good nation, what truly won him over."

"What is it?" Gary asked again.

"I think we can actually stop global warming if we build this tower."

Eva actually burst out laughing, but Franklin did not look offended.

"Let me pose a question. If we do agree that CO_2 emissions are the cause, then we agree it is fossil fuel burning that is killing us, and will eventually melt most of the ice in Antarctica and elsewhere above sea level. For these good people of Kiribati, a six- to eight-foot rise in water level will destroy their nation."

Gary nodded in agreement even as Eva remained silent.

"Or let's say it is all about solar cycles or whatever. Still we can agree that oil is reaching peak production, it is becoming more expensive by the day to extract each barrel. We will turn back to coal in our desperation, and forests will be leveled—and are being annihilated in most tropical regions. No one wants nukes in their backyard, and the dream of fusion power is decades away, perhaps even a century, and believe me, I am a dreamer and even looked at that seriously at one point as to where to put my money."

"I don't get that," Gary asked. "You thought about fusion as an investment but then switched to space elevators? What is the connection?"

Franklin grinned a bit self-consciously.

"You might think me crazy if I told you the full truth."

"You dragged us halfway around the world to stand on this baking-hot beach and stare at empty ocean. Maybe we are the ones who are crazy. So I'm ready to listen."

"In this age it is bad form to say you admire the industrialists of the Gilded Age of the nineteenth century. Nearly every history book brands them now as 'robber barons.' Hell, depending on who is in power politically, folks like me are either barely tolerated or outright hounded because someone thinks we built our billions unfairly and the government needs to take it all away. Ironic, because those preaching from such pulpits are using their pads, cell phones, and the Internet to send out their message, and if they get sick, expect the latest ultrasounds, MRIs, laser surgeries, and all the rest to put them back on their feet.

"But I digress. Carnegie built an empire of steel that transformed industrializing America. A few decades later, after turning us into a global power, not even he could see that in the future the foundations he built ensured we had the industrial strength to defeat totalitarianism. Commodore Vanderbilt created a transportation network, and ironically, if you go to western North Carolina, everyone loves the Vanderbilt mansion; their entire tourist economy is based on that, even while some living there would scream for Vanderbilt to be taxed to death if he were alive today. I could go on and on; I guess that historian I have on my staff pumped me up for this. J.P. Morgan builds a banking empire so strong, he actually bailed the entire United States government out of bankruptcy at one point. The Rothschilds created a global banking system; Ford transformed global transportation . . . The list is endless."

Again that smile.

"And all of them gave back. Amongst themselves, it was actually considered bad form to check out of life in this world without giving back to the world and trying to make it a better place. And I decided I'll add my name to the list by helping you two to build this pillar."

"I'll agree it will transform space transportation," Eva offered, "but dare I say, I'm not seeing the rest of your point."

"What do we have up there that is limitless and free but down here the world is scrambling for, and wars are fought for, and I fear ultimately a final cataclysmic war will eventually be waged over?"

He paused for dramatic effect.

"Energy."

It was so damn simple, Eva actually started to laugh.

"What in hell is so funny?" Gary asked.

"Solar panels. Hundreds of square miles of solar panels. Hang them from the side of the tower, or position them nearby. Once they're up high enough, you've got sunlight 24/7, 365 days a year," Franklin explained.

"Tens of gigawatts, hundreds of gigawatts, waiting to be harvested. Eventually the tower is a pipeline. Beam the energy partway down via lasers.

But you don't need hundreds of square miles of collecting stations on earth, which will only work part of the day, and weather messes it up even more, and no one wants to risk the impact to the upper atmosphere of sending it down via microwave. For the final leg down to earth, you have superconductivity cables."

As Franklin spoke, he traced out a pattern in the sand with the toe of his boot.

"But of course," Franklin continued, "it is all based here. Traffic going up from this island, limitless energy coming down. Let the oil sheiks have their fantasies awhile longer before sand again engulfs the palaces they build now. Twenty years from now, they'll be coming here to gaze in wonder, because this will be the energy station of the world."

His words caused Gary's initial burst of delight to dampen down significantly.

"Security," Gary said. "When the world catches on to how this could change the entire economic flow of the planet . . ." His voice trailed off.

Suddenly his dream had become infinitely more complex, and even a bit frightening.

Franklin did not reply, and walked down to the water's edge, looking out to sea.

"No one will stop this. We will build it."

Eva shrugged and smiled.

"You almost sound like a character in the old movies they used to show us in school about Soviet heroes looking off to the horizon, promising a workers' paradise someday," and there was a touch of teasing levity in her voice.

Franklin, not insulted, could only grin.

"What the hell, maybe someday they'll make a movie about us. If so, I want Morgan Freeman to play me, though by then he might be on a bit in years."

Franklin stood silent and now there was a cold, icy stare. So far they had seen one side of him, and Gary sensed they were also now seeing the other side, that of the businessman who had built an empire.

"What I just told you is in the strictest confidence, never to be repeated at least for a few more months. Any public discussion of this tower is strictly about what is going up, not what I dream will one day be returned. Do we understand each other?"

"Of course," Gary said, "but I must ask: Why this sudden change in tone?"

"Because, Drs. Morgan, if that half of this plan is ever known, do you realize what economic forces, dependent on fossil fuel for their economies, will unleash everything they have to stop us? They would rather see their profits grow for another generation, two at most, and then the hell with the resulting collapse, even at the cost of the destruction of this beautiful island nation or the kind of world their grandchildren will inherit at the end of this century. You are never to speak a word of this other aspect of the tower until the time is right. I'll let it leak out bit by bit, but let me decide when. I insist upon that and pray you understand why."

The two could only nod in agreement, and he relaxed, becoming his affable self again.

"Come on, I've got a sick kid to look after," Eva announced. "We'll figure out who plays us later in some movie after we build this thing and it works."

7

Six Months Later

Waking up earlier than usual, which was the norm of late, Gary sipped his coffee while waiting for Eva, gazing out the bay window of their home, which offered a spectacular view of Seattle and Mount Rainer in the distance. With a salary between them of nearly three million a year, and stock options never dreamed of, it was a reality beyond imagining: even though they had earned decent money at Goddard, a quarter of a million a year in D.C. meant living cheek by jowl with the neighbors in a suburb, with a maddening daily commute on the Beltway. They didn't even have to worry about that now, a company car met them every morning so they could relax and get some work in on the ride to the office. But this morning they were skipping work.

Eva came out of the bedroom dressed simply but as always elegantly in a calf-length white dress. She thanked Gary for the cup of tea he had prepared for her, saying nothing for a moment as she looked out the window.

"Every morning I look out this window and can't believe what is happening to us," she whispered. "But, damn, I wish they could change the weather. I'm Ukrainian; you know our flag: yellow bottom half, blue upper half, representing endless fields of grain and crystal-blue skies. What has it been, eight days since we've seen the sun?"

"I think ten," Gary said softly.

She didn't say anything more. They just walked out the door, taking two windbreakers off the coatrack, then went to the garage to their new Beemer and, still without comment, Eva got behind the wheel and turned on the ignition. It was a silent ride to the clinic that Franklin had insisted they go to as the best in the city. A half hour later, Dr. Bock, one of the country's leading neurologists, came out to the waiting room and gestured for them to come into his office.

This time there was no small talk, no jokes about what a boring pain Franklin could be if anyone at a party even remotely made a conversation opener about what many now called "Franklin's Folly."

"No sense in playing any games and delaying this," Bock said, and his voice was gentle, his eyes filled with compassion. "You know what I suspected and your tests came back positive."

Eva struggled for control, her hand reaching out to grasp Gary's.

"Gary, you have Parkinson's. In fact, the stage you are at, I suspect you've known for maybe a year or more but simply would not face it."

Gary nodded.

"Nothing worse than the Internet and a Google search when something is bothering you," Gary finally admitted.

"Why in hell did you not get yourself in to see a doctor on day one?"

"I was rather busy at the time," Gary offered.

"And you, miss?" Bock asked. "Didn't you pick up on the early symptoms?"

She gave Bock a guilty look.

"Call it denial," she whispered. "That and I wanted to believe that with everything that has been happening, it was just simple exhaustion. I thought we'd finally take a vacation for a month and all would be back to normal. The president of Kiribati offered us a cottage on the beach to relax."

"Some vacation," Bock muttered. "And let me guess: Franklin would have you two playing politics and, of course, you'd have to go down and see how work was going."

Gary smiled and shrugged.

"Never thought going to Tarawa would be a vacation," Gary remarked. "But frankly I really like the president: he's a decent guy with a vision of the future for his people, no matter how disruptive our presence is. He even offered to help me try to find where my great-uncle died and place a marker there for him. And if you forget about the history and look at the future, it is a beautiful place."

"Franklin Smith and I go way back," Bock said, "and unless you scream patient confidentiality, I'm tempted to call him as soon as you leave this office to suggest you two take a vacation even if it is to that island."

"I'd prefer not," Gary said.

"He already knows," Bock replied.

"How?"

"Come on, Gary, we're talking about one of the most brilliant men either of us knows. He made your referral to me and told me to cut the crap with waiting for an appointment and to see you the next day, which I did last week. He pretty well had it figured: your drooping right foot, the fact that you were stumbling at times, dropping things, when tired your speech slurred a bit even though you don't drink. So I bet he went to the same Internet sites you did, but unlike you he called in the doctor."

"We have to tell him anyhow," Eva said, trembling hand clenched tight in Gary's.

"And let me guess," Gary said, and there was a note of bitterness and frustration in his voice. "Now you're going to tell me to retire, take it easy, stare out the window, do some dumbass physical therapy sessions, find a counselor for the emotional stuff, and wait to die."

Bock smiled, got out from behind his desk, pulled up a chair, and sat directly in front of Gary, gazing at him intently as if examining him again.

"There are times I love my job," Bock said, "especially the winners and, with kids, when there is a cure and we get to the problem ahead of time. Mostly, though, I have days like this one."

He paused, and Eva wondered if this man was about to be overcome with emotion; she could sense his frustration.

"I am not going to con you, Gary. From your current state, I would guess onset at between twelve to eighteen months ago of the first physical signs that were noticeable."

Gary said nothing. Bock had spent their first hour together just getting a case history, so he already knew that.

"I could suggest retiring, both of you. I actually believe in Franklin's Folly and I know your role in it. You can sign out today and Franklin would make sure you were both set up for life; then go out and enjoy it. But then again, I have a sense of who the two of you are. And both of you would tell me to go to hell."

Gary answered yes. Eva sat silently and finally nodded in agreement with Gary. Bock smiled.

"Bully for you, as old Teddy Roosevelt used to say. I have patients who take five years off of their life just in the walk from here to their car. They go home, curl up, and wait to die. You two aren't the type. Stay at it, go to work today. I know Franklin: he'll say a few words, and then off to your next meeting."

"He better not tell anyone else," Gary said. "I'll be damned if I am treated like some dying man because of this."

"Gary, you can look at it this way. From the moment we're born, all of us are on the path of dying. There are nights I have to sit by the bed of a ten-year-old and look at his parents on the other side keeping watch on his final hour. Even as the parents cannot accept the reality of it, the child knows and even welcomes it. I believe in a gentle God, but I do have to ask why at such moments.

"I could give the old platitude about what a good life you've had so far, Gary. Just seeing the love between you and Eva, what I have heard about your wonderful daughter—all of it is a blessing. As to your future? I'm always asked, 'How long do I got?' "

He sighed.

"I can't tell you. That actor—such a young guy when this was found out—is still going strong after nearly twenty years. Others—and I do not BS my patients—five years. So let's cut the difference. I think you have a lot of good years ahead of you. Maybe not the best in the physical sense, but you're one of those egghead scientist types, and as long as you can think clearly and keep on working on your dream, I'm with you all the way. So go back to work and look for years more work ahead, but by heavens, you will let me be in charge of your treatment to help keep you going.

"OK?"

Gary nodded.

Bock smiled and leaned back in his chair, closing his eyes for a few seconds and Eva could sense that this man apparently had had a sleepless night, and chances were that when he made the comment about the ten-year-old, that was most likely how he had spent the previous night. He struck her as that kind of doctor, who put his heart and soul into his patients, and she whispered a silent prayer of blessing for him. He looked off for a moment, then forced a smile.

"I can deal with my body going down," Gary said, "but my mind? You kind of dodged that a bit."

"An answer? I can't say for now. Five years, maybe, before you'll start to sense a decline, if we are lucky. You stick to your medication, diet, and exercise, and for you I think the mental exercise is a key."

"Just great," Gary sighed, looking away in frustration. *I lose my mind before we finish the tower,* he thought, looking over at Eva, who he knew was thinking the same thing.

Bock put a reassuring hand on Gary's shoulder and squeezed it.

"I believe in you. I met Franklin a few days after the press conference when he announced the real plan behind Pillar Inc., dropping the veil of some super resort, which we all knew was bull, just not his style for an investment. I doubt if you remember me being there; you two were so obviously overwhelmed by the crowd. That character dragged me off and inside of ten minutes talked me out of several million to invest. So much for my 401(k)."

Bock chuckled, shaking his head.

"Anyhow, I like investing in dreams. I always kicked myself for not putting ten thousand into him when we first met twenty years ago . . . Hell, I'd be retired now and cruising the sky in my own fantasy, an original P-51 Mustang, if I had fallen for his first sell job on me."

Gary chuckled at that.

"I doubt that," Eva interjected. "You'd still be here doing what you are doing right now."

He looked at her and nodded, acknowledging her wisdom and insight.

"Anyhow, there's the old joke about putting doctors into high-performance planes and our life expectancy. But still, it is a nice fantasy."

Another laugh.

"Get that tower, pillar, whatever you call it, built and I am on my way. That was his pitch to me and some other doctors: the thought of geriatric research and life in low-gravity environments."

"Or maybe for Parkinson's," Gary replied. "Guess I'll be thinking of that now as well."

"A good goal, Gary Morgan," Bock said, leaning over to pat Gary on the shoulder again. "Maybe God's way of telling us there are other purposes behind this tower as well. A very good goal.

"So, you two. Go out to your car, have a good cry. Gary, play on this lovely lady a bit for some extra TLC, at least for a few days"—he smiled at her and actually winked—"and go back to work. We'll meet weekly for a while to do some tests, see how you take to the meds, and you can keep me posted on the work."

He stood up, indicating their time was up. Without doubt, by now there were half a dozen other patients in the waiting room, waiting for news, either good or bad, and Gary knew they would receive the same understanding and compassion he had just gotten with this gentle, good man.

"Since I'm an investor, though, no insider information as to how it is really going with the project," Bock said with a smile, taking Gary's hand with his left and Eva's with his right. "You're in my prayers; I'm one of those doctors that still believes in that, and honestly, I look forward to when we can one day do a consultation—up there," and he nodded toward the heavens.

"Yeah, part of how Franklin sold me was talking about the potential positive effects of low-gravity environments for patients who are no longer ambulatory. He wants me to consult on building the first clinic."

"And by then I'll be a patient there, I guess," Gary said, momentarily giving way to despair.

"Perhaps," Bock said, and now his voice was steady and forceful. "But it is worth thinking about as you work. Maybe you won't get the tower or pillar, as Franklin calls it, built in time for you, but for others? I would rather like the idea. In my line of work, I see things every day that I want to change but cannot. Maybe you two are working on something that can change lives for the better that no one, especially all you engineering types, have even thought about yet. Gary, hope is what life is all about, so when you walk out of here, decide whether you are dying or going on with living. It is why I am telling you to hell with retirement: now go back to work."

Back at the car, Gary did not even comment about who would drive. He felt OK to do so, but the spasm he had had several days back—when he felt no control over his right foot, which just drooped—spooked him a bit on the idea. Eva made the gesture of offering him the keys. There were some aspects of her old Ukrainian upbringing that drove their more feminist-oriented friends wild at times, and his old insistence that he drive whenever they traveled together was one of them. But she did offer the keys, he refused, they got in the car, and ten seconds later she disintegrated into tears and was holding him close.

"Why don't we just take the day off and go home," she gasped.

He forced a smile.

"No way in hell. We're getting paid more in a week than we used to make in half a year. Besides, what do we do once we're home? Sit and brood? Stare out the window at the rain?"

But then he did look over at her with a smile, a bit of a twinkle in his eye. Her tears stopped and she smiled back.

"Save that for later tonight, Gary Morgan!"

And they both laughed and hugged each other.

"Let's go to the office."

"One thing, though," Eva asked. "What do we tell Victoria?"

That question had been troubling him, too, since he already knew before they went in to see Bock what the prognosis was. The last six months . . . what a whirlwind. On signing the contracts with Franklin, he never imagined there could be such a mountain of paperwork for a simple hire in the private sector, but this was more about a partnership than a simple employee agreement. Then they went back to Goddard to pack up. They put their house on the market only days later; with that aspect of the economy still tottering, the appraisal and sale left them in shock, even though Franklin pointed out that a week's pay would more than make up what they lost in selling their home. Then it was off to the new home—some real sticker shock there—then moving, unpacking thousands of books, one of the treasured works a battered copy of de Camp's *Ancient Engineers* that Erich had given him, then seeing Victoria off to college. And all the time digging into work on the dream, which now actually seemed real at last.

Victoria. She had been home for two weeks at Christmas, and when she left it was even more painful than her first departure. At this moment it hit him hard just how much he missed their daughter.

"We tell her the truth," Eva said. "Besides, I think she suspected as well."

"'As well'?"

"She asked me before she left for college if something was wrong. Even mentioned Parkinson's. Remember, your little girl still worships her daddy and watches his every step."

He smiled and now his eyes filled up.

"She said she'll solo within the week?"

Eva nodded, not at all happy with that thought. They had signed the paperwork for her to join the flying club on campus, do ground school—which was worth three credit hours—and take flight lessons. In their conversation of just the night before, she casually dropped the word that she was about ready to solo, most likely this coming weekend.

"I think, given the situation, we can hit Franklin up for a favor," Gary said.

"And that is?"

"If his plane is free, let's fly out to see our little girl and tell her face-to-face. I'd prefer it that way."

Eva's tears vanished and she grinned with delight.

The Gulfstream touched down flawlessly on the main runway of the university. During the Second World War, Purdue had become a major training center for pilots, a program that had actually been started several years earlier by the legendary Amelia Earhart, for whom the field was named. He felt a swelling of nostalgia as the pilot crossed over the campus on final and he looked down on the place where he had spent four years of his life, building his dreams, and many a late night spending hours with the new Internet, exchanging e-mails with the Ukraine.

As they taxied up to the small somewhat run-down terminal, a crowd was outside, braving the cold January day to greet them. Actually it was not so much to greet them: Franklin had insisted upon coming along, saying there were a couple of other stops they could make over the weekend, so it would be a working trip for the three of them; and besides he wanted to watch his "intern" do her solo.

Gary had thought to call ahead, checking in with the professor, Brandon NeSmith, who was flight instructor for the air club. Yes, his daughter was ready to solo; NeSmith had figured he would take her around this Saturday—the weather forecast perfect for a new pilot—give her the classic "Give me three touch and goes" before getting out of the plane, and telling her to give him three more—on her own.

There had been some reluctance at first on the professor's part—he really did not like nervous parents hanging around—but when Gary explained the circumstances and who he would be coming with, the arrangement was sealed in a second.

Wind less than five knots, straight down the runway, a nice cold day, limitless visibility, and until the hatch of the Gulfstream opened, Victoria had no idea who was on the plane. There had only been an e-mail bulletin to all aerospace engineering majors late yesterday that they were invited to the campus airport for a surprise guest lecturer. Given that it came from the department chair, "invited" was all but an order, and as the Gulfstream taxied up, Gary could see a hundred or so students out early and braving the midwestern winter chill.

Back in the days of the shuttle, a "surprise guest lecturer" usually meant a visiting alumnus who was now an astronaut dropping in for a visit, but those days were gone. Few outside of Purdue knew that the university had graduated more astronauts than any other college, including the military academies. It was the place that astronauts in training were sent for master's degrees in aerospace engineering or whatever areas of work in space they were specializing in.

They had agreed that Franklin would disembark first, since he was the surprise guest lecturer. Chairs had already been set up in a freezing-cold hangar. When the crowd caught sight of him, it was like a rock star making an appearance for the collection of campus "nerds." Most had shown up because there was nothing else to do on campus on a Saturday morning. Purdue was definitely not a "party school," and more than a few figured it would impress their professors if they did show. But as the hatchway dropped and Franklin stepped out, there was a flurry of remarks, a few shouts of surprise, and then even applause.

Who did not know Franklin Smith, what with the hoopla and controversy raging around his insane project? Eva stepped out next: and one person did recognize her, Victoria breaking out of her group and racing up to embrace her, the two instantly in tears. Gary followed, and the joy of seeing his "little girl" simply overwhelmed him. She had grown so much in the last six months, maturing into such a beautiful young lady, taller by a couple of inches, with her mother's dark blond hair, still worn long, but pulled back, tied off into a ponytail this morning, tucked under a Purdue baseball cap, so that it wouldn't blow into her face if she hit some turbulence.

With the consent of Victoria's flight instructor, they had a few minutes to chat, but then he was dragging her off for her lesson. The last thing he or Victoria needed was anxious parents standing by the runway; the instructor reciting a cautionary tale where a student panicked and circled the field for a half hour, crying, while her father got on a handheld radio and started to cuss her out for embarrassing him. He finally talked the girl down, and the FAA had a long talk with the father about violations of radio usage. NeSmith's firm policy, ever since the incident with the hysterical parent, was zero tolerance for their clinging presence, but given who was coming to visit along with Gary and Eva, he would relent this one time as long as they obeyed *his* rules without question.

They had agreed that the crowd would follow Franklin into the hangar while Gary and Eva quietly slipped off with their daughter, and for heaven's sake, NeSmith absolutely forbade them to say anything more than that they were dropping in with Franklin so he could give a talk, and there would be time later to catch up on things after she did her flight.

Franklin was in his element. Those gathered round him pulled out cell phones to take pictures and call friends who had blown off the idea of actually getting up at nine in the morning to listen to some most likely boring guest speaker. This was *the* Franklin Smith, triggering the same reaction Steve Jobs used to when he showed up for the release of a new product at an electronics show. Franklin, knowing the game, gestured toward the open hangar, asking if there was any coffee to be found. Half a dozen students raced ahead for the honor of giving him a cup.

Gary and Eva stayed by the Gulfstream. Victoria was reluctant to leave them, but her instructor shouted good-naturedly that he didn't have all day and it was time to shoot some landings. As the two walked off, Brandon shot a glance back at Gary and Eva that was a clear enough warning. Gary forced a smile and waved. Eva held his hand and actually started to step forward.

"Don't," Gary whispered.

"I just want to look in the plane and make sure it's safe," she said, and he could sense her classic Ukrainian temper going up a few notches.

"You take one step toward the plane and the instructor told me he'd cancel her flight."

"Then maybe I should."

"And Victoria will all but kill you. Today is her day; we're just her parents and it's time we stepped back."

He felt her tense up but then nod in agreement.

While Franklin fell into an informal question-and-answer session around several coffeepots and some donuts set up in the hangar, Gary and Eva tried not to look nervous as their "baby" did a preflight check then hopped into the Cessna 172, suddenly all serious, went over the checklist, opened the side window to shout "Clear prop," started up the engine, let the oil pressure and temperature build, ran through her magneto and carb heat checks, and then taxied out to the end of the runway. Danny McMullen, their pilot with the Gulfstream, came up to them with a handheld radio so they could listen in.

"She's doing just fine," Danny offered. "No sweat. Today you see your girl get her wings, and she better not like that shirt she's wearing."

"Why so?" Eva asked.

"After she solos, the instructor and her friends will cut it off."

"All of it?" Eva cried.

Danny laughed. "No, just the tail. It is an ancient ritual."

They listened as Victoria announced she was taxiing onto the active runway and would left-turn depart runway 28. Just hearing her voice like that sent a nervous shiver through both her parents.

She lifted off easily in the cold morning air, climbed out, executed a neat left turn, then announced she was entering downwind for a "touch-and-go."

Danny, holding the radio, stood intently watching, nodding his approval as she turned from downwind, to base, to final. Eva turned away, unable to watch.

"The instructor is still on board, Eva," Danny said. "No sweat."

She came in, wings wobbling a bit, a touch of throttle sounding, then easing back as she "cleared the numbers," touched down, tires squealing on the pavement, throttled up, and seconds later lifted off again.

"Nicely done," Danny said reassuringly.

She did a second, even better than the first, tires barely brushing the pavement before throttling up, and then went around for a third.

"Lafayette traffic. Seven-seven-seven Bravo Xray, downwind for runway 28. Full stop."

Danny grinned.

"She's ready."

The Cessna touched down, came nearly to a stop, taxied halfway back to the hangar, and stopped. Then the right door opened and Brandon got out.

The plane turned, taxiing back to the end of the runway, and again her voice came over the radio; her parents could hear the excitement and tension. He had a flash memory of the day she first "soloed" on a two-wheeler bicycle, not aware at first that her father had stopped running alongside her and had let go. That look back over her shoulder, first grinning, then panic, and then ten seconds later tears as she held her skinned and bleeding knee, Eva furious with Gary that he had let go too soon. Then the argument about whether she should try again or not, until they both turned in amazement and saw Victoria flying down the street on her own, laughing with glee, having slipped from their grasp while they were arguing.

It felt the same now, and Gary felt his chest swelling with pride that he had been blessed with such a wonderful, gutsy daughter even though his stomach was a bit knotted up. That was his "baby" out there, about to solo a plane for the first time.

"Lafayette traffic. Cessna 777 Bravo Xray. Entering active runway 28, left-turn departure."

She started to throttle up, and Eva all but had a death grip on Gary's arm as the plane lifted off.

"Why in hell did we come here?" Eva gasped.

"Our kid is getting her wings," Gary whispered, trying to reassure her.

Victoria lifted off gracefully in the cold morning air, banked gently—no showing off—into a left turn, announced another turn on to downwind, then there was the cutting of the throttle. Eva's head was now buried in Gary's shoulder.

"Damn my grandfather," Eva said. "I never should have told her about him!"

"She's doing just fine, and, sweetheart, your grandfather is riding copilot with her, so don't worry, it's in her blood," Danny offered reassuringly, and Gary smiled wistfully at the thought that his grandfather and father were up there with her as well. The skill to actually fly might have skipped a generation with him, but it was continuing now with his girl. Gary could see that Danny was watching intently, completely focused on every nuance of what she was doing. It was part of being in the wonderful "brotherhood" of pilots: they were delighted to see someone about to get their wings, watching intently, whispering comments, sending along prayers, and in their hearts remembering their own first moments "up there" alone for the first time, knowing the joy so best described by a poet who wrote "because I fly I envy no man on earth."

Victoria turned on to final, throttle back, flaps down, a bit of waver, a touch of a gust sweeping across the field causing her to lift slightly. A bit too much throttle for a moment, then settling back down, still fifty feet too high as she cleared the faded numbers at the end of the runway, settling down; then the squeal of tires, full throttle, and she was back up several hundred feet later.

"Great, Victoria, now give me two more like that." It was her instructor standing down by the runway.

The second one was actually much worse: even Danny tensed up slightly as she came in too low this time, throttled up too much, and finally came to rest a thousand feet down the runway.

"A little long on that, Victoria. Just relax," her instructor clicked in.

"It's normal," Danny finally said as she lifted back off, all three of them exhaling nervously. "They always try to come in and want to kiss the numbers to impress their instructor, then get a bit antsy when they start to come in short and give it too much throttle. I did the same thing. She's got 6,000 feet of runway ahead of her, plenty of room in a 172 to land. She can play with short field landings later."

Eva had finally unclasped herself from her death grip on Gary's shoulder and was now watching intently, Danny providing a running commentary, all complimentary, as Victoria climbed up to pattern altitude, did her calls, cut clean ninety-degree turns from downwind to base, and then to final approach.

"Oh, she is going to kiss this one!" Danny announced gleefully.

Even her instructor clicked in.

"Looking great, Bravo Xray, you are in the groove. Now just let her land herself."

A dozen or so students had broken free from the crowd around Franklin, which was growing by the minute as students—and even some professors who obviously had been abed only a half hour ago—were racing out to the airport to see the man who was actually going to build a tower to the heavens.

Eva and Gary, with Danny by their side, did not notice. If prayers could give proper lift and glide to an airplane, it was certainly having its effect as she effortlessly cleared the threshold and this time did kiss the ground all so gently fifty feet beyond the numbers.

A brief announcement as she turned onto the taxiway, "Lafayette traffic, 777 Bravo Xray clear of active." She came to a full stop on the taxiway, her instructor going around behind the plane, then climbing in for the ride back to the terminal. As the Cessna came to a stop a hundred feet away, Gary felt such a swelling of pride with how his daughter was now all focus, intent, serious, nodding, listening to her instructor, holding up a checklist for a moment, then shutting the engine down. They climbed out of the plane, walking aft, never forward, as she had been taught, tying the plane down, chocking the wheels, doing a quick walk around for a visual postflight inspect, and only then, with childlike enthusiasm, she flung herself into her instructor's arms, hugging him, the instructor a bit red-faced, patting her on the back and twirling her around, while her friends at last raced forward to congratulate her.

Eva wanted to rush over as well, but Gary held her back.

"Give her a moment," he whispered. "She'll come to us."

Friends gathered around Victoria and NeSmith, some slapping her on the back, others hugging her, and then indeed the group pulled up her short jacket and sweatshirt, teasingly threatened to pull them up higher, then laughed as she shrieked that it was "too damn cold!" They pulled out the tail of her shirt from her trousers, and a lanky young man, producing scissors, cut her shirttail off and held it up triumphantly before handing it to her and kissing her on the lips.

Eva chuckled at that, but Gary felt a bit of an icy chill.

"Well, it does seem our young lady is growing up," Eva observed. "I wonder who *he* is."

Gary had nothing to say, and his wife squeezed his arm again, this time playfully.

"How old were we when we met?"

"I don't want to talk about it," Gary replied a bit sharply.

The exuberant group now made their way back to where Gary, Eva, and Danny were standing. Danny came forward first, looking all formal in his flight captain's uniform, and actually gave her a traditional military salute, which she laughingly returned. In the hours she had spent with him up in the cockpit of the Gulfstream, an obvious friendship had developed.

"You did great, young lady. I didn't tell your parents this, but on my third landing I just absolutely froze up, bounced it three times, my instructor yelling at me to go around, then I circled out there for fifteen minutes, struggling to get my nerve back, with him cussing at me to just bring it in."

"Oh, great," Gary whispered. "And we trust our butts to him?"

Danny looked back at him and laughed.

"Yup, you do. And I usually never confess that. The navy ain't so forgiving: I thought they'd wash me out that day, but I finally got my carrier wings."

He gave Victoria a warm hug.

Victoria's instructor was beaming.

"You are one of the best I've taught in a while, Victoria, even though that second landing was a bit shaky."

"Yes, sir."

"Next session with me, later this week, we'll work the schedule based on weather," and then he turned to the other students. "She did it in nine hours. Mr. Jenkins, you've had twelve hours now; listen to what she has to say later rather than the two of you staring at each other moon-eyed."

Mr. Jenkins was the young man who had cut off her shirttail. "So that's his name," Gary said as he looked at the redheaded youth, who obviously had more than a friendly interest in his only daughter.

Jenkins, aware of the way that Gary was staring at him, reddened.

"Now, the rest of you, you're missing out on what Franklin Smith has to say, and I want to hear it as well. Mr. Jenkins, one hour, I want you out to preflight the plane, and let's see if you can do the same, finally."

The group broke up and started to head to the hangar, but Victoria's flight instructor nodded to Gary, who followed after him while Victoria stood wrapped in her mother's arms, the two talking excitedly.

Gary extended his hand to the flight instructor, wondering if by chance this man remembered him from long ago.

"Thank you, sir."

"No, the thanks are mine," Brandon said. "Your daughter is a natural pilot. Piece of cake this morning. I'll confess that when I cut some of them loose, my stomach is in a knot. I make a wrong decision on that and I have a kid augering in. No such worry with your girl. You should be proud of her."

"We are, but still . . ."

Brandon nodded understandingly.

"Sir, I've been at this for thirty years. There was a time when the air force and navy sent their top-gun guys here who they were grooming for the astronaut corps. Those days are over, sadly. They had to keep their flight time up and would offer me a ride. Some of them scared the crap out of me when I'd go up with them. Too overconfident and hotshot. But maybe that was part of the formula back then. The ones I liked were the ones who knew where the edge of the envelope was and had the guts to admit when to not push it. I put your daughter in that class. She's told me all about your work, of course, and says her goal is one day to be on that tower and flying missions off of it."

Gary nodded. His years at NASA had made him privy to all the inside gossip about which pilots and crews really did have the "right stuff" to fly a dangerous machine like the shuttle, especially after *Challenger* and *Columbia*. The fantasy image of the hotshot pilot on the edge, as promulgated by such films as *The Right Stuff*, had long since passed. It required a lot of guts still, but balanced with an icy ability to analyze and work within the parameters. He wondered if, in building their tower, they would again have to go out to that "edge" and beyond, given how the concept was indeed "on the edge." The words of Victoria's instructor were both reassuring but also made him worry, as they would for any protective parent.

"Now, sir, I'm really dying to hear Smith's lecture. Can we join him?"

"One question," Gary said.

"Anything, sir."

"Who is this Jenkins kid?"

Brandon threw back his head and laughed.

"Oh, Peter? The usual freshman crush. They met in my ground school class and were staring at each other the first day." He shook his head and chuckled. "Sorry, sir, hate to break it to you, but I've been working this age group for thirty years. Your daughter is a fine young lady of darn good intellect and sense, I must add. Of course she is going to draw a bevy of admiring boys. Peter is OK in my book if that is what you mean, though, Lord help me, I will be nervous on the day he solos. He'll be an OK pilot—not the natural like your daughter, but not a washout.

"It's tough when I gotta tell a kid they should stick with radio-controlled aircraft and computer simulators and keep their feet on the ground."

Gary smiled, a bit embarrassed.

"You told me that, sir, over twenty years ago."

Brandon looked at him quizzically and then started to laugh.

"Oh my God, yes, Gary Morgan. When you called I thought the name sounded familiar beyond the incredible work you are doing. I was sorry to burst your bubble then."

Gary laughed softly.

"You were right. I'd've put it in nose-first sooner or later."

"And look at what you are creating now instead," Brandon said, and actually gave him a friendly pat on the shoulder.

"Well, your daughter didn't inherit your two left feet. She has a natural instinct for it."

The mention of two left feet did make Gary hesitate for a brief second, wondering if Parkinson's was haunting him even then.

Brandon nodded.

"Once your tower starts to go up, will you go up on it?"

Gary looked at him quizzically.

"Of course."

"Everything has risk, sir, if you are really living. Read some of the stuff by Richard Bach about flying. Not his seagull stuff, the articles about what I'd call the Zen of flying. Your daughter has that shot through her soul."

Gary looked back at his daughter, her mother, and the young man, who actually was holding her hand while the two girls talked.

"Back to the moment," Gary said. "This Peter, how does he check out in your book? I mean, as a young man who is obviously more than a bit interested in my daughter."

Brandon laughed.

"I have three daughters, sir. The oldest is thirty with two kids, the youngest your daughter's age. Days I wondered how I'd survive. Don't worry, you have a good kid. I promise to keep an eye on her."

Gary tried to smile.

Applause was erupting in the hangar as Smith stepped up to a podium raised up on a low platform: behind him was the perfect backdrop, one of the prizes of the university—an airplane once flown by Earhart.

"Come on, I don't want to miss this," Brandon said, pulling Gary along, dragging him out of his worries of the moment as a father as well.

Someone had thought to set up a projector hooked up to a laptop, and Franklin had tossed over a memory stick with the usual video loaded in.

The "program" started with a fifteen-minute presentation by a well-known actor who had once portrayed an astronaut in a movie; he was also the narrator for an excellent series on the Apollo program, was very "pro-space," had provided the voice-over for the video . . . and had also invested a sizable chunk of change in the project. When the tower was up, he'd be the perfect spokesman and laughingly agreed to do so for free as long as he could do the documentary from atop the tower. Franklin felt it was one of his better deals, given he'd have gladly paid the actor a million.

Applause did break out at the end when Franklin enjoyed his little ego stroke by appearing in the video, as if he were on board the capsule ascending to the heavens and talking to the audience about the limitless promise of the future ahead. Gary, of course, had seen the video a score of times, helping to add some technical points. Nevertheless, every time he saw it, it sent a shiver down his spine. "The limitless promise of the future ahead of us": such a different vision of the future from the one the kids around him were now fed on a daily basis. It was again like the days of his earliest childhood when he would watch the last of the moon landings with his father and grandfather, seeing tears in their eyes and hearing their talk about how when he was a man, the heavens awaited and space would transform their world back here on earth.

Seeing it again, he felt that shiver. A hand slipped into his: it was Eva's and he could see that her eyes were damp; it was not just her reunion with Victoria, who had gone off to join her friends.

"We have something to do with that, and I am so proud," Eva whispered, squeezing his hand tightly.

The video ended and Franklin launched into questions and answers, obviously delighted with the enthusiasm of this young audience versus the sometimes hard-nosed response he got when trying to sell another investor into sinking a couple of hundred million into the project.

Gary and Eva stood at the back of the hangar. As usual, he had absolutely insisted they not be introduced. He was a lousy public speaker, as was Eva; it was Franklin who was the magic. And besides, they did not want their daughter somehow singled out by students or even professors for special treatment. So far, only Brandon had made the connection.

"Doctor Smith." It was obviously a professor, standing up to be recognized.

"Ma'am?"

"Are you familiar with the thesis of disruptive technologies?" the professor asked.

"I am."

"You do realize if this tower—or, as you call it, this pillar—of yours actually works, it will put hundreds of thousands out of work. In fact, we might as well shut down an entire graduate program in rocketry research. It will disrupt all satellite placement clear out to geosynch orbit. And to be blunt, sir, it would put into your hands, and your hands alone, access to space. I am uncomfortable with that."

That did catch the audience by surprise. There was silence except for the creaking sound of the vast hangar's sheet metal walls and ceiling expanding with the heat of the morning sun.

Franklin stood silent for several seconds, nodding his head.

"Maybe you are right, Professor . . . ?

"Garlin. Professor Garlin," she replied sharply.

"Professor Garlin. In honesty, I must correct one point at the start: I am not Doctor Smith. Never got that far. MIT, in its wisdom, felt we should part company long before then."

There was a bit of a chuckle from the audience and whispers as those in the know explained to others why he had been expelled: because he had hacked into the registrar's computers. For this young audience it made him even more of a hero, a true hacker in their midst!

"Ah, yes," Garlin retorted, and it was obvious her misstatement was calculated.

"'Franklin' or 'Frank' is fine with me, Professor."

"Fine, then, Frank. Would you indulge us with the rest of your response?"

"I am familiar with your work and glad to meet you at last." There was no sarcasm in his voice, even though in recent months she had emerged as one of his sharpest critics. "I will not reply with the old line, never to be trusted: 'Do you trust me?'"

There were some nervous chuckles from the audience.

"I am familiar with the theory of disruptive technology: that a new technological innovation can have serious negative impacts on the service provided by a previous technology, and at times disastrous dislocation for those who work in the technology being disrupted by the new one—and even economic upheaval."

"You could, in fact, put NASA permanently out of business," she replied.

"And I must add that you have, essentially, taken the research of a team at Goddard into this tower design and, with slight variations, filed dozens of patents based on that work, I think obviously for your own profit."

Now there was an audience reaction, for more than one dreamed, as Gary had once dreamed, of working for that august agency. Even Gary had felt uncomfortable with that very fact: that Franklin had indeed cornered the market, as some were now saying, on some of the innovations that he, Eva, and others had labored over for nearly two decades, but inasmuch as it had been for a government entity, such research automatically became public domain and could not be patented.

"Regarding putting NASA out of business: I doubt that," Franklin replied, and now there was an edge to his voice. He did not respond to the question about the patents.

"NASA's business since its inception," Garlin countered, "has been to put astronauts—many of them trained here—satellites and interplanetary exploration programs like the recent *Curiosity* mission into space. Your Tower of Babel will at best interfere with that, at worst could shut it down. If ever built, every launch would have to take into account your tower. It will indeed be a pillar—like a pillar built smack in the middle of an interstate highway."

There were nods from more than a few regarding that tough point.

"Professor, need I remind you of the scores of other areas that NASA works in, from aerodynamic research within the atmosphere, to climate change studies, to anything and everything dealing not just with space but aviation in general?" Franklin replied, again dodging a tough point.

"But their bread and butter has been space."

"And at this moment their funding has all but put them out of business. And that is why I stepped in: for this moment."

"To make a profit whether this tower of yours goes up or not."

At that, Franklin did bristle, and Gary smiled. The audience reminded him of spectators at a tennis match, their heads shifting back and forth from the elderly professor to Franklin and then back again. It was Franklin's move now to return the volley just fired at him.

"My books are open as to my worth," Franklin said sharply. "Net worth approaching fifty billion, I didn't check the close of the stock market yesterday, so I can't give you an exact count. I'll give you my accounting firm's number if you wish to check on Monday, or just look at my last tax return: I paid enough taxes the last few years to have nearly provided NASA with one hundred percent of its budget last year."

He paused for effect.

"Give or take a few billion."

Again a few more chuckles, but Gary could sense the rising tension.

"Professor—and I assume you are a professor here at Purdue . . ."

"Yes, I am. Thirty-two years."

Gary remembered taking a couple of classes with Garlin. Boring as hell in the classroom, but nevertheless a woman he admired for her research into trans-atmospheric aircraft capable of taking off like a plane, achieve orbit, and then return.

She was right: if the tower went up, her life's work was finished. With the tower taking payloads and people aloft at a few dollars a pound, all the hundreds of billions of dollars of research and efforts for the last fifty years would be moot.

"I understand your perspective, Professor," Franklin said, "and I admire your work."

"That is not the answer I sought," she responded, "though I appreciate the platitude."

Franklin, going into these situations, Gary learned, always had his bases covered. So that was the portfolio he was studying while in flight: bios of professors who might be in the audience. Typical of him, Gary realized. Undoubtedly he had studied him and Eva for years before making his choice.

"Nor would I expect you to accept that as an answer, Professor. Will you indulge me in an explanation that might take a few minutes?"

Garlin could only agree but remained standing.

"First, regarding NASA. For the moment, in this economy, we all are in accord that it is receiving but a fraction of the funding that it should be getting. When we had trillion-dollar bailouts, I wish fifty billion of that had gone to NASA to take us back into space to stay."

It was an easy win line with this audience, and there was a round of applause.

"I cannot arrange trillion-dollar loans, but as an American I can invest in what I believe in. This country gave me opportunity against all the odds of the social system I was born into and not of my creation or that of my parents. Other heroes—Americans who believed in the first words of our Declaration of Independence—opened those doors for me by refusing to give up a seat on a bus or by facing police dogs on a bridge in Selma, Alabama. Without them going before me, I would not be standing here today in this honored position."

He paused for a moment as if overcome by emotion, which Gary knew was genuine.

"I believe that, given my age, it is time I started to pay back. The tower will be my payback to America and to the world for the chance I have been given."

No response for a moment, nor did he seek it as an applause line. Instead he pushed straight ahead.

"I do believe the work I have started I might not finish. It will cost far more than I have or can ever hope to raise, but if I start out on the path, I believe there will be a day when NASA is again at the fore. So let me have a bit of hubris here and say that I am fanning the waning fire of our dreams, keeping it alive until it bursts forth anew."

A scattering of applause did greet this.

"And when that day comes," Garlin interjected, "your profit?"

Franklin chuckled.

"Professor, this is America, and it was, if I remember my history, built on the profit motive. I never saw that as a sin as some do."

There were some chuckles in the audience from that one.

"But let me add," he quickly continued, "I will most likely be pushing eighty by the time this project becomes fully functional and, dare I say, on a profit-making base. I have no children; as for my other relatives, well, they'll be in for a sad shock when my will is read. And as one approaches eighty, profits really don't mean that much. What matters more and more is the thought of what you will leave behind that betters this world for all of us.

"I doubt if that will reassure you, but let me press to the next point of your query: disruptive technologies."

The hangar was silent as Franklin paused to take a sip from a bottle of water and clear his throat.

"You are absolutely right. A disruptive technology usually sneaks up and, in military terms, outflanks those ahead of it, then moves to the fore. I could go back to the nineteenth century and cite how steamships finally killed the industry of building sailing ships. How iron replaced wood and then Bessemer steel replaced iron. Some of you engineers out there with a history background might recall that when the first iron bridge, of less than two hundred feet, was built in the 1790s at Coalbrookedale, England, it was declared the new wonder of the world and people came from as far as London on canal barges to gaze at it with awe. Iron, precious iron, used to make a bridge?

"When was the last time any of us stopped on a highway overpass, got out of our cars, and gasped, 'Wow, this bridge is made not just of iron but of steel!'

"That was a disruptive technology at work, and perhaps a few stonemasons glared at the bridge and muttered this would certainly screw up their careers as bridge builders. I ask: Should they have taken the bridge down or blown it up?"

"That is not the point of the issue today of disruptive technologies and their economic impact on hundreds of thousands, even millions of careers and livelihoods," Garlin retorted.

"It is precisely that point, Professor," he replied a bit more sharply now. "Automobiles replaced carriages and eventually even railroads. But let me take three men as a modern example.

"Go back to 1978, to three guys named Jobs, Wozniak, and Gates. Who were they in 1978?"

He chuckled and pointed to the audience.

"They were nerds like us."

This did draw a lively round of applause.

"Consider the giants at IBM, Wang, and now all-but-forgotten-firms like Atari. The giants could not give those guys the right time of day. I do wonder about the fate of one executive in particular at IBM. Remember, they were the giants, the masters of the universe of computers in 1978. They got dragged nearly butt backward into the business of what was then called microcomputers. Everything for them was mainframe, or what they then called mini-frame. So they do start to make the micros, reluctantly in response to something called Apple, which they said only hobbyists and old hippie types would still be buying.

"Remember back then? In my world of 1964, of course, I could not go to the World's Fair in New York."

He smiled and shrugged, and Gary looked around at the audience of young students, realizing many might not even pick up on the fact that the South was still segregated in that year, and the thought of Franklin and his family venturing to New York City was nearly as great a leap as going to the moon.

"You can find old movies on YouTube from that fair in 1964, put out by Bell, IBM, and others, touting 'The World of Tomorrow.' "

Franklin pronounced those words in a halfway decent imitation of James Earl Jones's voice.

"The image of the computer of the future, of the year 2000, which seemed a long way off back then, was some giant mainframe, like Bell with its telephone switching stations—so big it needed an entire building, coming soon to a neighborhood near you. You'd dial in to the computer. Think of that: When was the last time any of us 'dialed' a phone? And then, there stood the joyous housewife in the kitchen, able to access a new recipe for dinner; Junior could get an answer to his homework question; and Pop could even order a part for the family hover car parked in the garage. That was the vision of the computer in 1964, until three nerds and others like them came along."

This did draw appreciative laughs and several in the audience already had their iPhones or iPads out and were checking out the videos seconds later.

"Anyhow. Nerds start making a new kind of computer in their basements and garages. One of the big giants finally stirs reluctantly. They need what was then called a disk operating system, which as you know is the absolute breakdown into strings of ones and zeroes to run the computer in such a way that regular English that everyone else can read appears on a twelve-inch-wide green screen monitor. Bill Gates writes it for them—an outside contractor, since no one in the firm could be bothered. And that savvy young man just casually throws into their contract for his services that he owns the copyright and they pay just a few bucks per copy.

" 'No big deal. Why, sure,' " and Franklin drew a laugh when pantomiming the executive shrugging and signing the contract.

"We know who is worth more today, Gates or IBM, and I wonder if that executive who signed that contract for his company had his golden parachute packed and ready, because he definitely was going to need it."

"You make light, sir, of a serious question," Garlin admonished.

Now Franklin bristled even more.

"I remember, Professor, a generation ago, when the impact of what was called the microcomputer really started to hit . . . and where it would lead. Meanwhile Jobs and Wozniak are playing around with something called a mouse. I recall when the mouse came out, even some nerds rejected it: real nerds type in their codes, none of this point-and-click crap."

Gary smiled at that. It was well into the middle of the 1990s when he finally decided a mouse was worth having.

"Meanwhile, other genius types are thinking about another crazy idea: Why even have a big computer when you could link every computer in the world together by just typing in a few words, or using that mouse thing to click on a line of words? Mr. Gates and the folks over at Apple better start building machines that can interface with that! And the race was on that transformed our entire world.

"The bottom line of the argument: if a computer can do the job better than a man or woman, then let it come. Is there a person in this room who would argue we should toss out computers and reopen factories to make slide rules?"

He paused and looked around the hangar.

"You know, slide rules?" he said, laughing, making a gesture as if working a calculation on one. "A gizmo sort of like an abacus. Don't laugh: more than a few in Mission Control on the day *Apollo 11* lifted off had them on their desks. And besides, you don't have to worry about batteries running dry."

One of the professors in the crowd opened his book bag and actually pulled one out, holding it up.

"I don't leave home without it. And it is virusproof as well!" he cried.

That drew a laugh from the crowd and a nod of thanks from Franklin.

"That is the bottom line of the disruptive technology argument. Do we let it happen and take our chances, or do we freeze development?

"And let us say we do freeze development somehow, which I can only see happening in some Orwellian 1984 state."

He snapped out those last words with cold intent, a challenge to provide a rational alternative to stopping technological innovation.

"In such a world some nerd in this very hangar will sneak off to their dorm room or garage and, like Jobs, Wozniak, and Gates, just keep on inventing anyhow, and the hell with what others say. And thirty years hence you might be standing here, talking about some sci-fi-sounding hyper drive that can take us to Alpha Centauri and beyond."

This received some applause, at least from those not sitting too close to Garlin, who had finally sat back down.

"Professor, I mean no insult to your stunning achievements," Franklin said to her, offering a flag of truce. "In fact, for the dream of my firm to be achieved, we still need heavy-lift vehicles, on the scale of the *Saturn V* of the Apollo age, to loft several hundred tons into geosynch orbit before we can even begin to build. At $100,000 a pound to geosynch that comes out to . . ." He paused dramatically as if running the numbers through his head but, having faced this argument before, he already had the figures down. ". . . that will come to something like fifty billion or more, give or take a few billion just to get the material up there to start construction . . . at which point I will be flat broke."

He then smiled.

"So if anyone here wishes to help me raise another fifty billion, I will be all ears."

It was obviously an exit line as he made it a point of checking his old-fashioned wristwatch.

"I regret I must leave, because my next stop, like a desperate politician on the eve of election, is to try to raise more money. I'll leave a stack of cards here; I have a partial feeling for Purdue. I cannot say why, because one of your alumni, who is a bit stage shy, has forbidden me to drag him up here."

Gary at that moment did give Franklin an icy gaze as his friend made a show of peering toward the back of the hangar, shading his eyes as if looking for someone.

"Anyone want an internship, you got my e-mail address for Pillar Inc. Anyone graduating who wants to take a shot at what I believe will be the greatest adventure of the twenty-first century, send in your résumé. My respects to you, Professor Garlin, and I pray someday we can shake hands in agreement—"

He paused.

"—while floating in zero-g, out at geosynch orbit."

Before Garlin could fire back, Franklin had already put down his mike, walked off the stage, and was heading for the open hangar doors. He tried to avoid getting inundated by members of the audience wanting to shake his hand, some even holding out pens and sheets of paper and asking for an autograph. Out in the parking area, it was turning into a traffic jam.

"Get on the plane and let's get outta here," he whispered as he strode by Gary and Eva, acting as if he did not know them.

The crowd surged after him, few barely noticing Gary, Eva, and Victoria, though Professor Garlin did. Gary was a bit anxious as she came up to him but then graciously extended his hand.

"Gary Morgan, isn't it?"

"Yes, Professor."

"Hope you don't think I was being rude, but it is a question that needs to be raised and which your friend will soon find increasing resistance from, if not outright blocking moves or far worse."

"I must confess, Professor, I never really thought much on it."

Garlin smiled.

"You, a student I remember from twenty years ago as one of the best?"

Gary reddened, his feelings toward her softening. Besides her traditional technology work, she also taught a course on the societal impacts of technological innovation, which he had found to be fascinating.

Gary introduced his wife and daughter.

"Given who your father is," Garlin said, smiling at Victoria, "I am actually running a graduate seminar on this exact topic of the ethical questions raised by disruptive technological advances. Would you be interested in auditing it, young lady?"

How could Victoria refuse such an offer, regardless of her workload? She gratefully accepted.

"I think your Mr. Franklin wishes to, as they say, 'get the hell out of Dodge,'" Garlin said, "so I will leave you three for your farewells. And, Morgan, even though I completely disagree with this whole scheme and think you are way beyond the edge of the envelope, I am proud you were once a student of mine."

She departed and Gary smiled inwardly. She was a formidable intellect, and highly respected. It was evident that she would use her influence to stand against the building of the tower, but nevertheless he did admire her.

The three stepped out of the hangar but did not head directly to the Gulfstream: it was evident it was going to take Franklin some time to get there as more and more cars parked along the access road to the airport and people who had come to see Franklin Smith got out and flocked in his direction.

Gary had his arm around Victoria, her mother by her other side, holding her hand. It was time to do it.

"If you said yes to Professor Garlin," Gary said, "you have to follow through."

"Oh, I will. It sounds interesting, and what I learn might help the project."

"Of course, dear."

He looked at Eva and swallowed nervously.

"I think you are here for more than just watching me fly," Victoria said, and there was a tightness in her voice.

"What do you mean?"

"Just that I can sense both of you are tense."

He stumbled trying to say the words and finally looked appealingly at Eva, who broke the news and answered Victoria's initial questions. He was unable to speak as he felt her arm slide around his waist and she leaned in against his shoulder, struggling to hold back tears.

He took a deep breath.

"Hey, sweetheart, remember what I always used to say when you were little and were freaked out by lightning storms, or when things just spooked you?"

" 'Until you see me get afraid, kid, there is no reason to be afraid.' "

She could barely say the words.

"Exactly. So keep that in mind, sweetness. The doc says with the new medications and such, I got plenty of years ahead of me. We wanted to tell you that face-to-face, and you know we never hide anything from you."

Victoria held him tightly.

Gary's cell phone rang, the tone indicating it was a call he could not ignore: it was Franklin, little more than a hundred feet away.

"We'll be along in a few minutes," Gary said.

"Gary, just got a call from our stop later this afternoon and the schedule's been changed a bit. Something's come up."

"We're on our way now, just saying good-bye to Victoria."

"Why say good-bye?"

"We're leaving, aren't we?"

"Bring her along."

"What?"

"You three need some time together. Kidnap her and bring her along; I'll see that she gets a flight back here in time for classes on Monday."

Franklin clicked off.

"We've got to get going, Victoria," Eva said, hugging her daughter.

"Sweetie, you have any plans for this weekend?" Gary asked.

"Well"—she blushed slightly—"I did promise Peter I'd hang around to watch him try for his solo."

"That was Franklin. He suggested you come along with us."

"What?"

Gary looked at her appealingly. Leave it to his friend to keep pulling these last-second surprises. Given where they were headed so late in the day, why did Franklin suddenly invite her along?

"Daddy, I don't have anything packed, half of my shirt just got cut off . . ."

Her voice trailed off as she looked into her father's eyes and smiled.

"Sure, Daddy, let's go."

He gave her a warm hug as Eva wondered aloud in Ukrainian what Smith had up his sleeve this time.

"Give me a moment to explain to Peter," she said, and broke away from his side.

"Who is this Peter guy?" he could not help but ask.

"Come on, Daddy, he's just a friend."

She waded into the crowd. He looked at Eva, who was smiling as she watched their daughter make her way up to Peter and say something inaudible. His smile transformed into a crestfallen look a few seconds later. She gave him a quick hug, then a kiss on the lips.

"Eva?" Gary asked, looking at his wife, who just stood there smiling.

"Save it for when she is home on vacation; she can tell us all about it then," she said, then laughed and gave him another kiss.

"I'm not sure about this," he said.

"No father is when it comes to his baby girl," Eva laughed. "My father wanted to fly to America just to 'check you out,' as he put it in a less-than-friendly tone when I first told him about you."

"You were twenty-two then; our girl just turned seventeen."

"Kids grow up faster now," was all she said in reply; then, letting go of his hand, she waved toward the Gulfstream.

He could see McMullen standing on the steps of the plane, looking their way while blocking entry to the crowd gathered around, Smith having already boarded.

Victoria's flight instructor, Brandon, was trying to do crowd control, shouting for the group to get a hundred feet back from the plane so it could start engines. As Gary and Eva reached the stairs, Danny extended a helping hand.

"We just got word that the college president is coming here, along with some congressmen, and we want to get wheels up now, otherwise we'll be stuck here for hours."

They gained the top of the stairs and Gary looked back. Victoria was pushing her way through the crowd. Danny reached out to grab her hand and pull her up the steps.

There were more than a few comments at the sight of her getting on the plane. Only a very few knew her connection to Franklin via her parents. The seventeen-year-old in her did come out, though, and playing a bit of a role she turned, bowed, and blew a kiss to Peter, which was greeted with more than a few comments Gary did not quite appreciate before ducking down and entering the cabin. Gary hoped that Franklin's offer to take her along for the rest of the weekend did not trigger any reactions, especially jealousy on the part of some professors, but it was too late to debate that now as Brandon shouted to McMullen to close the hatch and that he'd handle clearing the area around the plane.

Smith was already strapped in and jotting some notes on his iPad but folded it over as the three headed aft.

"Mr. Smith," Victoria bubbled, "thank you for inviting me along."

"Figured since you'll be my intern next summer, it's a chance for us to get to know each other. Besides, something in our schedule changed and I thought you might enjoy that, and just spending time with your parents as well."

"Again, thank you," she said, and actually leaned over to hug him.

"We're cleared for engine start-up," Danny said over the intercom. "Please take your seats and let's get out of here before the college president, the congressmen, and Lord knows who else show up."

The three did as ordered in the aft section, Victoria happily settling in beside her father while her mother did the same on his other side. She snuggled against him and took his hand. Nothing more was said about the news they had just broken to her, but it was obvious she was dealing with a flood of emotions.

They could hear Danny, up in the cockpit, side window open, shouting for everyone to please stand clear, and the distant voice of Brandon replying. Seconds later, the port-side engine started up.

8

It turned out that the meeting with the real estate agent out in Denver for lunch was merely a side trip. Franklin did not come away with the hundred million he had hoped for but did get an investment of fifty million. As they reboarded the plane, Smith mused that at fifty million a day, in a thousand days he would have the rest. To Victoria's delight, while Franklin was having his lunch meeting, there was enough time for the three of them to take a quick stop at a nearby mall and hurriedly pick up a change of clothes and the usual necessities no seventeen-year-old woman would think of not having with her for a weekend trip. She at least had her flight bag and more than once pulled out her log book and just sat and gazed at the entry by her instructor authorizing her for solo flight.

After Denver, the next stop was out to a remote airfield in New Mexico. It was headquarters now to a legendary aircraft designer and a billionaire friend from England who were successfully running a suborbital launch business and already hard at work on orbital manned launches as a commercial concern. At the moment, they were losing money hand over fist, but that did not deter them; as Franklin said of them more than once, these two beyond everything else were having a good time.

Gary had met both before and was still somewhat in awe of the circles he was traveling in of late. The two greeted him and Eva warmly as they disembarked from the Gulfstream. They were led straight to a Hummer taking them out to the hangar complex. The driver swung wide and slowed for a moment as they approached the launch vehicle, its wingspan nearly that of a 747, with the suborbital spacecraft nicknamed "*Enterprise*" slung between the twin-fuselage "mother ship."

"We have a launch later this afternoon; the passengers are going through their final prep over in that hangar," their British host said, and nodded to the massive hangar that housed the vehicle. "Going to give them a sunset launch; they'll have the sun to the west as they climb out, turning east across the demarcation line, at which point the sky will explode with stars. At sixty miles up, they'll have a view over six hundred miles out in every direction, well past Dallas, which will be in darkness and lit up.

"They'll catch moonrise at apogee at nearly seventy miles up, and then back down. We find our passengers really like that one."

Rather than stop they continued on, heading to a low, squat building that was obviously newly constructed, raw earth still plowed up into piles around it. It covered more than four acres, with low arcing roof studded with solar panel arrays to take advantage of the plentiful energy available, at least out here in the high desert of central New Mexico. They'd be a joke if installed in Seattle.

Pulling up to a side door, Franklin and their hosts got out first. The three were talking softly, and Gary suddenly felt a bit out of place as their driver opened their door and with a smiling gesture indicated he, Eva, and Victoria should follow. It was far warmer on this sunny day than the Seattle climate he had gotten used to in recent months and Gary was grateful for the blast of cold air that greeted them once they were in the building. It was actually a vast shed, most of it empty, but scores of men and women were at work erecting smaller structures under the high roof. Franklin and the other two had not slowed their pace, heading for a white-walled building to one side of the vast enclosed complex, disappearing within. Gary, Eva, and Victoria followed. Once through the first doorway Gary felt the pressure change in the air. They were inside an overpressured airlock.

It was reassuring, and he relaxed a bit. They were going into an airtight lab, the air pressure inside kept higher than outside to prevent dust from seeping in, and out in this desert there was certainly enough dust. He could see Franklin and their hosts through the next glass door, a white-suited tech sweeping them with a vacuum cleaner, paying particular attention to their hair and feet. Gary, Eva, and Victoria followed, and Franklin, as if remembering that the three existed, smiled and said it was time to strip down. A female tech pointed the ladies to a side room while the men stayed behind and removed shirts, trousers, shoes, and socks, which were sealed up in white duffel bags, and then donned white coveralls.

Gary was impressed. In nearly all the clean rooms in Goddard, you just simply slipped on the coveralls over your street clothes. This place was well up in the stratosphere as far as not taking any chances that a stray particle of dust was dragged in, following procedures that existed in only a few score other clean rooms around the world. Forced air was coming out of long louvered vents in the ceiling and being sucked into the grating in the floor. The lab was most likely clean down to a fraction of a micron. They donned hairnets with hoods over them, goggles, and, for this place, even respirators; then they donned gloves and oversize white slippers, a tech helping with the drawstrings. Not a square inch of bare skin was exposed when the tech gave him a final sweep with the vacuum cleaner.

The four men and their guardian of the clean room waited politely, saying nothing, not even making small talk, as they waited as Eva and Victoria emerged in their "bunny suits." Gary always smiled at the sight of Eva in a clean room outfit and the big "Mickey Mouse" shoes covering her feet. It was the first time Victoria had been decked out, and underneath her mask and goggles he guessed she was grinning, nearly out of her head with excitement. He could see her eyes were crinkled up with delight.

"I must say, you look fetching, Dr. Petrenko, and so do you, Miss Morgan," the Brit said, and pointed to the third door, this one solid metal. Their guide punched in a code to open it up, the pressure in this inner lab area higher than in the outside prep room, causing their ears to pop. Within it looked for all the world like nearly any clean room lab. The brilliant light, the steady hum of air filters at full blast, techs at work at various tasks, except for a small crowd gathered around a glass-walled chamber, obviously expecting the visitors. The air was dry and crisp, the temperature set at the low sixties.

The Brit and the aircraft designer, voices a bit muffled by the face mask respirators, exchanged greetings with and then made formal introduction to a tall slender person in baggy white coveralls. It was hard to figure out if it was a man or a woman, let alone his or her ethnicity, until Gary saw the ID tag on the man's white suit.

"My friends, it is my pleasure to introduce Dr. Fuchida, who will oversee this little demonstration."

My God, Gary thought, even as he extended his hand. Protocol in such a high-level lab meant that shaking hands was frowned upon, but he could not help himself.

For years this man had haunted him. He was the competition. Eva could barely contain her delight, because this man was her fulfillment. It was his team, twenty years earlier, that had led the world in carbon nanotube research.

Gary looked at Franklin, who actually winked at him, and he almost blurted out the question of how much did it cost to bring this man under his sway and how long had he been working here out in New Mexico. Fuchida had not published in several years, and the rumor was that, when funding dried up in his home country due to their flatlined economy, he had gone into a quiet but frustrated retirement, location unknown. Some even said he had gone over to the Chinese for a capitalistic sum that far exceeded the cost of an entire American baseball team. And Franklin most likely had him here all along.

Fuchida touched Gary's hand for a brief instant and then offered a traditional bow, which Gary returned.

"I am honored and humbled to meet the two of you. I wish you to know that for years I have followed your research and publications with keen interest."

He turned to Eva and bowed.

"And I thank you, madam, for your article published eight years ago, expressing belief in my work."

Gary nearly burst out laughing. It had actually been an article in a popular magazine blasting the American research community because "our side" was lagging behind in carbon nanotube development, and without doubt Fuchida and company would take the final steps in this field—and if their country did not exploit it, the Chinese would. It was her article that helped to trigger the rumor about Fuchida going to China when his research lab folded up without warning and he disappeared. In this high-level world of research, a leader does not simply disappear to go fish off some dock or go metal detecting on a beach while wearing Bermuda shorts and black socks. Someone had him at work somewhere, and now the mystery was solved.

Eva's features were all but concealed, but Gary could tell she was a bit embarrassed.

"And so now we are here together," Fuchida said graciously, "all on the same team."

As he spoke, he gestured to the enclosed chamber they were standing next to, its glass windows several inches thick.

"Dr. Fuchida," the Brit said, "I think we are ready for this long-anticipated demonstration."

Perhaps the Brit's interruption of the exchange of greetings was slightly rude, but the enthusiasm in his voice was almost like that of a boy screaming, *I wanna see it!*

Fuchida nodded and pointed to the chamber.

"We have two strands of carbon-60 nanotubing within the chamber," he proudly announced. "One strand is two meters in length."

"Two meters," Eva gasped.

Gary could sense Fuchida's smile beneath the face mask as he nodded.

"*Bozhe miĭ!*" Eva exclaimed in Ukrainian. "When did you get beyond the millimeter stage?"

"Oh, about six months ago," Franklin replied offhandedly.

"And you didn't tell us?" Gary asked, half good-naturedly, but with a touch of hurt as well.

"Recall that was just about the same time I brought you two on board. Regardless, you do know now."

The implication, though it did sting a bit, was obvious. No matter how he felt their friendship had evolved, Franklin did keep some cards close to his vest and separated as well. Of course, it was how he made his billions.

"Come on," the aircraft designer announced, "let's see it."

"Well, there it is," Fuchida said, pointing to the chamber. Everyone leaned forward to the view ports. They saw two claw-like clamps separated about two meters apart, and behind them two large steel cylinders separated by a few centimeters, and empty space in between. Nothing else could be seen. It reminded Gary of the hoodwink of a supposed flea circus when he was a kid, a few miniature carnival rides spinning around, the barker claiming fleas were on board.

It was disappointing but Gary knew what was coming.

"A single thread," Fuchida quickly said, "as we are now mastering manufacturing of for significant lengths. If our computer projections are correct we'll quickly have strands of any length that are two millimeters wide."

"How quickly?" Franklin asked.

"Give me six months for 0.2 and six months more for our goal of 2 millimeters at the length you desire, if all goes well today."

"I don't see a bloody thing," the Brit said, but it was obvious his question was rhetorical. He had, without doubt, along with his aviation designer friend, been hovering around this lab since it was built.

"It is, of course, invisible to the naked eye, though I do have microscopes which you can watch through and cameras operating at a thousand frames a second recording the test when we start," Fuchida pointed out. "Behind it, between the two pistons, with a clearance of 1.5 centimeters between them, there is a woven mesh of fifty such strands. At such scales, I must say it was difficult to weave and is less than ten millimeters in length, but it is sufficient for the second test."

"You're going for tensile and compression, aren't you?" Eva asked excitedly.

"Exactly."

"Then let's do it," the Brit announced. "Push the button."

Fuchida turned to Eva.

"Doctor, would you do me the honor, since we are on the same team now, of pushing that button?"

"I would not think of taking that away from you, sir," she said.

He laughed softly.

"Don't you think I already did it before you got here?"

Gary did laugh out loud at that. Of course Fuchida and his team would have made sure of it, rather than suffer the humiliation of a failure in front of their funding source, and Franklin was indeed not all he seemed to be if he did not know that as well; he had most likely checked ahead before even flying in.

There actually was a red button on a control panel that Fuchida pointed to, and, delighted, Eva made a dramatic display of depressing it. The two claw-like pistons began to move ever so slightly. Even though he had most likely tested this dozens of times, Fuchida kept a careful eye on the computer readouts and motioned for them to come and look over his shoulder.

"Those two pistons are being driven by a hydraulic compressor which is exerting over a hundred kilograms of outward pressure on that one thread one-tenth the diameter of a human hair to try to pull it apart."

Gary wondered for a moment, if the thread broke, what the kinetic energy would be as it flew apart and if the glass wall would be shattered.

"This exceeds by nearly 50 percent the anticipated outward load on a pillar. If you went in there right now and simply tried to wave your hand between the two pistons, though invisible to the naked eye, that strand is thousands of times sharper than a samurai sword; you would with ease slice your fingers or hand off on it and barely feel it at first as your fingers fell to the floor. Actually, rather dangerous stuff when this slender. I'll be glad when we move up to the visible range, as you know or maybe heard rumors that we have had several accidents."

There had been "talk" some years back of a careless tech in Japan, acting on his own before the project director could stop him, who had gone into a chamber after a test strand had shattered during a test like this one and part of a strand spinning through the air had neatly cut his jugular. He had bled out within the chamber. The project director, most likely Fuchida, ordered the door to be kept sealed and no one to venture in. It must have been a horrific few minutes watching a coworker die like that. The broken strands of carbon nanotube, at such a microscopic diameter, were impossible to see with the naked eye, weighing less than a mote of dust on the wind; if one came into contact with human flesh with sufficient velocity, it would just slice through; if inhaled, even through a respirator, it would pierce the respirator filters, then wreak havoc in the victim's lungs. As a precaution, the room had to be sealed off, the body still inside, because it was feared that the invisible strands would escape by piercing through the layers of air filters and go into the atmosphere. Fuchida, if he was indeed the project leader, ordered the filters shut down and the entire lab, worth tens of millions, shut down and encased in reinforced concrete. If true, it was most likely what killed the Japanese funding for his project.

It must have been a surreal funeral service outside that lab, Gary thought as he continued to gaze at the two pistons, wondering how they were designed to actually grasp and hold the microscopic thread while testing it.

After several minutes Fuchida powered down the pistons, then offered the button to Franklin for the compression test, saying that after all he had spent to reach this moment, he deserved the experience. Franklin casually hit the button without comment, eyes fixed on the chamber. The two pistons separated by less than two centimeters appeared to move, and after several seconds Gary actually took Eva by the arm and pulled her back away from the glass wall. The pistons had actually compressed and were now tightly wedged against each other. Something had gone wrong!

Even Franklin, seeing Gary's reaction, stepped back, but Fuchida just chuckled.

"Happens all the time," he announced. "Those pistons are of the highest-grade tungsten steel to be found anywhere in the world. They are now fused together. The mesh held up; I'll show you the close-up high-speed film later. The mesh cut right through the pistons when we attempted compression."

"So how do we know if we have true compression strength?" Eva asked, relaxing from Gary's protective grip.

"Right now, by the rate at which it cuts into the face of the pistons at a given pressure. Believe me, we were a bit bewildered at first until we figured that out. Eventually we'll coat the pistons with the nanotubing, just to make sure, since they are rather expensive and then useless after a test in which they are fused together, but I'm confident we will exceed what is needed."

There was evident pride in his voice and a round of congratulatory comments from the rest of the group. Then Franklin looked at the computer screen, announced that they had to leave, and asked Fuchida and his team to join them for dinner at eight.

Eva was obviously reluctant to leave. The question of developing a material strong enough to make a tower viable had consumed her for years. She wanted to hear the details, not just of the molecular arrangement, but how Fuchida had finally cracked the mystery of how to actually spin the material out lengthwise from a few millimeters to a strand two meters long and then spin them together into a mesh. Given the fibers' incredible strength, it was almost a paradox to make something stronger than the machines needed to produce it. Even with high-grade tungsten steel, it was like trying to spin wire rope when your tools were made of butter and the rope being made could rip the machinery apart.

It would have to wait, she thought, as their British host led them out of the lab and through the inner airlock. Once clear, he removed his respirator and hood; then, still wearing the rest of the jumpsuit and hairnet, he motioned for them to follow him through the middle door and then out into the main building.

He gestured to the vast open expanse within the four-acre building.

"You go to some of the museums of the Industrial Age in England," he said, "and you can see examples of the rope-making and wire-making works of the nineteenth century. They were called 'rope walks'; they took threads of manila and twisted them into strands and eventually into cables capable of hoisting a ship's anchor—rope thicker than my leg. A ship of the line in Nelson's time needed miles upon miles of rope; one whole part of the ship was even known as the 'cable tier' where the huge ropes for the anchor were stored. They were spun out in vast open sheds a hundred or more yards in length. When your Yank, Roebling, was making the Brooklyn Bridge, his wire works in Trenton where the suspension cables were first drawn out into thin wire stretched nearly a quarter mile.

"That is what this will be a year from now if all goes according to plan. Once our friend Fuchida gets up to two millimeters in diameter for our first thread, we'll start manufacturing it right here."

He grinned.

"Cables thousands of miles in length," he said proudly.

"You mean kilometers," Eva corrected him with a grin. "My prophecy of years ago was true with that Mars mission, what with you English and Americans insisting upon miles, or is it statute or nautical miles?"

There were reluctant nods of agreement over the now legendary screwup that had sent a mission worth several hundred million crashing into the surface of Mars. That was gone over again and again before the incredible *Curiosity* mission was launched using standardized metric measurements to ensure such an embarrassing mistake never happened again.

"Miles are longer," the Brit said with a grin.

"You men and your obsessions on that subject," Eva huffed, and they all laughed, though Victoria seemed a bit embarrassed by her mother's joke.

Franklin rolled up the sleeve of his coverall and realized he had removed his old-fashioned wristwatch before going into the clean room.

"I do think we are on a tight schedule, my friends. Gary, Eva, Miss Victoria, if you will excuse us, the three of us have some contracts and legal stuff to hammer out, which I know bores the two of you no end."

Gary actually felt a bit cut out by the comment. It was obvious that Franklin was separating them from the others.

He and Eva stood silently, both feeling a bit embarrassed, not sure if they should just go and put their clothes back on, then go stand in the hot Mojave sun.

Conspiratorial smiles were suddenly exchanged between the other three.

"You've got a flight to catch, so why don't you go change," the Brit said, as if shooing them off. Gary only nodded and started to turn back to the outer door of the airlock.

"No, you're heading the wrong way," the Brit said, and Gary looked back at him in confusion, then felt a flush of anger, sensing he was being teased.

"Oh, for God's sake, just tell them," the aircraft designer said, starting to laugh.

The Brit and Franklin looked at each other and Franklin nodded to his friend.

"You tell them."

The Brit flashed his winning smile.

"I hear, young lady, that you soloed this morning," the Brit said, looking at Victoria.

"Yes, sir."

He extended his hand and patted her on the shoulder.

"Shirttail still missing?"

She blushed a bit and nodded.

"Well, you got another first ahead of you today."

"How is that?"

"A driver is waiting outside to take you to hangar number one. We'll fetch along your street clothes after you get back."

"Back from what?"

The Brit now broke into a broad grin, like a parent about to give an ultimate gift on Christmas morning.

"Sadly, three of our passengers for this afternoon's flight had to cancel out. Transferring through a flight from Detroit, they ate at the wrong restaurant and are now in our infirmary with a nasty dose of food poisoning. Poor souls. Not their fault, and insurance covers it all, so they'll fly a few months from now. So there are three empty seats on today's suborbital flight."

Victoria looked at him wide-eyed.

"What are you saying?" Eva asked, with an excited but nervous edge to her voice, and she instinctively put a protective arm around Victoria, as if about ready to hold her back.

"Oh, just that there are three empty seats for this evening's flight to watch sunset from space. Those seats are yours."

"*Bozhe miĭ*," Eva gasped.

"You barely got time to suit up and fall in with the others."

Eva looked at Gary and her expression changed.

"But . . . but, I thought passengers had to have flight physicals," she said, looking at her husband.

"He's already had one," Franklin replied. "I asked Dr. Bock to check him out for this and he's cleared. As for Miss Victoria, I'll take a chance on a pilot who has already passed her class-three physical and flew solo today. Now haul out of here."

"But what about me?" Eva asked.

"You had a company physical three months ago and you check out OK as well," Franklin replied, sounding a bit exasperated. "That is, unless the two of you have another child on the way."

She looked at him angrily and blushed, then shook her head emphatically no.

"Dinner at eight," Franklin said.

The Brit pointed to the door leading out of the vast open building.

Victoria, with a shout of delight, was already heading for the door, but Eva protectively snagged her. She had already gone through one white-knuckled moment this morning and now their somewhat crazed friend was pushing their daughter into another adventure?

Franklin smiled with delight, but then his features turned serious under Eva's icy gaze and he looked at the Brit.

"You are one hundred percent sure this is safe?" he asked. "As I think about it now, looking at these three, I lose them and we are all screwed."

"I'll bet my life on it," the designer said. "Besides, it's good training, they'll be spending a lot of time up there soon. Victoria, do you have your logbook with you? We might give you a few minutes in the copilot seat and it should be noted."

The young woman was standing before one of the greatest heroes of the current aviation age.

"It's on board Mr. Smith's plane," she said. "I can go get it."

"No time for that now. But we'll have the captain of your flight make a log entry after you get back. Now come on, either get a move on or we'll call down and have them take off without you."

The way Victoria looked at her parents, Gary knew they'd never be forgiven if they backed out. And besides, he wanted to go, too: it was a childhood dream about to be fulfilled.

The prospect even overwhelmed Eva's protective motherly instincts, and the three ran out the door like kids embarking on the adventure of a lifetime . . . which it most certainly was.

9

The Flight

"Sixty seconds to separation and drop."

Victoria was unable to even remotely contain her excitement. The six passenger seats were arrayed port and starboard along the bulkhead walls, each with its own window, surprisingly large, oval, and slightly bigger than a standard airplane window, while overhead were half a dozen more view ports, which at the moment showed only the underside wing of the mother ship that was hauling them up to the drop altitude of 53,000 feet.

For the last hour they had climbed in a wide circular pattern, clearing past 40,000 feet, near the maximum altitude for commercial airlines, then up through 50,000, their pilot announcing that if they looked forward, literally over his shoulder (there was no barrier or door between pilot, copilot, and the six passengers), they could actually begin to detect the curvature of the earth.

It was a far cry from the thrill of being nine hundred feet above sea level on her solo flight of this morning. Victoria grinned, wondering what Professor NeSmith would say at this moment! Her parents were sitting behind her, and she craned her head to try to look back, but was securely locked in with a four-point harness and could barely move. From the corner of her eye she caught a nervous smile on her mother's face; behind her, her father was actually grinning and gave her a thumbs-up, which she returned.

The aisle separating the port and starboard side of the cabin was ninety inches wide, a bit more cramped than Franklin's Gulfstream. Getting aboard and strapped in had required a bit of gymnastics, including maneuvering through a very narrow pathway between the six seats. Across from her was a middle-aged couple, Brits and relatives of the owner, accompanied by their son, Jason, a history major at Oxford with a keen interest in early aviation and turn-of-the-twentieth-century industrial technology who had interned with Franklin to do historical research on nineteenth-century technological advances and their societal impacts. She caught his eye; he was nervous, eyes wide, but forced a smile and gave her a thumbs-up as well.

"Thirty seconds to drop," the pilot announced. "Keep your arms folded across your torso. Legs tucked in under your seats. The mother ship will nose over ten degrees and then release us. We'll be in free fall for ten seconds, just like if you were skydiving, and then I'll fire up our engines. Then the fun really starts! The pad screen mounted in the seat in front of you will provide readouts of engine performance, velocity, g-force, and elevation. Emergency sickness bags are in your right vest pocket."

He chuckled.

"Don't be embarrassed; use them if you need them, though you'll all be OK: that little shot we gave you before you boarded usually does the trick.

"Ten seconds to drop," and even as he spoke, the mother ship, with their craft still secured, nosed over into a shallow dive.

Victoria had been reluctant to take the shot, but when running over her flight experience, the medical tech urged it, assuring her she might feel a touch drowsy but not like the old days when the med would all but knock you out. She felt secure and ready.

"Edith, I don't give a bloody damn if he is your cousin who built this damn contraption," the elder Brit snapped to his wife, who just laughed with delight as they continued to nose over.

"Drop in five, four . . ."

Victoria looked out the window again. The pilot of the mother ship was looking down at them and actually gave a formal salute, which was quickly returned by their pilot.

"Drop!"

All six of the passengers let out a yell; for some it was a yell of delight, like that of passengers on a roller coaster topping the first climb; for a couple—and Victoria could tell that one was her mother—it was a yell of distress as *Enterprise* dropped free of the mother ship and let gravity do its work. Several seconds later Victoria was looking straight up at the mother ship through a topside window as it banked into a port-side turn at the same time *Enterprise* banked to starboard, the same as with a glider release. The free fall continued for ten seconds, nose pitching down, as they fell a couple of thousand feet and gradually started to level out, now well clear of the mother ship.

"Engine ignition in five . . . four . . ."

She took a deep breath, a bit nervous now. This was a hell of a lot different than being in a 172 or even Franklin Smith's plane. She was strapped in as a passenger, with no control, and did not like the sensation.

And then the hybrid liquid-and-solid-fuel engine ignited.

A "Yeah haaa!" barely escaped her when within five seconds they accelerated up to over two and a half g's. *Enterprise,* a glider only seconds before, was now a true rocket ship, accelerating with startling rapidity, nose above the horizon, and then just continuing to climb and climb, nose pointed up at forty-five degrees, still accelerating.

"Mach one and climbing!" the pilot announced, his calm voice audible through her headphones, the ship buffeting slightly, nose continuing to point up. A moment of tension on Victoria's part: at this attitude, her Cessna 172 would be into a full stall and plummeting back to earth.

"Mach 2!"

She could sense the excitement of the pilot even though he was thoroughly trained, like the most seasoned airline pilot, to sound calm and nonplussed no matter what the situation. The nose of the ship continued to rise, the horizon ahead no longer visible. They were heading nearly straight up and still accelerating!

She looked out the side window and gasped. She could see the curvature of the earth! And above it, the light blue band of the atmosphere, the sky above it darkening. On the port side, the sun still shone, kissing the horizon, but on her side it was darkness. And then . . .

"Oh my God," she whispered, even as the pilot announced they had just punched through 100,000 feet and were at full thrust, the velocity now at Mach 3, over 2,200 miles per hour. At this speed, if they leveled out, they could hop clear to New York in less than an hour.

The view from the pilot's position though . . . The darkening sky was a sea of stars.

"Maximum velocity 2,423 miles per hour."

They were heading nearly straight up, the three g's of thrust keeping her wedged in her seat. The pilot offered a soft reassuring commentary, announcing the 150,000-foot mark, 200,000 . . .

In spite of the headphones she could hear her mother behind her, saying a prayer in Ukrainian, but then repeatedly exclaiming, "My God, ohhh my God," not in fear, her voice filled with awe.

She wished she could turn around and see her father's expression but already knew what it was. That wondrous nerdy childlike grin of his. So loving for his daughter, so reassuring when she needed it, so delighted when he knew she was happy, so calming in moments of stress and fear. Her heart filled with love knowing that he was embraced by his childhood dream to reach to the stars.

"Love ya, Dad!" she shouted, and she thought she could hear his reply.

"Five seconds to shutdown!"

It hit with a jolt. One second she was slammed back into her seat, pulling g's, and then, with the shutdown of the engine, a second later weightless. They were not yet in free fall. The velocity of the ship would continue to carry it heavenward until gravity finally canceled out upward thrust. They would now enter a long parabolic curving climb and then eventual drop. But now came the six minutes or so of total freedom and she did feel a twinge of fear. *Can I handle this?*

She had experienced free fall before and never really liked it when Brandon had put her through full-power stalls and accelerated stalls, and, contrary to what most flight instructors did these days, had even taken her through a spin. But at 3,000 feet up in a 172, the sensation lasted only a couple of seconds. In spite of her wild enthusiasm for this flight, the next few moments did scare her a bit.

She felt her stomach rise up. The deep undertone of the rocket astern fell silent. In fact, all was silence for a moment.

"Welcome to space," their pilot announced, turning to look back at his passengers.

"Everyone OK? If so, give me a thumbs-up!"

She offered a thumbs-up. Turning to look back, she saw her mother, eyes wide with wonder, thumb up, and her father, that beautiful, childlike smile creasing his face. Jason on the other side by her father, thumb up.

Poor Edith suddenly did not look so happy, though her husband, complaining a few minutes before, was laughing.

"Bloody hell, yes!" he cried.

"Unbuckle your harnesses, we have just under six minutes. A real good burn, folks, best yet; you are definitely the top of the club at 117 kilometers up, so we have a few extra seconds. Float about, but be careful. If you feel queasy, do the ground crew a favor and hang on to that bag, and don't be ashamed to use it."

The copilot, a young woman—Victoria guessed she was from India—floated up out of her seat, motioning for the others to join her, and, then pushing off from the forward cab, floated past them, laughing, knees tucked to chest, somersaulting over their heads. Victoria fumbled with her harness for a few seconds, unbuckled, took a deep breath, pushed off from her seat, rose up, head bumping against the ceiling, and tried to follow suit, but like a marble in slow motion she bounced back and forth against the cabin. But she didn't care.

Is this is how angels feel? she wondered.

Her father was up, and as she drifted past him she reached out a hand, brushing his face.

"How are you, Daddy?" she cried.

"I can't believe it!" he shouted. She caught a glimpse of her mother. She had unbuckled but still held the armrests.

"Come on, Mom!" Victoria cried as her father floated up beside her.

Eva floated but, as if glued in place, hands resting on either side of the large overhead window, she was looking out, mesmerized. The sun to their port side was setting. To the east, hundreds of miles off, far, far below, the distant surface of the earth glowed with the lights of Dallas, El Paso, Oklahoma City. On the horizon above, the moon, two days shy of full, was rising as their ship glided eastward at over 2,000 miles an hour. And overhead it was a sea of stars. An endless sea of stars.

Eva was crying as she gazed upon it with reverence and wonder.

Victoria felt a hand slip into hers. It was her dad, and she looked at him, the fear of earlier in the day forgotten.

"Come on!" he cried, and, pushing off the ceiling with his other hand, he propelled himself and her down the length of the cabin, both laughing hysterically. The copilot, though joyful in her first somersault, was aft, doing her job now, reaching out to brake them before they slapped into the aft bulkhead, offering a word of caution; then, taking hold of Gary, she gently pushed him forward.

She felt like Superman, floating down the length of the cabin, playing at having her arms stretched forward, floating over her mother, looking down at her. And yet, still her mother was glued to the window and was now openly crying, saying something in Ukrainian.

The British family. The father was trying to somersault like their copilot, without much success, instead bumping back and forth. Jason was up, just floating and laughing, but his poor mother would have none of it, and had her bag out now and, between retches, was soundly cursing her "bloody damn crazy" cousin who had talked them into this.

The copilot, seeing her distress, floated over by her side to offer words of reassurance.

Jason drifted past Victoria and reached a hand out.

"Care to dance, fair lady?" he cried, taking her hands, and for a moment they tumbled head over heels, laughing wildly. She caught a glimpse of her father, just floating, his gaze now glued to a top-side window.

"Excuse me, good sir," she said with a smile, and, breaking free from Jason, pushed off a bulkhead to float up by her father, reaching out to grab his shoulder as she drifted up to him. He pulled her in by his side, nodding to the window.

"My God," he whispered, "it is so beautiful. Remember when I taught you the constellations?"

There was a catch in his voice as he looked at her and smiled, pointing to the window.

She looked out and gasped. Never had she seen so many stars.

"Orion, isn't it, Daddy?"

"Yup!"

"And there's Gemini. And, oh, that's Sirius."

"Two-minute warning," echoed in the cabin. "Everyone back in their seats at one minute, please."

"We only have a few seconds, angel," her father said, and in her heart she suddenly wondered if he was speaking in a metaphor. That against that eternity of stars they did indeed only have a flicker of time, a few seconds to gaze in wonder and questioning and desire.

There was a long moment of silence, father and daughter floating side by side, glued to the window.

"Imagine a day when we can watch like this for hours on end," he whispered.

"You'll be there with me, Daddy."

"Of course I will," he said, and kissed her lightly on the cheek.

"'For I have slipped the surly bonds of earth, and reached out to touch the face of God,'" Gary whispered. She could see her mother, turning to look up at him, eyes still filled with tears. And she teared up as well; it was a quote from his favorite poem.

"One minute. Back to your seats, please."

"I love you, Daddy," Victoria whispered, and kissed him on the cheek, reluctant to let go.

"Back now," he whispered, voice choked with emotion.

She gently pushed off from his side, reaching down as she floated over her mother, hand brushing the top of her mother's head. Eva looked up, smiling, and blew her a kiss. She tried to grab hold of a recessed handhold in the bulkhead to steady herself above her seat. A hand reached out; it was Jason, and she smiled a thanks as he steadied her.

"Thirty seconds. Back in your seats, please, and buckle in."

She managed to coil her feet under her seat, grabbed hold of the armrests, and pulled herself down, fumbling to get her harness back on. The copilot, carefully and with cheerful professionalism, having left poor Edith's side (the woman was decidedly green and miserable), worked her way from aft forward, checking with each passenger to ensure they were buckled in, reaching her position just as the pilot announced they were at zero for microgravity and starting reentry.

The remarkable design of this craft now came into play as the wings began to rotate from what most would think to be standard position to nearly vertical, the wings now upright to act as brakes, to slow the craft as it reentered the atmosphere.

Victoria was buckled in and then felt the first faint tug of gravity returning as the spacecraft, soon to be an earthbound glider again, having arced through its apogee and free fall, entered the upper atmosphere. The faint wisp of molecules of nitrogen and oxygen, the shield under which life existed on the surface below, struck the upturned wings, the friction of their passage slowing the spacecraft, the energy of their passage heating the passing molecules so that a plasma glow soon engulfed the spacecraft, gravity imparted by their deceleration building, reaching a full one g and then sliding up to more than two g's, pressing Victoria deep into her contoured seat.

She had learned to love the thrill of what she thought were high-speed turns in a plane, but nothing equaled this! And yet, already a burning nostalgia filled her—nostalgia for the few brief moments of freedom she had known above . . . in space.

A hum echoed through the ship; outside the window the glow of superheated plasma, triggered by the braking effect of the upturned wings, pulsed and shimmered. The craft was coming into the atmosphere nose high, the glow shimmering in the forward view from the cockpit.

"Maximum g's 2.3," the pilot announced.

No big deal, she loved the sensation, such a transition from the zero g of but a few minutes before. A thought did strike her: the comments by Professor Garlin only a few hours ago. When the tower was finished, this experience would be gone forever; a simple ride up a very long elevator was how future generations would start their journey to the stars. No thundering rockets, no fiery returns like a blazing comet through the upper atmosphere, as ancient and soon lost as steam locomotives and horse-drawn carriages. Would there be a romantic nostalgia for this, as there existed for other things lost? Was Garlin right to anticipate resistance from the very people her mother and father assumed would be with them? She felt a tug in her heart, because at this instant she was having the ride of a lifetime and loving it, already addicted to it.

She could feel the g load easing off, the glow dissipating, a rumble of servos as the pilot shifted the wings from vertical to act as brakes, returning back down to the "normal" position for flight, a slight thump as they locked into place. She looked straight up, a final glimpse of a star—was it Sirius?—and then the blackness of space shifted to deep blue, nose pitched forward, the horizon visible, still a glimpse of the curvature of the earth, the space plane, now a glider, turning into a forty-five-degree bank, away from the approaching darkness of night turning 180 degrees, the ground below clad in twilight and dusk. They were somewhere over central New Mexico, mountains, desert—was that Albuquerque far, far below off their starboard side?

"Sixty thousand feet, speed 1.3 Mach," and now the copilot called out the numbers. Another forty-five-degree bank, nose a bit high, a slight buffet as they bled off speed and altitude, dropping below mach speed. Looking down, she caught a glimpse of the runway, lights on in the early twilight.

"We're on the numbers, folks: touchdown in two minutes thirty seconds."

One more banking turn, a final glimpse of the runway, now looming large, talk between pilot and copilot and ground control, all business now, as if she were just listening in on a standard commercial flight. She had learned enough as a student pilot to be able to follow most of it as they turned on to final approach, nose going up a bit, the thump of landing gear locking into place.

The ground seemed to be racing in; they were coming in far "hotter" than any 172 or commercial jet. Nose dropped slightly; the four-point harness kept her locked in place as she tried to crane her head up higher to catch a glimpse of the final seconds, of final approach of the array of green lights to either side of the runway, a visual that they were on the proper glide slope, too low and the lights are red, too high and they shift to yellow. Now over the numbers and then a bit of a lurch, the audible squeal of tires striking pavement, and then a long rollout, at last coming to a full stop.

"If you could please remain seated, harnesses secured, while our tug hooks up and tows us back to the hangar."

A moment later there was a bit of a lurch, the tow tractor hooking on to the forward wheel, and slowly they were pulled off the runway, the copilot out of her seat, grinning, squeezing her way past Victoria, bending over to check on poor Edith, patting her on the shoulder reassuringly, the woman looking up at her wanly.

They came to a stop, a bit of chatter on the radio and intercom as the pilot ran through a shut-down checklist, the copilot unlatching the aft door.

"All right, crew, we can disembark now. Start with the aft row seats."

Victoria unbuckled, stood up, her father already up, the copilot offering a hand. She felt a flash of concern; he did seem a bit wobbly as she guided him to the door, followed by Jason, then her mother and the British couple. She hesitated, then took a few steps forward to look over the pilot's shoulder. He paused in his checklist and she knew protocol well enough not to interrupt at such a moment, but he looked up at her with a grin.

"We'll let you back in later: you can take the right seat and I'll walk you through whatever you want to learn."

She smiled gratefully.

"Just one quick question, sir."

"Sure."

"How was it for you?"

He chuckled.

"You're the first one to ever ask me that.

"How was it for me?" he repeated, as if to himself.

"I was one of the last to be recruited for the astronaut corps. I started training to fly the *Constellation* but then the program was killed, as you know. Our friends building this snatched me up, thank God. This was my eighth flight, my fourth in the left-hand seat."

He looked forward, saying nothing for a moment.

"To tell you the truth, of course I love it. It's crazy that I am actually getting paid to do this. But"—he hesitated—"I'll confess to you since you ask, as we reach apogee, I find myself looking straight up, wishing I could just go on forever, straight out to the stars."

She reached out to shake his hand.

"I know" was all she could say in reply.

"I'll run you through the whole checklist later if you wish, but for now I've got a lot to do here and I suspect folks are waiting for you."

She headed aft, thanking the copilot, then took the few steps down the ladder and hit the pavement. Her parents were standing there grinning like kids, talking excitedly with their hosts. The Brit now made a show of going up to each and pinning wings to their collars.

"Each one is numbered," he announced. "Yuri Gagarin was number one, the first person to achieve space. You six are numbers 673 through 678. Someday I believe it will be in the millions. Wear them with pride."

He shook her hand after pinning the button to her collar, wings that she knew she would wear henceforth whenever she took to the air, and on the day she returned to space.

"Now dinner awaits."

Wheels up on the Gulfstream the following morning was decidedly anticlimactic for Gary after the experience of the evening before. If Franklin had planned all this out as some sort of therapy, it had most certainly worked. It had refocused the dream.

They had said farewell to Victoria on the tarmac. The Brit was flying back to England and had offered Victoria a hop to Lafayette. He just hoped this did not blow things for her at Purdue. Fly out with Franklin Smith, fly back in with one of the most famous aviation and space innovators in the world. Jealousy in any field, especially academia, could surface in an ugly way at times. He also wondered how the boy back there would be treated. At dinner and later, standing outside the hangar, he noticed that the young man, Jason, seemed to have struck a chord with Victoria, the two standing somewhat close while looking up at the heavens and talking about their experience, and as that family boarded a plane for the flight back to Albuquerque and home, the farewell hug and kiss seemed to suggest they were more than "just friends."

Clearing 10,000 feet, Danny announced it was OK to unbuckle and move about. Gary and Eva went up to where Franklin was sitting, staring out the window, for once not already buried in his iPad. He motioned for them to shift the seats in front of him aft and sit down.

"Everything all right, Franklin?" Eva asked.

He nodded and forced a smile.

"Those two guys are just about the toughest damn negotiators in the world, and that Fuchida—my God, he is one hard partner."

"How so?" she asked.

He hesitated.

"Look, I apologize if I did not let you in on the fact I had Fuchida all but locked up two years ago. They had the lead on nanotube development until that accident, and it was no rumor, it really happened. It was the perfect excuse for someone to kill his funding for, as they always say, 'more practical things down to earth.' The Japanese blew their lead at that moment, and that was when I moved in. I had to have the corner on the only material that could actually build a tower, and the assurance it could be manufactured at an industrial level before I took the next step of bringing in you two and going public with Pillar Inc.

"Sorry I didn't tell both of you up front, but in this game some things have to be compartmentalized."

"We understand," Eva offered. Having started her education when the

Soviet Union still existed, she definitely understood better than most to what extremes secrecy could go.

"The Chinese wanted him, of course, and I had to outbid them. Let's just say it was a bit tense and still is."

He was silent for a moment.

"He will hold most of the patents, but I've locked him in on an exclusive ten-year right to production, though it will cost a bit more than I expected."

He chuckled and shook his head.

"By the time this is done he'll be the billionaire and I'll be broke. Beyond that our two friends in New Mexico have some controlling interest in it as well and the manufacturing facility you were standing in yesterday."

"How much more?" Gary asked.

"Oh, several billion more," he replied vaguely.

The way he said "several billion" was still startling for the two of them, who were used to decades of tight budgets defined as a few million.

"I finally did get a contractual guarantee on first delivery with a penalty if delayed, with a bonus if ahead of schedule."

"How soon?" Gary asked.

"Two years."

They said nothing. The way Franklin pitched his sales to investors, it seemed as if construction would start the moment he had the money in place, which was, of course, absurd. There was no telling how many billions had already been spent just getting to this point, and with the construction of the base at Kiribati, which was now employing thousands.

"The problem now is our heavy lift vehicle.

"Our two friends are also contracted for that. They promise delivery of the first in two years as well. Essentially it is a hybrid of the old *Saturn V* design augmented with solid boosters. There was a claim some years ago that the old blueprints for the *Saturn V* were lost. That's crap. I have them; the original contractors still had the plans but no interest in building them again. So our new team is taking on the job."

"My God, that is putting a lot of eggs in one basket," Eva said.

"They're the best at it. Why do you think they want a lock on the carbon nanotube design? It is not just about the tower. It will revolutionize earthbound and low trans-atmosphere flight forever. Once they get mass production going and fulfill our contracts, they'll be turning out new aircraft with one-tenth the frame weight, capable of cost-efficient flights from here to halfway around the world in little more than an hour. But first we got to get enough 'wire,' as we're calling it, and the heavy lift vehicles to loft the first strand, and I'll confess I'm sweating it."

He looked out the window.

"I just, shall we say, wrote out checks for twenty billion dollars last night for a—I hate to phrase it this way—a crash program to have the first test and beginning of actual tower construction in little more than two years."

He sighed.

"There was a time when investors did think long-term, ten years or more, before they saw a return, such as the backers for the Brooklyn Bridge. But today? With some, if they can't turn a profit within six hours, they aren't interested; with government, it's only as good as to when whoever is pitching it stands again for election and has to show a payoff back to the voters. It's part of the reason the space program stalled. When Bush senior proposed returning to Mars but then said fifteen to twenty years, all it drew was a mighty yawn and only marginal funding—and then no funding. If on the day of his inauguration he had set it as a goal for the year 2001, or his son said by 2010, it would have lit a fire in the national soul. If I want to keep my investors, we need to start something within two years or it will start to collapse, and I fear then, as we languish, the Chinese will jump to the fore."

Neither Gary nor Eva spoke. Locked in their own world of design of the tower, the time factor all but disappeared, though the shock of the news Gary had received just a few days back did make him aware of his own mortality and the desire to see the job done within his now apparently limited lifetime.

"I have to move swiftly. I have to move so fast with this that those who wish to oppose it—and will oppose it, for a multitude of reasons—do not have time to react. Never argue for permission. Get it done, then ask them if they now want it torn down. Or a fundamental lesson of Sun Tzu: to seize control of the conflict before it even starts and you then control the conflict. I can act in ways a government bureaucracy cannot. I must do it swiftly, and to do it swiftly, well, our good friends knew how to negotiate for the money to get it done."

He forced a smile.

"It's like trying to compress Apollo from seven years into two years from concept to launch."

"At least we have the R & D already in place," Gary offered. "We didn't back in 1961."

Franklin did not reply for a moment. Then he looked at the two and smiled.

"There are times, my friends, I wish I had never read some of your articles, and this is one of those times."

Gary did not know how to reply, but Eva extended a reassuring hand and patted his knee.

"What an adventure," she whispered. "That is what you are buying, dear friend. Anything else would be boring to you now."

"Yeah, what an adventure," Franklin replied, shaking his head, but smiling. "In two years it is going to be one hell of an adventure."

10

Two Years Later
Kiribati

"We are at five minutes and holding. An automatic hold at five minutes for final flight readiness review."

Gary had been out to Kiribati five times over the last two years, and each visit was stunning; if his own morale was flagging, it was always a boost. Thousands were at work. The entire southern half of the island was now blanketed with barracks for the construction teams. There was a dining hall that could feed a thousand an hour, a recreation center, a base hospital headed, of course, by George's wife, and a power plant to air-condition every unit under the daily boiling heat of an equatorial sun. The 6,000-foot landing strip had been completed a year earlier, and even now an additional 5,000 feet, projecting out over the north end of the island, were nearly finished. Building the airstrip was ironic in a way: it was there for the hauling in of materials during construction, but once the tower was firmly in place, for security reasons more than anything, it would be shut down, with nearly all air traffic except for specially designated aircraft landing in Tarawa instead. Back at Tarawa another strip, eventually 12,000 feet in length, was going in, along with harbor facilities for heavy shipping.

If the residents of the island had concerns about the environmental impacts on the reefs and their way of life in general, it had gone by the wayside for the moment. Billions of dollars had been poured into the nation of little more than 100,000; unemployment, which had been over 30 percent before this project had started, was at zero for any capable of work. There had indeed been the problems of cultural dislocation: in a nation where many of the island's communities lived much as their great-grandparents—and overnight were overwhelmed with thousands of "outsiders" pouring in—the populations of two entire islands had been dislocated. Franklin, thinking ahead on the advice of his young intern Victoria, actually had a team of experts funded to handle the societal dislocation issues. The last thing they wanted, with the fate of the entire project invested in this one location, was to go under due to a societal collapse, a revolution, or even an outright coup and the nationalization of all assets, that was suddenly "allied" to a hostile power overseas.

The sale of alcohol was banned on the islands where construction was taking place; if workers wanted to get boozed up, they could fly back to Tahiti, New Zealand, or Hawaii. Drunkenness or the use of drugs was cause for immediate dismissal and a flight out the same day. There was a weekly meeting with Franklin, and the team handling societal issues was always on schedule to head off problems before they hit. Fortunately the president of Kiribati easily won another term against a candidate who actually was calling for the project to be stopped and a return to their traditional way of life. It didn't hurt the president that he had a rather sufficient campaign chest and more than a few experts on global climate change pointing out that Kiribati was in a race to find ways to either slow or stop global warming or their nation would be the first to disappear if sea level rose even by a meter.

Part of the plan, and the ever-spiraling expense, was the construction of schools, hospitals, and education centers for the citizens of Kiribati, who then had first shot at jobs they were qualified for after training, at Western rates of pay. Scholarship funds were established for those who wished to pursue university degrees off the island, in New Zealand, Australia, or America, as well as for private schooling for younger children. Franklin was able to raise money for that foundation with the argument that the best people to run most of the management of the spaceport were those who had the claim to the land it was built on.

Not to say he was not already facing resistance. Several international environmental groups, when the full extent of what was going on could no longer be contained, had staged protests; one of their ships attempted to block the building of the airport in Tarawa by anchoring in the path of the dredging. It had not been pleasant removing them; Franklin's appeal that the "Pillar" was the only answer for the long-term health of the planet—that "robbing Peter of a few dollars will give Paul billions in return when it comes to saving the planet"—just did not register with some.

Even the UN was trying to step in now. Several of the nations on the equator had filed appeals, claiming that the tower would interfere with their claim that they did own space directly above them clear out to geosynch, a battle that had actually been waged decades earlier when the first geosynch communications satellites were going up.

As for those nations with satellites in orbit, it was getting ugly quick. Franklin's lawyers had actually turned back to a famed case from the 1850s when the steamboat interests tried to block the building of railroad bridges across the Mississippi after one of the boats ran into a bridge pier. Their claim was that the bridges presented a navigation hazard to the public. It was obvious, though, that the real intent was to kill the ability of the newer technology of railroads, a "disruptive technology," from spanning the country and impacting the trade controlled by boats. The railroads won their case, a crucial federal ruling. It just so happened the lawyer leading the case for the railroads was Abraham Lincoln. Interestingly, it was Jason Fitzhugh, who was now a serious subject in Victoria's life, who had passed that suggestion up to Franklin with his graduate studies in the history of industrial technology of the nineteenth century and its societal impact.

The other resistance, subtle but perhaps far more troubling, was from oil-producing countries, who sensed in the tower a profound threat to their dominance of the global economy for the last fifty years. Nothing directly overt, but there were rumors afloat and yet more tens of millions were being poured into security. The fact that their friend Senator Mary Dennison was on the Senate oversight committee for the Department of Defense was a major help, and on a regular basis now American destroyers and even an Aegis-class cruiser were conducting "exercises" in the waters around Kiribati. On this most crucial of days, a cruiser just so happened to be patrolling over the horizon.

As the countdown continued on hold, Gary looked over to where Jason and Victoria stood nearby, hands clasped together. How she had matured in two years since the day of her solo and their shared flight into space always left him startled. She had indeed interned over the next two summers in Franklin's office, would graduate in another year, and did indeed have her private pilot's rating and had just completed her instrument rating and was starting in on multiengine and commercial ratings.

She was following in her parents' path, to a certain degree. Garlin's "disruptive technology" thesis had left an impact, and like any young man or woman with a social conscience she did question the impact on the citizens of Kiribati, though so far Franklin had always been able to trump that concern with the global warming argument: that if they did not find a way out of the use of fossil fuels and the environmental trap of a closed ecosystem contained on the surface of the earth, this nation would cease to exist in another two generations, three at most. They had to adapt or die. It was a hard but realistic answer, and so far the islanders agreed and as an intern she had devoted most of her energy to working on this aspect of the project and thus endeared herself to George, his wife, and even the president of Kiribati.

"All systems are go. Resuming countdown in ten seconds."

Their attention was fixed on the island of Abernama, four miles away, now designated as Launch Site One. It was the island the Japanese had mysteriously taken an option on fifteen years earlier but then let drop. Pillar Inc. had poured a billion into it to create a heavy launch platform, which was about to get its first use. When the time came they'd name it after some multibillion-dollar supporter or for the first one to be killed working on this mad scheme.

"Resuming count at T-minus four minutes and fifty-five seconds and counting with all systems go."

All work had stopped on the runway, the living quarters, the start of the maglev track that would finally connect this island clear back to Tarawa, and the massive platform taking shape a mile off the coast. That platform would, if all went well, become the anchor point for the tower, as Gary kept insisting on calling it, and Franklin said was the pillar. A dozen square acres, built using the technology learned from the construction of hundreds of oil-drilling platforms that went ever deeper and ever farther to draw up, at yet more expense, the very oil that kept this world running at 150 dollars a barrel. The miracle of it was that it had a flexible mounting that would allow it to shift up to two hundred meters north or south.

That had taken one hell of a lot of head scratching and calculating, the idea being that if there was no way to avert a satellite impact, then the entire tower could actually be moved laterally. Not much, but enough to send up a controlled harmonic wave since the first strand to be anchored in place would be just that, a strand two millimeters in diameter, eventually to be woven out to three centimeters, designated for right now as Construction Pillar One.

He and Eva had approved the design reluctantly. Controlling a harmonic wave along a strand of "wire" that would eventually be 40,000 miles in length was frightful to them both until thrusters could be mounted in place as the tower was woven, just as the wires of a suspension bridge were woven after the first strand was in place. Talk of a different design concept—of an actual ribbon five meters wide, now referred to as Primary Pillar One—was still more than half a decade off and dependent on getting Construction Pillar One in place first. The construction pillar was needed before the actual work on a commercially functional "primary pillar" could begin, because the cost of lofting the "ribbon," as it was called, up to geosynch—along with all the other equipment necessary for its deployment—cost more than actually building this first strand or "wire." But that hard fact was "classified" out of fear investors would bolt when the true length of time until a financial return was realized.

Also, the building of the wire would serve the same purpose that the half-forgotten Gemini Program served long ago. When President Kennedy called for the Apollo program in 1961, America's total flight time in space was little more than fifteen minutes with Alan Shepard's suborbital trip, and it would be more than half a year before John Glenn's epic three-orbit flight. Back then it was going to take half of the decade, at least, to build the first Apollo rockets, command modules, and lunar landers. What was needed was a "training program," a halfway point, and that was Gemini, a two-man spacecraft with about as much room inside for the crew as an old-fashioned telephone booth, in which the future Apollo astronauts, including both Neil Armstrong and "Buzz" Aldrin, flew in space, practicing rendezvous, docking, even "space walks," while Apollo was still on the drawing boards. It had paid off handsomely, and the first "wire" now was the Gemini Program for the ribbon design, the "Apollo" program to come: the ribbon design that would place a truly commercial pillar into space.

"Three minutes and counting, all systems are go."

Gary raised his binoculars again. In the last two years the island of Abernama had been converted into a launch pad for the project. The rocket was a squat, ugly thing, not the tall, graceful pillar of Apollo but just as powerful. The primary stage was powered by four liquid fuel engines, scaled-up knockoffs of the old Soviet Soyuz design, simple and cheap, after royalties were paid, with four solid boosters strapped around it. The second stage was powered by two more Soyuz-based engines, and the payload above it in the third stage, most of it dummy weight with a single engine. No crew was on board, but there was a robotic unit carrying a five-hundred-mile spool of the "wire." Once at geosynch the robotic unit would separate from the vehicle and maneuver into proper geosynch position directly above them, and then a small thruster unit attached to the end of the spool would pull the "wire" out to its full length, like a seamstress unwinding a bobbin of all but invisible thread, to test out all systems before the real launches to go up after this first test flight with enough wire to string out a strand clear back to earth, and a crew of three astronauts to oversee the project from geosynch.

This day was a move aggressive in the extreme. No launch just to low earth orbit with but a few miles of wire to unwind. It was going all the way to geosynch as the first step.

Franklin, increasingly concerned about security, especially regarding the inner workings of how the wire would be managed in space, insisted that the launch take place here. *Why not test out our entire infrastructure at the same time?* was his argument to increasingly reluctant investors. Test the launch facility, their own rocket system, and beyond that, as all knew, directly along the equatorial line, which they had to do anyhow, rather than the high inclination of a launch from Russia or even from the Kennedy Center. Launching from the equator also meant a heavier payload, since the rotation of the earth imparted the most energy for any object going in an easterly direction.

Bringing it all together in this amount of time? Franklin could only shrug in private and whisper that there was never a problem that could not be solved on time if enough money was thrown at it. It had been done in the 1960s and, given fifty years of research and development after that, it could be done again . . . and he was about to prove it.

He had billions and a lifetime of prestige riding on this "throwing of money."

"T-minus one minute and counting. All systems now on internal control, all command switched to onboard computers."

Gary drew in his breath, his free hand reaching out to grasp Eva's. He needed a cane now if standing or walking for any length of time. Their dreams of a lifetime were now riding on what would happen in the next few minutes.

The old drama, which triggered an adrenaline rush for any who believed in the dream of Apollo—for any who had ever witnessed a shuttle launch from up close and felt its power and thunder—was unfolding yet again before them. This would be the most powerful launch of a private venture vehicle ever attempted.

There were no formal viewing stands. The media simply had cameras deployed along the beach, although there was a cordoned off area where Franklin, the design team of the Brit and the American aircraft designer, key supporters (including now a few pro-space members of the House and Senate, with Mary Dennison leading that group), Gary, Eva, Victoria, and her boyfriend, Jason, stood silently, all with binoculars raised.

"Fifteen seconds and counting. All systems go, gantry rollback complete and clear. Ten, nine, eight . . . we have liquid engine start . . . six, five . . ."

A plume of smoke blew out sideways from the base of the rocket on the hastily built pad; odds were that liftoff with the blast from the solid boosters would shatter the pad, but a far more sturdy platform was already under construction a half mile away at the south end of the island.

"Two . . . one . . . ignition of solid boosters! We have liftoff!"

Gary drew in a deep breath, a gasp of surprise as the four solid boosters ignited and the nearly eight million pounds of rocket appeared to leap from the pad. From nearly four miles away he was startled that he could actually feel the heat radiating from the engines, the glare so bright that he had to squint as he followed it upward with his binoculars. The shock wave, traveling much faster through land and water, sent out a ripple across the surface of the ocean, and he could feel it in the soles of his feet—at least his left foot.

"All systems go, we are on proper trajectory, roll complete at twelve seconds for trajectory to orbit. One kilometer downrange, all systems nominal . . ."

He kept his binoculars focused on the rocket as it angled over, the sound of its thunderous ignition at last reaching them, washing over the gathering, the shock wave rippling the surface of the ocean between them and the island.

"We have . . ." There was a pause.

And in that instant it all just disappeared into an ever-increasing fireball. Gary let his binoculars drop. The fireball expanded outward, ever outward, the sound of the engines from the first seconds of launch drowning out the cries of shock, dismay, even fear. All had been warned that if the rocket detonated on the pad, they should start running to the other side of the island and find whatever shelter they could.

Eva screamed for Victoria to run, then Gary tried to pull them back.

"It was arcing away from us!" he shouted. "We'll be OK."

He looked over at Franklin and felt reassured in his thinking. The man just stood erect, unmoving, binoculars focused on the expanding fireball, though more than a few around him were beating a path to the west side of the island. The Brit and the American remained unflinchingly by his side.

The fireball reached its maximum; it appeared to actually touch the ocean's surface, aboil now as debris rained down, water foaming. The third stage of the rocket, which had continued on up out of the explosion, was beginning to tumble, ground control hitting the auto-destruct so that it, too, blew apart, the sight of which made Franklin wince. The sound of the explosion now washed over them and was like the roar of a hurricane, which then gradually subsided into absolute silence.

Gary limped up to Franklin, who just remained silent. There was shouting now from the press corps, who were storming toward them, cameras raised, swooping in like buzzards eager for a feast, held back by a cordon of burly islanders, construction workers.

Gary stood in the circle of mourners and finally the Brit stirred.

"Bloody hell," was all he could whisper. "There goes three billion."

There would be plenty of time for the arguing, the blame casting, the postmortem that would finally reach the conclusion, revealed by one of the cameras positioned on the island that had survived the blast, that an oxygen fuel tank on the second stage ruptured at ignition, wisps of liquid oxy visible in the high-speed film pouring out from the side of the second stage until at twenty-six seconds it completely let go.

Franklin turned to head back to his helicopter, making only one comment to the press, that "stuff just happens when you fly rockets" (though he didn't quite phrase it that way) and that work would resume the following morning.

Gary and Eva flew back in another chopper along with their daughter and Jason—there was no airsickness this time with Victoria; she was seasoned now—the four in mournful silence, her parents wondering if after all of this they would still be employed come tomorrow.

At the staff meeting that evening, when the first film from the cameras on the island was run for review and the liquid oxygen plume became clearly visible when the images were computer enhanced, along with telemetry of a pressure drop in the LOX fuel tank, the Brit calmly sat back and said it was his team's fault and that they would take the bite for it.

"We move ahead, then," Franklin announced calmly. "We must assume the wire in space and deployment reel works exactly as our computer simulators said they will. Step two, next launch in six months."

He finished the last sentence looking over at the phlegmatic Englishman and his American partner. They looked at each other and nodded.

"What the hell," the American said. "You guys remember what Chuck Yeager said after we lost *Challenger*? They had it pegged to a frozen O ring in little more than a month. He said, 'Go back to flying and don't launch if the temperature is below fifty,' but no one listened and it took nearly three years to get back in space. We can't afford that. My friend and I have agreed we'll hock the rest of our holdings for this. The oxygen tank will be reviewed. I suspect that with the high temperature out there, 107 degrees at launch, either a pressure relief valve failed, cracking the tank, or the valve jammed open and the liquid oxygen just flooded out."

He paused.

"It won't happen again."

"Thank God we are not dependent on Senator Proxley anymore," Gary whispered, "or this thing would be over with."

"They'll find a way to tangle their fingers into us anyhow," Eva said in reply, and as usual her prediction was correct.

The second launch took place six months and three days after the first. Though never proven conclusively, the assumption that a relief valve in the primary liquid oxygen fuel tank of the second stage did bear out in testing back in New Mexico, when a tank using the same valve developed a leak when temperatures went over 105 degrees and then hit a high level of vibration. Of course the old Russian design, with launches from Kazakhstan, had never encountered such temperature extremes prior to launch; usually it was the exact opposite.

This time they did achieve orbit, the heaviest payload ever lofted by a private venture firm: over fifty-two tons to low earth orbit, and from there over six tons to geosynch. Unfortunately, with this test the reel used to deploy over a thousand miles of "wire" and keep it stationary utterly failed after only seventy-eight miles had been taken out. Remote cameras showed the two-millimeter-wide thread had jammed the deployment, the jam occurring in the "shuttlecock," which moved back and forth, like in the old spinning mills, guiding the thread through a narrow aperture as it came off its spool. Conclusion: an astronaut with the right tools could have cleared the jam in five minutes, though more than a few baleful eyes were turned toward Fuchida's team, which had promised that a deployment drum and reel guide—also made of carbon-60 nanotubing—was simple and foolproof. It settled once and for all the question of attempting an unmanned deployment of the actual "first thread," as it was being called.

This fateful decision, which would cost three billion more, was to send up a three-person team—which was inevitable anyhow once the first thread was actually deployed and the "spinning" process along the primary thread began.

Fuchida's firm lost a nine-figure bonus because of this failure, and it was never discussed that several of the designers were unemployed a day later.

Both the Brit and his partner argued they should go as the first crew—they absolutely wanted to go—but there was no way in hell Franklin would ever risk that. Drawing from their increasing ranks of astronauts for their suborbital firm and their first test flights of low-earth-orbit manned flights, the two-man-and-one-woman crew—the woman had been the copilot on Victoria's flight—was selected.

They would launch independently of the cargo vessel lofting up the "space station" and rendezvous with it at geosynch. Their capsule was increasingly referred to as "Spam in a can." It was basically off-the-shelf, a throwback to the *Apollo* designs, but lacking most of the backups and redundancies that had come to be expected in this, the second decade of the twenty-first century and more than fifty years into manned space flight. Given that they would be in deep space for two weeks—far beyond the Van Allen belt, and thus exposed to significant solar radiation—the answer was to simply keep the spacecraft aligned with its reentry shield always pointed at the sun.

After the first wire was deployed, a very primitive crew base would be positioned at geosynch, another throwback to 1970s technology: a hollowed-out third stage from a rocket, almost identical to the *Skylab* of the post-Apollo days, which would be parked and then anchored to the "wire," then occupied by subsequent crews after the first wire was in place. These crews would monitor the "spinners" that would build up the wire until eventually it could handle a useful load.

Once in place at geosynch, this primitive crew base would become the operational point as the "threads" of the first tower were spun out. As the tower was gradually "built up" with additional threads, it could be used to carry up the real payload—the still-under-development and testing of the ribbon design—at a fraction of the cost of sending the material up via rockets. This first "thread" was like the first wire across the East River, nearly 150 years ago, out of which the mighty cables of the Brooklyn Bridge were eventually put into place.

Franklin increasingly turned to young Jason Fitzhugh, the historian, to write his comments and counterarguments, drawing on the great technological advances of the nineteenth and early twentieth centuries, along with their risks.

"If men and women are willing to put their lives on the line for the greater good of all, then we should say Godspeed and go! Fear never held back Columbus, Magellan, Cook, or those who came to first settle America. Let that spirit flow in our veins yet again!" became a frequent closing line to his speeches.

So far the suborbital and test-orbital manned flights of the firm he was partnered with had a sterling safety record, though one flight had been a near disaster when a port-side wing did not lock back into place properly on descent. It was one hell of a piloting job bringing it in and *Enterprise One* was all but totaled on landing, but the six passengers and two pilots walked away from the wreck. The pilot on that flight, Miss Selena Singh, who had copiloted the flight the Morgans flew on, was now heading up the team that would be the first to go to geosynch.

Franklin's publicity team was at last talking about the environmental aspects of the Pillar's construction after he had adroitly lined up a few more patents on upgrades to solar panels that yielded a 40 percent increase in their energy output, and in high orbit attached to the tower would deliver a magnitude increase in energy that the same panel could achieve if put out in the Sahara. Popular Web sites and old-fashioned print media dedicated to science were soon awash with articles and debate about the prospects of harvesting not just gigawatts, but hundreds of gigawatts of electricity out in space and "piping" it down to earth via superconductivity cables and lasers.

Talk in the past had speculated about solar panel arrays larger than all of Manhattan and their potential, but the fundamental stop point was always the same. If the energy was beamed down to the surface as microwave, it would require hundreds of square miles of collection stations around the planet, and the potential impact to the upper atmosphere would only hasten global warming and heaven help any bird or plane that flew through the microwave beam. For the first time, a logical answer of harvesting limitless energy for earth—along with another "disruptive technology"—was offered: once solar panels in space had a means to transfer that electrical energy to earth, every coal-fired, oil-fired, and even fission energy plant on earth would soon be obsolete and shut down.

It was, Franklin and his supporters declared, like a wanderer dying of thirst in the desert when just on the other side of the hill there was an oasis waiting to be tapped. Limitless energy from the sun constantly flowed around our planet; it was now time to use it and end our dependency on CO_2 fuels. The secrecy he had kept wrapped around this concept was at last falling aside as he judged they were far enough along to ensure public support and block the resistance that was to come from oil-producing nations.

What did not go smoothly was the increasing protest. Eva's prophecy about Proxley had been on the mark. Suits had been filed that "Franklin's Folly" would be an obstruction to space navigation, placing even the International Space Station in jeopardy, even though supporters in NASA pointed out that, if need be, the built-in maneuvering thrusters aboard the station could provide the necessary boost to steer safely clear when, it was now estimated, every eight months or so, it would pass within half a kilometer of the Pillar.

Calculations were run across every known object in orbit, from functional satellites to space debris from the thousands of launches that had taken place since 1957. When Gary and Eva were first presented with the analysis, all they could do was sit there, numb. Several hundred functional satellites were in low- to mid-range earth orbit, but so was space debris: factor against that an initial strand two millimeters wide, not yet shielded with Eva's mesh (the final design would, at least on paper, include high-energy lasers drawing their power from the solar arrays to all but vaporize debris, along with a harmonic wave to oscillate the tower out of the way of impact as an object passed), and the odds were unsettling. Within a year they could expect at least one significant impact.

There was one thing they could not accurately calculate: the strength of the carbon nanotubing against the kinetic energy of an unknown object striking with a velocity of perhaps five miles per second or more. Tests were run, but the variables were the velocity of the impacting object and its mass and the diameter of the first strand when impacted. Within the first few weeks, a strike by an object weighing as little as ten grams traveling at eight kilometers a second would be catastrophic. But given enough time to spin a few dozen additional strands onto the first one, out to the first thousand kilometers from earth, and the odds of survival increased significantly. There were too many variables, though, and when Eva, at one meeting, finally just sat back, stared at the ceiling, and told the staff, "Learn to pray," the room was silent.

But there was no turning back now, and Franklin, as their public persona, dodged the tough questions like an accomplished politician while continuing to sell the dream of the future. As to the threatened hearings and some attempt by the UN to block the tower, his response, though never "on the record," was: "How many rogue nations, bent on evil, have been doing their chicanery right up to making nuclear weapons and the world did nothing? We in contrast are doing something that, once proven, all humanity—except those who wish to see the old collapsing economic system remain in place—will come to support."

There had been several debris strikes in space on the shuttle during its 135-plus flights and total flight time far exceeding a year in orbit, as well as on the space station during its nearly twenty-plus-year record. One gouged a crater over a centimeter deep to the forward windshield of a shuttle, striking with a loud bang that echoed inside the crew compartment and giving everyone a scare. Analysis later indicated it was most likely a bolt, of all things, but if it had been ten times the mass, it might have penetrated and caused a catastrophic decompression. Only those who carefully followed the news about space flight were even aware of it. It was the type of thing that simply didn't get a major press release. It did not ground the program, it came down to a calculation of risk aversion versus the benefits of building the space station, and NASA had kept its fleet flying . . . and replaced the nearly cracked windshield.

Franklin more openly compared this situation to that of the legendary Captain "Sully" Sullenberger. Bird strikes had been a reality of aviation since Wilbur and Orville. Every private pilot with enough hours under their lap belt had taken a deep gulp at least once on lifting off when a flock of ducks came soaring up out of a nearby marsh or lake. Every aviator learned that ducks and geese, unlike most other birds, will go for altitude when panicked—meaning they will come up under you where you can't see them until that final split second before impact—and that could spell disaster, yet it did not stop pilots from flying. Commercial airlines regularly suffered bird strikes, but a total engine loss? God put Captain Sully on board that flight out of New York that day, Franklin would say with a smile, and they were designing the Pillar with that in mind. There would always be a Captain Sully on board and in control of the Pillar.

It was, Gary and Eva knew, an argument that did not hold much water until their second phase, when the actual commercial tower rather than the construction tower was in place. The ribbon design had evolved over the last few years: unlike the initial "strand" tower, the commercial tower in its final form would be a ribbon that could easily have additional layers stitched onto either side and could be made any width—a dozen meters or more—so that even if one of the individual ribbons, each about the width of old-fashioned 35mm film, was hit and taken out, the ribbons stitched to either side would remain intact, and repairing the broken section would be a simple enough task. The first tower was simply to haul up the hundreds of tons of "ribbon" at reasonable cost to build the primary tower for actual commercial use.

Until then, it was hoped that the space-faring nations would at least attempt to cooperate and nudge their satellites a few hundred meters to one side or the other if on a collision course.

However, that had not stopped a few opponents in the Senate from demanding high-profile hearings on this "new hazard that can shut down space travel," even though those same senators for years had systematically choked off funding to NASA for their own projects and driven engineers like Gary and Eva into the arms of Franklin Smith and his team.

The harassment built. Franklin appeared before one hearing in which he was shredded. The following day he flew to Kiribati, and within a week most of his key administrative staff had followed. He ignored the next summons to appear in Washington.

He was in near exile now, but his project was in full swing. And although those in power at that moment vilified him, those who supported him—who understood the science involved, and the dire prospects if new answers were not found—grew in number. Franklin's eternal optimism captured something about the American spirit. An older generation began to speak more to the younger one about a time in their own youth when a young president challenged the nation to dream of new and higher frontiers. The current dystopic vision of America's future—economic collapse, its decline into a second-rate power, threats of war, gas at twenty dollars a gallon, even zombie invasion—was gradually changing. The belief that a resurgence was at hand for America, and with it the entire world, just might be taking hold.

11

Two Years Later

"Kiribati control, this is Pillar One, we have hard dock."

"Pillar One, Kiribati Control. Great work. You have a lot of men and women down here about to turn blue."

Victoria could not help but smile at that one. She looked over at Jason and squeezed his hand, for he had quietly passed along the suggestion that Mission Control say those exact words. It was a direct salute to the famous exchange between Neil Armstrong and Houston when he announced touchdown on the moon: "Houston, Tranquility Base here. The Eagle has landed."

The control room on the floating platform, positioned a mile south of the island of Aranuka, was minuscule compared to the once sprawling complex at Houston where hundreds of tech heads and engineers had monitored the Apollo launches. The team numbered fewer than fifty at that moment. If all the dreams came true, it would one day house more than a thousand monitoring the daily operations of the Pillar and its construction.

Victoria looked back at her father, who was seated near Franklin: his gaze still fixed on his monitor, he did not even look up while applause and self-congratulatory backslapping resounded in the room.

It had been a tense five days. Not since the days of the old Gemini Program, when *Gemini 7* and then *Gemini 6* had been launched within a few days of each other to achieve the first "rendezvous" in space, had there been such a launch. It had actually required two launches. First up was the precious payload of "wire," 40,000 miles of it. And now the manned crew of three to oversee that deployment, two men and one woman, in the first private venture—or, for that matter, any venture—to geosynch orbit.

If all went precisely to plan, they would just spend the next two weeks relaxing inside their "Spam-in-a-can" capsule, monitoring the reels as they deployed the wire down to the earth's surface. The design was simple and yet stunning, actually drawing upon the early attempts at laying a 3,000-mile-long transoceanic cable 160 years earlier. The wire was wound on to two drums. The "counterweight wire" would climb up out of geosynch, extending outward 13,000 miles to act as the weight balance. The second drum which the manned capsule was docked to would actually remain at geosynch, its end attached to a "descent thruster," which, starting with a low thrust burn, would begin to pull 23,000 miles of wire off the second drum, guiding it down to the platform at Kiribati.

Eva, Gary, and the entire team had been worn to exhaustion working out this plan. The one ascending, to act as a counterweight, was not so crucial. If jammed, they would just leave it in place for the time being and worry about it later.

The trick, the real trick—what the entire operation now hinged on—was anchoring the first wire in place. They would have only one shot at it; it had to go flawlessly. Thus Gary's proposal that the deployment drum be kept at geosynch, with the astronaut crew just a few meters away, while a thruster pack, with the end of the wire attached to it, did the descent, the drum unrolling the wire out at two hundred kilometers per hour.

There were hundreds of questions to be answered, calculations to be made, the matter of how to counteract the torque of the drum spinning out wire, and the incredibly complex problem of actually guiding the wire down to a fixed point on earth. Eva's analogy that it was like trying to toss out a thread so that the end would go perfectly through the eye of a needle 23,000 miles away was apt.

For the entire operation, this was the crucial moment. In private Franklin had made it clear to his inner circle that, just like the high-risk *Curiosity* mission to Mars, they had one chance and one chance only to get it right and, like *Curiosity*, must do so with technologies never actually tested in space before. If the descent thruster system didn't work, if the drum deploying the wire down jammed up, if the tensile strength of this first wire was exceeded—a hundred other ifs—they were finished. Opponents were just praying for a screwup to jump on, and his network of investors had been stretched to the limit and would fall away if this one failed.

To the public Franklin still spoke with great enthusiasm, as any leader should and must at such times. He asked them to try to imagine Eisenhower, on the day before the invasion to Normandy, telling the troops they stood a 50 percent chance of failure and they would all die, or the very real number predicted by some that Armstrong and Aldrin had only an even chance of actually landing on the moon and returning safely to earth. It was known by some, but at such moments belief in victory had to transcend fears or no dream would ever be achieved.

On a very personal level, the frightening part that had everyone on edge was that if there were problems with the drum and extra-vehicular activity was required to get it functioning or perhaps to untangle a snag, they would be working with a wire strand two millimeters in diameter, all but invisible. If it even brushed against their EVA space suits, it could slice them open like a hot knife through butter. Of course, there were emergency backups: for example, one astronaut would do the repair work while a second hovered back by their primary vehicle, and each would carry an emergency patch kit to slap over a tear in a space suit. The real nightmare was a break in a cable that somehow looped around the manned unit. It would cut through the titanium body, and if it sliced into the service module aft that held their oxygen and fuel, there would not even be a whisper of a chance of getting home. And it would be one hell of an explosion.

It was the riskiest manned mission ever attempted.

The other completely untested unit was the descent thruster, which took up over a third of the weight of the entire vehicle lofted to geosynch orbit. The end of the first spool of wire was already attached to it. The two tons of the descent thrust was mostly fuel. The orbital dynamics were insanely complex, but if all went according to plan, 220 hours after deployment the thruster would enter the upper atmosphere. That would indeed be the hairy part, as Franklin put it.

The last 100,000 feet would be the toughest. There had been talk of a high-flying aircraft snagging it, bringing the entire unit down, and releasing it above the anchor point, or even somehow transferring it to some kind of helicopter with a vast bay aft of its rotors that would drag it down to the platform. It was Gary who vetoed all of it, saying that if they could trust the thruster to bring the wire in 99.9 percent of the way, then they shouldn't make things more complex but should trust it for the last twenty miles. Besides, to try to snag an out-of-control thruster and wire would be a suicidal gesture. The thruster had to bring the wire in.

The world was startled by the realization of what this plan really meant. Nearly everyone assumed that Franklin's Folly would be built from the ground up—that first a huge tower, kilometers high, would be constructed and a cable anchored to it would be carried aloft into space, then other rockets would carry it farther.

Absurd. Better to use gravity itself to build the Pillar from the top down. Start at geosynch, then simply lower the cable, though the word "simply" was very much an exaggeration.

The crew set up basic housekeeping, prepping up so that at any moment one of them could go EVA. Then with the entire team in space and on earth taking a collective deep breath, Franklin ordered for the deployment to begin.

The drum carrying the wire up beyond geosynch began its ascent, while at the exact same instant the thruster, with the wire from the second drum attached, fired up for a short burst of six seconds, and the wire attached to it started to play out—silently, of course, in the vacuum of space. It was soon unspooling at the full speed of almost two hundred kilometers of wire an hour, following a complex trajectory downward, with timed stops of the thruster to allow a certain amount of slack to spin out from the drum, the slack providing reserve time if a snag should develop; the snag would then be untangled before too much tension built up on the wire. In fact, the wire was nearly a thousand miles longer than necessary, to provide for that slack; it could be taken in later once the end was firmly anchored to the ground.

The calculation of this had been a magnificent venture into the unknown that had given Gary and Eva many a sleepless night. The influence of solar wind on the strand, or a collision with debris, a functional satellite, or even an untrackable meteor the size of a pebble, could end it all. Once locked in place, perhaps better calculations could be made, but at this stage the variables changed second by second as the wire spun out and down. And the tough one: the tug thruster, as it was now being called. When it fired up, it was indeed towing a wire thousands of miles long, but the longer the cable, the more time it would take until the tensile stress reached the deployment reels. If that stress was too great, it would pull the entire unit out of position; if there was not enough, the wire spinning off the reels would just float and coil, and if it ever wrapped around the manned module or the deployment unit itself, it would probably destroy it.

Those on the ground, even when ordered in a four-hour rotation to sleep, could barely rest, the tension was so high. Franklin looked as if he had aged ten years in the last two weeks, and of the members of the ever-present media—many of whom were cheering the team on in the tradition of Walter Cronkite and CBS—more than a few were the kind who just waited for a disaster to occur so they could breathlessly report the end to this project, with plenty of "investigations" to follow.

For nearly two hundred hours, all went flawlessly. The counterweight drum rolled out nearly 16,000 of its intended 17,000 miles before jamming. But that was more than sufficient for the present. Everything was riding on the next twenty-four hours as the thruster, zeroing in on its anchor point, would do the final burns that would drop it into the atmosphere and guide it to the platform off of Aranuka and thus lock the first thread in place. The game was at its most complex moment, guiding descent, but the closer to earth, the stronger the gravitational pull, so at times it had to fire extended counterburns to keep velocity down.

With twenty-one hours to go, the reason for investing billions in putting three astronauts up to geosynch finally arrived. The drum began to jam up, a nearly invisible strand of wire overlapping, tangling on the drum, and in under a minute it had stopped unwinding. Fortunately the clutch design prevented an instantaneous stoppage, which would have snapped the wire, though it did "backspin" onto the drum for several hundred revolutions. Only human hands could sort out the tangle, and in less than ninety minutes, when by the immutable laws of orbital mechanics the thruster had to fire up again if they were to drop straight in on the platform at Kiribati, rather than come smashing down somewhere in the Pacific or even Brazil.

As Selena Singh was opening the airlock, she paused for a few seconds.

If I have but one more flight in life, this is it, she thought. Far, far below was earth, its face fully illuminated by the sun behind her shoulder, the glorious blue-green sphere . . . and her first thought was that they needed to send up someone like Ray Bradbury or Richard Bach to really tell the rest of humanity of the beauty and wonder of it all.

The mission was indeed forgotten for a brief moment as she took in the glorious splendor of it all, the brilliant sphere that contained the entire world she knew; to its right, beginning to rise, a quarter moon, the reflected light so brilliant she immediately snapped down her polarized filter, regretting she had to; she had so dreamed of just seeing a sea of stars.

The mission. Focus on the mission. You can take a few minutes to play tourist after it's over.

She had one of the new, smaller thruster packs on her back; there was no way they could have fitted the full-size units carried on board the old shuttles and the space station. Besides, they were docked to the deployment reel platform, and she elected to use the handholds to pull herself over while telling her backup, Kevin Malady, to fire up the high-intensity lights. Someone had come up with the simple idea of actually putting a dab of reflective paint on the wire at one-meter intervals. That caused intense debate, as it was calculated to add over two hundred kilos to the total weight, and there was speculation on whether the paint would even adhere in the vacuum of space or else flake off, perhaps jamming up the whole works.

In the wonderful days of NASA such things would have been tested and retested before ever being used. But not now, not on this project, for which Singh was being paid half a million a year for this moment—to risk her life—and to dedicate an entire flight just to testing dabs of paint would delay everything yet again and cost millions.

Singh knew her heart and breathing rates were being monitored, as they should be for all EVAs, and it annoyed her. As she approached the reel, of course she was scared. It looked as if the paint had flecked off as predicted. Wherever the hell the cable was, it was hard to discern.

She flipped up her polarizing sun shield and now she could see it, the brilliant sunlight glinting off the cable.

"I can see it!" she exclaimed. "Up here in this sunlight I can actually see the wire. It is like a string of diamonds!"

She looked to her left. The string of diamonds, as she had called it, snaked off, down toward earth. There was no tension to it; it was loose, slack, like a rope drifting on a slow-moving river.

"MB One, Kiribati, we have initiated renewed thrust. That line will begin to tense out in under thirty minutes."

"Kiribati, Singh. You must have it cleared before then."

She switched on the high-intensity lights mounted to her helmet and could easily see the problem: the overlay in the wire on the reel, which threatened to snag when renewed tension snaked up the line from the thruster unit now closing in on the earth's surface.

It meant going inside the open pod bay of the deployment unit, being careful not to brush against the diamond-like wire, and then, by hand, gently move the wire, which was nearly wrapped around the guide spindle. It reminded her, of all things, of a tangled reel of fishing line when she was a little girl, crying while her brother was reeling in a big catch, and how her loving father untangled the mess and then showed her how to cast her line back out without it tangling.

She braced herself with her right hand on a handhold built into the spindle deployment unit, careful not to let her legs touch the lose wire coiling about.

"Singh, Kiribati. Thruster has fired again; watch your time."

The spindle guide was the first thing she had to focus on. It had jammed in place, and she caught glimpses of the wire: it had slackened for an instant, then coiled around the spindle guide, triggering the drum to stop deployment; but while slowing down the wire had "back tangled" exactly the way it would on a fishing reel.

"Kiribati, Singh. We have a back snag on the drum; you should be able to see it with my helmet camera. I will clear the spindle first, then manually work the snag off the drum."

Ever so gingerly she took hold of the wire. Her gloves, which cost over a million dollars a pair, were coated with the same material as the wire; otherwise they would be sliced open as she carefully worked the tangle clear. It was a simple enough operation, only taking several minutes. The billion dollars spent to put her there had just paid off. If they had gone with the original idea of actually lowering the drum, without manned back up it would have been the end of the entire program.

The next step was to clear the back tangle. Using a computer control strapped to her forearm, she activated the reverse on the drum. The back snag started to play out, and she gingerly took hold of the wire, guiding it out, pulling it clear, and letting it drift out behind her. Checking the chronometer in her heads-up display, she could see that time was running short; but the back tangle was just about cleared and in two minutes the drum would start spinning again, feeding out more line as the thruster, 22,000 miles below, continued its descent.

It was finally cleared, and with a sigh she carefully backed away from inside the drum.

"Kiribati, Singh. We're cleared."

"Singh. Exceptional work!" It was Franklin rather than Mission Control.

She could actually see the wire going tense, the reel beginning to rotate, within seconds spinning up to a blur, the spindle that guided the wire deployment effortlessly moving back and forth the same way spindles had moved in spinning mills two hundred years ago.

"Kiribati, Singh. All is nominal. Returning to MB One."

"Singh, Kiribati. Incredible work. You earned your pay today."

But as she let go of the handhold to reach out to the capsule, the movement caused a slight torque effect, making her feet rise up. It was one thing to practice on the ground, or even in a water tank to simulate weightlessness, but out here there was no volume and mass of water to prevent her feet from rising.

Singh's left foot brushed against the wire behind her, which was again spinning out at over one hundred miles an hour. All the talk about a red-hot knife slicing though butter was true. Carbon-60 nanotubing in a two-millimeter strand was far more dangerous than a string of razor blades unreeling at the same speed. In less than a second the wire had sliced through Singh's boot, tissue, tendons, and bones, entirely severing three toes and finishing the job by cutting clean through the sole of the boot.

Kevin Malady, her backup for the EVA, reacted before Singh could even cry out. He saw the toe of her boot being sliced off, the surreal pattern made by liquid, blood, spilling into the vacuum and near-absolute-zero temperature of space. Pushing off the side of MB One, he grabbed hold of her within seconds, making sure his own legs cleared the wire spinning out.

The radio chatter now was overwhelming, between Singh's gasp of pain, the call from Kiribati asking what happened, and the doctor monitoring her vitals in the control room shouting that something had gone wrong.

Kevin already had the emergency patch out and was pulling off the cover that exposed the adhesive surface. It was awkward: the patch had been designed to be used when an astronaut lost fingers or sliced open his or her space suit . . . but not this.

While holding Singh with one arm, he opened the packet containing the patch and slapped it over the cut-open boot. It would not be the wound that killed her in the next thirty seconds; it would be depressurization as a result of the hole in her suit. As the suit decompressed, it would not be like all the ridiculous movies of decades past in which bodies exploded. Hopefully the pressure cuffs positioned above the knees and elbows would activate, but even then, exposed to space, she could lose her leg from the knee down. If the cuff didn't fully activate, she would just simply depressurize, the last breath of air sucked out of her lungs. They had been trained in such an event to keep exhaling, otherwise the imbalance of external and internal pressure would actually cause their lungs to fatally rupture even if they could be hauled back into a pressurized environment.

"Tom, be ready with that door!" Kevin shouted.

The only words out of Singh were "Kiribati, I screwed up. I think I cut my foot off."

Kevin kept a forceful hold on the patch to insure it did not blow out, pressing it in, feeling the outward pressure at five pounds per square inch trying to blow it off even as it solidified into place. He continued to hold it tightly in place as he hung on to Singh, while the wire continued to spin out; if either brushed against it, they were dead, and he would be damned if he would lose her. They had trained for maneuvering in zero gravity, but it was still delicate work; all the while he kept reassuring her, telling her not to move, to let him guide her back to safety.

He pushed off, taking Singh with him, and nearly drifted past the hatch when their crewmate, Tom McMurtry, snagged him by the left leg and pulled him back in feet-first.

Kevin slammed the hatch shut, sealing it, while Tom hit the pressurization and air, at five pounds per square inch, flooded back into the capsule.

The radio was still chattering: the doctor on the ground, Kiribati control, and amazingly even some damn press who had tapped into their frequency were shouting questions about what in hell had just happened. Kevin ignored them.

Tom, cursing soundly, reached up and slapped off the switch to the main radio feed, then switched to the secured and scrambled link back to Kiribati.

Singh was remarkably calm, taking off her own helmet as pressurization reached five pounds, although she was crying, not with pain but in frustration.

"I screwed up—damn all to hell, I screwed up!"

"I gotta get your boot off," Kevin said. "It's gonna hurt."

"Get it off," she said, voice still breaking. "Oh my God, I screwed up. I'm so sorry."

"Shut up!" Tom shouted, arms around her shoulder, working to get the upper part of her EVA suit off so he could give her an injection of painkiller and start an IV.

"Hang on, angel," Tom said.

"I'm not an angel," Singh snapped. "I'm captain of this mission and I screwed up."

Her two male companions could not help but laugh for a few seconds at that.

"All right, Captain," Malady replied, "but don't cuss me out. Now, here goes . . ."

He twisted the coupling to her EVA boot, unlocking it, and as he did so she gasped and let fly with some decidedly unladylike comments. Kiribati control maintained a secured shut down on the comm link, blocking off what was happening to the rest of the world, the staff listening in on the secured channel, in spite of the anxiety there was more than one smile over her command of Anglo-Saxon expletives. It showed as well that she was still very much alive.

Kevin and Tom's comments were instantly added as the blood that had pooled in Singh's boot now floated out in the zero-gravity environment. The emergency patch Kevin had slapped on her boot had saved her life from depressurization but, of course, had done nothing to staunch the flow of blood from three severed toes, her "pinky" toe up to her middle toe; her big toe and second toe had been cut open at the tips but not completely severed.

"MB One, Kiribati here. How is she?"

For a moment Kevin did not even answer as he tried to figure out how to stop the blood cascading out of her severed digits, forming globules that floated about the cabin. He had the sun shield visor up but was still in his suit, a globule of blood splattering against the inner faceplate. He tore his helmet off and let it float free while Tom pulled out the emergency medical kit, which had been packed with everything up to and including a full surgical kit and defibrillator.

"Damn it, someone answer!"

It was the Brit, his voice finally penetrating through the cacophony of chatter.

"Kevin here, sir."

"What in bloody hell happened?"

Kevin gave a brief rundown, during which Singh remained stoically silent as Tom maneuvered the top half of her EVA suit off. As soon as he pushed it clear, he jabbed her forearm with a morphine surret. She cussed at him over that, saying she didn't need it, but he ignored her complaints.

"I'm putting the doc on the line now." Franklin snapped. "Listen to him. Tell him exactly what you see and follow his directions."

Kevin followed the doctor's directions as they were passed up to him. He now had a video link on the wound and was more than a bit annoyed when the doctor exclaimed, almost with professional admiration, that a surgeon's laser or knife could not have done a cleaner cut and even mused about trying to retrieve her toes to sew them back on.

The compresses were secured while Tom, giving perhaps the first IV transfer in the history of space flight and zero-g medicine, inserted an IV of plasma into Singh's arm and, since there was no gravity to provide a proper drip, gently squeezed the bag, forcing the contents into her.

The bleeding eased and then stopped. Singh was less than amused when Kevin insisted upon pulling off the lower half of her IV suit, since she did not even have a jumpsuit on underneath. Without asking for permission, he scissored off the long johns underneath to check her leg to make sure there was no damage from depressurization or frostbite. Though a bit drugged, she was still lucid and asked for at least a pair of shorts, which Kevin handed to her; in spite of her pain and a touch of drowsiness from the injury, she slipped them on while the two men made a point of trying to politely look the other way.

"MB One, Kiribati. This is Franklin. Prepare for immediate undocking and emergency return."

With that, Singh stirred.

"Repeat, please."

Franklin repeated the command.

"Ah, sir, may I speak frankly."

"Of course, MB One."

"Open mike."

"If you wish."

"Fine, then. Sir, fire me when we get back for my screwup. But as to abandoning mission before completion, you can go to hell."

There was a pause, and she could actually hear some laughter in the background after the last half hour of tension and fear.

No response came back.

"We came up here for a mission. OK, I screwed up and sliced some toes off. It'll hurt like hell once the painkiller wears off, but then what? Whether we get back two days from now or three it won't change things much here for me. And whoever the doctor is, tell him he's an idiot. I am not sending my two comrades out to look for my missing toes, which are by now frozen stiff anyhow. We see the final deployment and lock into place, then we come home—and that, sir, is final."

There was no reply.

The laughter had drifted off to silence.

"MB One to Kiribati," and she fought to control her voice as if it were a matter-of-fact transmission, "anything else you need us to do other than monitor reel deployment?"

"No . . ." A pause. "God bless you. Will keep you advised if there is. We have twenty hours to touchdown of the first wire. Wish us luck."

"Good luck down there," Singh replied. "I asked for a mission and I got it. Now, do it right down there."

She paused.

"After this, I think my flight days are over," she sighed mournfully, "so might as well do my job while I can."

"Not by a long shot," came the reply from Franklin. "You've only just started flying, Captain Singh."

12

"Two hours and eleven minutes to touchdown and counting. We have visual on the descent stage."

More than a few of the "hangers-on," the major investors, and the four pool reporters allowed on the platform were outside, gazing up, binoculars raised, as if they could actually see something through the scattering of afternoon tropical clouds. On the monitor, though, the image was clear. The Brit's "mother ship one" was circling at a maximum altitude of just over 60,000 feet, cameras trained on the two-ton thruster, the nearly invisible wire trailing behind it.

Now was the time to sweat. One of the multitude of reasons for choosing Kiribati was its weather. Typhoons and hurricanes were all but unknown along the equator. It was a zone free of earthquakes as well, but that was not to say that heavy equatorial thunderstorms might not occur due to the strong convections triggered by the boiling equatorial heat over the ocean.

They were committed, there was no turning back, and a major thunderstorm engulfing the thruster and its wire just prior to anchoring—buffeting it with updrafts and downdrafts that could exceed a hundred miles an hour—could be a disaster.

The local islanders, so enthusiastic for this project to succeed and perhaps eventually save their homeland, had even indulged in an ancient ritual, to appease the ocean and pray for calm seas and blue skies. It had appeared to work, at least in their eyes, but winds aloft at 40,000 feet were brisk at over 100 miles per hour and fuel for the descent stage was down to less than 5 percent. It was going to be a nail-biter. The last-ditch alternative, which literally was last-ditch, if the descent unit ran out of fuel was to let it drop into the ocean, hopefully close by, with a ship standing by to try to pick it up and tow it to the platform. Risky all around with 23,000-plus miles of wire behind it.

To add to the anxiety, warships of several nations were hovering at the edges of Kiribati waters; a no-fly zone of one hundred nautical miles had already been declared by the island nation based on extending its claims outward to several atolls that barely broke the surface at low tide. Kiribati had no army, no air force, no means of enforcing its sovereign rules, and for the moment its appeals to New Zealand and Australia for some kind of protective efforts had disappeared into bureaucratic double-talk. Half a dozen other ships, identities murky, were nearby as well, and there had been rumors of some sort of terrorist attempt. The long-term implications of what the Pillar might bode for global oil demand just might induce some entity to pass money and the technology of a surface-to-air missile to another entity.

Though considering himself something of a persona non grata in his home country at the moment, Franklin had pleaded hard with several senators who were indeed on his side and that of NASA, and the day before, an Aegis-class cruiser had positioned itself off the island nation, thanks to their friend Senator Dennison's direct appeal to the president. Though not outright stated, the message was that if a missile was launched at the thruster, it would fire to shoot the attacking missile down, for the logical reason that the "wire," if loose and unanchored, could pose a serious threat to navigation, both within the atmosphere and in space. Two hours earlier the Aegis had fired up its high-gain X-band radar, the preliminary to a near-instant launch of an antimissile if required. It had also deployed a number of passive listening devices and active sonar buoys in the surrounding waters to detect any submarine activity.

Thus Franklin and his team were not entirely on their own. The only threat that did bear some weight was that one news channel aircraft circling outside the no-fly zone actually strayed a few miles in until warned in no uncertain terms that if they did not turn about at once, the network would be forever banned from entering the country. The Brit had personally called the CEO of the network on that one, and within seconds the message was conveyed to the wandering aircraft.

Gary, conceding he needed a wheelchair on this day, sat in front of a wide-screen monitor, Eva by his side and joined now by Victoria, watching the images being fed back from the Brit's high-circling aircraft, which focused in on the descent stage, thrusters pulsing to counteract the lateral force of the wisps of air of the upper atmosphere. There were occasional glints off the cable catching the afternoon sun. It seemed taut, rigid.

"I wish we had a read on the stress load," Gary whispered. "If it severs now . . ."

"It won't sever," Victoria whispered reassuringly.

"Fifty thousand feet, winds at 72 knots, bearing 235 degrees—all looks nominal."

The thruster had rotated on its axis, putting one of its engines in direct opposition to the crosswind, firing pulses every few seconds.

"We have good comm between ground and the package," the mission director announced. "We are on the beam; it is coming straight in."

No one spoke now. It was out of the control of everyone present except for the mission director, the communications tech monitoring the computer guidance linking the base on the platform to the thruster, and a young lady, not much older than Victoria, who was working a joystick and wearing a headset that gave her a stereo-optical view from the camera mounted to the bottom of the thruster. The camera had just switched on, and there was a two-dimensional image up on the main screen of the platform below.

The twelve-acre platform that was its target was lost to view as clouds shifted between it and the ground; when this happened a radar image of a blinking target appeared in the center of the screen, which now started to shift to the left. The young lady added more thrust, lining it back up.

"Fuel at 2 percent," the mission director whispered. She nodded, saying nothing, looking almost alien with her stereoview headset covering most of her face, the only giveaways her tension, the tight set of her jaw, and the sweat trickling down the back of her neck, staining her T-shirt.

"Twenty thousand feet. We have visual from the ground."

Gary spared a quick glance at a secondary monitor, a camera mounted on the platform magnifying to high gain, showing the boxlike unit descending.

The dynamics playing out were the tension and drag of the wire clear back to geosynch and the lateral force of the wind, which, the closer the unit got to the surface, would now start to play on the wire itself, even if it was but two millimeters wide. There were no monitors built into the cable itself to measure stress loads of tension, compression, and lateral forces; those would come later. The only source of actual data was from the thruster, its read on the tension imparted to it by the attached cable, which was approaching 90 percent of tensile strength as the thruster pulled it down through the atmosphere, and from the astronaut crew monitoring from the deployment reel, which was still spinning out cable. The cable, once anchored, would actually be slack for nearly a thousand miles as the earth rotated, the centrifugal force imparted by that rotation whipping it along. The reel would then start to climb up and away from geosynch, laying out the last of the cable on board to act as additional counterweight to pull the cable taut. As more strands were then woven on, the reels would eventually act as a counterweight, holding the wire rigid and in place.

The crisis was at hand and the thousands of hours of calculations and speculations by Gary, Eva, and their team about this moment were now about to be proven out. Would the drag of the cable actually overcome the power of the thruster so that it dangled helplessly just short of its goal and then was actually whipped back into space? He half wished the backup of using a plane with a snag—the way the early photo recon satellites of the 1960s would be caught while dropping through the upper atmosphere—had been adopted, but the risk to the crew would have been infinitely worse than what the three astronauts had just faced. A loose cable caught up in a turbojet intake would shear the plane in half in a heartbeat.

"One percent fuel remaining, at 8,500 feet, descending 135 feet per second. One-minute warning."

Eva muttered in Ukrainian about someone making up their mind once and for all to use kilometers.

Victoria drifted from their side to move half a dozen feet over to the young lady remotely piloting the thruster. They had become rather good friends during the weeks of planning and her training leading up to this moment. Gretchen, who had started as an intern like Victoria, just had an uncanny knack for playing computer simulator games, trouncing Victoria, Jason, and anyone else on the team. Word had reached Franklin through

Victoria as to Gretchen's skills as they planned out exactly how to do this, and now the twenty-five-year-old was playing the ultimate game: dropping the thruster with wire attached into the middle of the platform and guiding it down into its locking port, lined with carbon nanotubing, which would shut around it. It would then be wrapped with anchoring cables, also of carbon nanotubing, looking like vast oversize vise grips driven by hydraulic pistons encasing the first dozen meters of the precious cable, holding it firmly in place.

"Point six percent fuel remaining, at 3,200 feet, 130 feet per second descent . . ." A pause. "Gretchen, you got less than thirty seconds remaining."

She simply nodded, jaw clenched tight.

The image on the main monitor, transmitted from the bottom of the thruster unit, was filled now by the platform, the docking bay for the thruster clearly visible in the center, crosshairs off by fifty feet or more.

"Fifteen seconds . . ."

"OK, guys, expect a hard landing," she announced, trying to sound calm.

She flicked a button on the left-hand throttle, subtly moving the joystick, the crosshairs swinging dead-on over the docking bay, which was racing up as she jacked up the rate of descent.

The crosshairs missed the docking bay.

"Two seconds . . . one . . . cut off!"

"Hang on," she gasped, slamming the joystick over to the left. The crosshairs barely aligned and she gave full reverse throttle.

The reverse thrusters actually did sputter up, firing for a few seconds. Gary tore his gaze from his monitor to look out the window at the docking bay in the middle of the platform. The thruster seemed to be dropping like a rock, but there was a flicker of flame under it. Gretchen was planning on some fuel still being in the fuel line and in the pumps, and just plain fumes.

The thruster disappeared through the floor of the platform into the docking bay, which was fifty feet lower than the main platform, the thruster striking the side of the bay and bouncing off, a loud bang and vibration resounding through the control room. Part of the thruster sheared off, along with the platform siding. If the unit had been filled with fuel, there would have been one hell of an explosion.

"Throw the locks!" the mission controller and Franklin shouted.

Another crash and vibration as the thruster hit the floor at the base of the docking bay, disintegrating into a heap of twisted metal, smoke, and a wisp of flame and fragments soaring back up through the top of the bay and sweeping across the platform. But the hydraulic locks were already slamming shut, closing the bay door, while above them the "vise grips," as everyone called them, closed in. The cable was nearly invisible, but the inertia of the descent was bringing the strand down onto the platform, a safety railing lining the edge of the tower simply sliced off as the wire hit it.

There had been debate about the wisdom of putting the control center on the platform at all until a mesh, nearly ten million dollars' worth of the nanotubing, had been attached to the roof and draped around the building. There had been no time or budget for that precaution, which would have to come later.

The vise grips, looking like two halves of a press, closed in, shifting back and forth laterally, reminding Gary of a baseball shortstop trying to position himself to catch a tricky bounce. The grips came together, their operator shouting that he had the wire dead center, straight line, no kinks, pressure rising to over fifty tons per square inch. The rumble of the engines driving the hydraulics vibrated through the entire platform and would continue for hours until the two plates were firmly bolted together, then bolted down to the main deck of the platform as well.

"All systems nominal," the mission controller announced. "Locking plates secured and holding, auxiliary backup pumps up to full power." He paused. "Fire contained in the docking bay, hatch with cable attached secure."

Again a pause.

"Centrifugal force of the earth's rotation taking effect on the wire. It is beginning to straighten out. Wire is holding."

Another pause.

"This is Kiribati base. First wire to geosynchronous orbit is now secured. Closing down drop operations. This is Pillar One, signing off for now."

"Pillar One." The words were as momentous as "Tranquility Base here. Job well done."

The mission controller rolled backward in his chair and took off his headset, features pale, and he looked up at Franklin and then over at Gretchen, extending his hand to grasp hers.

She ever so slowly took off her stereo-optical viewer, eyes wide, features pale, short red hair drenched with sweat. She offered a weak smile.

"Piece of cake" was all she could say; then, turning, she frantically looked about. It was Franklin who grasped what was going to happen and handed her a plastic wastebasket, and she promptly got sick to her stomach. No one commented as, gasping, she sat back up, now thoroughly embarrassed, Franklin taking the basket from her grasp, the mission controller taking it from Franklin and heading with it to the bathroom, where chances were he was about to get sick as well.

"Never do that on a greasy burger, fries, and coffee," she said weakly. "Are we still being videoed?"

Franklin laughed.

"Yes, and you deserve this," he said as he pulled her out of the chair, hugged her, and kissed her on the forehead, the room breaking into cheers, the group swarming around her.

Gary, tears in his eyes, watched from one side, Eva leaning in against him. She was in tears as well.

"Remember the day we met and you basically called me a sci-fi dreamer and an idiot?" she whispered, hugging his arm.

"Vaguely."

"I think I am owed an apology now."

Turning to kiss her, he was more than happy to make up for that moment.

It was always surprising to him just how quickly the transition from sunset to total darkness hit at the equator. Eva still complained about it at times, given the far northern latitude of Kiev and Moscow, where in the summertime twilight, with its beautiful golden glow, lasted for hours. But not tonight as they stood with their daughter; Jason, who it was obvious would soon be introduced as their son-in-law; Franklin; and Gretchen, who had endured plenty of kidding about her first response but was also viewed with admiration and outright awe for her nerve.

In the final seconds she had known they just might fall short, looking up helplessly as the thruster dangled several hundred feet overhead and then just started drifting away. She took the risk of using up the last seconds of fuel to go to a maximum burn, whereas the plan had been for the deceleration thrusters to slow the unit down for a soft landing. Her second bet was that some of the fuel had pooled down into the bottom of the tank and into the line and pumps for the deceleration thrusters, just enough to break the fall and go from a catastrophic to just a darn hard landing—and according to conventional pilot wisdom any landing you can walk away from is a good one.

She had made it by a matter of a few dozen feet. If the entire unit had slammed onto the platform deck rather than gain the hole through which the thruster was supposed to descend, it would most likely have been blown apart, with the possibility that the wire would have detached and gone whipping off the side of the platform. Like a child chasing the string of an escaped balloon, everyone would have been stuck watching the wire, years of effort, and billions of dollars, blow away with the wind.

Even now the tech team was inspecting and inspecting again the efforts of the construction crew to firmly bolt down and weld into place the nanotube-lined pressure plates holding the wire securely to the platform, then checking the stress loads on the interlocking beams, massively overbuilt to hold everything firmly in place with the platform itself.

At times, the setting sun would catch the wire at just the right angle and there would be gasps of wonder when, for a brief moment, thousands of feet up, they could actually see a sparkling line of light piercing a cloud. Seconds later half a dozen spotlights, tens of millions of candelas, snapped on, and there shouts of exhilaration as the wire reflected the light so that it looked like a string of diamonds pointing straight up to the heavens.

A message came in from the Aegis cruiser congratulating them on a remarkable effort and asking if Gretchen wanted a career in the navy: they needed personnel like her with nerves of steel, and besides, everyone got seasick on board at one time or another.

Franklin watched indulgently, like a proud father, as the pool reporters gathered round her. She had become the personal side of this story, along with astronaut Singh, who had just sent down word that they were undocking from the reel, which was beginning to play out wire beyond geosynch to assume position as a counterweight while they began the two-day spiral back down to earth and an at-sea splashdown off the Kiribati coast.

And then another message came in, this one from the States. Hearing it, Gary felt absolutely drained and passed the phone to Eva, who, closing off the call, went over to Franklin to tell him the news.

"Why don't we go take a closer look," Franklin finally said in reply, his arm around Eva's shoulder and looking over at Gary.

Gary, still in shock, took a moment to react and then nodded in agreement.

They approached the locking plates, which rose up nearly thirty feet, a scaffold surrounding the vise grips as the tech crews and construction workers continued to labor with the anchoring.

"Gary, think you can manage the stairs?" Franklin asked softly.

"Hell yes."

He got out of his chair. Victoria came over to his side, hovering, ready to help. He smiled and shook his head but did take her hand.

"Come on, angel, let's take a look at our dream and say thank you to a friend," Gary said.

There was a numbed tingling in both his legs; he wasn't sure if he actually had motor control of his feet or not but, grabbing hold of the handrail, he started up the steps, one at a time. Victoria held his other hand, and he could sense she was ready to hold him tightly if necessary, but he would not let that happen now. They turned a corner, gaining the second flight. It looked like a long climb the next ten steps. *Damn this body*, he thought, embarrassed, knowing that the others were keeping pace patiently, not saying anything, but hovering just behind him in case he should stumble.

Not now, not now, don't let me fall now.

They turned the corner to the third flight up to the top of the scaffolding. He knew he was trembling with the effort but pushed on, the others silent now. And when at last he gained the final step and stood atop the scaffold, he felt a touch of vertigo as he looked about: just an open platform twenty feet across, with no safety rails yet in place. Franklin reached into a haversack that had been handed to him by one of the techs and pulled out gloves made of nanotubing, passing them to the others.

The glow from the spotlights revealed the wire.

"Go on, Eva, you first," Franklin said softly. "Don't wrap your hand around it; just lay your hand lightly against it."

She looked back at him, at her daughter, and then over at Gary.

"No, Gary, you first."

He shook his head, laughing.

"You were the first one to believe in it, not me," he said with a smile.

She looked back to her daughter, offering her the moment, but Victoria, laughing, refused. "It's all yours, Mom."

Eva nodded, donning the gloves, then nervously stepped forward and stretched out her hand.

"You are touching the heavens," Franklin whispered.

She began to cry. "I know. It's vibrating, like a violin string. Listen!"

Noise still rose up from below, the hydraulic pumps gradually easing off pressure to test if the bolting and welding were holding everything in place. Dozens gathered round below them, looking up, but then, yes, he could hear it, faint, ethereal, an actual humming as the wire vibrated from the effect of winds far above, and beyond that the pressure of the solar wind and even perhaps the vibration as the upper reel deployed the counterweight.

"The music of the spheres," she whispered.

"Join me," she said, looking at the other three, and then stepped forward, reaching out, Gary's hand half atop hers, their daughter, her voice choked, saying, "Hey, me in the middle, between you two," and their hands slipped apart to let her hand slip in between theirs, and then Franklin towering above them at nearly six and a half feet, leaning forward, laying his hand atop the three of theirs.

"My God, I can feel it too," Franklin whispered.

All were silent for a moment, looking at each other and then up at the pillar, which really did look like a string of diamonds climbing straight to the heavens.

"Erich, I know you're here," Gary whispered. "Thank you, sir, for inspiring the dream."

Less than an hour after docking had been achieved, word had come that Erich Rothenberg, watching the news in a hospice near Goddard, had smiled, whispered, "Now I can leave," and then slipped away.

There would be no time to return for his memorial service—according to Jewish rite he would be buried the next day—but hundreds from Goddard and the last of the old Apollo team, including two who had walked on the moon, would be there to see his mortal remains off. His one vanity: a request that his Victoria Cross, earned in what seemed now to be another age, would one day be taken aloft and placed somewhere on the tower.

There was a moment of silence, and then to Gary's amazement Franklin whispered in Hebrew the "Shema": "Sh'ma Yisra'el Adonai, Eloheinu Adonia Eḥad . . ." (Hear O Israel, the Lord is our God, the Lord is One.)

They stood silently for several minutes, each lost in their own thoughts. He could feel Victoria's hand slip over his and squeeze it, guiding her mother's hand up to join them.

"I am so proud of both of you," she whispered.

"And we of you," Gary replied.

Her voice began to break.

"I promise you," Victoria said. "We know this will still take years and this is just the first step. But I promise you, I will see it through to completion."

It was a strange comment at the moment, but his heart filled with pride in her. Though barely into her twenties, it was the promise of someone far beyond her years acknowledging the mortality of her parents and now reassuring them that their dream would continue, no matter what.

Franklin's hand engulfed theirs.

"This is just the first step to the stars, and Victoria, if need be I know you will get it done."

13

The Spinners

The actual load-bearing capacity of the first strand was little more than several hundred kilograms, but it was a start. The next step was to use that first thread as a guide wire, with additional threads to be woven around it in nearly the identical manner as in the nineteenth century when a first guide wire would be suspended between the two towers of a suspension bridge, then additional wires spun around it. With the building of the Brooklyn Bridge, eight to ten strands a day woven onto the first cable was considered magnificent progress. But at that long-ago rate of ten miles a day, and fifty strands to be woven around the first in some places, it would take only about four hundred years to complete the Pillar.

For the Pillar, the weaving would start at both ends. For the spinners working at the top of the tower, it would be easier in a sense, because at geosynch they would be working essentially in zero gravity, and as they descended and gravity gradually increased, it would help propel them. For the upper end the cable still had to be lofted into place by rockets at the usual cost of nearly a quarter of a million dollars a kilo. But after several such launches, with the Pillar "beefed up" enough to handle heavier loads, spinners sent up from the ground could operate along half a dozen sections at the same time.

So it would be a slow and expensive start, but then after a year the pace would increase dramatically.

No matter what advances there were in hybrid engine designs, from jet to "scramjet" or "ramjet" and then to rocket in the final step through the atmosphere, carrying payloads all the way to the precious "high ground" of geosynch orbit was expensive business. To put several astronauts up there cost nearly the same amount of energy as nudging them a bit farther to orbit around the moon. And once up there working, if one of them had a craving for a pizza, cost on the ground would still be ten to fifteen bucks but delivery (without tip) was still around a quarter of a million dollars.

The ground launched spinner was built around a slender tube, made of nano-filament, that encased the tower to guide the spinner on its ascent. Energy for lift provided initially by a jet engine pack would loft it the first 50,000 feet; the jet pack would be ejected, recovered, and used again. After that a rocket pack would take over. Maximum gain at the start would be two hundred miles, at which point the end of the wire being spun on would be sealed tight against the main tower and the lift unit separated to reenter the atmosphere, and recycled for another lift up. As quickly as it was detached, another unit would begin to ascend, weaving another strand on. The strengthening of the cable within the atmosphere and eventually for its first thousand miles out was absolutely crucial. It was where there was maximum compression stress from the load above as well as horizontal stresses due to weather; it was also the primary impact zone for orbital debris.

Once the support wires were built up, some of the cables sent aloft would be of a slightly different molecular structure, not anywhere near as strong in terms of bearing loads, but designed to be highly conductive for electrical flow; thus the later spinners would have electric motors and actually be driven by power "piped" into the tower.

The spinners labored day after day. There were the usual glitches. The third launch from the ground jammed at just under 100,000 feet and finally had to be blown clear, an extremely tense moment: they were all fearful that blowing off the load might damage the tower or set up a harmonic wave, but it broke clean away and the remaining wire was even recovered for later use.

Fuchida's firm, which had an exclusivity agreement with Franklin for the next ten years, was now charging just over two dollars a foot for two-millimeter nanotubing. The rule of mass production, as with all products, held sway, and by contract he was allowed to add 20 percent to operating cost, but by totaling up the number of strands for a viable tower 23,000 miles, the numbers did rapidly add up. There had been a surge of investors clamoring to get in on Pillar Inc. in the days after the successful linkup, but as the months passed without even any remote talk of the first commercial payload that would actually begin to generate income, interest had waned. In a world of computerized instant trading with fortunes made or lost in a matter of minutes, investments for the long term without payback for ten years or more were hard to find.

This was not like Franklin's earlier schemes that had made him famous, with a half dozen investors each throwing in ten thousand and then cashing out a few years later with a million or more, or the later ones when backers with a million to invest suddenly had twenty times that three years later. Now he was scrounging for billions with no promise other than the charisma of his past record as a promise that in the end all would win.

And then at last Franklin dropped the bomb publicly. He had, of course, referred to this first strand as the "construction tower" and said that another, stronger one would be built, but he was vague about whether the construction tower itself, once "beefed up," would have commercial use.

Eva and Gary had been in on the debate regarding the reality of their designs long before the failed launch of the first test ship; they knew the inherent long-term flaws of using a strand, but the cost of developing "ribbons" and lifting their far heavier load to geosynch without a construction strand in place would exceed anything Franklin could ever hope to raise in terms of backing.

Research and development on the ribbon concept had moved ahead dramatically and in secret even while preparations were being made for the launching of the first "strand," and even now while it was being strengthened, and that research had changed the entire paradigm of how Franklin and his team saw the real future of this project.

Of course, Gary, Eva, and the team working with them were the ones who had come up with the ribbon concept years earlier, but Franklin had sworn them to secrecy, preferring to keep public attention and investor interest focused on what was already in place. Eva and Gary had learned a lot about the difference between working at Goddard and being part of a private venture, otherwise they would have felt no constraints about publishing their revised concepts, even repudiating the original design of the tower, given the technological advances that had been made since the mass production of carbon nanotubing had begun. But they knew, even if Franklin had not extracted a promise from them, that publicizing their misgivings would destroy the program; thus their work was kept at a level of secrecy equal to that of a highest-classified military program. Even as Fuchida was turning out strands, he was now secretly manufacturing their first reels of ribbon as well.

It was Jason Fitzhugh who had come up with the right analogy. When the Roeblings, father and son, had designed the Brooklyn Bridge, mass-produced steel was still a dream. But even before the first tower of that bridge had been set in place, Bessemer's new process of blast furnacing was soon turning out high-grade steel at a fraction of the cost. The Roeblings were already committed to using old-fashioned iron for the bridge's cables and thus stayed with that material. A hundred and fifty years later that bridge carried tens of thousands of automobiles daily and no one thought twice about it, even though nearly every bridge built afterward had steel cables of far better strength.

Franklin had not left Kiribati since the tower linkup: things were still hot with Senator Proxley, who was demanding another grandstand public hearing and even claimed now that by building the first strand, Pillar Inc. had become a monopoly that had to be broken up. But the winds were beginning to shift back in the States. Private firms were now routinely offering suborbital launches, and thousands of passengers, all of them voters, proudly wore on their lapels the "astronaut" wings given to them after their flights. They had actually become something of a status symbol. America was becoming pro-space again.

A private venture firm had even gotten within a hairsbreadth of a manned flight to the moon, but the first stage had detonated seconds after liftoff. Fortunately this system was similar to *Apollo*, with the built-in safety feature of a rocket-powered escape tower that pulled the capsule with its two passengers free of the explosion.

And there had been disasters as well. So far fifteen had died trying to reach the heavens. Two of the Brit's competitors were out of business after their spacecraft broke up in flight.

Although no one ever said it directly, it was clear that rocket-powered space flight would always be much too risky for high-volume commercial use at even one-tenth of 1 percent the level of daily jet travel around the world.

But rather than decreasing, there was actually a resurgence in public interest in space. Going into space, for the younger generation, was the new extreme sport that made base jumping in "flying squirrel" suits look tame. Extremely high-altitude jumps from balloons were now "in" as well, and fascination with the potentials of the tower was growing.

The unmanned work of NASA, especially its Mars landings, had created intense enthusiasm and received much support. There had even been a slight increase in NASA's budget, but it was human exploration that held and would always hold the key to public and therefore taxpayer interest. And with that, the promise of the Pillar was stirring public interest.

Where once there had been negative press about Franklin's Folly, now there was growing fascination in the Pillar, with hundreds of blogs and discussion sites dedicated to it. The comparisons had been made so often that they had become the standard retorts to critics: Where would aviation be today if after the first plane crash all flying had been stopped in order to investigate? Thousands had died and thousands had been injured in the first generations of flight up until World War II while simply learning how to get off the ground for a few seconds, or during high-speed, instrument-based cross-country flights at night in heavy weather. Hardly anyone thought twice about the reality and sacrifice behind their getting into a hollow tube with wings and jets strapped to it, leaving New York, and seven hours later waking up in London, a journey that took weeks and was fraught with such perils as collisions with icebergs only a hundred years earlier. The same thing was true today as we reached for the stars within our lifetimes, the arguments ran, provided we had the guts to do it, and this resonated especially with a younger generation around the world eager for challenge and adventure.

It was Victoria, of that same generation, who convinced Franklin that he should put up multiple Web sites dedicated to different niche audiences—not with the usual boring stuff like some photos and videos, but with active daily videoconferences with team members, discussions of future plans (only the "unclassified" ones, of course), and live cameras feeds of the spinners at work. The spinners were actually rotating around the Pillar at more than one revolution a second as they built up the cable's diameter, but someone with a bit of computer savvy figured out how to snap an image every second from the precise same spot and thus stream it as a live video. The spinners were even on the social networks with their own names, putting out bulletins about their progress, and a couple of full-time staffers handled the uplink traffic, answering serious questions as if they themselves were the spinners, or cooking up witty replies that at times went viral.

The names of the spinners were inspired by a popular computer-generated cartoon of a few years earlier about two robots who fall in love and in the process save humanity and restore earth's environment. The firm that created the cartoon was more than eager to join in the fun, allowing use of the names of the two smitten robots, one of which was given to a spinner working from the top of the Pillar downward, the other to a spinner below that was working its way upward; longing to one day meet in the middle. Their ongoing romance was a hit; and the parent company who created the cartoon was soon turning out short "outtakes," as had been run during the film credits at the end of the movie, of the antics and interplay of the two spinners and other characters. It had definitely gone viral, a hit with schoolkids around the world.

Other Web sites went up, for elementary, middle, and high school and high-tech college-level conversations and information. Victoria's fiancé, Jason, had pushed as well for a site dedicated to the history of technological innovations that had transformed how humanity lived; it was a proactive measure to mollify a significant technophobic minority. A critic of NASA long ago had made the slashing comment that the agency had taken the most exciting adventure in the history of humanity, the Apollo program, and made it almost boring and routine. Victoria, Jason, and others of their generation who were computer and social network savvy were making sure that would not happen again. There was even rumor that in a year Proxley would face stiff opposition from a very pro-space opponent. Perhaps the tide was indeed turning after a long moribund period in which the heavens were calling but no one felt like making the investment to answer the call.

But what was increasingly the hot topic was Franklin's remarks that the ultimate intent of the Pillar was not just inexpensive transportation to space but the piping down of limitless energy from solar arrays deployed around it. It could mean an end to the dependence on fossil fuels, even fission power, thus in fairly short order slamming on a brake against global warming.

The weight load for such a power system, though, was magnitudes higher than what the tower could bear . . . and thus the ribbon was the ultimate answer: stitching layers of ribbon side by side and atop each other could build the tower out to any strength load desired, and it was ultimately why the construction tower was already obsolete as soon as it went up. But to say as much to the world and investors would have ended the project on the same day.

"In for a penny, in for quite a few pounds more," was Franklin's favorite line . . . in private, of course.

It was the problem that consumed Gary and Eva now that the tower was up, with the spinners reinforcing it day by day so that it could eventually withstand the stress of carrying a viable load of ribbon clear out to geosynch. Franklin slipped out word of a meeting for his "inner circle"—Gary, Eva, Fuchida, and a few others—to discuss the next step.

Franklin had picked the location for this meeting well. To get into this room required connecting flights from Hawaii or Fiji and then to Tarawa. If need be a lot of "sudden" paperwork could tie up uninvited visitors forever at Tarawa. Permission to land on the island of Aranuka, now that the tower was up, was strictly limited to aircraft that had first landed at Tarawa for a rigorous security inspection before being cleared to bring in supplies, with carefully selected pilots at the controls for the final leg, hauling in the reels of wire and personnel with what were called "blue pass tags." These pilots were armed and if that defense failed, they were instructed to fly straight into the ocean before allowing anyone to take control of their planes. There would be no repeat of 9/11, at least by any aircraft.

Though no one spoke openly of it, the United States Navy did seem to have a special interest in events around Kiribati, and at times an Aegis-class cruiser or destroyer could be sighted lingering on the horizon. The few times an unauthorized aircraft started to approach the island, the ship's high-gain X-band target acquisition radar would switch on, "painting" the aircraft and then suggesting it turn about back to Fiji or land in Tarawa for clearance. At other times an Australian or British ship would take up position as well.

It was obvious that although he was in semi-exile, Franklin had friends somewhere who understood America had a stake in the successful completion of the tower, and Australia and New Zealand could already sense the potential economic impact of the tower on the entire region in the years to come.

The room where this very private meeting was about to be held could seat fifty comfortably and had a curving glass ceiling that offered a spectacular view of the tower from its base; at night its illuminated surface rose arrowlike to the heavens. Everyone present was definitely blue pass only. Gary could not help but notice with pride that Victoria and Jason had been invited. Like any father, he had a lot of doubts at first about who his daughter's heart had settled on, but over time this young man, with his decidedly Oxford accent and British manners and mannerisms, had won his heart. Jason had really won Gary over when, over a bottle of good Scotch that Jason had provided, the young Briton had actually managed to explain how the game of cricket worked. The two were laughing uproariously by the end of the evening, and the following day Gary took him out for the male bonding ritual of shooting flintlock rifles at a nearby range where security personnel, nearly all of them citizens of Kiribati in constant training with some former American and British military types, put them through their paces. Whenever Gary showed up with his treasured flintlock, he always caused a stir, not just because of the uniqueness of his gun, but because he was one of the two people who had played the greatest role in making the dream that was transforming their world a reality.

It was a hobby Gary had indulged in as a young man, and he was embarrassed by the extent that Parkinson's had affected his ability to hold a Pennsylvania long rifle steady; he could barely hit the target when seated and resting the weapon. Jason, with his fascination and professional interest in early technologies, waxed on at great length about the historical debate and mythology of "Yankee riflemen" versus "lobsterbacks." His aim was little better than Gary's, who could sense the young man was deliberately missing in order to be polite. As they talked about the technology behind the weapon, Jason reminded him that it was a British officer named Ferguson who had invented a breech-loading rifle seventy years ahead of its time, which if adopted rather than mockingly rejected by higher-ups, would have changed the course of the Revolution. Unfortunately "for our side," as Jason defined it, Ferguson was killed at the Battle of Kings Mountain early in 1781, though at that point it was already too late to "bring you colonials to your senses."

On the trip back to the platform, the topic shifted to disruptive technologies and the impact of that thesis on further development of the Pillar. Professor Garlin had actually written a book denouncing its construction, pointing out all the hazards both to low-orbit navigation and the stream of seventy years of technological development of rocket-powered flight. The tower, she contended, would end that research, putting hundreds of thousands out of work at a time when some firms were finally proving that traditional methods of access to space were becoming viable. Sounding like an anthropologist, she then went on a lengthy diatribe about how it was technology that was destroying humanity, not saving it, and raised the old argument that space would not be the answer to humanity's woes until its problems "down here" were solved. Garlin's book had gained favorable notice in several major papers and journals. She was now a regular on the talk show circuit as a critic of the program and had suddenly become close friends with Senator Proxley.

By the time Gary and Jason returned from the shooting range, they reeked of black powder and their hands and faces were covered in soot, but they reveled in their appearance. Gary said but one thing to Victoria when she greeted them at the door to their small apartment on the platform: "If you don't marry him, you're crazy."

Franklin stepped up to the podium, turned to take in the view—a spinner just beginning its ascent, jet engine thundering—then nodded to his audience, who stood to applaud. But it was obvious he was nervous as he extended a hand and gestured for all to sit down.

"I only hope you will applaud when I am done speaking," he said, and there was actually a bit of a tremor in his voice.

Only a few in the room—Gary, Eva, the Brit and his American partner, and Fuchida—knew what was coming.

He paused for a moment and looked back at the tower, the roar of the spinner's jet engine piercing the room as it rotated around the Pillar, spinning another layer into place.

"It is a magnificent sight, is it not?"

He paused, and, of course, there were nods of agreement, even some more applause.

"And who of us just seven years ago would have dreamed that we could have reached this far."

More nods of approval, but the audience could sense something was up.

"But it will never be economically viable."

Now there was total silence.

"If you wish to drag me out and toss me into the sea when this meeting is done, that is your right. However, given my ethnic heritage, I do detest lynching, so let us refrain from that."

He turned his back to the audience, watching as the spinner continued to climb heavenward.

"Perhaps I have led all but a few of you a little bit astray. Let me say in my defense, though, that I had to in order to get us this far. Remember in the old Westerns, when a group got lost in the desert, the leader promised that water was just over the next ridge, even though he knew it was still fifty miles off? I had to play that role, my friends, in order for us to get to this point, and now that we are within sight of the real goal, I hope you will hear me out."

"Some of you might have picked up a hint when I referred to this as Pillar One. You see, all along I saw it as that. The first pillar. Most of you smiled and nodded, realizing that once we proved our point with this one, more would surely follow—and I did say that this was simply the first tower and a second would follow. Already there is an indication that the Chinese, having recruited a few renegades, shall we say, from Dr. Fuchida's team, are now preparing to start construction in Indonesia, and I wish them well. Competition fuels innovation."

That had indeed been troublesome for Fuchida and now for a host of lawyers in Japan, America, Kiribati, and China who were arguing whether the three men who Fuchida had fired early in the project—and who were now living somewhere in China, without doubt in great luxury—had engaged in patent violations. One could always get by even the tightest security with terabytes of data, if planned for sufficiently in advance. Regardless of who won or lost the legal battle, the Chinese were rapidly moving toward the start of their own tower.

"I will confess to you now that early on I realized one fundamental flaw with our current design, but at that stage we were already committed to building the Pillar as it was originally designed. That, and technological innovation is always racing ahead, and before this first strand went up, a far better concept was laid before me.

"Often with rapid technological innovations, in the time it takes to get from what they used to call the drawing board to actual construction, a newer technology is developed. Thus it is now with our tower. It is obsolete even as we build it."

Now there was a stir in the room, and one of his primary investors asked loud enough for all to hear, with plenty of expletives added in, why in hell were they building it in the first place.

Franklin nodded to him, thinking that the investor was about to become a former friend.

"Because we *are* building it," Franklin replied. "Building it and here is the entire point of this meeting. We are building it not to be used as a commercial launch system. We are building it not to be eventually used as a commercial platform, to put satellites into geosynch orbit at a fraction of the cost, or from that high point atop the tower to hurl spacecraft to the moon, Mars, and beyond, again at a fraction of the cost. We are building a tower in order to prove we can build it, then use it to haul up the hundreds of tons of additional material needed to build the *real* Pillar, the ribbon design you already know we have been working on."

"My God, Franklin, what in hell are you talking about?" the investor shouted. "We've sunk nearly forty billion into this so far. Let this ribbon thing of yours wait. Start sending up commercial launches, we could be doing that by year's end and at least starting some return cash flow. And at least get some payback for a while."

"Before we can even do that," Franklin replied, "we all know we still have to spend another ten billion to strengthen Pillar One for survivability from debris impacts and to handle any kind of real commercial load, unless Dr. Fuchida wishes to give us wire for free, and our allies in the launch business give us eight more launches to geosynch—three of them manned for long duration work up there—for free as well."

The Brit smiled and shook his head.

"You have the launches at cost, I'll concede that, my friend, but I am barely keeping my head above water as is. I've all but put into receivership all my other ventures to keep this one going."

"So what are you driving at, then?" the investor shouted.

Franklin, still a bit of a showman at heart, put on a glove lined with nanotubes, reached under the podium, and produced what appeared to be a black but highly reflective ribbon nearly a foot across. He slowly turned it edgewise, and as he did so, it became almost invisible. It did not flutter, though, the way a ribbon of fabric would; it was perfectly rigid, like a ribbon of tungsten steel. As he turned it back toward his audience again that mirror-like sheen made it almost invisible.

"This, my friends, is the stuff of the real tower, but we need what we are building right now in order to finally get this up there," and as he spoke he nodded back to the tower, the spinner that had been timed to lift off just as he began speaking now a barely visible dot in the sky above.

The room fell silent as he held the length of ribbon aloft. Although he did have a protective glove on, he did not seem all that nervous or careful handling it—unlike the time he first held up the nearly invisible wire before many in this group, wearing not just gloves but a protective suit in case an errant puff of air caused it to brush against his body.

"The real tower—the tower I realized five years ago would have to be the real tower—will not be made out of the carbon nanotube strands we are now weaving behind me even as I speak. This, my friends, is the future of tower technology for at least the next twenty years or so, until someone smarter than all of us here thinks up a better idea that none of our team has cooked up yet. As wood and stone were replaced by iron, and iron by steel, so this will replace what we call wire, not just for building the Pillar but a whole new generation of construction projects down here on earth as well."

He spoke quickly now, so as not to be interrupted and deluged with questions.

"Dr. Fuchida told me five years ago, when he started to mass-produce thread for the first time, that if you threw enough money at the problem and gave him enough time, he could weave what I am holding before you, but it would take at least several years. He finally achieved it three months before we launched our first thread.

"Once Pillar One is sufficiently strengthened its cargo will consist solely of ribbon for several years to come, that and supplies for our astronauts working out at geosynch. There is no time to waste on commercial loads. It means delayed payoff for all of us, but the payoff will be there when we have completed Pillar Two.

"With the first ribbon anchored, adding dozens more ribbons of carbon-60 nanotubing will become easier and cheaper. Haul them up on Pillar One, then drop them down and weave them in place for Pillar Two. Additional ribbons will be deployed as layers atop the first one to strengthen it, or could be run down either side of the first one and stapled or laminated in place, extending the Pillar outward—a dozen meters or more in width, if desired—with stunning load-bearing capacities.

"Then the real payoff begins, my friends. This is not so much about what goes up but what comes down. We've gone public with that concept already, this is about clean solar energy. We're weaving several threads into Pillar One to test the concept. But once Pillar Two, made of ribbon, starts to go online, we can layer in super conductive carbon nanotubing that eventually will handle gigawatts of power. There is the ultimate payoff."

He paused, taking a deep breath.

"But it will take time. Five years or more at least and not five or six months, as some of you thought, would be the case for financial return."

"Financial return you promised us," the angry investor retorted with barely concealed rage.

Franklin hesitated for a moment.

"I'm in this for the long haul, my friends. Not just for the long haul when it comes to how much money is still in my account on the day I die. I'm in it for the long haul of what it means to future generations."

He fell silent and nodded toward where Victoria and Jason were seated. Such a gesture from nearly anyone else would have triggered chuckles of derision by the hard-edged investors in the room. But no one dared snicker when a man with the reputation of Franklin Smith made such a gesture. All knew it was from his heart.

"A foot of ribbon, even with everything Fuchida's team had learned with mass production of wire, will still cost thirty times more than a similar strand of nanotubing," he continued, protests silenced for the moment. "Cost for a functional ribbon tower, as a starter, will run an additional hundred billion.

"What we are gaining from our Pillar One, as I call it, is not just the ability to haul up the construction material for Pillar Two at dollars per pound versus a hundred thousand per pound; we are training ourselves in how to do it, safer, cheaper, and better. Without Pillar One, Pillar Two will be impossible, or so prohibitive in cost no individual, firm, or nation will ever dare to venture it, and thus, we will continue to slowly stew in our own juices and in another fifty years, a hundred at most, our technological civilization will collapse.

"With that thought in mind, I am asking you to stick with me through this. I have a fondness for Lincoln that transcends the fact that my great-grandparents were born into slavery. I have a fondness for his vision of the future of America as the preeminent technological power of the world if the crisis of the Civil War could be transcended. At this moment I think of one of my favorite quotes from him that 'we shall either nobly save, or meanly lose the last best hope of mankind.' Pillar One is the last best hope of mankind."

He held up the ribbon again.

"After that then this is the future."

"The bottom line for all of us as a team . . . ?" someone asked.

"How long before this next Pillar is capable of doing anything useful?" The investor, who was now pale-faced, shaking his head ruefully, finally asked, breaking the silence.

Franklin hesitated. He rarely spoke from note cards and it was obvious to Gary that the answer had escaped him. Gary held up five fingers and mouthed the reply.

"Five years," Franklin replied. "Commercial loads on Pillar Two in five years and viable energy coming back down."

He caught his stride again and now offered an idea, suggested by one of his young staff which he knew just might capture the group's imagination and the global press as well. "For a very sharp turnaround in investment, they could quickly expand the pillar, which would have to be done anyhow, to six meters in width up to five hundred miles and build the first substation there, leasing facilities for scientific observation and most definitely for tourists, who would be eager to spend a few nights at a hotel and stand on a platform to look straight down for five hundred miles. Victoria Morgan has even proposed a new sport out there.

"What happens if at five hundred miles, while wearing a space suit, you just climbed over the safety railing of our facility there and jumped? Would you go into orbit?"

Most knew the simple answer, but a few did look at him quizzically.

Franklin nodded to Victoria, who stood up to speak.

"At five hundred miles up," she began calmly and with an authoritative voice, already used to speaking to large gatherings, though usually of students and the general public and not this hard-edged group, "the effect of gravity relative to the earth's surface will only be 10 percent less. All this nonsense about zero gravity once in space, as you all know, is exactly that: nonsense. Astronauts appear to feel that they are in zero gravity when orbiting the earth aboard the space station, but in reality, as they zip along at something like 17,000 miles an hour, 200 miles above the surface of the earth, they are actually falling around the earth. Gravity is still trying to pull them down, but as they fall back toward earth, their rate of fall exactly matches the curvature of the earth; therefore, they are forever 'falling' around the earth and thus have the illusion of being in zero gravity.

"With our second pillar, with a station attached to it at the five-hundred-mile level, if you step over the safety rail at the platform, you will start to fall, though the angular momentum imparted by the tower will cause you to drift away from the tower even as you plummet to earth.

"Recall a while back the jump from nearly twenty-five miles up by an ultimate skydiver leaping from a balloon taking him to the edge of space. In the near vacuum of that altitude, recall how startlingly quickly he accelerated up to past Mach 1. The tower will make that experience pale in comparison and draw thousands to try it.

"It will be the ultimate sport. I call it space diving: fall until you hit the atmosphere, then deploy a mini heat shield; to decelerate, the heat shield folds up once well into the atmosphere, and a drogue chute at 50,000 feet deploys to stabilize to subsonic speeds; then free fall again and finally deploy a regular parachute to land. I see it as an Olympic sport in twelve years' time, along with low-gravity soccer inside a contained sphere; and imagine the potentials for ballet, dance, how it will transform so many of our sports and arts . . ."

Her voice trailed off. Talking about sports that might appeal to her generation was a rather low item on the agenda at the moment. Victoria started to sit down but Franklin shook his head and motioned to her to come up to the podium.

"Most of you know Victoria Morgan, daughter of our esteemed colleagues Drs. Eva and Gary Morgan."

There were polite nods from the audience, a few smiles, but in general silence.

"Victoria is working on her Ph.D. in electrical engineering at Purdue and it is her specialization that I wish her to talk about for a moment."

He stepped back and nodded to her to proceed.

"There is a second purpose to the Five Hundred Mile Station," she said. "It will be the power transfer station of the twenty-first century."

A few of the insiders were smiling but the rest looked a bit confused.

"May I interrupt for just a moment here, Miss Morgan?" Franklin said. "I remind all of you that you signed some very stringent confidentiality papers in order to be part of this meeting. What is said in this room stays here until the board of Pillar Inc. decides to go public, because when it does, I think you will see just how disruptive the information can be to the global economic system we are now stuck with. But it will, as well, be the largest arrow in our quiver when it comes to gaining political support in some very key areas."

He stepped back, nodding for Victoria to continue, while on one side of the room a large screen flickered to life. It was an image of Pillar Two, but rather than just being a single ribbon into space, close to its base it looked more like a spiderweb, or a wagon wheel with a dozen spokes radiating out from it.

This was not part of the plan, for her to explain the solar energy aspect of the tower, but he just smiled at her as he turned off his mike and affixed it to the lapel of her lightweight blazer.

"It's all yours, Victoria," he whispered before switching the mike back on. "Your dissertation and dream, now go for it."

She looked at the image on the screen, smiled, took a deep breath, and faced the audience, launching in as if she had practiced this presentation for weeks. The only problem was to avoid eye contact with her parents who were obviously about to explode with pride.

"This tower will be connected to solar arrays each a mile or more in width down its length. We already know that solar panels in space are the true clean source of energy for our world, it was postulated as far back as the 1970s by such visionaries as Dr. Jerry O'Neill and writers such as Clarke and Asimov. But the insurmountable question has always been how to get the energy the last two hundred miles from space to where it is needed on the earth's surface.

"There was talk of microwaving it, or using lasers, but we all know the absurdity of such proposals: even the most disbelieving when it comes to environmental impacts would quickly see the profound negative results, even if willing to accept the absurd costs involved for receiving stations. Pillar Two finally solves those questions."

She fished in her pockets for a laser pointer, a bit embarrassed to realize she had left it in her room; and there were some chuckles when her mother stood up, approached the podium and handed her one, with several people applauding Eva's motherly gesture as she smiled at her daughter and returned to her seat.

Victoria flicked it on and pointed at the screen.

"Each of those spokes is yet another fascinating by-product of carbon-60 nanotubes. There were reports more than a decade ago that the tubes could be arranged for superconductivity. The team I am working with on this—and why I decided to get a Ph.D. electrical engineering with a specialization in space-related electrical engineering—relates not just to the solar panels but those spokes radiating out from the Five Hundred Mile Station, though in actuality I think positioning it closer to a thousand miles up is optimal."

She traced the line of one of the spokes attached the Pillar from its point of origin toward Hawaii.

"The gigawatts of energy we harvest in space will be beamed down to the transfer station, and from there, via the radiating spokes of superconductive nanotubing, it will be piped the rest of the way to the earth's surface, in this case to Hawaii."

No one spoke for a moment until the once angry investor, confused by this new twist, quietly asked, "But the weight of the cables? The transmission distance? How?"

"That is why we need Pillar Two. Some in this room are understandably focused on what will go up that pillar. I have become far more interested in what will come down.

"I will have to offer a nod to one of my professors, who we know is an opponent of this tower because of what she considers its disruptive technology. I took a course with her and it set me to thinking. I and most of my generation believe that, environmentally, we are approaching a dead end. Far more a concern to me at my age. And it struck me, to just disrupt the whole damn thing with a revolutionary answer, the same way problems of the past were solved with revolutionary answers. Think up something entirely new and off the charts, that once initiated will seem absolutely logical, even if disruptive to existing systems. It is the way coal replaced wood, and I bet a hell of a lot of wood choppers were upset with that one."

There were actually some chuckles at that.

"When oil replaced coal as the primary driver of the industrial revolution of the early twentieth century there were massive economic disruptions in the coal fields of England and America, but should we ever go back to that fuel as many now claim we should? Now, we find ourselves running low on oil unless we increasingly pursue fracking and drill ever deeper at greater and greater cost. We need a new answer, a clean answer, and those of you in this room, when you look at the Pillar and the plan Franklin has laid out for Pillar Two, I see the answer for the future, not just in terms of energy, but our collapsing environment as well, and even the very existence of this nation which has hosted our project."

She gave a polite nod to the president of Kiribati who was front and center in the audience; he half stood, bowed in reply and there was a scattering of applause at their gesture of mutual respect.

"We look at the two great wars of the twentieth century, a number of smaller ones, and the first major conflict of the twenty-first, and what has been the underlying cause? Energy. Oil. And as we run short, we know the economic disruption will grow worse while the environmental issues become ever more grave."

She paused, scanning her audience.

"But I digress and, sir, I have not yet answered your question," she said calmly while looking at the confused investor.

"To begin with, each of those spokes, in order to address the weight and stress factors, will be but single ribbons, capable of transmitting an output of one of those supposedly clean but rather inefficient windmills now marring the landscapes and seascapes of the world, and the revelations of their negative impact on wildlife and true efficiency. But in time . . ."

She smiled.

"The potential is limitless. That, ladies and gentlemen, is your true profit motive for building the tower. Fifty years hence, when the palaces of the current rulers of the world's energy are disappearing into the sand, carbon nanotube towers—of which ours will be the first—will be the energy hubs of the twenty-first century. And you, supporters of this program, will be in on the ground floor of that investment."

She smiled and subtly nodded to Jason who had planted the idea.

"If you lived a hundred and fifty years ago, think of the return on a ten-thousand-dollar investment with Carnegie, Rockefeller, or Tesla. I see an investment with Franklin Smith in the same light."

She paused, scanning her audience.

Gary felt such an explosion of pride at this moment. His young lady had most definitely found a mentor as he had found one in Erich. It was Franklin Smith: his style of delivery, the way he could work an audience, that indefinable "something," of a natural-born public speaker that Gary most definitely lacked. She had pulled it off with charming ease.

The room was silent and Franklin came to her side.

"And there is one final point here, my friends," Franklin said with a smile. "Political support."

"How is that?" the investor asked, but all the anger was gone from his voice.

"Taxes."

A mutter ran through the audience on hearing that one word. The economic picture of the last half of a decade was only getting worse as government after government sank deeper and deeper in red ink and felt the only answer was to just keep raising taxes yet higher.

Franklin held up his hand in a friendly calming gesture.

"Let's just say, for argument's sake, we visit the governor of California, which is struggling with deficits, and I single that individual out because I've known him for decades, and though politically we might disagree on many an issue, there is one issue we have always seen eye to eye on, and that is space. He even picked up a mocking nickname because of his outspoken support of space exploration. Now, just imagine I first ask him if we could anchor an "energy spoke" to an offshore platform. And then just add that eventually it will deliver not just megawatts but gigawatts of clean, green electricity, making his state a net exporter of electricity . . . and he can tax it. Dare I suggest we have a governor, two senators, and about fifty members of Congress from the state of California supporting our Pillar and demanding that NASA gets in to lend a hand?"

There was a moment of silence and then a chuckle and finally applause echoing in the room.

"That, my friends, is why we need to build Pillar Two."

Franklin smiled at Victoria.

"I am certain Miss Victoria—who will soon be Dr. Morgan, following in the tradition of her parents—could wax for hours about the various potentials, which, my friends, if your souls are only those of hard-nosed investors, will see profit in as well."

Victoria smiled, nodded in agreement, and—knowing she had successfully "sold the pitch"—returned to her seat.

"We have eight more launches planned and paid for to haul additional wire up to geosynch, and that is with the built-in expectation of upwards of two failures at launch," Franklin continued quickly, shifting back to the hard-core issue of the moment.

"Two of the missions will be manned, perhaps a third if all the other launches go without a glitch. The next mission, which I pray there is no failure, will loft permanent living and work quarters and supplies to maintain a team of four men and women in geosynch for months. Their primary purpose is to oversee the spinning from the upper level and the deployment of empty reels and equipment up the length of cable beyond geosynch to act as an ever-increasing counter mass. We're also sending up a manned 'crawler' that can go up and down the tower's entire length for inspection and to clear a problem if a spinner jams."

Now there was a stir.

"Then why the cost of sending a manned team up by rocket?" the investor asked.

"It is one thing to send up a man or woman on a climb with just enough air and supplies to reach geosynch versus sending them up as a viable workforce. We will still need rockets for that for some time to come to get that tonnage aloft and, yes, at a thousand times the cost. If we have a glitch along the line, I want a manned crawler up there that can much more easily drop down to handle the problem, then return to the manned station or just come back down to earth. It is the economics of energy and time to deal with a problem, particularly in the upper section."

He looked about the room. There were no objections.

"Eventually we can send people and supplies up by a crawler, but for now the additional expense of lofting one up is worth the insurance it provides. Eventually, if for no other purpose than to prove we can do it, we'll send somebody up."

Again the touch of the showman there.

"And on the day a human does the first ascent, the whole world will be watching.

"But their real mission is to lay the groundwork for Pillar Two, the real Pillar to Heaven and what Miss Morgan has just outlined for you."

He paused and now actually smiled at his audience.

"Until that pillar behind me can bear the weight, and we have our astronaut crews in place, and Dr. Fuchida starts mass-producing ribbon rather than single strands of thread, the first spools will go up by traditional rocket launch, but after that we are going to use that tower behind me to start hauling the material heavenward, at several tons every three days, to build the next tower. That is why I have put any thought of commercial launches on hold. Absolutely first priority of Pillar use must go to the construction of the second pillar."

He pointed back to the first wire again.

"Without that in place, we are talking somewhere into the hundreds of billion dollars to make our dreams and our future come true of building the truly viable commercial Pillar for energy production and transportation to space. That is why I am asking you to stick with me in this decision."

He took a deep breath.

"If not, vote to disband this effort for I see no other way than the path I, Miss Victoria, and the rest of our team have labored for years to create. You'll still have Pillar One, you can earn back some of your investment, but it will never be commercially viable, and it will never fulfill the real goal of not just reaching space, but providing limitless energy and saving our planet from environmental disaster as well.

"If there are no further questions, will someone move to put it to a vote?"

He fell silent, his gaze sweeping his audience.

The vote was unanimous to endorse the project, and before the last of those carrying a "blue pass" for access to Aranuka had left, Franklin had another fifty billion pledged. But even that was not enough. And when word hit the press a day later—leaked by someone who had signed the usual oaths of confidentiality but, once home, pulled out his stock from the venture before going to the press—the true uproar and accusations that the entire project was a fraud began. As for those who saw the potential for the ultimate "disruptive technology," darker thoughts began to form as well.

14

In the following eight months, seven of the eight launches went without a hitch. Fortunately the one that did fail four minutes into flight, carried a cargo of wire and the first reels of ribbon but no personnel or crucial supplies. The two manned launches and the launch of the cramped and barely adequate workstation—simply a hollowed-out third stage unit not unlike the old *Skylab* of the 1970s—were flawless. After six months aloft the first crew rotated out to be replaced by the second team of four, commanded by Miss Selena Singh, now overall flight mission commander for the entire operation. In space, she readily pointed out, what others saw as a minor disability was not a problem at all.

There was a coronal mass ejection, or CME, a fairly strong one at a G3 intensity that caused the atmosphere to expand for over a week. For whoever was tracking objects in orbit, it was their worst nightmare, because it meant a recalculation for every single object out there, right up to the massive space station and its orbital position. The teams at Kiribati, America, China, the European Space Agency, and Russia at least shared those calculations and doubled-checked each other's efforts. The International Space Station had to shift several hundred meters to avoid an impact with a long-defunct American weather satellite from the 1970s, and there was a cold-sweat moment when a fragment of a satellite, destroyed by the Chinese some years ago in an antiballistic missile test, had shifted in its orbit and passed less than a dozen meters from the wire, with a velocity relative to the wire of over five miles per second, which would have been a killing blow.

The Chinese offered some mild apologies while forging ahead with their own planned launch of a wire to be anchored in Indonesia.

As for the reaction to Franklin's announcement that the tower was not the real deal, but merely a means to loft up to the geosynch sufficient material to build the "real" tower, at first there was a massive outcry of fraud. The following day, stock in Pillar Inc. plummeted nearly 40 percent, but ironically there were not many sellers other than a few disgruntled individuals, and by the end of the first day of what some feared would be a panic—and Proxley predicted would spell the end of the venture—the stock started to climb back up again and stabilized by the end of the month.

Gary found it fascinating that Franklin, who, of course, owned 51 percent of the shares and therefore held the controlling interest, seemed nonplussed when on paper he had lost over $20 billion in a single day.

"Hey, it keeps capital gain taxes down for a while, and zero dividends for a long time to come as well" was his phlegmatic response.

The spinners did their job well. Diameter up to three hundred miles was well over a centimeter, and in the atmosphere over three centimeters. What had been a nearly invisible thread was now a clearly visible presence, though it was a bit unnerving to sit and watch it, to see it ever so slightly shift, and turn in response to the dynamics of forces exerted far above, often thousands of miles away.

On the ground, the maglev from the island of Tarawa down to Aranuka was progressing rapidly, a good 10 percent of the actual cost of all this so far, not counting the start-up of ribbon product and the launches. A second platform four miles to the east of Aranuka was now under way—the eventual anchor point for the "real" tower, as everyone now called it. The two-track maglev connecting to the airport and shipping terminal at Tarawa would at start-up be handling a thousand or more tons of equipment and hundreds of personnel a day; no one knew what it would do twenty years hence, but Franklin was building it with that exact purpose in mind, unlike the "first" pillar, which he had admitted was but temporary. Everything else being constructed had an air of permanence. His plans for the final "station" where cars would be loaded with supplies and passengers would board for their ascent to the heavens had the look of a massive Gothic cathedral resting on the northeast side of Aranuka with tracks then diverging out to the construction tower and the much-anticipated "ribbon pillar," as it was increasingly called. By the time the "cars" actually reached the location where the permanent tower would be based, they would have accelerated up to over three hundred miles an hour, giving impetus to their ascent before it even started.

Victoria's doctoral dissertation, the design of the "wagon spoke" system of power distribution that would "pipe" energy to anywhere in the Pacific basin, was presenting something of a political and ethical problem. A dissertation was supposed to be open for public scrutiny, but at the same time some things that Victoria was proposing were so revolutionary that Franklin, when queried about her work, simply said that she was a part-time employee taking time off for her graduate work and she was entitled to speculate however she wished as long as it was within the parameters of real science and not science fiction. He put emphasis on the term "science fiction" as if to dismiss his young intern's efforts, though Gary, Eva, and a select few knew he studied everything she wrote with keen interest, and it seemed as if new start-up companies were popping up out of nowhere and quietly applying for patents on some of the concepts she had mapped out. Victoria was winding up with some rather nice stock options in those companies.

Franklin had even provided a small grant to Purdue to set up electric vehicle charging stations on campus. No one called it a coincidence that one was in the parking lot next to Victoria's office on campus, causing more than a little jealousy over the fact that, though still a graduate student and the only grad student to own an electric car, she had a prime parking space only a few feet from the entryway to the electrical engineering building. Such small perks can fuel intense rivalries in graduate programs, especially when the wind chill was twenty below zero. It was obvious that Franklin, who had taken a liking to a gangly sixteen-year-old who had stood up to a U.S. senator, now saw her as the daughter he never had and was grooming her for crucial work ahead.

"The game is to feed folks often but only a little bit at time," Franklin said. "When Jack Kennedy first spoke about going to the moon in May 1961, our total flight time in space was under fifteen minutes with a suborbital by Alan Shepard. The goal of going to the moon by the end of the decade, when you thought about it back then, seemed damn near crazy, but then again just perhaps reachable.

"Suppose instead he had said, 'We are going to Mars by 1975'? More than a few advisers said the Russians were so far ahead that they would reach the moon well ahead of us and we should aim for Mars instead. But Mars? We could beat them to Mars by 1975. In fact, the technology to go to the moon is 90 percent of the way to go to Mars. It is not a question of distance, as you know, but of lofting power. Three *Saturn V* launches to low earth orbit could have then assembled a Mars vehicle and sent it on its way. But would the public have bought it?"

He was right, of course. Kennedy would have been mocked off the stage rather than cheered that day. And, of course, the tragedy was that we could have indeed gone to Mars in another five to ten years after Neil Armstrong and "Buzz" Aldrin first set foot on the moon, given the technology mastered by Apollo, but the dream of the mission and the goals had been lost by then.

"We take it one step at a time," Franklin counseled Gary. "Victoria's plan will work, the same way as when I first came across the papers you and Eva wrote while still graduate students; even before you completed your dissertations, I knew your idea for a tower would work. But let's not talk about it just yet."

And then a glitch finally occurred, this time a human one.

One of the four crew members aboard the geosynch station overseeing the spinning process and testing the first segments of ribbon, for lack of a better term, simply "freaked out." The team up there had signed on for a six-month tour of duty; a couple of Russian crew members aboard the old *Mir* and the International Space Station had stayed aloft far longer. At a billion dollars a launch for a replacement crew, it was sign on for the long term or someone else would, and there were volunteers aplenty. The long-term effects of zero gravity and cosmic ray and CME exposure in high orbit were a concern. The station did not have upgraded shielding, a major weight and therefore cost factor for the launch, therefore in the event of a major solar storm they would retreat to their reentry vehicle and place the heat shield between them and the sun until the storm abated.

The launches to start bringing up sections of ribbon, which they would "park" until enough was in place, had started. Short sections were taken out on EVAs to practice deployment, stitching, and laminating, since it was a whole new approach versus the single wire on a drum and then spinners building upon the first wire. As it was, there were now concerns about the effectiveness of spinning and getting the new cables to adhere to the existing ones. The potential problems of laminating and stapling ribbon sections thousands of miles long had to be clarified before tens of billions of dollars more would be spent on assembly and lowering down to the earth's surface.

The human crisis, however, put all of that planning on the back burner for the moment. Mission Control in Kiribati had been made aware of the situation on the ground regarding one of their crew member's family within an hour of the tragedy, and even while Franklin debated what to do and how to convey the information, the news was all over the Internet, which the crew had full access to and unfortunately not blocked in time so that the tragic news could be broken in a gentle civil manner. An astronaut's wife had been killed in an auto accident, hit by a drunk driver, and one of their five-month-old twins had been killed as well; the other was in critical condition. Singh finally had to sedate the crewman to stop him from popping a hatch to "space" himself, he was so overcome with grief.

If they used the capsule they rode up in to send him back, it would leave the other three truly stranded for at least three months until their replacement crew was scheduled to be lofted. Singh and the others offered the capsule for their comrade to return home in, more pragmatically to get him off the small station before he harmed himself or, by blowing a hatch, killed all of them. However, the capsule also served as a fallout shelter in the event of a major solar storm, its heat shield blocking out the potentially deadly levels of gamma rays produced by a CME. If the capsule was sent back down, all four crew members would have to return together, and work on the upper end of the Pillar would cease for at least three months.

There was only one alternative: the small descent pod used on the tower. Sent up by the last launch, it could house one person and was intended to be used to descend the tower to work on a jammed spinner and then return to geosynch, but if necessary it could go all the way back down to the earth's surface. It had a rocket pack on board to provide deceleration or lift and the first experimental transmission of energy via the super conductive wires woven into the tower. A friction braking system could actually take it all the way back to the earth's surface. At least that was the theory but it had to be tried out, for to do so would mean that the spinners, which were operating now at several different levels would have to be cleared. So it was still an untested concept.

Regardless, the following day, after being heavily sedated, the tragic young man who now held the attention of the entire world was bundled aboard the pod, a chamber little bigger than that of an old-fashioned telephone booth, and about the same size as what a *Gemini* astronaut once had. Audio and video transmission except directly to Kiribati control was cut off as he descended, and in one of those rare moments of global unity, there was understanding for one man's grief, though those in Mission Control had more than a few tense moments with Franklin and a team of psychiatrists talking him through it, convincing him to remain sedated and in the last twelve hours lying to him that his other son was pulling through just fine. They would break that ultimate tragedy once he was safely back on the ground, knowing with certainty that if given the truth that his other son had died as well he would indeed "space" himself. Franklin and so many throughout the world damned all drunk drivers who had destroyed three lives and the life of the young man returning from space as well, and a communications block had indeed been maintained. More than once after Franklin had linked to the young man, he kept the full reality concealed to encourage him to stick it through the last few hours; once off-line there was not a dry eye in the control room, and even Franklin broke down into tears.

Three spinners had to be blown clear of the tower to allow the pod to pass, at a cost of a hundred million each, but that did not matter at the moment, in the same way no one ever spoke of the cost involved in saving *Apollo 13*.

Once the pod landed on the platform, a medical team was waiting and the grieving man was flown home to face the terrible reality of a life and a dream shattered by one drunk, who—as always seemed to be the case—had walked away from the accident unharmed and now some claimed was a victim in all of this because the whole world hated him. Which was indeed deservedly true.

As for the program, there was a pause.

For the first time a human had actually used the tower, traveling its 23,000-mile length to return from deep space back to earth. But never would an account of his story be told out of respect for his privacy, which Franklin went to great lengths to assure and again something which the world respected.

The pod was detached from the wire, cleaned out, and restocked, and it was agreed that it should be returned back to geosynch. The equipment to do so was on hand, but no one had anticipated having to for at least another year or so. It would involve a launch package similar to the spinners', consisting of a jet engine, which would drop away once all the fuel was expended, and a pulse rocket. The carbon nanotubing that the pod clung to would serve as a guide wire but was nearly friction-free unless a braking clamp was applied during the descent. They had yet to test it all out on the ascent. The rocket to take it all the way out to the geosynch station simply did not exist, and instead a fair portion of the final ascent would be achieved by the clamp adhering to the tower, while energy which so far had only been tested on the conductive wires down the cable would power up the batteries that drove the electric lift motor.

The logic behind using the jet pack and rocket was to get it through the atmosphere and at least part of the way out of the gravity well of earth. The higher it climbed after that, the less electricity it would need as the struggle against gravity lessened with each mile gained above the center of the earth. At least, that is how they thought it would work.

Even as the design was being cooked up, Gary remembered a cartoon series popular when he was a kid that had inspired a yearly competition at Purdue, the Rube Goldberg Competition, involving some strange, overly sophisticated combination of machines to do some absurdly simple task, like fry an egg. The journey up would take over three days, and though the prospect seemed thrilling, most people expressed pity for whoever would ride aboard a pod not much bigger than a coffin. If it failed or jammed, there was no backup, no second "climber" already up there, and the air supply would run out after six days. If all else failed, the pod would be allowed to drop and hopefully brake, and the passenger would do an old-fashioned bailout at 50,000 feet when the pod was blown clear of the tower.

For this worse-case scenario, the betting was that the passenger stood maybe a one-in-ten chance of actually surviving if the pod had to do an emergency return. Zero chance if it became firmly stuck once out into deep space. With an emergency return, chances were they would lose control of the unit as it descended without any power and it would just burn up as it hit the upper atmosphere. Over the next day, as the pod was prepared to send back up, the macabre betting odds in the control room were fifty-fifty that Franklin would not send someone to round out the crew "upstairs." The workload had been designed for a team of four, with a rotation of watches, including a safety backup whenever there was an EVA. With only three up there, they would soon be worked to exhaustion, and when people were exhausted in space, that was when simple mistakes could turn into fatal mistakes. It was the balancing of one risk, sending someone up the Pillar, versus ratcheting up the workload for those up there and telling them they'd have to tough it out.

But even with the risk involved, all four members of the crew that was scheduled to go up as replacements in another three months clamored for the chance to "ride the pillar to heaven, and odds be damned."

More than a few media sources, now caught up in the enthusiasm for the tower even as they showed respect and sympathy for the tragic reason the pod had to be used in the first place, pointed out that fifty-fifty odds had been the going rate for Lindbergh, who did make it after several others had died trying, and for Amelia Earhart who did die trying, but it had not stopped aviation from moving forward . . . the same odds that years later were finally discussed openly regarding *Apollo 11*. More and more the media was shifting from criticism to support of the program.

At least the farther from earth, gravity would drop off, and there was even a new iPad system on board to provide communications and entertainment, a system jammed for the passenger on the way down who was told it had glitched off. Some called it a flying coffin; others pointed out that at least the passenger would have one hell of a view and adventure before checking out of this life and could give the world a first glimpse of what the future would hold when anyone "rode the pillar."

The question that consumed the media and Internet chats in the hours after the pod had reached earth with its heartbreaking passenger: Who would be the first one to ride it back up?

And then Gary, needing crutches, came into Franklin's small office on the platform.

Franklin pointed to a chair next to his desk. Gary, Eva, and Victoria were just about the only personnel on the island or platform who did not need an appointment days in advance; indeed, absorbed in their own work, rare was the time they would impose during work hours, although many an evening, in a ritual that Franklin insisted on, there would be a "happy hour" atop the observation deck (no alcohol, of course, since it was still banned on the island) to enjoy the slight cooling of the equatorial breeze, to gaze in contemplation at the Pillar, and to freely exchange ideas, some logical, some off-the-wall entirely. More than one major breakthrough had occurred during those happy hours, which any good manager knew was when at times the best work really occurred because people felt free to speak their minds.

The fact that Gary had timed his arrival for the half hour that he knew Franklin usually took off to just sit and meditate or, of all things, relax, playing a game of chess against the computer, was a tip-off that this was serious, and his friend suspected what was to come.

Gary nodded as he took the chair, laying his crutches to one side, shoulders slightly hunched over, another indicator of the advancing ravages of Parkinson's. Over the last few months Franklin could not help but note that Gary's face had begun to assume a mask-like appearance and that he stuttered more and more.

"I want to take the pod back up to geosynch," Gary announced without any preamble.

Franklin blew out noisily and sat back in his chair.

"Come on, Gary, you know we already have someone picked: one of the rotation crew. He's well trained and we need him up there for when we finally start unspinning the first reel of ribbon for deployment and to weld it together as each reel reaches the end of its load and the next one has to be hooked in."

"And remember, I wrote the concept and the plans for it years ago."

Franklin could not deny that.

"Have you talked to Eva and Victoria about this?" he fell back upon.

"Not yet, but I know they will understand."

"Oh, really. I think both of them will, as we used to say, freak out."

"Then let them. Victoria is well launched, thank God," and even in that rigid face there was a look of pride. "She defends her dissertation in another two and a half months, and we know that is a walk-in, and then her plans are to marry Jason the week after."

"Don't you want to be there for that?"

"Of course I do, but I can do so just as easily from up there. Besides if I'm actually present, I fear I'll get too emotional the way some fathers do, so it is a good excuse."

And as he spoke he looked past Franklin to the Pillar reflecting the mid-afternoon sun.

"Why, then?"

Gary actually laughed.

"If you could find a legitimate excuse, wouldn't you go, my friend?"

"In a heartbeat."

"Well, this is my heartbeat now. Come on, Franklin, we both know where this game is going with me. I can barely walk; to go more than a hundred yards, I need a wheelchair. That I can deal with. But of late, Franklin, I can feel that it is at last beginning to attack my mind."

He paused, and his eyes filled with tears of frustration.

"My mind, Franklin—my *mind*. Take my body away from me, and maybe I can deal with that, though for dear Eva I know it is torture to see it happen."

He smiled sadly, remembering what only seemed to be yesterday: their second summer together as graduate students on internships at Goddard, and what it was like to be twenty-two years old and in love. Was that only yesterday?

"Remember the movie *2001*, with HAL, when the astronaut began to turn his brain off and HAL begged him to stop, to please stop, that he could feel his mind slipping away?"

Franklin could only nod, gaze fixed on this man, who along with his wife and their departed mentor, Erich, had kindled this dream to reach for the stars.

"I am slipping, Franklin. Little things, but I know it is starting. Not enough yet to affect my work, but in six months, a year? When I know I have reached that point, you will have my resignation."

"Like hell."

"Come on, Franklin, you don't need me helping to head up a team that, if we make one mistake, this whole thing comes crashing down. Oh, sure, you'll name me 'emeritus' or something like that, but we both know what that means and, damn it, I am not even fifty yet. Not like Erich, who still had it with him well into his nineties, and it was only his heart and lungs that gave out first, not his mind. For me it is the reverse."

Franklin remained silent, and finally Gary continued.

"I am still putting the project first. We have three good personnel up there at geosynch; hell, Singh is worth two or three in herself. It is time that the person who helped design it all had a personal look. Just on the ascent stage I can pick up nuances others might not catch. Once up there, I can observe every step of what is going on, with the wrapping up of the spinning and the beginning of deployment of the ribbon. I have been living this dream for over twenty-five years and know every nuance inside and out. What better pair of eyes to have on it?"

Franklin could not argue with that point.

Gary sighed.

"In a year at most, I will have to be replaced, and thus, my dearest of friends, I am now asking for this final chance, which at the same time I know you will turn into a beautiful publicity coup to garner continued support, which is my goal as well."

"Gary, I could argue the exact opposite, then. My going up would prove the viability of the entire project."

Gary shook his head in sharp response.

"Oh, come on, buddy. You are the financial brains for this. A helluva lot of good you'd do 23,000 miles up while trying to con someone out of a few billion more or arguing with Fuchida about the cost of ribbon."

He hesitated.

"As for Eva, she's got a lot of healthy years ahead, and I think for this moment I would prefer her to still be close by Victoria and guide her."

Franklin gazed at him, eyes filled with concern.

"You speak as if you have no plans to come back."

Gary leaned back and laughed hoarsely.

"Of course I do. I'll return with the next crew transfer."

"Why not go up with them? Let the astronaut I've selected ride the pod and I'll consider giving you the empty chair in his launch capsule."

"You got a lift pod sitting there," Gary replied, pointing out the window. "What the world should have witnessed as a triumph—the first person to actually journey from geosynch to the earth's surface via the tower—was essentially a news blackout, and rightly so out of respect for what that poor man was enduring. I'm offering you a public relations coup now. 'Co-designer of the Tower Goes Aloft to Inspect and Help with Guiding the Beginning of Pillar Two.' And yeah, throw in that I have Parkinson's and long for zero gravity to free me of its infirmity. What the hell, we might even find that exposure to zero-g and solar radiation might actually have a palliative effect."

"Damn you," Franklin sighed.

"I am the perfect candidate to go up and you know it, Franklin. No need for training, I helped design the damn thing, though I must confess the whole toilet arrangement is rather crude. You'll have world press focused on it; I'll do the usual announcements and interviews, and throw in how eventually, besides everything else, I believe the real tower will be a destination for those in my situation or with other debilitating infirmities to free us from gravity and again float and play like a child. I'd rather like that, my friend . . ."

He hesitated.

". . . while I still have a mind that can enjoy it."

In tears, all Franklin could do was nod in agreement.

"Gary, you are one royal pain in the butt at this moment," he sighed, swiveling about in his chair to look out across the platform. "We had to drop three spinners to clear the way for the pod to come down. I'm not complaining about that—we always had that as a contingency plan anyhow—and that poor guy, no one can blame him for wigging out. I'm not blessed as you are to be a parent, but I think I do understand the anguish."

"I honestly think neither of us can fully grasp the intensity of his loss; even trying to grasp it brings me to tears," Gary said quietly. "Thank God we have not had to face it, but Eva and I sweat bullets every time Victoria goes off on some new flight escapade, or her recent trick of trying out base jumping in one of those damn squirrel suits. Even Jason was flipping out over that one."

Franklin looked back at him and chuckled.

"Didn't tell you this before, but I threatened to fire her from the company if she did that crazy stunt. She laughed—actually laughed—though most respectfully argued it gave her a better 'perspective' on certain things and more respect for her position with the company at such a young age. It was proving to others that she had the 'right stuff' to eventually help oversee operations in space."

Gary laughed softly.

"And, damn it, your public relations team was there to film the whole thing and ensure it went viral," he pointed out. "I damn near resigned that day myself in protest."

The two laughed once more, and it touched Gary's heart yet again, as it had on their first night together—flying to Seattle with his daughter up in the jump seat, peppering Franklin with questions—that this man loved Victoria as if she was his own daughter . . . and worried about her as much as Gary did.

"A brain like hers—the best of both of you—doing silly stunts like that. But then again, it does play well with the press.

"Then I read the final draft of her dissertation. To think that kid has worked out the model for energy transfer from geosynch to anywhere on earth . . . Once they stamp her paperwork at her dissertation defense, I'm giving her control of that division."

"What division?"

"Exactly that, my ultimate goal all along with the Pillar rates right up there with perpetual motion . . . and that is limitless energy. She's going to run it. Hell, from the first day I met her as a gangly high schooler, I knew she had a future that might be even more brilliant than that of her parents."

Gary could not help swelling with pride at this news. And then it struck him.

"And you are telling me this now to talk me out of what I am asking for."

"Ah, Gary, you are mastering the art of political persuasion. That has always been the problem where I felt I fit in. The minds of engineers like you, Eva—the team that once flourished at Goddard—always left me overawed, humbled. But, damn it, it was rare that one of you could translate what you were doing into the elegant beauty and wonder of it all and then fill the public's imagination with dreams. Think of the irony of it. Even as the public turned its back on Apollo, at the same time they were enthralled with the adventures Hollywood portrayed of our future in space.

"Eva is heading more in that direction with her increasing talk about sociological change, impact on the arts, and the way we perceive ourselves in relationship to the universe that awaits us. During the Apollo program, one of the mistakes they made was that they should have sent up Walter Cronkite himself with his 'Gee whiz, this is incredible' schoolboy enthusiasm, which was so infectious. Or a poet—I mean a real poet, like Frost, Sandburg, or my favorite, Bradbury—someone who could capture in words the wonder of it all."

"So is that an argument against my taking that pod back up?"

"One of them. Though I daresay Victoria will have that eloquence when her day comes to go up."

"I can do it. I'll never be as good as my daughter, but I'll open up the way I do in private, just as long as a camera is not sticking in my face. The guy you selected is a darn good space structural engineer"—Gary sighed—"and is about as exciting as watching paint peel from a wall."

"Oh, that is rather cruel," Franklin said, even as he laughed at the very apt description. "Come on, Gary, you are no poet; you dread even getting in front of a microphone in public. On the basis of that, if that was the criterion, I'd send up Eva rather than you."

"Eva is not dying; I am," Gary said coldly.

Franklin swiveled his chair around to Gary, who was sitting hunched over, embarrassed that an uncontrollable tremor was causing his right leg to shake.

"We are all dying, Gary," Franklin replied seriously.

"Well, the difference is, for most of us, it'll come as a surprise. As for me, I can feel the clock winding down within me. Franklin, I can come to terms with some of it. The fact is I can barely walk and a flight of stairs looks like Mount Everest now; I've noticed that decline just in the months since we climbed but three flights to touch our first strand."

Franklin said nothing. Though he had never discussed it with Gary, Franklin had made sure that every square foot of the platform was handicapped accessible, with Gary specifically in mind. And no longer did he even try to put on a show of climbing a flight of stairs, let alone join in the evening walks around the platform at sunset to enjoy the view in what had become semiformal staff meetings. He took the specially installed elevator up to join the group.

"It is my mind that is starting to scare me, Franklin," Gary said, his voice barely a whisper.

"I haven't noticed one iota of difference, Gary," Franklin said, leaning forward, staring him straight in the eyes. "And that, my friend, is the God's honest truth, so help me."

"But I have. Little things: not remembering a name, or where the hell I put my ID badge. Stuff like that."

"Oh, come on, we all deal with that, even me,"

Gary shook his head.

"No, it's starting to worm its way in and I can feel it. I lie awake at night, Eva snuggled up close by my side, and I make believe I am asleep, because ever since we found out about this, my wife has this thing about not falling asleep until I do, fearful that I might need something and not tell her."

Franklin smiled sadly, nodding. His wife was gone fifteen years now, and to cover over his grief, he had thrown himself into the start of this project. It had become such a routine that his life was indeed a monastic one. Just the way Gary spoke of Eva asleep by his side hit him deeply, and he lowered his head for a moment, remembering . . .

"In the last few months I'll lie there quietly, breathing softly so as not to disturb her, but wide-awake, playing mind games with myself. Dr. Bock, God bless him, told me that the best weapon in this stage of the fight is mental exercise."

Gary smiled.

"He is a remarkably gifted man, Bock. Joked that if ever there was a career ahead for mental exercise, it was mine, and to keep at it. So I'll lay awake and play mental games. From simple formulas clear up to trying to re-create in my mind the pages of calculations Eva and I handed old Erich the end of our first summer together working for him."

He looked past Franklin to the tower, bathed in the morning sunlight. Without a spinner in operation there was very little activity out on the deck, many of the work crew taking advantage of the hiatus to grab a day off, back on a beach at Aranuka or hop the shuttle back to Tarawa for a change of scenery. For some reason, perhaps because of its once storied and bitter legacy of long ago, there was now a club there that put on swing dances, playing music from the 1940s. Gary felt that drifting music just might somehow float along the coral rock and sands to where his lost uncle and his marine comrades, whose remains had never been found, still rested in hallowed memory, and that their spirits just might smile. It had become a favorite haunt for Victoria and Jason, and Gary and Eva, on their rare days off together.

"I can no longer work some of those formulas in my head, Franklin," Gary said, his voice flat, not looking for pity, just making a simple statement of fact. "Time was I could snap them off in a heartbeat; give me a diameter of wire, its molecular structure, OK, maybe a pocket calculator for a few of the tougher calculations, and I could tell you what you wanted. Now?"

He shrugged.

"What level chess do you play to unwind?" he asked.

"On the computer? Level six was all I could ever beat more than half the time"—Franklin smiled—"unless I cheated a bit and took back a few moves to play over."

"I could play a game in less than ten minutes at level eight," Gary said. "Give me an hour and I could break even at level nine."

"And now?"

"Nowhere near it, and don't ask me what level," Gary replied. His voice, as with those who fought Parkinson's, had taken on a strained, trembling tone, his right hand shaking slightly. Of late he had taken to hooking his thumb through a belt loop to hide the trembling.

"Franklin, we've been at it for how long? Seven years, isn't it?"

Franklin nodded.

"Have I ever asked you for anything?"

Franklin smiled and just sighed.

"I am asking for this. While there is still time. Let me see it. Let me ride that throne, as some now call it, to the heavens. It won't be a joyride. I'll talk every damn foot of the way up and your public relations people can pull out the best sound bytes. You can play the angle, make it public at last that I have Parkinson's, and in space I can again be free of a body that has to struggle just to walk across a room."

He chuckled.

"Hell, you'll market that alone into another few billion for the development of medical facilities once the ribbon pillar is in place. Get Bock down here to help sell that idea while I'm on my ride to the heavens."

"You really are conning me with that argument," Franklin said.

"That from one of the best cons of all when it comes to raising money for mad schemes. I take that as a compliment."

Franklin could not help but chuckle softly, his deep baritone voice filling the room. And then Gary pressed on.

"And what we are preparing for up there? The positioning of the ribbon canisters, tests stapling them together, prepping for deployment of the real tower while we finish beefing up the construction tower . . . Is there anyone on this planet, other than my wife, who understands the dynamics better than me?"

He paused.

"At least for a few more months, maybe a year at most, I'll understand it," he whispered, "and then it shall be a gradual slipping into the night. My friend, let me do this before my mind goes into the night, and I shall be content then."

Gary fell silent, not moving, Franklin's tears streaming down his face as he gazed at his friend. At last he nodded in agreement.

15

He had not slept a wink. Part of the reason was a rushing thrill, mind racing, for the moment at least focused as to what this day would bring. And then there was Eva, who wanted to soak up every moment possible with him. Several times during the night they would talk, remember, laugh, go to the window to stare at the floodlit tower, sip tea, since coffee no longer agreed with him, then return to bed, and a few times there were tears.

There was no need for the alarm that beeped at 3:30 and then softly played a piece by Gary's favorite composer, Constance Demby. He had discovered her work while in graduate school. Her album *Novus Magnificat: Through the Stargate*—which combined the spiritual, even Gregorian chants, with what some called "space music"—was a stunning synthesis, and spoke to him of the mystical beauty of reaching for the heavens. He had made sure all her works were loaded on his iPad; the music would most certainly fit the experience to come. Back at their home in Seattle he still had the original CDs and even a rare vinyl recording, the cover jacket signed by her when they had met at a public conference on the tower years back, and Gary had asked her to one day take a trip up, an offer which she enthusiastically embraced.

Eva helped him dress; he was embarrassed that he could barely tie his own shoelaces now. Though hungry, he had been advised to avoid eating breakfast in case of vertigo; the food packed for him would be rather bland, with no fiber—tasteless stuff—and loaded in as well were the array of medications he had come to live with, enough to carry him through six months if need be.

In the kitchen Gary found that sometime during the night Eva had taped together some soda straws with a little handmade card placed beside them. “Remember that day with Erich and the straws? Have a grand time, my love, and kiss the stars for me.”

There was a tap on the door, and Eva opened it. It was Victoria, with Jason standing politely to one side out in the corridor. Gary was filled with emotion at the sight of her. Like any parent, he found it hard to see the lovely young lady she had grown into: in his mind she was still the skinny, slightly gawky, acned sixteen-year-old who was so filled with promise and so obviously loved her father. Then his heart took him to imagining his four-year-old who would smother him with “smoochies,” then insist that they give flying lessons to her collection of “my little ponies.” Too swiftly, all too swiftly that had passed, and yet with each day there were still new adventures, and he felt such pride in what she was and what she was becoming.

She tried to say something but then just broke into tears and threw her arms around him.

He laughed softly. “Hey, you two, I’ll be back safe and sound in four months at most. Come on, now, if anything, you two should be cussing at me out of jealousy that I get to go up first!”

Victoria nodded as she leaned against his shoulder.

“Promise, Daddy?”

“Sweetie, remember what I always used to tell you: Don’t be afraid of anything unless you see me afraid. We designed this thing and I get to ride it at last. Afraid? Hell! It’s going to be darn near the best time of my life!”

He paused and looked at the two women.

“Except for the day your mother finally admitted after a year of coaxing that she was in love with me.” He smiled at Eva. “Come on, you knew it the first time you laid eyes on me!”

Eva exchanged a glance that spoke of a lifetime of love and smiled back. “Oh, but of course,” she said in Ukrainian.

Then he looked to his daughter.

“And the other best day was the first time I held you.”

That got both of them crying and he extended his arms to embrace them.

There was another polite tap on the open door of their small apartment on the platform. It was one of the crew members from Mission Control: Gretchen, who had gained such fame for guiding the descent system for the first wire and was now heading up the division overseeing the pod he was about to ride in. Franklin, with his genius, was seeking out so many people Victoria and Gretchen's age to form his team, and through them reaching out to the world with a new youthful vision of the future of space exploration. It was no longer a realm of straightlaced males with pencil-thin neckties and pocket protectors. One of the best of the spinner operators sported a tattoo of the Pillar on his forearm. Gretchen had at least abandoned her purple hair dye for today as she stood smiling but obviously moved by what she was seeing.

"Dr. Morgan. Time to get you suited up; you have a flight to catch."

Wife and daughter flanking him, they took the elevator down to the ground level and into the Mission Control room, which to his surprise was packed. As they entered the room, all were on their feet, applauding. He was never one for speeches or any form of public speaking and now felt a bit embarrassed, glad he was not suffering any tremors as he braced his shoulders back and walked through the room, not using crutches, but with Eva and Victoria on either side to support him if need be. This inner team knew his condition, that if he stopped and tried to shake everyone's hand it might be difficult, and more than a few had tears in their eyes, not of fear but of joy, as he carefully walked past them. Now, in a small ready room, he was delighted to see Dr. Bock, bleary-eyed from what must have been a grueling flight from the States.

"Damn it, Gary, I think I just set a record for the farthest a doctor ever traveled for a house call," Bock said.

Gary gladly took his hand, but Bock was instantly all business, grasping his hand for a second but then squeezing it, asking if Gary could feel the pressure, then seconds later listening to his heart and rattling off questions, with Gary lying in response to more than a few.

"I know if I said I was grounding you, you'd all tell me to go to hell," Bock said, and then there was a genuine smile. "Godspeed, Gary Morgan, my prayers go with you."

Gone were the days of heavy pressure suits; he would be in shirtsleeves throughout. For one thing, staying locked up in a suit for nearly four days would be decidedly unpleasant, and secondly, a cold, pragmatic decision was that if the pod was "spaced," there was precious little that could be done to get him safely out. The now hundreds of passengers going up each month aboard the various commercial suborbital flights did so in jump suits similar to what Dr. Bock and a couple of Mission Control personnel helped him get into, and he was delighted to see his name embroidered over the left pocket, the logo of Pillar Inc., a Gothic tower rising to the heavens with the disk of the sun creasing the top, the curvature of a blue-green earth at the bottom, a diamond like stitching representing the tower bisecting the middle of the patch. Bock did insist that a blood pressure cuff, a heart monitor, and an oxygenation meter be hooked up, and made noises that if anything started to go offline, they would abort the ascent and bring him back down—to which he replied that he would pull the wires off and use a manual override if they tried, whispering it so that Eva and Victoria, standing out in the corridor, did not hear the exchange.

Bock looked at him with his compassionate, but piercing, intelligent gaze.

"I think you're crazy," he whispered back, "and I'm tempted even now to put a stop to this."

"And if you do, I'm firing you as my physician," Gary replied, "and it really would put our friendship in serious jeopardy."

Bock continued to look him straight in the eyes and then grinned slightly.

"You crazy bastard, I envy you."

"You'll get your ride up soon enough, Doc. Hell, you'll get a publication in the *Journal of the American Medicine Association* about the effects of microgravity on Parkinson's; might open up a whole new field of medicine, my going up."

Bock, falling out of the role as Gary's physician, could only nod and, grasping his shoulder, squeezed it tight.

"Don't do anything stupid. You got a wife, a daughter, and I suspect someday grandkids to come back to and plenty of good years left, my friend."

Gary simply smiled.

"Nothing stupid. So, all of you, stop acting so glum," and now he spoke loudly enough for his family to hear: "I'm getting the ride of a lifetime—of my dreams—today!"

As he settled into the pod and waited for the techs to seal it shut, he looked around. It actually seemed a bit more spacious once inside. The unit could rotate on its axis which was already clamped to the tower. It was at this moment in the horizontal position; strapped beneath it was the rocket pack, and beneath that the first stage of a jet engine. The couch he was resting on was really quite comfortable, and as he settled back he could feel the high-tech foam shifting to fit the contours of his body. To his right, there were several portholes and two more overhead that would offer splendid views; to his left, sealed storage bins containing food, water, his medications. A checklist of what was stored and where was attached to the bulkhead at eye level. He had gone through a briefing on the toilet facilities when taken to the pod the afternoon before for a rundown on how it all worked. A bit embarrassing, and he hoped that the designers knew what they were doing. Strange but how "that was done" in space seemed to be a question everyone wanted to ask. Once into low gravity, there was enough room that he could actually move about a bit, at least turn.

Settled in, Gary's four-point harness secured, the tech crew stepped back. He had made Eva and Victoria promise no emotional scenes, just a quick kiss, a few words, then they would step back as well, since it was going out on the news feeds and if anything he was fearful that the emotion might trigger tremors or affect his voice.

Victoria finally managed to grin as she leaned into the open hatchway to kiss him.

"Proud of you, Daddy, and frankly jealous. Now, come back to me."

"You'll get your chance up there soon enough, sweetheart."

Eva then leaned in and simply whispered in Ukrainian, "Be safe, my love, and God be with you. We are soul mates and I will love you forever."

And then one more person stepped forward. It was Franklin. He was, of course, on camera and knew it—he had an instinct for that—but there was no acting now.

"Like Bock told you, don't do anything stupid while you're up there. And by the way, you forgot this."

He pulled out of his pocket two sets of astronaut's wings. The first one, the back engraved with "678" on it, was from his flight long ago on the Brit's suborbital plane. Franklin pinned it to his collar and then pinned on a second, with the numeral "1" etched in gold.

"For this flight," Franklin said, holding it up for a moment so the news feeds could focus in on it, "for the first man to ride the Pillar to the Sky," and then he pinned it next to the first. He grasped Gary's hand and then said something that caught him off guard.

"See you at sundown, Gary."

It was from an old favorite movie they both loved, starring Spencer Tracy, about adventure on the colonial frontier of so long ago. It was Franklin who sealed the hatch, Gary settling back into the couch, breathing deeply, a bit nervous now and trying not to hyperventilate. His legs were trembling and he was tempted to pull the monitoring wires off right now, but he knew Bock would pitch a fit and perhaps even stop the ascent until he was rewired. Clipping on his headset, he listened in as Mission Control ran through the checklist; it was all so automated now in contrast to the long-ago days of the Shuttle and Apollo. The monitor screen above his head was within arm's reach, a touch screen showing the rundown of the checklist.

"Ascent Pod Morgan, Tower Control. You are number one on the runway and cleared for takeoff."

Gary smiled at that, the compliment of naming it after him and his family, but making it sound to the public like the standard chatter of an airplane departure. They had even changed the name from Mission Control, which sounded very space flight and rockets, to Tower Control, as if they were indeed almost an airport.

"Tower Control, Ascent Pod. Ready when you are."

There was no countdown—again, the stuff of another technology. Franklin knew that a fair part of the world might be looking in on this moment or check the podcast later, and in his perpetual sell job to keep this project alive, he wanted it to look routine.

He felt the vibration as the jet pack beneath him fired up, idled, a check run by Tower Control flashing across the screen, and then throttled up. It had the thrust of an engine for an F-22. Slow at first, a glimpse out the window of a crowd on the roof of the observatory and the Mission Control—now Tower Control—building looking up, waving. He raised a hand to wave back; chances were Franklin had a telephoto camera aimed at the window. He could feel the vertical acceleration picking up, feeling like a helicopter rising at first but then more like being in the Brit's suborbital ship, pressing him down into the couch, the screen above registering ascent at 1.5 g's.

A moment of a few deep breaths, some lateral movement, the tower itself flexing from the passage of the pod, wavering back and forth. He knew they were well within structural limits; what the hell, he was half the team that designed it.

The pod punched through 10,000 feet, still accelerating, a brief flash of dark gray tropical clouds, then through them. His ascent had been timed so that he would punch through to sunrise at 20,000 feet, cameras mounted on the vehicle catching the view.

"How we doing, Gary?"

It was Bock, on the private comm channel, and Gary just laughed.

"Wow! This is one helluva ride!" he cried.

He heard laughter on the open channel; someone had switched that through as a live feed after a few seconds' delay in case any comments slipped out that were deemed inappropriate for the world audience. He knew he had to start doing his job.

"It's fantastic . . . I can see dawn has already lit up some high cirrus clouds above me . . . The tower above, it is glowing red with the dawn . . ."

As they gained altitude, the air thinning out, the jet pack throttled up to full thrust, pressing him down into the couch. A bit more wobble and lateral movement from the tower. *Don't comment on that,* he thought. It was a bit disconcerting; he knew his heart rate must be going up.

And then through the starboard window he saw the sun breaking the horizon.

"My God," he cried, "there's the sunrise! This is beautiful, so beautiful. Smooth ride." He was lying on that point, there was definitely a lot of flexing going on with the tower as it swayed from the stress load of the pod racing up its side. He thought of the first man who rode across the two towers of the Brooklyn Bridge in a small boatswain's chair on the first strand of wire that had been strung across that technological wonder of the nineteenth century. The rush he was feeling now must have been the same.

He glanced at the monitor screen. Jet fuel was burning off quickly: five hundred pounds left. Once that was burned and dropped off, the stress on the tower would be reduced. He shot through another thin layer of cirrus clouds at 30,000 feet, still accelerating, staying below supersonic to avoid the shock wave that they definitely did not want slamming against the tower, speed holding steady at Mach 0.9 now. Which was still going up vertically at nearly seven hundred miles an hour, nearly a mile higher every five seconds. Six miles down behind him now, still about 23,000 to go.

Forty thousand feet little more than ten seconds later, 50,000 nine seconds after that. He was actually laughing. It was incredible. He flashed on memories of so many years ago, summer nights with Eva after they were engaged, at night, back at Goddard, going up to the observatory, lying together on the cool grass, watching as the observatory fired calibrating laser beams to various satellites, cheering and applauding as the beams flashed into the heavens, then they snuggled in closer and shared a kiss, looking up at the stars and talking about their dreams.

And now he was living the dream.

"Five seconds to jet pack shutdown."

It was nothing dramatic, not like the old days of solid booster separations or the first stage dropping away from a rocket launch. A shudder, an actual sensation of something falling away, acceleration easing a bit, the g level dropping down to 0.5 with the deceleration, a bit of a light feeling in the stomach.

"How we doing, Gary?" Again it was Bock, and Gary just laughed.

"Fire the rocket up. Let's get going!"

He knew Franklin and the publicity department were now loving every second of this. Some years back, hundreds of millions had watched on their televisions, computers, and iPads as a man slowly rode a balloon nearly twenty-five miles up then jumped out. Franklin had guessed they just might get a billion watching this, and his estimate would turn out to be rather close to the mark.

He got what he asked for a few seconds later, even as Tower Control announced the clear breakaway of the jet pack, a side thruster pushing it away from the tower and deployment of a drogue chute to guide it back for a splashdown near the platform.

The rocket pack hit like a kick in the butt. Throttled up, and seconds later he was at two g's and 60,000 feet up, when the climb really started. A mile every four seconds. At 75,000 feet they broke sonic, the stress load against the side of the tower low enough as to not be of much concern.

And then he saw it!

Turning his head sideways, he saw the curvature of the earth, the blue band of the lower atmosphere above an ever-darkening sky in spite of the distant sunrise to the east, rays of dawning light splashing across a turquoise and indigo blue sea. While straight overhead the sky became ever darker.

"Stars," he gasped. "My God, I can see stars!"

And now the rocket pack was at full throttle. The thread of the tower, but a few centimeters wide here, was but a blur in the overhead window. One hundred and fifty thousand feet above was a vast ocean of darkness, except for the stars, and the sunlight reflecting off the tower, which sparkled like an arrow of diamonds pointing straight up.

He struggled to keep up a running account of it all, and felt a sudden longing for Eva to be at his side. In Ukrainian, which he had somehow learned in their years together, he knew her rich, descriptive language would have found the right adjectives, adverbs, and superlatives to describe the absolute wonder of this transcending moment.

"Eva, Victoria, I love you both. I wish you were here with me to share this. My soul would be complete."

"We're with you, sweetheart," Eva replied, voice choked. "I can see it on the cameras—we all can," and she lapsed into Ukrainian to express her wonder and joy for the adventure her beloved husband had embarked upon.

Two hundred and fifty thousand feet. Less than a minute later 300,000 and still climbing.

"Ascent Pod Morgan, Tower Control, Franklin here." Gary smiled. "You just got another set of astronaut's wings. You've crossed the hundred-kilometer mark, my friend: you are in space."

"No need to tell me!" Gary cried. "Eva, I'm swiveling a camera so you can see what I can see out my right-side window." He fumbled with the touch pad. The g load was still up there at 1.7 but he got the view focused in, angling down, a view across the vast Pacific and what might be Fiji, bathed in light, hundreds of miles away.

"How we feeling, Gary?"

It was the ever-hovering Bock on the private channel.

"Doc, I'm doing great." It was a lie: the trembling in his legs from the Parkinson's was hitting him hard. Before departure he had refused to take any sedative or relaxants other than a mild shot for motion sickness, but the hell with that, there was no way they could turn him around now unless he started screaming for help and told them to slam on the brakes.

"OK, Gary," was all Bock said.

"Believe me Doc, you're gonna love this when your chance comes."

And then he hit the line that would be the headlines around the world that day.

". . . We must preserve our beautiful world for all those who come after us. That is why we are building this Pillar to Heaven."

"I can see it on the camera," Eva replied, and her voice was choked. "It is beyond what I ever dreamed."

"We, all of us, did this together . . . and thank you, Franklin—all of the team—for this moment."

"Rocket pack fuel depletion in thirty seconds," Tower Control announced.

Gary regretted that news, they were pulling just over two g's again and he absolutely loved the sensation. He knew what was coming next, and it was his first real worry about this ascent.

He was soaring up the face of the tower at over 2,000 miles an hour, the maximum they dared to try; the lateral stress load on the tower of his passage at this speed was near maximum, given the diameter of the Pillar at this altitude.

It was not the way the design would one day work: with maglev cars riding up and down the sides of the ribbon tower at a slow and steady speed. They needed a "fast and dirty" system for right now until they had the ribbon tower in place where cars would ascend at a stately five hundred miles per hour for the two-day journey to geosynch, with room for a couple of dozen passengers—room to stand up and stretch—along with hot food, tea, even a selection of drinks, and definitely an adequate bathroom arrangement. It was like comparing Lindbergh's *Spirit of St. Louis* to a routine transatlantic flight on a 747.

Regardless, he was grinning like a kid, because he was the first to take this ride, and to hell with the risks.

"Ascent Pod Morgan, Tower Control. Rocket pack shutdown then separation in fifteen seconds. Be ready for a little jolt."

Actually there was no real jolt. He felt a slight shudder and then a most disturbing sensation in his stomach as the rocket pack winked off, the final few pounds of fuel firing from a lateral thruster that pushed the rocket pack clear of the tower.

"Ascent Pod Morgan, Tower Control. Clean breakaway of the rocket thruster. How are you doing?"

With the cutting off of the rocket pack, his vertical velocity, in little more than a second, dropped from two g's to a momentary zero g. He was not, as most assumed, now weightless because he was in space; it was a simple reality of vertical thrust one second, cutting off the next second. In a jet plane, even a prop-driven plane climbing straight up, if power was cut, the pilot and passengers on board might suddenly feel, for some the disturbing sensation, for others the exhiliration, of just floating "weightlessly."

The guide tube wrapped around the wire was nearly friction-free, the gravity of the earth the only counterforce to his upward acceleration. With each passing second it exerted an influence to slow him down. He easily soared up past the orbital height of the old Mercury and Gemini space flights, of the likes of John Glenn and Gordon Cooper. Unbelievable to him that he was now zooming past their altitudes, still soaring straight up, on inertia only; but as he looked up at his monitor screen, he could see that the numbers of his vertical ascent were no longer a near blur as gravity slowed his ascent. He still felt weightless. A touch of nausea from it, but not dangerous. He could even sense his heart rate settling, and then the most wondrous sensation of all: he was floating, and imagined that if, rather than being stuck in a pod, he had a vast open field before him, he could soar across it like a hawk or eagle, no longer confined by trembling legs and pounding heart.

"I feel all so free, like an eagle soaring on wings," he whispered.

His speed continued to drop. The blur of the tower above was becoming a visible line, the wire with the dozen or more cables wrapped around it since the first strand was anchored now coming into focus. A bit troubling now: he clicked to a private channel, reporting that in some places it looked as if the spun cables added on were not adhering well, but then again it could be an optical illusion; it warranted closer scrutiny. The adhesive to bond the carbon nanotubes together in the vacuum of space had been a serious question, and he wondered how much support each strand was lending to the others. This, too, would have to be looked into.

Speed was down to below subsonic if he was still inside earth's atmosphere, but that was an absurd definition out here in the near total vacuum of more than 250 miles up.

"How's the view, Gary?" It was Franklin, prompting him.

He looked out his starboard window.

"My God, is that Australia I'm looking at now? I definitely can clearly see Australia, still night there. Guess those are the lights of Melbourne and Sydney.

"Hey, will they blink them for me the way they did for John Glenn?"

That had been a wonderful gesture when Glenn passed over the continent, the citizens having been coached by a television station to flick their house lights on and off at the same time in a gesture of "Good luck and Godspeed" he could clearly see in space.

"I'll throw in the request, but no promises."

Speed continued to bleed off; he was coasting now. When the descent/ascent pod was first being designed, there was a lot of debate about how to power it, the consensus leaning at first to using an electrical lift motor right from the ground up. But there were concerns about condensation on the wire from the tropical air getting into the wheels and motor and then, in the vacuum of space, freezing and perhaps shorting the unit out, and the amount of energy needed to throttle it up to even a stately three hundred miles an hour, which would take the pod to geosynch in just under four days. Some thought the combination of the jet pack and the hybrid rocket motor from the Brit's space plane was overplaying it, but it was a sure way of getting the unit well above the atmosphere quickly, and frankly it did have a certain public appeal to it, with a dramatic sendoff. Eventually, with the ribbon tower, it would be the maglev that would be friction-free, but it would also require a tremendous amount of electrical power for the track, and that was still years off.

All things considered, Gary was delighted with this design: rather than just being several miles up and slowly accelerating, the traction wheels struggling to build up speed, he was now at an altitude beyond that of the space station. He could feel the vibration of the wheels spinning up to nearly 5,000 revolutions per minute, so that when engaged their rotational speed at the edge would match up exactly with the speed at which the wire was racing past them. Too fast or too slow could cause an overstress that might rip the wheels and gearing apart, or perhaps even damage the tower itself.

"Pod One Morgan, Tower Control. Activation of electrical lift in ten seconds."

Gary took a deep breath on hearing this announcement. The energy for the rest of his climb would transfer from the Pillar to the three small wheels, made of conductive tubing as well that would take in the power from the tower, feed it into lightweight batteries to keep them charged up which in turn then powered the traction motor that would then drive the wheels. Slow compared to the ride of but minutes before, but still sufficient to get him to geosynch in three and a half days' time.

"Pod One, Tower Control. Engaging traction wheels in five seconds."

He watched the monitor screen and held his breath. It had worked on the first test spinner to lay out the conductive cables when a thread of the material had been spun from geosynch clear down to earth. It had worked for the spinners. Would it work now? If not, the battery packs on board could get him most of the way there, but not the full distance. They had a second, backup laser beam transferring energy from the geosynch station down to the pod, but that would be one hell of a trick, given how lateral movements as the pod moved up the tower could throw aim off. Even Gary had expressed concern about a laser of such intensity actually hitting the tower.

"Engage."

There was a shudder, a slight lurch, and for the first few seconds the battery packs spun up the traction wheels before pressing them in tightly against the wire. They held, and then, as Gary watched his monitor, he saw that indeed they were getting electricity off the tower itself, but not quite enough to match the energy output. A momentary pause while the gauge on the screen fluctuated slightly, measuring energy coming in via the wire, energy output, then calculating whether there would be enough to reach geosynch. And then the gauge went green. At the present rate he would indeed make it!

It was working!

"Mission Control"—he forgot himself for a second—"Ascent Pod One. We have good contact, good energy. We are on our way to geosynch!"

Again he could hear the cheers.

"Godspeed, Gary Morgan," someone said, again harkening back to the glory days and the words spoken to John Glenn as he lifted off. Gary looked off to the west, where he actually thought he could see that the good people of Sydney were indeed flicking their lights on and off in support of his climb to the stars above.

16

Docking

A hard shudder jarred the pod, more than a little disconcerting.

He was trembling slightly from the Parkinson's, but also the temperature control in the pod had gone a bit offline and it was getting damn cold—a strange balance, actually, with the pod on one side at hundreds of degrees below zero on its outer skin, while on the side facing the sun it was several hundred degrees hot.

He felt the latches snapping loose and nervously took a deep breath. This was the first time this had ever been tried, and then the hatch slid open and a dark, bright, smiling facing looked down at him and grinned.

"Dr. Morgan, I presume!"

That almost did make him laugh. A well-thought-out line indeed, especially for the video feeds, and although his hand was trembling, he reached up.

"Commander Singh, I presume!"

She reached down, taking his hand, and then leaned into the pod and helped unsnap his harness. He was a bit embarrassed: the Parkinson's was causing some uncontrollable trembling of his legs. Singh effortlessly backed out of the pod, holding his hand to guide him, telling him to just take it easy, float free, and she'd guide him up through the airlock. He let her take control, and she did so with casual ease, used to the months of weightlessness, as they floated straight on "up" into the main chamber of the station.

He entered it headfirst, disoriented for a moment, confused as to what was up, down, or sideways. During the three-day climb he was the first human to experience something absolutely unique: the slow dropping away of the effect of earth's gravity. It was not the sudden mind- and inner-ear-blowing experience of sitting on a launch pad at one gravity, then two minutes later being slammed back into your seat at anywhere from two to five g's, then at engine burnout on achieving orbit feeling the false sensation of zero g, which was actually an illusion created by literally "falling" around the curvature of the earth.

At five hundred miles up he wondered if he was noticing the difference because at that altitude the force exerted by the gravity of the earth was one-tenth less than on the surface of his home world. The effect of the earth's gravity actually did radiate out to near infinity, as it did with all bodies, but the farther he climbed from the center of the earth, it did lessen. At the same time the angular momentum of the tower gradually started to increase the effect of falling around the curvature of the earth, even while remaining stationary directly above the islands of Kiribati. At 2,000 miles up it actually was noticeably different, and the sensation was delightful.

Of course, the effect of earth's gravity extended far past geosynch, otherwise how else would the moon remain in orbit and not instead just go flying off? For that matter the moon's gravity did have an impact on the surface of the earth, or else there would be no tides to speak of except from that of the sun. It came down to the whole complex formula of mass of the object in inverse proportion to its distance. The moon's gravitation influence was something they had to factor into the tower design as well. The moon was but a minute fraction of the mass of the sun, but it was almost five hundred times closer.

So as he continued up the tower, the rotation of the earth, imparted to the tower, was giving him more and more angular motion relative to the surface, thus imparting the dynamics of being in orbit, while distance itself lessened the actual "feel" of gravity.

To keep his mind occupied while not listening to his favorite music by Constance Demby, Debussy, and from his early youth some Emerson, Lake & Palmer, he tried to run through the mental calculations and formulas regarding the "force" of gravity at any particular height, the incredibly complex formulas he and Eva had struggled through when it came to the stress, tension, and compression loads on the tower at any given point. To his dismay, he found at times he had to shut his thoughts down, turn up the volume on the music, and just stare out the window and try not to think about what he was losing more and more with each passing day. But at least, in these few blessed days, how much more he had gained. The first human to actually ride a tower to the stars! What would Alexander, Caesar, da Vinci, and Newton have given for these precious moments? He had laughed at that thought, the legend of Newton playing around with apples, perhaps trying to drop one in the confines of the pod and then rattling off a calculation.

Now free of the pod, jackknifing up to follow Singh's lead, turning about as he did so, his inner ear started to send out a major distress signal to his stomach; but seeing that one of the crew was holding a handycam unit, filming his entry, he forced a smile and an exclamation of delight. Once clear of the hatch, the other crew member went down the hatch and into the pod to start off-loading Gary's gear, and a shout of delight echoed up that someone had thought to pack some southern barbecue sandwiches, New York–style pizzas, and some "damn strange curry dish," the woman holding the camera shouting that the sandwiches were hers and then calling out thanks to whoever it was on the ground who had thought to order from Phil's Bar-B-Que Pit from her hometown in North Carolina. Franklin had made sure that the favorites of all three were on board the pod. It had been found long ago that food could become a major obsession for those on long-term missions into space . . .

Singh did a half somersault and steadied herself at what appeared to be "right-side up" beside Gary.

"Tower Control, *Station One*. As you can see, we have Dr. Gary Morgan, one of the original designers of this project, safely aboard. And our thanks for the treats sent along. We'll have a regular feast tonight."

The mention of the food did not help Gary. He forced a weak grin for the camera, Singh giving him a sidelong glance.

"We're signing off for now," she said a bit hurriedly. "It's been a long journey up for the good doctor. We have to get back to work stowing the pod and hooking on a new spinner, but will be back online later. Tower Control, *Station One* off the air."

The young woman behind the camera nodded and shut it off, and a second later Singh was forcing a sickness bag into Gary's trembling hands and in an almost motherly fashion holding him while what little was in his stomach let go.

"Don't be embarrassed," she said soothingly. "You've been cooped up for three days in that pod. Your inner ear goes crazy when you are suddenly in an open room out of it; there's no feeling of gravity to orient you when you are floating around like this."

She took the bag from him, sealing it and stuffing it into a convenient disposal bin.

He gasped out a thanks.

"Afraid I was about to vomit in front of the entire world," he said.

The girl behind the camera laughed.

"I did, but fortunately our friends on the ground have a five-second delay loop on all broadcasts, so they cut that part out. But they played it back up to me for laughs as part of some fake broadcast."

Gary, on Singh's advice, took a few deep breaths and settled into what was an actual chair with a small table in front of it, and she floated into the chair on the other side.

"Let me get you oriented, sir. It'll help you settle down."

"Miss Singh, it's 'Gary,' please."

She smiled and extended her hand again.

"All right, then, Gary, Selena here, and our friend behind the camera is Jenna Philips, a good southern girl who has been complaining for weeks about a craving for a barbecue sandwich from some joint in her hometown. Kevin Malady is the gentleman cleaning out the pod at the moment and preparing it for undocking and stowage. We call him Conan; you'll see why once he comes back up."

As Kevin stuck his head back through the hatch and floated some of the provisions off to Jenna, Gary looked at him with open admiration. He was the astronaut who had kept his head and saved Singh's life. When this work crew was detailed to go, it was a given that Singh would lead it, and she had insisted that though Kevin was outside the rotation schedule, to hell with schedules: if he did not go, she didn't go. Some had whispered that there was "something going on" between the two, but that was not the case at all. Singh, all professionalism, had remained aloof from emotional attachments; it was just that she knew Kevin was not just a darn good medic, he was without a doubt the best mechanical engineer in the lineup for this project.

"Stomach OK?" Singh asked gently.

"For the moment I think so."

She reached into a pocket on her coverall sleeve, took out a small pill container, and handed it to him.

"Ginger root. Take two"—she paused—"as long as that's OK with your other medications."

He nodded as he swallowed the pills.

"Just keep your eyes focused on me and imagine that we are sitting down at a kitchen table: down is toward your feet and up is over your head. The station is designed to create that illusion, and it works."

He did as suggested and found that it actually did work, recalling that the old space station was designed that way, with an illusion of up and down, and it was considered very bad etiquette and even an indicator that someone was getting a bit "spacey" if they started floating about in opposition to everyone else. The human brain was wired to seek out points of spatial orientation and even read facial expressions "right-side up." If someone floats upside down or sideways in relation to you, the nuances of expression become mixed and even disquieting if the person who is "spacey" remains that way for too long. There were old stories about life aboard the now long-gone Soviet space station *Mir,* where one of the cosmonauts had insisted that his version of right-side up was the rule and the others on the crew came close to sedating and tying him up. He was finally rotated back down to earth.

"I have to ask this first, sir"—she smiled—"I mean Gary. I'm cross-trained as the medical tech for the crew and will have to give you a full check over as soon as possible. Any major symptoms troubling you? And, Gary, you don't have to give me any bull for answers: you can't be grounded now."

She smiled.

"Dr. Bock said he figured you were lying through your teeth to him, so I'm to get the straight line on how you are feeling."

He nodded and sighed, and then was a bit surprised that the simple gesture of nodding, in the weightless environment, actually caused his entire body to start to move back and forth and up from his "seat" so that he had to grab hold of the table with trembling hands to steady himself.

He ran down the list: the usual tremors, some cramping, which he attributed more than anything else to the confinement in the pod for three and a half days, a bit of dizziness, which Singh assured him was just his adjusting to the open space of their station . . . She extended a warm hand to check his pulse; took out a pocket flashlight and shined it in his eyes, causing him to wince, and asked him to track the light as she moved it back and forth; took an oxygenation meter and pressure cuff out, clipped the meter to a fingertip, the cuff to his lower forearm, and after a moment smiled.

"Ninety-eight percent pulse of 77, blood pressure 125 over 73. That's good, darn good. I'll do the rest later after you've had time to get oriented and relaxed.

"Now, without you moving around, let me give you a bit of a tour of our palace in the sky," Jenna laughed, a comment floating up from the pod from Kevin that was not as polite.

"This was lofted up as an empty third stage instead of being a cargo unit. It's twenty-two feet in diameter and forty-four feet long. It's divided down its length by a partition, giving us two floors. You'll notice we have our living quarters all oriented down toward the floor, which we just call the 'ground floor.' Kitchen area here, bathroom, and even a rather ingenious shower stall which you'll get a kick out of twenty feet farther aft. Kevin will teach you how to use all of that."

"He sure as hell needs one," Kevin called up from below. "Man, this pod stinks!"

"Ignore him," Jenna whispered, floating down to "sit" next to Selena. "Best mechanical tech head on this crew but a bit short on breeding."

"I heard that!"

The two women laughed.

"New York versus North Carolina between these two," Selena said with a fake sigh. "I thought you Americans had settled your sectional differences 150 years ago.

"Anyhow. Your bunk and private area is over there." She pointed to the far end of the station. "We'll get your gear moved in there. You'll find that sleeping might come hard the first day or so: you'll jolt awake feeling like you are falling, but believe me, after a few days you'll sleep like a baby. Exercise area is across from your bunk. I'll run you through the routine. Two hours a day mandatory, and believe me, the computer will monitor that, and if you are one minute off, Bock will raise hell with both you and me. That was one of the conditions for you being up here."

Now there was a bit of a command authority in her voice, and he nodded in reply, this time holding on to the edge of the table.

"We prefer to share our meals together, around this table. We rotate cooking duties; it's all microwave and simple enough. As to other duties, our command and communications center is over there on the other side of the docking port you came through. I'll run you through the ropes on that, even though I know you designed some of it. We operate on Kiribati rather than Zulu time: it coordinates better with the folks on the ground. You have two duty shifts of three hours each a day. Mainly we are monitoring the spinners deployed from up here, though all of us are on duty when a supply ship is docking and we off-load supplies. The three of us are EVA qualified; you'll be trained as our backup. Usually only two of us are out when we are hooking on a new spinner, though you and Jenna will be suited up as well.

"Upper deck is all our life support systems, storage, and supplies. Primary docking port for the supply runs is upstairs. The lower docking port you just came through was designed for the pod and also direct access to the Pillar, which we are hooked to. Our ascent and return vehicle is docked topside as well as aft. If we get a solar storm or CME alert, you are to don your EVA suit and do so fast; we retreat to our craft and sit it out.

"So far, as you know, we've only had one brief alert and had to hole up for six hours, but if we get an alert you move fast, sir. And the same stands true for a hull puncture. If it hits the upper level, we seal the hatch, don EVA, pump the air out here, then go up to see what can be done."

She paused for a moment.

"If it hits this lower chamber, you are to head for the upper level."

Again a pause.

"If the rest of us do not make it, you are to seal the hatch, don the reserve EVA suit there, get in the escape vehicle, and wait for orders from the ground."

Another pause, voice firm, definitely that of someone in command.

"And, sir, if you do not make it to the hatch in time, I must tell you: whoever does make it up there is under orders to seal the hatch. I am telling you that straight out now and know that you understand what I mean."

"The survival of at least one of us comes first," he said softly.

"Exactly."

"I understand."

"I hold the record for survival while depressurizing." She paused, actually smiling, looking over and nodding at Kevin, who didn't even return the gesture, just continued with his work. "They tell you to exhale sharply, if you try to hold the air in, you rupture your lungs. I did as trained and then there was just nothing, a strange drifting-away sensation because the pressure cuff above my knee did not get a firm lock and the rest of my suit started to drain out until Kevin slapped that emergency patch on and my suit repressurized. If we face an emergency depressurization we'll try to pull you through but if worst comes to worst and instead you are the only one to make it to the upper level you seal the hatch, get into the command module, and await orders from down below. Do you understand me, sir?"

He could only nod.

"Actually, if I had to choose a way to go," she whispered, "that would be it."

She was silent again for a moment.

"Thought I should let you know."

"Understood."

She relaxed and smiled again.

Kevin had returned from Gary's ascent pod, grinning and holding up a vacuum-packed cooler, "Compliments of Phil's Bar-B-Que Pit" stenciled on the side of it. Jenna, with a shout of delight, left the table and floated over to grab it.

Gary could see why they called him Conan: Kevin was a rare combination of sheer physical brawn combined with a sharp mathematical mind and icy nerves. From the looks of him, Gary guessed that every spare minute of the day, when the rest of the crew was not on the exercise machine, Kevin was pounding away on it. He had let his black hair grow long. The left side of his face was scarred by third-degree burns from the crash landing of a suborbital flight for a competitor of the Brit's. He was something of a legend in the fledgling suborbital business. He had started off as a mechanic but quickly showed he knew the operation of the craft better than some of those who flew it; went through flight school; rated as a pilot, and when an engine fire caused an abort, he guided the ship in and managed to get all the passengers out, then spent a month in a burn unit.

Looking at him again, Gary decided that this was one no-nonsense man who looked almost like a throwback to the "high steel" construction workers of a century earlier.

"Now, how are you feeling, sir?"

"'Gary,' remember?"

She relaxed.

"Sure, Gary. Honestly, how do you feel?"

He slowly turned his head left and right, looked up and down, the others watching him, perhaps a bit nervous. This was, after all, the legendary co-designer of the Pillar. They had been fully briefed on his physical condition and, unknown to Gary, had been given the option of vetoing his joining the crew; the vote, anonymous, had been two to one in favor. All were now seasoned veterans aboard the station, and prior to that had experience in the suborbital business—and all had experienced the extreme displeasure of someone getting sick in zero gravity. A few never acclimated and were useless for any work for days, even weeks in space. Gary forced a smile of reassurance. Though the air was, of course, artificially pumped and constantly recycled, the atmosphere did have a slight gamey scent to it after months of continuous occupation.

"I wouldn't mind checking out the view," he finally said.

"Just go about cautiously at first. You'll get the hang of it all in a few days. Kevin, why don't you lend him a hand; I got to get back to my duties."

Kevin pushed off from the table, extending a rough hand, which Gary took while Jenna started working on stowing the food and other supplies that had been jammed into the pod, since it was still months out until the next resupply launch. Meanwhile Singh floated over to her station at the control center, settled into a chair, and buckled herself in.

"Glad to have you aboard, Doc," Kevin said.

"Hey, it's 'Gary.'"

"Nah, you're 'Doc' to me. You're the wizard who designed this dang thing we're working on. Believe me, I know mechanical design even though I didn't get the degrees you did, and I gotta say, you did one helluva job."

There was actual admiration in the man's voice, and Gary could not help but smile. Huge, tough exterior but inside, the soul of a dreamer of space like he was.

"Now check this out!" and Kevin guided him to a circular porthole, eighteen inches in diameter, set nearly in the "floor" of the station. Kevin guided Gary's grasp to a recessed handhold.

He could not help but gasp in wonder.

He was now one of the privileged few out of all humanity: a total of nine Apollo crews who had ventured to the moon and back, and the teams across the last year who had lofted up here to guide the first wire deployment and now occupied this station. Only they across all of history had been granted the vision to see the full disk of the earth below, luminescent; the wondrous blue-green of the vast Pacific; but also the western half of South America, the east coast of Asia, all of Australia, and what must be the east coast of India cloaked in clouds. There was no sense of motion, as those flying in low earth orbit knew, with the landscape but a few hundred miles below rapidly drifting by. Instead it felt as if they were just hovering, which in fact they were, almost like angels looking down from celestial heights.

They were not traveling in the fast orbit of the lower reaches of space, where one actually did sense motion over an ever-changing landscape below; they were firmly locked in place, 23,000 miles directly above the platform, a mile south of Aranuka. He had half expected to actually be able to see that, but of course not from this altitude. Even the "wire" itself quickly disappeared from view in its long descent, adding to the sensation of hovering like guardian angels over their home world.

But as he watched, there was indeed now a sense of movement as the demarcation line of sunset and sunrise half a hemisphere wide shifted along at nearly a thousand miles an hour at the equator.

It actually was disorienting for a moment, even with the awareness that they were stationary above one spot, and that it was the earth rotating that was causing the demarcation lines of sunrise and sunset to shift below them.

A strange, wondrous feeling, and he felt such a swelling of pride and joy.

"Commander Singh"—he laughed—"I mean Selena, can I patch in a call to my wife and daughter?"

She looked back from her station, smiled, spoke a few words into her headset, unbuckled herself from her seat, and brought an iPad over. A few seconds of static and then there was Eva looking at him, grinning, eyes tearing up.

"Thank God you are safe!" she cried in Ukrainian.

"Safe and sound. You got Victoria with you?"

"Getting her now," and as Eva spoke she was walking out on to the deck of the platform and actually looked a bit foolish as she gazed straight up as if she could actually see him, and then back at the iPad's camera.

"I can't believe you are really up there!"

"Believe it!"

"Hey, Daddy!"

Victoria now crowded into view beside Eva.

"Hi, angel."

"How you doing up there?"

"You two have to see this," he cried, and switched the camera view on the iPad, pointing it out the window, Kevin quietly leaning in to help steady it, since Gary's hands were trembling. Kevin made eye contact with him, gesturing that he'd hold the unit for him. It was a simple but so compassionate gesture. Gary talked excitedly for several minutes about the view, exclaiming with delight that he thought he could actually see Honolulu lighting up for the night.

His two girls let him ramble on until finally he realized he was hogging the conversation and then tried to sound casual as he asked, "So how are things down there today?"

It was a delight to hear both of them laugh. He knew they were worried sick about his ascent and relieved at last that he was safely aboard and in safe hands.

"Just green with envy, Daddy!" Victoria cried with delight.

"Won't be long before you two are up here as well, and then after you millions more will eventually follow. Eva, you're right: just this view, it changes everything. Everything about how we see our world, ourselves, our futures"—his voice choked a bit—"our daughter's future. I can't wait for you to see it, to paint it, for my favorite composer to come up here and write her music while seeing what I am seeing. Maybe words cannot do it, but music by someone like Constance Demby can explain it all, though if old Ray Bradbury was still alive I bet he could almost reach it."

He fell silent, afraid emotion would completely overtake him if he continued.

His two "girls" were silent as well, gazing at him, smiling with joy for him.

He looked over at Singh.

"This is a secured channel, right?" he asked.

She nodded.

"Private channel," she said.

He looked back at the iPad, switching the camera view back to focus on him.

"And don't worry, I'm feeling just fine. Tell that busybody Dr. Bock I think we are onto something when it comes to therapy and treatment in this environment—for a lot of things."

He let go of the handhold and then did something reckless, pushing up, tucking his legs in, and actually somersaulting, laughing at first but then seconds later wishing he had not as Singh hurried over to steady him, Kevin reaching up to guide him back to the view port. But it had the effect he wanted down there: both Eva and Victoria were laughing with delight.

He forced a smile, willing himself to focus back on the earth, doing as Singh had advised, thinking above him was up and he was just looking down while the fluid in his inner ear continued to slosh around.

"I'm going to sign off for now," he said. "Got to stow my gear and see what zero-g sleep is like. I just want the two of you to know how much I love you; Victoria, how proud I am of you. Don't worry, up here I am actually free to again move around as I darn well please. And oh, yeah, tell Franklin thanks for what he spent on this: best damn investment in the history of humanity."

"I know that."

It was Franklin. Eva shifted the camera on her iPad to one side and his friend was standing there, grinning at him.

"God bless you, Franklin. I look forward to the day you see from up here what you created."

Franklin's dark features were creased with a wide grin.

"What you and Eva convinced me could be real," he replied. "Now go get some rest. The ever-hovering Dr. Bock is just out of range of this camera and ready to start swearing at you for pulling off your monitoring wires once you got a thousand miles up and we knew the lift pod would take you all the way."

"You're damn right I'm upset with him," Gary could hear off camera. "Tell Singh I want a full physical report 1800 hours our time here."

Gary laughed.

"I'll think about it," and then he reached over and touched the iPad to turn the camera off.

"Thanks, Kevin."

"Sure, Doc. Now, two things. See those smudge marks on the window?"

"Yes,"

"That's from our noses pressed to it. There are times we actually argue about who gets the window, so we have a schedule for that. If the window is free, it's yours, but if it's on someone's schedule . . . well, then it's mine!"

Gary could not help but laugh with understanding.

"Technically it's my scheduled time right now, but what the hell. You take it and enjoy it. We'll get your bunk made up, I'll show ya how the shower and head work, and between us two guys you do need a shower. Physical for you at 1800 hours, dinner at 1900. I'm the cook for tonight and I just might share a slice or two of Luigi's Pizza from New York, if you think your stomach can handle it."

"Damn straight."

"Don't push it too much at the start," Singh called from her post back at the monitoring station. "And, Kevin, you're on EVA standby at 2100 along with Jenna, so you know the rules: no eating for six hours before EVA. We'll have dinner after the next spinner is hooked up and on its way down."

"Ah, damn it."

"All right, then, a midnight snack."

Gary could hear Jenna cussing in the background that her beloved Phil's Bar-B-Que, imported all the way from Black Mountain, North Carolina, was going to have to wait as well.

"Doc, you just hang here for a while, enjoy the best view in the universe," Kevin said. "The orbital mechanics are awesome with this. The only time we are in total darkness is for a few minutes when our rotation carries us around so that the earth below eclipses the sun. My God, it is incredible: everything below is dark, but the entire band of the atmosphere from pole to pole is glowing. Or just as wild when the moon behind us eclipses the sun, but down below, the earth is illuminated. That is why there are so many nose smears on the window."

Kevin laughed.

"When the earth eclipses the sun, we draw cards for who gets the longest look-see. You have a small nine-inch port in your private bunk but that kinda looks just straight out. But still, you get to see the stars and, depending on the time of day, the sun or moon, but it's not the same as looking straight down."

He paused.

"You feel a need for the head right now?" Kevin asked.

He did actually but shook his head. His stomach was settling down, and it did make him feel like a little kid in need of someone to show him how to use the various sanitary devices on board.

"Sure, Doc," and he clapped him on the shoulder with his big, beefy hand. "Couple of days from now when you get a feel for the place we'll show you a couple of games."

"Games?"

"Tag, for one," and he looked back at Singh with a bit of a sly grin.

"I heard that, and the rules are tag only the other person's head."

Kevin chuckled.

"Heck, locked up here for a tour of duty, it does get to you," he whispered in a guy-to-guy voice.

"We do some gymnastics. Jenna is the wiz on that: she can do an octuple somersault within the length of the ship. I prefer just doing the Superman routine of flying back and forth. Once your inner ear settles down, we'll teach you the ropes."

Though it sounded appealing, he said nothing, keeping his focus on the earth below and trying not to think about attempting even one more somersault at the moment.

"I'll come back and fetch you, Doc, when we're ready to take you around for the rest of the stuff."

Kevin left his side, giving him a gentle slap on the back and another "Glad to have ya aboard, sir."

It was so reassuring. He had worried about how these three professionals would greet what they might see as an intrusion looking over their shoulders rather than a fully trained replacement crew member even if everyone had quietly agreed that the man who had been "bumped" was a well-trained genius but had the personality of a dead wet fish. It was obvious that so far they were enjoying the fact that one of the designers of the "world" they now lived and worked in was sharing it with them.

He hoped that in the months to come he could prove his worth.

That wish would come true sooner than he thought.

17

The "Perfect Storm"

In the two and a half months after Gary's epic ascent, which had indeed captured the imagination of the world in the same way the Mars *Curiosity* mission and the advent of the suborbital launch business had triggered a renewed interest in space, much had changed 23,000 miles below.

Proxley had barely survived a primary challenge from a very pro-space advocate and the message to him was clear. Senator Dennison had become chair of the Senate committee that had oversight on the NASA budget and she was making it abundantly clear what her vision was for America's future: that vision was a revitalized space program and, while fiscal responsibility and budget cuts would be the order of the day, it was time NASA was placed back on the front burner of public support as a path to a better future. And the public support was growing.

The Chinese had attempted their first launch of a wire to geosynch, and though on a professional level all with Franklin's team wished them well, there was some tension until the announcement that the unit had failed to deploy. Franklin had actually been magnanimous and without the slightest sarcasm offered to advise and consult for free, stating that the world could eventually use a dozen towers and he held no monopoly on the concept. So far the Chinese had politely refused his offer.

But there were problems as well. Professor Garlin's increasingly strident attacks on the disruptive technology of the tower were gaining notice. Her latest book had reached best-seller status and she was a guest speaker at an EU conference about the future of space policy, calling for a moratorium on the entire project until its full impacts—not just on space navigation but on the actual global economy—could be "studied and evaluated."

Such a study, she and other opponents knew, would drag out for years, as such things tend to do, until the project just died as investors drifted away and public opinion shifted. It was an age-old tactic and usually it worked. But in defiance of a UN vote for just such a study, the nation of Kiribati stood firm in its support, and short of an actual invasion or coup that overthrew a democratically elected government, how could anyone stop them? Franklin's wisdom of going to an independent nation which would be the first to be overwhelmed by global warming was now abundantly clear. A nation of little more than a hundred thousand citizens was telling the rest of the world what it could go do with their so-called injunctions and studies and reports and just continued to forge ahead with the dream.

Gary thought it highly ironic that the university that had trained and launched his career also harbored someone who was now hell-bent on stopping it. At least his daughter was ready to go for her dissertation defense, and interestingly it was even drawing some national media coverage, with Franklin broadly hinting that once Victoria had her Ph.D. in hand, she was taking over as head of the subsidiary of the Pillar Inc. conglomerate dedicated to developing and distributing limitless electricity from space. There was even a flurry of news when another company, obviously with the intent of sidetracking her work, offered her ten times what Franklin was rumored to be paying her. She laughingly turned it down.

The truly disturbing aspect was the realization, in that perpetual hot zone of global politics, the Middle East, as to what a successful ribbon tower, capable of sending nearly limitless energy back to earth, could do to the economy of nations pumping out what was left of a diminishing oil supply at ever-higher prices was now becoming clear. Oil was nearing two hundred a barrel as the nearly eight billion inhabitants of the planet scrambled for what was left, even in the face of the most optimistic projections of oil still to be found in substrata shale. Whether it was twenty years or a hundred, calculated on present demand, that demand would continue to rise almost regardless of price. Granted, oil output was nearly the same as in peak years, but it was the cost per barrel to extract from ever-greater depths that was driving prices ever higher. The long-ago days of "gushers" in the Texas plains shooting geysers of oil hundreds of feet into the air with every other drilling were now just a dream of generations past. Now half a billion or more might be spent on a deep-sea rig to explore, perhaps tap into a few million barrels and then go dry, not even recouping the investment.

Beyond that, with each passing year—as China, India, and other former "third world" countries leapt forward to achieve the living standard of what had been once called "first world" countries—not just the demand for energy but with it the dark after-effect of CO_2 output spiraling ever upward was increasingly converting even the most die-hard critics of global warming that, be it a generation from now, or a hundred years hence, the world would be in deep trouble.

And with all these issues it was inevitable that the region of the world still seen as the primary supplier of oil, the Middle East, saw the handwriting on the wall: that their decades-long run of economic exploitation, and the political power that came with oil, was now threatened and dark rumors circulated as to the steps that might be taken.

Someone had leaked Victoria's dissertation, which she would soon have to defend before her graduate committee. A sudden, revolutionary undercutting of that energy system, as proposed in Victoria's dissertation, would trigger an economic dislocation unknown in modern history, far exceeding that of workers in nineteenth-century England and northern Europe.

Out of the vast industrial transition of the nineteenth and twentieth centuries, in spite of some of the darker moments of societal transition there had emerged a better life for future generations. The downside that Garlin and others dwelled on with their Cassandra-like warnings, and at times outright scare tactics, were the tragedies that had come as well and now the ever-present threat of another global war in the twenty-first century as humanity scrambled for ever dwindling resources. It was the eternal struggle between the belief in progress on one side, and the fear of the change it will create on the other side.

As Victoria prepared for her dissertation defense, Garlin argued most persuasively that overnight there could be economic dislocation of billions, from those working in auto plants still turning out gasoline- and diesel-fueled vehicles and across the entire economy absolute disruption of a system built up over the last hundred years based on oil. The "disruption" theory was gaining strong supporters that paid lip service to agreement that the global climate had to be addressed but to do so in a slower, more carefully thought-out pace . . . again the standard tactic of delay until interest and investments waned and then disappeared.

In the academic world that Victoria still inhabited, more than a few had turned against her, and there was even pressure on her graduate committee, tasked with reviewing and expected to approve her dissertation, to instead veto it and deny her the advanced degree she had studied for. There were daily protests in the commons area of the campus, organized by graduate students of Garlin's, to have Victoria's work dismissed, and her dismissed as well from the university.

To try and calm the controversy, the president of the university suggested a dialogue between the two sides, which filled the entire auditorium, one of the largest of any campus in the country. It only added fuel to the fire that a twenty-three-year-old graduate student was about to stand up to an esteemed professor as she had once stood up to a senator.

Garlin cut deep to the millions dependent for their livelihoods on existing and so-called "proven" technologies.

And yet, in the next breath she maintained that of course she was for a green planet and the reversal of global warming from the use of fossil fuels. But was the answer truly to be found in space rather than on earth, where green solutions could be found that would not disrupt the global economy? Were there not viable alternatives to putting the fate of the world into the hands of a Franklin Smith, who would make the economic impact of men such as Carnegie, Vanderbilt, the Rockefellers, and the Rothschilds seem insignificant by comparison?

Once in place, what was to prevent Franklin and company putting a stranglehold on the global economy, enriching themselves by trillions of dollars while billions of workers would see their livelihoods vanish?

By the end of the "discussion," Garlin, with two generations of experience over her young rival, had gained something of an upper hand, though Victoria's poise, eloquence, and solid scientific arguments—even if they fell on some deaf ears—essentially ensured that her graduate committee would not succumb to any kind of pressure when in a few weeks she went before them.

The two views of the future were on a collision course, but then again, throughout most of history, that had always been the case.

Thus, even while the arguments were fought out at a university in Indiana, there were increasing warnings coming to Franklin via friends in

Washington that covetous eyes and even dangerous gazes were shifting toward the Pillar.

Gary followed the news on the daily uplinks or was informed by Eva of the latest gossip, while Franklin briefed him every day on what was happening and sought his advice as he always did.

His initial childlike enthusiasm of the first few weeks on board the station had never fully settled down. Though of course he was deeply concerned for his daughter, especially when told by Franklin on a private encoded link that Victoria for the time being had an armed security detail.

In contrast he felt totally free of all constraints. He was free from daily meetings, seemingly endless debates, and he was free as well from the confines of wheelchair and crutches, and for a while he argued with himself over whether the palliative effect was psychosomatic or real. He actually felt better and his mind had regained a certain acuity that it had been losing of late. He had enjoyed the "zero-gravity" dances—all proper, of course, since he was a married man—and beamed down to Eva endless thoughts about the prospects of art, ballet, and even sports when they would one day construct a sphere several hundred meters across for such activities. His musings on a game of zero-gravity soccer or a sport he dubbed "falcon flying"—in which competitors would don small wings for propulsion, have a streamer tied to one of their feet, then swoop and dive as they attempted to take the streamers from their opponents until only one was left—had triggered an entire issue of *Sports Illustrated* titled "Sports of the 21st Century."

He had settled into the routine of life aboard the station, gaining favor with his crewmates by taking on the daily tasks of cooking dinner, thereby freeing each of them up for an additional hour. He had trained with the EVA suit but had not been let outside, other than to briefly poke his head out of the airlock while Kevin labored to properly secure a spinner and send it on its way downward.

They had gone to the new upgrade of spinners now that the tower was strengthening, and his own ascent had proven its overall capability. Spools twice as big as before were being sent up, and although there was concern about the adhesiveness of the primary cable, it was hoped that subsequent layers would tamp the first threads into place. Another conductivity layer was added in as the first "wire" was buried under subsequent layers and an additional spool was sent up to reinforce the counterweight out to 40,000 miles.

He had helped monitor the docking of the supply ship, the off-loading of the rolls of thread and the first rolls of the new ribbon with which they were to beginning to test deployment, stapling, and lamination.

And then the first warning came in. The solar cycle, quiet at the moment, had nevertheless put out enough storms and CMEs to affect the upper atmosphere, one of them of such intensity that the crew had to spend nearly a day in the tight confines of the descent capsule, heat shield pointed straight at the sun to block out the dangerous gamma rays. It had, as a result, shifted orbits of thousands of items, from satellites to bolt-size debris in the lower and even middle zone thousands of miles up, and after a couple of days of tracking and computing it looked as if two strikes on the tower would occur within the month: one by a fist-size piece of debris, but then, chillingly, another by a long-defunct Soviet surveillance satellite of several tons, expected to hit the tower dead-on.

The fist-size chunk was a remnant of a booster stage that had lofted a satellite to geosynch. It had been on a long, slow retrograde spiral down for years, and only in the last month had it finally shown up on the complex tracking computers as a threat, its trajectory calculated for impact, followed only hours later by the catastrophic threat of the surveillance sat.

It was thirteen days off, plenty of time for debate uplinked and downlinked over the secured lines.

The fist-size chunk of metal, if off even by a few centimeters, would pass harmlessly by, and it was admitted that calculations down to a few centimeters would not be accurate until minutes before impact. But the large Soviet-era satellite? That was all but a guaranteed hit. Thus Franklin, with the concurrence of Gary and Eva, decided they were going to have to go for a harmonic wave by shifting the base and at the same time using the positioning thruster on *Station One*. The concept had haunted Gary's nightmares for over two decades, always the memory of "Galloping Gertie," the bridge over the Tacoma Narrows. And he thanked God he was up here, at least able to play an active part, even though he could feel that, regardless of the joyful rejuvenation of being in microgravity, Parkinson's was still working its ravages.

The planning session the night before the potential impact was an intense meeting of the four on board the station, and he wondered for a moment if Singh trusted his judgment after all as he reviewed the plan that he, Eva, and a hundred techs had hatched on the ground. Six hours before the impact of the first object, the station would start to set up a wave that would vibrate down the tower like the vibration on a string plucked on a violin. They needed only shift by several meters to save the wire from a nearly five-mile-per-second impact by an object weighing several kilos, which, when one did the math, was a lot of kinetic energy—something that a ribbon could easily endure, but a single strand? Final calculations had yet to be run on its trajectory, but the probability of a hit by "the fist," as it was being called, was going up.

The big one was six hours later. Hours before that, the base platform itself would shift back and forth laterally, timing each shift to match the upward pulse and then magnify that pulse as it raced back down the wire, until they were shifting the entire tower nearly thirty meters away from where the satellite would pass, thus avoiding collision. They then set up a counter pulse to dampen out the harmonic wave.

The reassuring argument was that if Galloping Gertie had had modern technology and computing power as backup, the destructive wave could have been dampened down in a few minutes and the structure preserved intact.

Easy to say; now it was time to prove it.

The plan for the station was that all would don for EVA; there was the threat that the harmonic wave would tear the entire unit clear of the tower with possible hull puncture. Spinners were dropped to clear the path down the entire length. The manned ascent and descent pod was loaded with emergency repair equipment if part of the tower was damaged.

Then it was hang on and wait.

Franklin did make this crisis public. It was impossible not to when the Russians announced that it would be their satellite that would apparently strike the tower, offering many apologies and then a shrug that there was nothing to do about it; then shortly after that they claimed that the satellite was still functional and, if damaged by the tower, they would hold Franklin's firm liable for damage, which, of course, would run into the billions. Given that the tower was the realm of primarily American investors, they really had nothing to lose and much to gain by just sitting back, though the close-knit community of space scientists, who often transcend the foolishness of nationalism, privately communicated that there was not an ounce of thruster fuel left on that long-abandoned satellite. Their own calculations showed that the game of orbital pinball between a strand of filament now a couple of centimeters wide and 23,000 miles long, versus 20,000 objects whizzing around the earth, had finally come up as a hit.

The fact that a smaller object was supposed to strike several hours earlier up near geosynch had triggered more than a few bloggers and media casters to call this the first real test of the tower and the "perfect storm" scenario. At least, down on the surface, the tropical weather was calm, though winds aloft for the day at 20,000 feet were predicted at nearly one hundred miles per hour. Nothing major, but still, an additional factor.

At upper impact zero minus thirty-one minutes, Singh was ordered to fire up the lateral thrusters for thirty seconds, and Gary could feel the disconcerting nudge as the tower they were attached to actually did shift. And like the crack of a whip, the bowing-out of the tower started to race down its length. With far more distance to travel, the shifting of the tower at ground level was initiated six hours and fifty minutes before potential impact, the massive support frame anchoring the tower in place shifting to the south by the entire width of the platform off of Aranuka, then rapidly shifting back via the tracks embedded on the ocean floor.

Gary—and for that matter everyone around the world who was watching—could sense the tension; nothing like this had occurred since the days of shuttle launches, when all held their breath as Mission Control told the ascending vehicle "You are go at throttle up," the last words spoken to *Challenger* before it disintegrated.

There was really nothing dramatic to watch after the platform had shifted back and forth three times, sending up three "bows" in case the calculations of the satellite passage were off by even a few seconds—still hard to calculate, given the fluctuations in the earth's atmosphere even as the solar storm sent out a final short burst of intensity.

"We are ten seconds from potential upper impact," Singh announced, and Gary could actually feel the tower shifting back and forth and then heard Singh exhale with relief.

"Whoever did this calculation is a jerk!" she snapped, whipping off her headset and turning off the open comm link. "Our radar is showing at least a hundred-meter miss without even having to shift!"

The "whip" that was coming up from below now buffeted them, traveled on up to the top of the ever-extending outer counterweight, made up of expended launch vehicles and empty spinner reels, then came racing back down, jarring them again.

Nightmare images of Galloping Gertie flooded Gary's mind as he strapped himself in beside Singh, watching the monitors, and for the moment his mind did feel clear, even though his legs were trembling uncontrollably.

"I think we got it," he muttered, "but we should deploy the pod out on to the tower, manned and ready to go instantly."

"For what?" Singh asked.

"We've got one of four scenarios. The second object misses and in space one inch off is as good as a thousand miles. Second, it hits and does not cut us in half, but there is damage. We need a repair unit on the spot and the only way to really do that is with an EVA. We can drop down a hell of a lot faster than sending a unit up via the cable.

"The strike point is calculated at 10,200 miles, give or take a few miles, which makes me doubt their calculation anyhow."

She nodded in agreement.

"Scenario three," he continued, "it cuts the cable, and then we are all screwed anyhow, though supposedly anything above 12,700 miles will remain in orbit, while everything below that will collapse."

"Nightmare," Singh whispered.

"Or fourth, my big fear, we've triggered a harmonic wave. It's going to take split-second timing to dampen that out along 23,000 miles. Someone should be down near the halfway point to measure the exact intensity of the wave and feed information both up and down. The small thrusters aboard the pod can even help dampen it as well."

Singh looked at him.

"And you are suggesting . . . ?"

He smiled.

"Yes: me. I helped design this. This whole Galloping Gertie nightmare: the first summer my wife and I worked on this back at Goddard, our mentor told us to find the movie of it at the National Archives, and it has haunted me ever since. I see it as much of, if not more than, a threat as any impact. We need precise, down-to-the-millisecond measurements of the harmonic passages—how much of a lateral shift—and that means someone at the midway point to feed the data. We have yet to install any sensing devices on this tower; we are blind as to what is happening along most of it. We need somebody in the middle to at least try to coordinate. The pod has a small rocket unit on board, transferred from one of the reels; if stationed near the impact point, it can help nudge the tower to help suppress the harmonic wave afterward."

"That would be Kevin's job," she said softly, nodding to where his friend was floating at the far end of the station, fully suited up and ready to go.

"You need him up here. Come on, Singh, if the crap really hits the fan and this tower fractures apart, who do you want up here more, him or me?"

She said nothing.

"Have the guts to make a command decision, damn it, right now, and don't go asking for advice back on the ground. Make your decision based on what you need up here."

She sighed.

"I'll need him more."

"End of debate," Gary said with a smile.

The pod having already been swung into place, Singh simply announced they had decided to start sending the pod down to monitor the harmonic and be ready for potential impact and repair, to which ground concurred. No one even mentioned who was going, the assumption simply being it was Kevin.

When told to get Gary ready to take his place, Kevin kicked up one hell of a cussing streak, threatening to get on the comm link, but Singh shouted him down in the most direct New York City language she could muster, saying that if the stuff hit the fan, and there was a cut in the tower, he would be needed up here.

There was an icy glare from Kevin to Gary.

"You are making me out to be the wimp in all of this," Kevin snapped.

"Kevin, chances are we'll get this under control, but if not, who is needed more aboard this station? You know the answer to that."

Kevin continued to glare even as he locked Gary's helmet into place and guided him to the airlock. It was far more difficult getting in wearing an EVA suit than it had been on his ascent two and a half months earlier. Kevin, muttering under his breath, helped buckle him into the couch, then finally did extend a hand, which Gary grasped.

"Don't do anything stupid, Doc. I'm the one trained in repair."

"And I wrote the training manual years ago," Gary shot back.

Kevin forced a smile.

"Doc, once down there, if all works out, maybe you should just head for home. You can go into a free drop once below 12,700 miles and be on the surface within a day. A climb back up will take three days."

"Let me guess: you want the pod returned with a real astronaut and a half dozen more pizzas, is that it?"

Kevin smiled but shook his head.

"I've loved working with you, Doc. I prefer your company to that other guy they were going to send up."

He hesitated.

"It's been an honor. Now, damn it, take care of your ass, OK?"

Gary smiled, shook his hand, then settled back in as Kevin closed the pod hatch, secured the locks, slammed shut the outer airlock to the station, and then retreated, closing the inner airlock.

"Pod initiate detachment on my mark," Singh announced. "I'll give the signal when you can fire off for rapid descent."

Gary found he was actually enjoying himself as he felt the traction wheels engage. Looking up, he saw the station appear to move away from him as he started the downward trek. At times up there he had felt like a third wheel on a scooter, in everyone's way; but as he fell into the rituals and rotations of duty, he had come to bond closely to the team. During their rare free moments they had, like wide-eyed kids, peppered him with a host of questions about how he and Eva had first conceived this dream, their meeting with Franklin, and what the legendary Erich was like, and in turn inspired him with their generation's absolute belief that they were the pioneers of the future and would stake their lives on the years of calculations and planning that he and Eva had started with long ago as interns even younger than they were now.

"Station, Pod. You are cleared for descent fire."

It hit with a kick, slamming him up against his harness, pushing up to three negative g's; but after two and a half months up there he felt like an old space hand, though he did swallow hard more than once. Kevin, while briefing him, said the real fear of astronauts on EVA was vomiting inside their helmets, as chances were they would asphyxiate; if Gary was going to be sick and he was still inside the pod, he should snap his visor up and to hell with where it went.

No need: he was feeling fine, even enjoying the ride. The Parkinson's tremors were hitting him rather hard, though, and to divert himself in those first minutes he tried to run through the calculations of harmonic waves and how to dampen them out; but he was also aware that if the tower was damaged by an impact, he would actually have to go EVA at the impact point and use a patch kit—again part of the team that had worked with him and Eva had designed it.

He was a good fifteen minutes into his drop, traction wheels withdrawn, guidance tube around the tower keeping him attached while barely touching it, dropping down at nearly 2,000 miles an hour. The velocity would have been impossible for the tower to sustain when only the first strand was connected; they were pushing the edge of it now, but the long months of work by the spinners enabled it to withstand the stress of the pod dropping at high velocity. Expected impact at 10,000 miles was now five hours off; he would barely get there in time to witness what, if anything, happened.

It was only then that Tower Control finally caught on to who was actually in the pod.

After repeated queries to "Kevin Malady, Pod One," he finally responded. "Wrong number, Tower Control. This is Morgan in the pod."

"Who?"

"You heard me right the first time."

"Sir, please hold," and Gary laughed: it almost sounded like the phone operators of long ago. A few minutes passed and then the private comm link channel blinked on his screen and he touched it.

"Just what in hell kind of stunt is this, Gary?" It was Franklin, and for once his friend's self-control was really shredded.

For the next fifteen minutes there was mutual shouting, with one barely able to catch what the other was saying as Gary laid out his justifications for this decision and said that if Franklin dared to fire Singh for going along with it, he would resign. She had made the right choice for the good of the mission.

"Damn it, Franklin," Gary finally yelled, "I'm committed! This is our only shot and you know damn well a fatal flaw in this tower was not having thrusters in place to dampen out harmonic waves, and the pod was our fallback. I designed it, I'm here, so shut the hell up and let's start working this problem."

"Eva will have my ass for this," Franklin sighed.

Gary laughed.

"Chances are once we get past this, the easier bet is for me to just come down. Leave the explaining to me. Where is she?"

"Fortunately not here, Gary. She's back in Seattle doing her pitch about getting the arts community, of all things, behind us. Victoria's back at Purdue prepping for her defense this week."

"That's good."

"Gary, I can't keep this from the news feeds."

"Figured that," Gary chuckled. "So let's go public and make the most of it. You'll have the whole world watching this one and another ten billion in investments after the fun is over with."

For the first time Franklin smiled on the screen.

"All right, damn you. I'm patching you back to open mike with Tower Control. We play the game as no big deal. But once this is over, I want you back down here; fun and games have lasted long enough, and it will be a lot easier bringing you down than sending you back up."

"Kinda figured that, even though I wanted to serve out a full tour."

"It just might appease Eva and Victoria a little, so do me that favor. Eva can be hell on wheels if she feels someone she loves is threatened, but then, I guess you already knew that," Franklin replied, and he was dead serious. "That is the trade-off."

Gary hesitated. His tour of duty was the journey of a lifetime, and he doubted if, once down, he would ever get the chance again. But he knew the logic—based not just on emotion but on simple physics—that bringing him down the rest of the way was a lot easier than sending him back up.

"Agreed."

"Handing you off to Ground Control, you royal pain in the butt."

For the next two hours the descent went smoothly until the next harmonic hit. Trying to move a cumbersome anchor point on the ground to set the wave up and get it to the frequency needed to sway the tower to one side of the potential impact had to be timed to within hundredths of a second.

That was always the design problem with a wire and cable versus a ribbon.

With a ribbon, a vehicle could rise and descend on one edge, while instrumentation and such essentials as small thruster units to control such moments could be mounted at multiple points along the other edge. A cable could never do that until built up enough to allow space for ascent and descent stages and spinners to pass, with enough diameter on the cable itself to mount such essentials to one on the opposite side.

There was still a reasonable margin of time. The old Soviet sat had cleared the equator nearly a thousand miles away in its last orbital pass. Of course its actual path was constant; the variable was the earth's rotation beneath it. Gary got word that Eva was on her way back from Seattle, raging mad, and he asked that her transmission be blocked as he forced his mind to focus on the variables, definitely feeling the next harmonic wave coming up, the shock of its lateral movement jarring his vision for a second. It would peak, come racing back down, and would supposedly move the tower just as the defunct Russian sat passed exactly where the cable should have been, except that it was now flexed more a hundred meters off the satellite's path. Another wave had been activated from the ground, calculated to meet and merge with the first one to ensure the distance, while small waves from the somewhat minimal move to avoid the earlier hunk of debris—which had actually passed far wide of the tower—continued to resonate along the Pillar. Again, in space, a miss by an inch was as good as a miss by thirty meters or a hundred miles.

"We are thirty minutes till passage," the voice of tower control whispered in his headset.

He was in free fall now, a feeling no longer disconcerting and actually pleasant, and he briefly wondered how normal gravity would feel once back on earth. He did not look forward to the prospect.

"Let's stop half a kilometer short of projected impact," Gary requested. "I can observe from there and, once past, start dampening out the wave from near the midpoint."

There was an assertion from the ground, which was repeated by Singh, now far above. He could tell they were getting tense. The calculations of where the harmonic would be at the precise microsecond of passage of the sat was everything, if the calculations offered by the Russians and confirmed by Tower Control were accurate. As the defunct satellite approached, with every passing minute the calculations were updated. It did not look good.

"Two minutes to passage."

Gary could feel the traction wheels starting to engage, to act as brakes, a brief burn from the rocket pad kicking in as well to slow him down. A couple of g's now as he decelerated. The Parkinson's was triggering a lot of tremors, but for this crucial moment, by force of will, he was keeping his mind clear, watching the display monitor only inches away from his helmet, modeling the harmonic waves that were racing both down- and upward to merge at the point of potential impact.

All was looking good, with thirty seconds to go. He was now at full stop a half kilometer above the predicted point of impact.

"Ten seconds . . ."

He half expected to see the sat go whizzing by. Absurd, as it was moving at over five miles a second relative to his position; despite its size, it was like trying to spot a bullet in flight, though Gary did switch on the high-speed cameras, filming at 5,000 shots a second to capture the passage for later analysis.

He felt the harmonic from above hit him, the view of the tower below on his monitor screen. Everything lurched from the wave passing.

"Passage!" someone shouted on the comm link.

He actually did see a blur on the screen, and then, merciful God, was that a spark, a flash of light?

He felt a shudder run up through the tower. Was that a spray of debris trailing out from the sat, which was already gone from view?

He focused the camera in on where he saw the spark. Had there been an impact?

It was impossible to tell.

"Tower Control, I saw a flash of light." His voice was shaky even as he spoke, the harmonic wave rattling him in the pod.

"Pod One, Tower Control. Yet to confirm. Proceed with caution."

He punched the monitor screen, ever so gradually edging up the speed of the traction wheels that kept him firmly locked to the tower. Just a few miles per hour, barely crawling, but he could feel a vibration running through the pod. Something was wrong.

And then came the word from down below, a near mimic of a similar announcement generations ago:

"Pod One, we have a problem here."

On the Platform

The alarms had gone off seconds before the passage of the sat and it had caught all by surprise. With all attention focused on the sat passage and controlling the wave to try to avoid a direct impact, the usual duty detail of local radar monitoring was a lonely post. But the elderly, bespectacled man in charge of it, Bill Webster—a long ago operative with a government agency that still had good contacts with "the corporation"—had been expressing concern for weeks that something was "building up."

In a world in which wars and rumors of wars had been part of life since the beginning of recorded history, when conflict in the Middle East, in Central Asia, Southwest Asia, and East Africa, threats of nuclear deployment, EMP attacks, and in the last year increasing agitation over how the tower might impact the global economy, the tension was there. But like all such things it had almost become background noise, except for the dedicated few who did take it seriously and monitored it closely . . . while the rest of the world continued to wonder who would be the next dancing champion, win the various games that weekend, or what was the newest scandal with some airheaded bimbo in Hollywood.

The alarm sounded, overriding the chatter as Gary announced that he thought there had been a partial impact.

"I am tracking two trajectories, submarine launched, 220 degrees relative to our position," Webster announced, whispered a curse, then switched his comm link into the open circuit for the entire control center back on. "Make that confirmation of two—I repeat, two—submarine-launched ballistic missiles 224 miles west-southwest of here, trajectory bearing 245 degrees."

He paused for a moment, waiting for the next data sweep from the high-gain X-band radar installed at Tarawa.

"Climbing through 33,000 feet and still accelerating," Webster announced, then paused again as Franklin ran over to stand behind him. "Tentative trajectory intersect with the Pillar at 210 miles above the earth."

"Nuclear?" Franklin gasped.

The old man, having lived through and monitored dozens of crises clear back to the 1970s, was absolutely calm.

"Negative on radioactive read from the warheads. Nonnuclear."

"Then what the hell?" Franklin cried.

"Still climbing, first-stage booster release."

Franklin turned away, cursing. His "friends" in the American and British military had suggested that there was no major security concern now. There was, however, a new crisis off Taiwan, and Pacific assets had to be shifted there; thus the Aegis that had lingered off their coast was long gone, though an Australian ship, delayed by rough seas, was due to take up station in another day.

Franklin's first thought was China, but then doubted that. China would be the last player to want to initiate a game of strike and then counterstrike on their own tower. Russia, given its high latitude, with no friendly nations on the equator, was out of the game entirely, and their negotiations with Brazil and Kenya had fallen through. Their leader was far too savvy to have his fingerprints on this kind of attack. But at this moment it didn't matter who it was. Franklin had to focus on what was going to happen in the next three minutes.

There was no Aegis system in place to respond, and even if there was, Franklin already knew that with the missiles now streaking clear of the atmosphere, an interception was already impossible. He had anticipated some damn plane-launched attack and had quietly negotiated with Australia to provide coverage in the form of four Harriers based at Tarawa, supposedly there on extended "exercises." But this?

"Two rockets still accelerating," Webster announced, voice still icy calm. "I am picking up high-gain radar tracking on their part."

A pause.

"Damn sophisticated. The missiles appear to be tracking on the tower cable. Estimated impact: ninety-five seconds and closing."

A chatter started in the control room, which only a few minutes before had been entirely focused on the sat passage and the harmonic.

"Everyone, shut up!" Franklin cried, one of the very few times in his entire life when emotions overcame his calm exterior.

"Any thoughts on the source of launch?" he whispered.

"Negative, sir," Webster replied. "Outside our sonar buoy range, and no ships on our side anywhere within two hundred miles."

"Forty seconds . . ."

Webster was indeed accurate in his assertion about the accuracy of the missiles, though to try to hit a target only a few centimeters wide by a missile boosted up to 6,000 miles an hour was almost impossible—as opposed to trying to hit a static satellite, in which case the detonation of half a dozen tons of explosive, designed to send out thousands of shards of fragmentation, could very well be destructive. Moreover, missiles like this, which were in the same class as the Aegis, were designed to track and close on a target that was also moving thousands of miles an hour—not one that was stationary.

The first missile blew past its target with more than a mile to spare before it exploded, but the second one detonated straight toward the tower from a quarter mile out, with only slight deflection, striking it with frightful kinetic energy and half a dozen high-velocity shards partly spun out of carbon nanotubing. The impact was catastrophic.

The Pillar, though damaged by the Soviet satellite's passage (half of its diameter had been sliced away), still managed to hold. It was the impact of the missile fragments and the shock wave from the detonation that sent it sheering laterally by several hundred meters. The harmonic wave that seemed manageable only three minutes earlier had turned into a tsunami that now raced up and down the length of the tower, coming at Gary at several thousand miles per hour.

It was indeed the "perfect storm" that could take the tower apart. Those who had engineered this coup de grace apparently planned it to coincide with the worries about the twin passages of debris. It was as if they had timed it to coincide with the threat of the debris passages. This attack had been long planned and just got lucky when the crisis over the debris hit. What was transpiring fulfilled and even exceeded expectations of those intent on destroying the dream. And they had timed it perfectly.

The submarine that launched the missiles had already submerged 1,000 feet and was silently running for home, ready to collect a multibillion-dollar reward for their country and, it was believed, for those aboard as well. In reality, for most—especially the sub's lowly crew members—the reward would be a bullet in the back of the head to keep them silent forever. For others, it was tens of billions of dollars in various offshore accounts, until called upon again, if need be.

The threat to the price of global oil, the threat of a new technology disrupting the old power structure was dying.

18

"Work the problem, people," Franklin announced, snapping on his headset back at his control station, trying to sound his usual calm self. He then indicated to the senior tower controller that he was taking charge.

"Do we have a break at point of missile impact?" was his first question.

A moment's pause as his team checked the tensile stress exerted at the base of the tower. If it had been severed, they should already be observing it going slack as the lower two hundred miles of the tower fell back to earth.

"We still have contact. It appears to be holding, but tensile is going up over 100 percent of bearing capacity as the shock wave heads out in both directions."

"Try to compensate here for starters," Franklin said calmly. But the still clumsy system of actually moving the entire base back and forth to stop a "Galloping Gertie" from developing was indeed their weak point. The shock wave from the detonation came down like the crack of a whip, hit the tower, literally sending a vibration through the entire structure, then rebounded and snapped back up the tower. They were now facing several waves racing up and down the tower: the ones they had purposely caused in order to avoid being struck by the satellite, and the waves generated by the missile impact.

The computer model up on the primary screen, fed in from radar aimed at the tower, showed the waves moving up and down. Someone whispered, "Looks like a damn Slinky toy about to shake itself apart."

Gary had inched his pod down to within a few meters of the damage inflicted by the satellite. It was not as bad as he first feared. It had not been a full-on blow—most likely it had been made by an antenna extension—but it had cut some of the strands, which were now drifting about loose, each two- to four-millimeter-wide strand laid around the initial core by the spinners drifting back and forth, weaving in space like deadly snakes. If one of them struck the pod with enough velocity, it could cut the vehicle open. He watched for several minutes, shifting the high-gain camera back and forth and zooming in, and finally perceived that three strands out of the twelve spun at this level had been completely severed.

What to do?

"Pod, you have a shock wave coming in less than thirty seconds. Hang on."

He said nothing in reply. Hang on to what? He was already strapped in tight. He refocused the camera down the length of the tower and actually could see the whiplike wave racing up toward him. It looked bad.

It *was* bad, displacing him a hundred meters or more in less than a second, blurring his vision. Shifting to the topside camera view, he watched from that angle as the wave raced upward. There was no atmospheric pressure to act as some sort of dampening; instead, the wave's passage triggered a reverse action, in the opposite direction, so that the entire tower was a cycle of back-and-forth waves.

It was becoming a "Galloping Gertie," a continuous series of waves triggered by the passage of previous waves. If the harmonics continued, those waves would start to move together, increasing the intensity and the stress loads.

"Control, Pod. You get my camera feeds?"

"Got them" was the terse reply.

He refocused his attention on the partial break. The passage of the waves and the resulting secondary waves had indeed caused the severed strands to whip around like deadly snakes snapping back and forth.

He just stared at them, his entire body trembling, but his mind, thank God, had a sudden clarity to it. Those bastards were not going to destroy his dream.

It took but a few seconds for a plan to form in his head.

"Control, this is Pod. I'll focus on the problem here. I'm going to slowly move the pod down over the partial break. The guide cylinder for the pod is wrapped around all the cables. My passage will force the strands above the break back into place. As I pass below the break, it should bend over the strands that are loose, causing them either to snap off or fold back against the tower. Then I'll apply the patch, wrapping it around as I pass."

The tower controller looked back at Franklin.

"Open a line to Eva," Franklin said. "I want her input."

They spoke for less than a minute, Franklin's features fixed, showing no emotion. Keeping the line open to her, he looked back at the controller.

"She said if that is how he sees it, then do it."

Gary took a deep breath, working the monitor pad, fearful that his trembling hands might hit the wrong icon. He could hear the traction wheels engaging, turning ever so slowly, and watched as a side screen focused on the tube encasing the tower, which kept the pod attached; saw the first errant wire, illuminated by high intensity lighting from the pod, being forced into the guide tube. The exterior patch unit, a small spinner with several hundred meters of wire on board, worked its way around the cable on the upper side of the guide tube. So far it was working: the first severed wire was being wound back in tightly against the main cable.

The second one behaved the same way, as did the third. He slowed to a stop for a moment. The partial cut was now only several meters below, and he studied it carefully.

"Pod, you've got an upbound wave, estimate thirty seconds."

As he hung on, trying to focus on the partial cut, the wave hit with a sharp jolt and he winced, not sure if another wire had loosened or snapped at the partial break.

"Control, Pod here. How is it going?"

A pause.

"We got bad harmonics, Pod."

"Getting worse?"

Another pause, and then just a single-word answer: "Yes."

The rocket thruster beneath the pod could rotate 360 degrees. On descent and ascent, it was actually angled several degrees away from the tower itself. It was a scenario they had talked about, using several pods to try to dampen a harmonic at the midpoint. He ran through the plan with Tower Control; they had the computing power to run it through and turn around an answer.

"Worth a try," came the final reply. "We're going to have to let the computers down here run it, and don't worry, we'll factor in the time delay for transmit. So keep your hands off the monitor and hang on: you have another wave in four minutes and thirty."

He settled back, watching the partial break on his screen and the severed wires below it whipping back and forth, again the mental image of angry snakes.

"Pod, thirty seconds to the next harmonic wave."

He braced himself, saw it coming on the screen, then the jolt and with it the counterthrust of the rocket firing for little more than half a second.

He watched the wave recede and hoped there was a difference. He waited for the feedback.

"Not too bad," Tower Control finally announced, indicating that the pod had dampened the wave down by several meters.

Gary grinned but then ran through the mental calculations. It was going to take a lot of firings—over a couple of days, perhaps—and one that was even a fraction of a second off could actually make the situation worse. Then he looked back down at the impact point. Were the loose cables separating farther out, given angular momentum by the passing waves, like strands of rope drifting out from a floundering ship, whipped back and forth by the pounding surf?

"A couple of the waves are synchronizing," Tower Control said, and he took a hard swallow on that one.

"How bad is the break down where the missiles impacted?" Gary queried.

"We're getting ready to send up a spinner. We think more than half are still intact.

At that altitude they had already spun the tower out to several centimeters in diameter. He and Eva had designed that section to withstand fairly significant impacts and even upper atmospheric influences, but they had never worked the calculations for a nonnuclear detonation close by. Up here, at nearly 11,000 miles? This was the strange transition point where the downward pull of gravity was all but counteracted by the upward thrust created by the angular momentum of the earth's rotation on the tower. It was the hardest part on the entire tower to reach with spinners; the upper and lower sections had to be beefed up first. And the fact that the pod was hanging here was not helping the stress loads.

He made his decision about what to do next and called it in.

"Tower Control, Pod here. I am going to slowly cross over the impact point up here and try to spin on a patch. Regarding the broken wires below that, I figure the cable lock around the tower as it passes over the place where they are still attached to the tower will either bend them back down against the tower, where the repair unit will spin them down tight, or snap them clear. I'll work a patch over where they have sheared off, then move back up past the partial break, spin on another patch, then move farther up and resume work on counterthrusting."

A long pause this time. He could hear the debate on Franklin's private comm line, which both had kept open. He'd have fifteen minutes until the next wave hit. They had to strengthen the weakest point on the tower. Someone argued that he could snag on the loose wires and be permanently stuck. Finally Franklin asked if anyone had a better solution, because if not, he was giving it a go.

"Go for it, Gary." Franklin announced.

Gary ever so slowly nudged the pod over the partial break, creeping along at a little more than a tenth of a meter a second. The repair spinner was still working atop the pod, wrapping wire around the cable. He cleared the break, putting down a wrapped single strand of wire on the damaged section. About six meters ahead, one of the loose cables was floating back and forth in an arcing circle, gradually breaking free of the tower. This would be the tricky part: the circular clamp anchoring the pod to the tower would eventually overlap where the broken wire was still attached. It would then either fold it over, pressing it against the tower, where the spinner laying a new wire over it could lock it back in place, or it would snap it off completely. He thought he caught a flash of one of the loose cables swaying back and forth just outside his side porthole. The camera focused on the spinner, and the clamp below it showed that the plan had indeed worked: the broken cable had been folded over and was being wrapped in place!

"Got one of the loose cables," Gary announced. "Wrapping it in place. Two more to go."

"That's my man, Doc! Couldn't have done it better myself!" It was Kevin up in the station, and Gary felt himself swell with pride at having earned a compliment from his friend.

"Get a move on, Pod, next wave is only five minutes out."

He spotted the second loose cable where it was attached to the tower, but as the circular clamp eased over it, the wire snapped off. With it gone, wrapping the damaged section would become easier.

But then, only a few seconds later, the pod lurched to a stop.

"What the hell?" Gary muttered, and he carefully, because of his trembling, hit the button to activate the drive.

A grinding noise echoed in the pod, but zero motion. He hit the button several more times. Nothing.

"Pod, we're reading your problem. Wave due in one minute and forty-five seconds. Hang on, then let's try to sort it out."

The next wave, bouncing up from below, was not as intense as the last one. The programmed thruster fired to try to dampen it. He wasn't sure of the effect, but after the wave passed, he focused a camera in on the partial break and took it up in magnification. The spinning was not resulting in a flat overlay; it looked like a bandage that was splitting apart down the middle.

"You get the feed?" Gary asked, and there was an acknowledgment.

"I'm jammed here," he said, and as he focused a camera on the drive wheels, he caught glints of reflected light. The damn broken wire had wrapped around a wheel, locking it in place.

He took a deep breath, thoughts racing, but staying focused.

"You see this, Tower Control?"

"Got it."

"I'm going to try to reverse and climb back up; maybe it will unwind the jam."

"Pod, we concur."

He was beginning to sweat, and he opened the faceplate on his EVA suit to wipe his eyes clear so he could focus on the monitor. He carefully punched in the reverse command, ignoring Tower Control's suggestion that they handle the controls from down there.

He tapped the engage button, programmed to reverse climb at ten centimeters a second. The wheel actually made several revolutions, but then, perversely, the wire unraveling from the top wheel now spun into the gearing of the second wheel and he lurched to a stop yet again.

He was truly stuck.

The decision was obvious. He clicked up to Kevin, who gave an immediate concurrence and said he'd "walk" Gary "through it."

The next wave hit. This was indeed a bad one. The spinner patch he had put over the partial break was definitely separating, while nearly 12,000 miles below, the crew on the ground was racing to send an automated spinner up to try to patch the partial break from the missile strike and act as another thruster unit to dampen out the waves.

"Tower Control, Pod. I'm going EVA."

"What in hell are you doing, Gary?" It was Franklin.

"You got any other suggestions, then tell me," Gary snapped back.

Silence on the other end.

"OK, Doc, punch up the decompression-of-pod checklist now. I'll talk you through it," Kevin interjected. "We don't have time to screw around with this and arguing with those down below."

A minute later he popped the hatch, an ever-so-slight rush of air pressing against the inside of the hatch nearly causing him to lose his grip.

"You got handholds all over the place out there," Kevin said. "Just don't look down for starters; it can get disorienting. Time later to play sightseeing. Now work your way up over the top of the pod; just use your hands, let your legs float free."

He did as instructed, saying nothing, but it certainly was damn exhilarating. He was actually outside the pod. Kevin guided him to the tool compartment atop the hatch, its contents having been thought out and argued about long before the first strand was ever lofted. There was even an old-fashioned roll of duct tape inside. He was reminded of how such a roll of tape had helped save *Apollo 13*.

There was also a roll of the new "ribbon" with an adhesive attachment. A momentary debate ensued on the comm link between Tower Control and Kevin as to whether Gary should just unjam the wheels and then get back inside or actually do a hand over hand the half dozen meters up to the fracture and try to manually wrap the tape around it. The side in favor of unjamming the wheels and getting back inside won out. The tape would have to be wound on with a pressure no human could apply. He needed the spinner unit to do that, but first he had to position it back over the damaged section.

Now, to unjam the wheels . . .

Kevin guided him to what looked almost like ordinary cable cutters, though far more high-tech, with blades of nanotubing: just guide the blade in, press a button, and the motorized unit would compress and shear. To do so manually would be darn near impossible, and also require using both hands. This was going to be tricky and dangerous: the bits of wire that would float about, if propelled point first, could easily puncture his space suit.

It was nearly impossible to see the individual strands that jammed the wheels. He guided the cutter around them, repeatedly pressing the activation button, hoping he was doing something constructive to clear the jam. It was tense work, made infinitely more difficult by the tremors of Parkinson's. He had nightmare flashes that he might accidentally cut the entire tower, but the shears were torsion stressed not to cut more than one wire.

He caught a glimpse of a shard, a foot or more in length, drifting past his faceplate.

"You got five minutes to get back inside," Kevin whispered. "Next wave is coming down fast. Don't want you knocked off, Doc. Have your butt inside the pod when it hits, then head back out again if you need to finish your job."

"Got that."

He felt he had cleared the tangle of wire and fumbled to put the shears back into the toolbox, Kevin urging him to hurry and be certain to seal the lid of the box.

He did so with two minutes to spare, sweating profusely, breathing hard; moving about in zero g was far tougher than he imagined. He tried to jackknife himself back into the open pod door.

He was halfway in when the wave hit.

For the first time in his life he actually did feel pure terror. The entire unit lurched. He lost his grip but kept his legs locked around the inside of the hatchway. The pod was then whipped back the other way, a hundred meters or more, and then . . . the momentum just kept carrying it.

He looked up and gasped.

Merciful God, the tower had snapped in half.

The lower half, to which the pod was attached, was now drifting away at a dozen or more meters per second from the upper half.

He fought down a blind urge, like a drowning sailor, to try to leap to a distant lifeboat on a storm-tossed sea, but already knew it was out of reach.

An impulsive thought flashed to get out of the pod, secure an emergency spool of cable from the tool box, hold on to one end then leap and try to grab the still-dangling strand of the upper half that was drifting away.

Absurd, with the thousands of tons of forces now at work. It would be like using a kite string to try to hold on to a battleship and tie it back in place.

The distance widened with every passing second. The upper half of the tower would actually remain "up" coiling about. There was enough mass in orbit farther up the line to keep it in orbit.

But he was now attached to the lower half, and he had a chilling thought.

At least this is better than dying of Parkinson's.

19

"It's gone!"

Franklin tore his gaze from a side monitor supplying video from Gary's pod, pointed straight up, showing the separation.

"Silence in this room!" Franklin shouted. "Secure the doors; no one is to leave the room. I want calm analysis and no other comments."

Several people looked back at him. One of the controllers lowered his head and tried to stifle his sobs. There was a numbed silence.

"Kill any outside feeds," Franklin ordered. In the moments after he thought they had control of the harmonics due to the shifting of the tower to avoid two collisions, he had again allowed an open feed to the world. It was another demonstration of the Pillar's viability. And he had allowed, as well, the entire world to witness the submarine-launched missile strike. He had already received word from the president of the United States, the prime minister of Great Britain, and even the Chinese government that they were dispatching ships to track down the sub.

But in the hours since the incident, the sub could already be anywhere within 15,000 or more square miles of ocean, and with each passing hour that search area would nearly double yet again. And even if they cornered it, what then? Fire on it? Perhaps trigger a world war?

The damage had been done.

"Can we keep a secured feed to Dr. Petrenko's flight?" he asked.

"We can encrypt but others will listen in and try to unscramble," someone replied.

He nodded. He'd make an open-line call to her, though she without doubt already knew.

"Patch me through to Dr. Petrenko and to Miss Victoria Morgan, and do it now. And the rest of you, work the problem. Is there any way we can perhaps use the thruster on the pod to try to maneuver back to a position to reconnect?"

His question was greeted at first with blank stares. No one had ever thought of this desperate scenario.

"We could at least try, sir." It was Gretchen, tears streaming down her cheeks.

Gary accepted the rapid fire orders coming up from Tower Control without comment. After the terrifying moment of dangling half out of the pod, he had used what little strength he had left to ease his way back in, pulling the hatch shut and repressurizing the unit, with Kevin coaxing him along every inch of the way.

He patched in to Tower Control, offering a running observation as the upper and lower halves of the tower drifted farther and farther apart. He knew the dynamics better than anyone except Eva. If the tower ever snapped, the angular velocity imparted by the rotation of the earth would still hold sway. The section of the tower above 12,700 miles would actually remain in orbit. Every part of the tower below that point would eventually fall back to earth.

And it would bring with it an incredible mess of thousands of miles of dangerous wire. Most would actually burn up on reentry, but enough would just slowly coil down through the atmosphere to create one hell of a problem on the surface, frightfully dangerous to any who might step on it or try to pick a section up barehanded, and absolutely deadly for any air traffic as it rained down.

"Gary . . ." It was Franklin, now four minutes after the separation. "How you doing?"

"I've had better days," Gary replied, trying to keep the trembling out of his voice, triggered by Parkinson's and outright fear.

"We've come up with two options here."

"Why do there always seem to be two options at moments like this?" Gary replied, and then added, "Are we on an open or closed mike?"

"I think closed."

"OK, go ahead, Franklin."

"You know you are below the demarcation point for eventual reentry, and you know what that means?"

"Crispy critter," Gary said softly.

"I wouldn't put it that crudely, my friend, but yeah, you're right.

"Option one: break free of the lower half now. Every second counts. Your rocket pack just might have enough energy to get you back to the severed end of the upper tower. Hook back on to it. Take a deep breath, let batteries charge up, and start to climb back up. With luck, you'll be back in the station in four days and then you return with the crew up there."

"Anyone work the math on that yet?" Gary asked. "Disconnect from the tower, then chase the upper strand, rendezvous and lock on to it. Sounds doubtful. Give me the second option."

"Stay attached to the lower half, use your rocket pack to try to guide it back to the upper half, then do an EVA and we'll try to figure out some way to reconnect the upper and lower halves."

"I'll take the second option."

There was a pause.

"Gary, the second option stands a snowball's chance in hell. There are dynamics playing out now that we cannot even begin to get a handle on with the way the wires are behaving, and the harmonics are still playing."

Both options were near to impossible, Gary realized, but at least with the second, there was a chance, a very slim chance he could still save the Pillar.

He sighed.

"You sure this is a secured line?"

Franklin paused, shouting a query to his communications director, and she gave the reply he wanted.

"It's secure."

"I'd rather die trying to save our dream than die trying to save my own ass, Franklin. You got that?"

A pause and then just one word.

"Yes."

"Send up the programming to control the thruster to Kevin on the station; he's the pro with this. He'll send it back down and try to coach me through controlling the burn. Who knows, I just might save it after all."

He could hear the tension in Kevin's voice as the guidance data was sent up to the station.

"Damn it, Doc, you know it should be my ass in that pod, not you!" Kevin snapped, while Singh loaded in the guidance information that would then be downloaded to the pod's onboard computer.

"I think you got a more important job ahead of you," Gary replied.

"Cut the crap, Doc. We both got jobs ahead of us, so don't lay any more guilt on me than I already feel."

Gary chuckled, glad for the reassuring voice of his friend. Franklin asked if he wished to talk with Eva, but when told that half the world would be trying to listen in, he had refused, telling Franklin to give the excuse that he was focused on this effort to save the tower.

There was no old-fashioned joystick to grab hold of and maneuver, not that he would even remotely know how to use one, though Victoria would. A flash thought of her. *Thank you, God, this is about me rather than her.* For this burn, he was just along for the ride; it would be Singh and Kevin who would be doing the fine-tuning from above.

"Burn in five, four, three . . ."

He felt the rocket pack beneath the pod kick in, pressing him sideways. He actually wondered how many terabytes of data were running this show, calculating not just the movement of the pod but also the mass of the wire he was still attached to, its fluctuations from both the harmonics and the fact that it was cut free, then trying to match it all up with the end of the wire floating above him and now more than a kilometer away.

"We have good burn, Doc," Kevin whispered, voice tense.

He did not reply. Eyes glued to the monitor, the topside camera supposedly focused on where the bottom of the severed strand was located.

"Still a good burn. We are closing in, Doc. You're doing great."

"I'm not doing a damn thing," Gary whispered back.

"You will once we got rendezvous. Your suit pressurized, full oxygen load, ready for EVA?"

"Yes on that."

He always felt that saying "Roger," "Affirmative," or "Check" would sound stupid coming from him.

"Hey, Franklin."

"Here, Gary."

"Bet you got the entire world watching this."

"We've shut it down, Gary."

He said nothing, glad to hear that. He was petrified. Strangely, he was not fearful regarding the next few minutes but about whether the tremors of Parkinson's would somehow hinder him once he was EVA. That would be an utter humiliation, to be so close to saving the Pillar but then have his own disability prevent it.

"Depressurize cabin, then open the hatch but stay strapped in for now. If we score this, you'll have to move fast," Kevin said.

He did as ordered, and for a moment he actually did catch a glimpse of the upper half of the tower. Inwardly he sighed.

He knew that they knew; the radar aboard the pod would already be showing it. They were moving to directly underneath where the wire had once been, but already it had drifted more than a kilometer upward and was accelerating away from him, its lateral movements random and out of control, orbital dynamics swinging it up and away.

No one spoke. He could feel the thrust shifting, the adjustable nozzle moving directly underneath him despite the threat that the wire coiling beneath the pod might be cut by the high-intensity flame of the hybrid oxygen and solid propellant engine.

The pod started to thrust upward. He watched the monitor, the amount of fuel remaining, the gauge dropping down, color coding on the computer screen.

"Three percent fuel remaining," Gary whispered.

"I know, Doc." It was Kevin, his voice trembling.

"We'll make it."

"Of course."

He could see the wire—at least, the onboard radar could—so tantalizingly close, less than half a kilometer above, but shifting several hundred meters now to his right.

Even more than in a plane, where at least if you had your stick or wheel directly wired to the ailerons, elevator, and rudder you still had some control, in space, once you lost thrusters, you were locked on the trajectory, fated to follow the path in your last second of burn. The engine, never designed for this kind of duration of burn, or for nudging such a mass back into position, sputtered out. The drag of the wire he was still attached to rapidly slowed his upward thrust.

"Doc, abandon the pod! If you EVA now, you might be able to grab the upper wire," Kevin shouted.

Gary actually laughed.

"Then what, hang there until I run out of air?"

"We could think of something. Sending a spinner down ASAP might work."

"Dream on," Gary replied. "Remember, I designed most of this. It'll never work."

He didn't speak after that, ignoring Kevin's repeated appeals to go for the EVA, instead just watching the monitor, the upper half of the tower, the focus of a lifetime of dreams so close and yet now an eternity away.

Upward velocity of the pod ceased as the thousands of miles of wire beneath him acted like an anchor line. He gazed at the radar image of the wire above, smiled sadly, then switched off the image.

"Franklin, can you patch me through to Eva and Victoria?"

The choice was easy enough once made. There were enough oxygen and supplies on board the pod for four days. Four days of what? Melodrama? Breathless, teary-eyed reporters flooding the Internet and airwaves with hourly bulletins? The already sick demands for exclusive interviews by tabloid writers trying to get into Tower Control? There was one piece of scum who had cornered Victoria at the Purdue airport and offered her a million dollars for a ten-minute exclusive. If Gary had been on earth, he would have knocked the guy flat. When he heard how physical her response was—about the shrieking reporter writhing on the pavement as her flight took off—he actually forgot his own situation for a moment and laughed. That was indeed his girl!

He still had friends at Goddard and in the government, who opened up a very secure channel so he could chat freely with his "girls" as they raced to New Mexico to catch a supersonic four-hour flight to Kiribati, personally piloted by their British friend.

It did give him time to compose his thoughts and, amazingly, even to sleep for a while. He had a wonderful dream, very private, of a time early on with Eva, and he awoke with a smile.

The retrograde motion of the lower half of the wire was increasing. The point of near impact by the missile had finally fractured completely from the stress loads. On the ground at the platform they were hurriedly trying to reel in the lower two hundred miles of wire. Parts of the wire farther up were into the upper atmosphere with enough velocity to burn up, with more fractures breaking other sections apart. He thought he could actually feel the vibrations of those breaks—or was it that so much of his soul was tied to this dream that he could feel it breaking apart and dying?

He clicked on one of his favorite albums by Constance Demby, *Sanctum Sanctorum*. It was comforting; there was a spiritual sense to it that had always moved him and seemed so appropriate now. *Novus Magnificat: Through the Stargate* was perfect for his ride up, but now? *Sanctum* was the comfort he needed as he gazed out the window of the pod, soaking in a sunrise, the moon setting on the western horizon and, above him, the sea of stars. Some more messages, to old friends, professors who had helped; a general message to Goddard to read to the staff sometime in the future, leaving it to Franklin to determine when; and a less-than-pleasant sign-off to Professor Garlin and her anti-technology friends. To be able to plan all that out and deliver it diverted him for a few hours and actually gave a certain pleasure, especially the messages to his favorite composer and friends.

Again settling back. What the hell, he had the finest view ever offered to an inhabitant of earth. He wondered just how many billions over the course of history had looked heavenward and would have gladly offered their lives just for a few minutes of the view he now had, especially when facing what he now faced. Far better than the ceiling and fluorescent lights of some damn hospital emergency room with a bunch of strangers staring down at him, he realized with a smile.

No longer locked to one place, and due to the vagaries of the lower part of the tower as it broke apart, he even caught a flash of what he assumed was part of it burning up on entering the atmosphere. He actually found himself feeling light, even free, though the sight of parts of his tower burning up was painful.

He was, of course, weightless, though confined by his EVA suit. Such a wonderful sense of freedom . . . He spent nearly a quarter of an hour talking with his friend Dr. Bock about the potentials of space for medical treatment in the near future, as a destination for those who were paralyzed or suffering from a debilitating disease who, in lower-gravity environments, could regain the freedom of movement of a child. The hours he had spent playfully somersaulting the length of the station while Kevin, imitating Superman, just glided back and forth, were times of joy and forgetfulness, even if after enjoying the antics one was then condemned to agonizing hours on the exercise machines to keep in tone.

And then word finally came up from Franklin.

"Gary, Eva has just come in with Victoria. I'm clearing the room so you three can talk. Our friends with NASA assure us the comm line is absolutely private, and I am leaving the room as well."

"Thanks, my good friend."

"Gary?"

The image of Franklin filled the screen, and he could see the tears.

"What, Franklin?"

A pause.

"Thanks."

Gary smiled.

"And thanks to you, even now. Thanks, you dear friend. Now keep the dream alive."

"Give my best to Erich when you see him," Franklin whispered, and turned away.

A moment later Eva and Victoria filled the screen. He smiled gently, telling them to not cry, and for more than an hour they spoke. At times he asked for Victoria to leave the room so that he and his wife could share a private memory, and then he asked Eva to leave the room so he could offer Victoria some fatherly advice and reassurances.

And then he knew they were dragging it out, that they did not want to let go, that somehow if they kept talking, what was to come would never happen. But in life—everyone's life, he told them—such a moment does come, and they should consider it a blessing that they had been given the time to share just how much they really loved each other.

"Victoria?"

"Yes, Daddy."

"Remember what I said about being afraid?"

She nodded, trying not to sob.

"Don't be afraid unless I see you're afraid," she whispered.

He smiled again.

"I'm not afraid, angel. Now do me a favor."

"Anything, Daddy."

"Work with your mother and get this job done. My love will be with you always."

Before they could see his own tears, he switched the private comm link off, but then switched on the open link—audio only, no video.

He had already depressurized the pod; opening the hatch was easy enough. He bent double, the Parkinson's making it difficult to control movement, but he felt no frustration that it took a few extra seconds. And then he pushed free of the pod.

His suit had a small, built-in thruster-control backpack, only a few pounds of propellant, but enough to turn him about so he was looking straight down at earth.

Such a magnificent view, a magnificent world.

"Earth is the cradle, but we cannot remain in the cradle forever. It is time now to reach for the stars," he whispered, knowing that the world below was listening. "My God, it is such a heavenly view."

Then he unlatched the faceplate to his helmet and raised it.

And it was indeed a heavenly view.

20

Fourteen months had passed since the death of Gary Morgan, the collapse of the tower, the near collapse of Franklin Smith's financial conglomerate, and all was now coming to a head . . . at last.

Like the harmonic waves that had set the stage for the disaster, harmonic waves of public opinion, debate, point, and counterpoint had swept the entire world.

As for who had actually launched the two missiles, at least in the realm of public media that was still declared to be a mystery. There were rumors aplenty and more than a few books out on what was called the "mystery of the century." The focus was on the oil interests in the Middle East and there was evidence that quite a few billion had certainly flowed through various accounts in an unexplained manner to North Korea. At times a good accountant can be almost as dangerous as a commando.

Fragments of the first stage of one of the missiles had been recovered by a deep-diving submersible. The design was Russian, which triggered hot, even threatening denials, with the Russians pointing out that such systems had been built in China as well and that the few identification markers were forgeries; the Chinese responded with equally angry denials. Shortly thereafter, a mysterious explosion in a submarine pen in North Korea destroyed two of their submarines. This caused a new flurry of speculation, with Western sources just shrugging and saying someone over there must have screwed up, while North Korea claimed sabotage. But then, after the usual bellicose rhetoric from that tragic nation ruled by insanity, there had been no further military response to what was apparently a brilliantly engineered strike by forces unknown, at least publicly.

In terms of a potential war, the situation cooled down rapidly, almost too rapidly for more than a few who wondered if there was a deep conspiracy to take out a revolutionary new technology that most definitely would have global economic impacts. As with all such impacts, there would be winners and also some major losers.

There had been other changes in the wind. The moribund issue of the future of NASA had taken a decided upswing in the recent presidential election when one of the two candidates had forcefully declared that she felt it was time to resume the dream of Jack Kennedy and reach for the stars. This time, not as a race against a former foe but as a broader mission for all mankind, to open a pathway to the heavens that any with peaceful intent could use, as well as to seek a source of limitless energy that could transform the world of the twenty-first century.

It was a unique welding of two constituencies that traditionally had been at odds, with those who were "green" and saw global warming as a top priority finding common ground with those who saw high technology, especially space-based technology, as the path to the future. There had even been a super PAC ad of a beloved but aged star of one of the most popular sci-fi series in history standing side by side with one of the remaining Apollo heroes, challenging voters to support the pro-space candidate and thus "boldly go where no one has gone before."

For a wide variety of reasons she had won the election, and those who had been frustrated supporters of NASA for so many years again felt some hope for the future.

But there was a countercurrent as well: those who supported Garlin. She had actually made a bid for elected office as a congresswomen and gained a seat, then pushed for a position on the committee that oversaw the NASA budget in the house. She became one of the agency's fiercest critics. Garlin appealed to all those who believed that the problems of earth had been created on earth, and until such problems were solved, it was all but obscene to carry such problems to other worlds.

A private venture to reach Mars had been launched with great fanfare, and had actually succeeded in touching down with ten on board, five couples who were to establish the first permanent base on that planet. It had been a one-way trip, their ship named *Mayflower One.* It was a wild venture and ended in disaster. Only one was still alive, but would not be for much longer. Plans for hydroponic food raising, and the conversion of subsurface water to oxygen and even fuel, had not worked as planned. The European firm that had sent them up continued to praise their spirit of discovery—which it indeed was—pointing out they had all been volunteers . . . But the firm was already bankrupt, and a rescue mission costing tens of billions of dollars to save the last survivor, who would most likely perish before help arrived, had long since been abandoned. The daily broadcasts from this dying "Martian," unlike Gary's, were profoundly bitter and now distinctly anti-exploration; he asserted that Mars was useless for humanity other than as a fantasy to waste huge amounts of money on that would merely be scooped up by a cynical few back on earth while the idealists they sent out died.

A sick reality show had even been built around the experience and had millions of followers. There was something perverse about watching a person slowly die, although Gary Morgan's final hours, by contrast, had been marked by quiet dignity, and the utter refusal of his wife and daughter to make a single comment about his passing had drawn universal admiration and respect . . . and woe to the reporter who tried to seek an "exclusive" with millions in hand. More than one got the same treatment as the heartless fool who had tried to corner Victoria as she set off from Purdue to Kiribati on the day her father died.

As for Franklin's venture, Pillar Inc. tottered on bankruptcy. No one was willing now to venture the many billions necessary to continue the project. There had been speculation about sending another strand down from geosynch, first using the nearly 14,000 miles or more of wire already in place, which the space-based crew had carefully reeled back in, and then building from there. But there was no longer financial backing for it.

The fate of the three astronauts—or "Pillar Builders," as someone had tagged them—had drawn global interest as well. It was assumed in the days after the disaster that they would simply board their descent capsule, depart the station, and return home, and that the entire project would be abandoned.

Their reaction had been the exact opposite, and when Franklin, in a despondent moment, had ordered them to return to earth, it was fortunate that the conversation was on the private secured link that NASA had kept open for him. Singh and Philips's "Hell no!" had been relatively polite compared to Malady's far more graphic response.

Gary had been right when it came to which of them would be of far greater service after the disaster, and his words seemed to act as a goad for Kevin Malady, who in the ensuing months raked up more EVA time than nearly every other astronaut combined since the start of space exploration. Though each venture was fraught with the potential of death, he made it almost look easy, like a "roustabout" of a century or more ago, manhandling empty reels into place, spinning up their deployment motors in reverse to crank up the "wire," then anchoring them to the first deployed stretch of ribbon extending a dozen kilometers out from the station.

Dr. Bock had more than one private consultation with the crew on their exposure to radiation, which exceeded any other man's six times over; Kevin's response was that, given the close but decidedly professional relationship with the "two ladies" on board, he had abandoned any thoughts as to the possible long-term effects.

The idea of a crew transfer had been abandoned at their insistence as well, and besides the money to send a transfer crew aloft had dried up. There was just enough still in the bank to fund the resupply missions to the three, but nothing beyond that. They soon clocked and then far exceeded a year in space. As Jenna put it: "Gravity sucks; we prefer it up here." Much better to send up supplies and, in an act of supreme optimism, that they should loft up the ribbon and a newly designed pod instead, given the cost of nearly a billion dollars a launch.

Franklin finally agreed, and more than a few in the media went straight at him then, claiming that he was putting some mad dream of actually trying to build a second tower ahead of the safety of the three still up there. The entire concept was dead anyhow.

Singh, with Philips and Malady floating by her side, had killed that argument in a most memorable broadcast back down to earth. In no uncertain terms she read the riot act to all of humanity that the decision was theirs, not Franklin's or anyone else's. They were volunteers, and in the tradition of volunteers they had elected to stay and decide their own fates, in the same way Gary Morgan had volunteered for his fate, knowing the odds better than any of them. That the three of them were leading the project from above meant it was not over yet, and they would be damned if they would follow what anyone told them to do from the ground.

Then Kevin spoke, starting off with a classic New York "Now listen, youse guys, I got somethin' to say about my own life and what I'm gonna do with it!" There was a pause as he looked off screen to Singh, who was whispering some sort of warning to keep his language G-rated . . . and then emotion hit hard when he said, "Gary went instead of me. I loved that guy as I would my own father. He had guts and I'll be . . ." He paused, his words carrying such power because such a tough-looking guy had tears in his eyes, his voice near to breaking . . . "I'll be damned if I back off now from what I know is right. We're up here to stay, so all you down there, get some guts as well and make a future for your kids . . ."

Jenna, with her distinct North Carolina accent, threw in that her ancestors had settled the mountains of her native state, knowing the odds, and as Americans had fought to defend what they believed in, in revolution and civil war; that she had Cherokee heritage as well from her home state and believed the spirits of her ancestors were with her and she was following their tradition, and any who tried to tell her different—Her features darkened and she fell silent, closing with "My parents taught me never to say what I want to say to some of you right now trying to tell us what to do with our own lives and this project we believe in" before she signed off.

With Singh there was a moment of emotion when she broke and spoke of their friend Gary Morgan and his final words and announced they would be waiting for someone with guts to come and follow in his path and see the construction of "their Pillar" completed.

She had made this declaration even more effective by repeating it in a somewhat more polite and circumspect tone in her native Hindi, then yet again, albeit more briefly, in Mandarin, offering the hope that China would actually pursue its own program or throw in with theirs.

Overnight, if such a term could be applied to people orbiting in the near perpetual daylight of geosynch, the team aloft had become a global sensation and as much a spokesperson for the future as Franklin was . . . or as Gary had been.

And yet there was, as always, the pragmatic side. Three supply ships, which had already been bought and paid for before the disaster, apart from the costs of fueling and launching, had been sent aloft, carrying with them thousands of miles of the new ribbon and supplies for the astronauts—including a few delicacies for the three, even though the cost of a single pizza delivery or deluxe barbecue dinner from Phil's Bar-B-Que Pit was well over two hundred thousand dollars; but then that was the end of the pipeline. They had a year's worth of supplies on board; when they ran out, like it or not, they would have to abandon their posts and return home.

And so they waited, surpassing in duration the longest flight times in space ever attempted aboard *Mir* or the International Space Station.

The few remaining Apollo astronauts, now in their late eighties and nineties, and the retired and long-since-grounded crews of the space shuttle program, in their sixties and seventies, held a joint press conference and rally at Kennedy, Houston, and then Goddard to lobby for support.

The message was becoming clear.

Do we stay in this cradle, and eventually perish in it because of our own follies, or do we seek the limitless growth potential of above?

And then at last had come the day.

The House had passed a budget for NASA undreamed of but a few years earlier, but it was locked in the Senate oversight committee that Proxley still was a member of. After winning reelection by only a few thousand votes, he took up his old litany, as if he could never learn another. Senator Dennison of Maine was now chair, but Proxley still had clout and was backed now by Garlin of Indiana and more than a few others who argued that the public was being swayed by emotion rather than logic. The fact that a savvy supporter who first wrote the proposal called it the "Morgan Space Bill" had enraged Proxley, but public opinion and now pressure from a president who was of the opposing party had finally forced a hearing.

Proxley had loaded the hearing with opposition for three days straight, led by Garlin from the House, who was lauded as a professor who was an expert on the subject of the impact of a tower.

She gave damning testimony about the disruptive technologies that could shatter entire industries and cause massive economic upheaval and shocks to the stock market, reminding everyone of the finger-pointing of the first decade of the twenty-first century. The nation after a decade and a half of moribund or collapsing markets and spiraling debt was barely back on an even keel, and she maintained that now was not the time for risk but for well-thought-out plans for a steady recovery. Space had been there since the origins of man; it would still be there fifty years hence and, all sentimental appeals aside, it was time to think of the present and not some sci-fi future more than likely filled with similar disasters rather than hope. She then raised the fear that continued pursuit of energy sources in space could so destabilize the national and regional economies that out of desperation a global war would be all but inevitable—that the missile strike against the tower had been the result of disabling economic threats. Did our nation wish to incur such a threat again, perhaps this time with nuclear rather than nonnuclear missiles on board?

There were more than a few, particularly those who had always mistrusted any technology—even as they carried their iPads, drove hybrid cars, and built personal wealth through the instant trading of stock on the Internet—who sided with Garlin.

After the first two days of hearings—which Proxley had carefully stacked in his favor even though Dennison chaired the proceedings—it was the turn for those who supported NASA to testify.

Franklin Smith, who had aged significantly since the disaster—and there at his side, the widow of a man renowned for his iconic final words, joined by Victoria, who Smith announced would increasingly take charge of their mission in spite of her youth—sat down before the committee.

Much had changed in their dynamic over the last fourteen months. Victoria had easily earned her Ph.D. Her department, in the aftermath of her father's death, had graciously postponed the final defense of her dissertation until two months later. Would anyone have dared to reject it, even though several hundred protesters without any sense of decency shouted right outside the office window while she defended her work? When they were finished, her committee, proudly and without dissent, congratulated her in the grand tradition: the head of her committee was the first to take her hand and address her as "Dr. Morgan."

Until this crisis was past, she and Jason had decided to postpone their wedding as he finished up his own dissertation, which was a comparative analysis of disruptive technologies of the early to mid-nineteenth century and the lessons to be applied today, in particular the Pillar. And yet, in the months that passed, though the couple remained close, there was still a certain distance between them as she single-mindedly threw herself into honoring her father's final wish and to stand as well by Franklin's side. Though Franklin did not show it publicly, Victoria's father's death had indeed shaken him to the core, and he even had moments of self-doubt.

Their relationship had changed. He was indeed more than ever the substitute for a lost father, and she the daughter he never had, but now did.

The disaster had worn down Franklin far more than he would ever admit, but it was evident to all. It was not just the loss of the tower. It was his deep anguish over Gary's death. He had bonded closely to Eva and Victoria as a result, and increasingly turned to them and even deferred to them regarding decisions about what to do next.

Operations on the ground had all but ceased except that Fuchida was still cranking out ribbon at a phenomenal rate at his factory in New Mexico. Franklin could no longer afford to purchase it, but there were many from overseas who were eager to buy; some, like the Chinese, had acquired the secret of making the wire but were not yet able to spin it into ribbon. Fuchida refused to sell. He had a ten-year contract with Franklin, and whether Franklin could actually purchase it or not, it was being stored in a heavily guarded warehouse in New Mexico, waiting to be delivered. Fuchida, the hard-nosed businessman, then just started handing it over to Franklin on credit. Others had offered astronomical sums for his entire stockpile, which he angrily refused, rightly surmising any purchaser other than the Chinese would simply dump it all in the deepest part of the ocean to prevent its proper use. He'd rather give it away for free and go bankrupt than see such an end to his lifetime of work.

The third day of the Senate hearings was at last at hand, and Victoria, Eva, Franklin, and their staff and allies—including the Brit and his American partner—arrived in Washington. The two pilots handled the controls on their trans-atmospheric flight from Tarawa, landing at Reagan Airport and barely acknowledging that the flight had set a new distance and time record in transit as they dodged their way through a sea of press.

As they approached Capitol Hill, Victoria could not help but flash back to the day when she, at age sixteen, had accompanied her parents to this same hallowed place, only to see them defeated. Sitting in the back of the limo, scanning over her notes on her iPad, she looked across at Franklin. The last year had indeed taken its toll. He was no longer a towering six foot six, his features conveying power with his slight fringe of gray hair offsetting his dark face and his bright dancing eyes, his well-modulated voice that sounded nearly identical to that of a certain beloved actor. The actor had portrayed characters ranging from Civil War sergeants to presidents, and when he and Franklin finally met, they had joked together about whether Franklin had imitated him or if it was the other way around. The actor was now an active spokesman for the project as well.

Franklin's shoulders were slightly slumped now, nothing serious other than the reality of advancing age. He was no longer in his mid-sixties. On the day he and Victoria first met, he had come across to her as a man of near-infinite wisdom, a true legend of the dot-com days—days long forgotten in the economic turmoil that followed. He was a man who had risen from the poverty of the segregated South to become one of the financial leaders of those who had not given up hope in the future and believed there could still be a bright century ahead. As he had so often said, he believed his mission now was to give back what he had received in spite of the barriers of the racism and economic poverty of his youth. But in the last year he seemed to have retreated into circumspection and even depression, and now he was going into a hearing to face one of his fiercest foes. An opponent who, under the previous administration, had actually sworn he would bring down "a monopoly created by an egotist out of control."

Victoria looked over at her mother, born during the Cold War, in a nation under the thumb of their masters in Moscow. She carried with her memories of ancestors who, despite their oppression, had risen up to fight against the fascist evil invading their land, even though the iron fist of Stalin hung over them and despised them and kept them imprisoned after the fascists were defeated. It had become a running joke between mother and daughter that she wished she had never told Victoria of her own grandfather and hero of Stalingrad.

As Victoria looked to her mother, she recalled Eva's stories of how, as a child, she would visit her grandfather in the military hospital and glory in the moments when he would pin his medal to her blouse. How, as a young teenager, she had fled her hometown, never to return, when the nearby nuclear reactor at Chernobyl had melted down. How she had gone to the University of Moscow with a belief that in space was not only humanity's future energy resources but also a means of staving off yet another conflict if only old rivals could see their common future in the universe above.

On many a night over the last fourteen months, she had awakened to hear her mother softly crying, and more than once had tapped on her bedroom door, gone in, and lain by her side and held her as they both wept for a man of such simple outward bearing who had shown the world a dream and the courage to face his fate while in pursuit of that dream.

The thought of that, of her father, steadied her nerves for what lay ahead.

Settling into the chairs facing the Senate committee, Victoria did spare a quick glance around the room. C-SPAN, this time, thought the hearing worthy enough to give it live coverage, as did several other networks. She saw old supporters and friends, nodding to them, and of course Jason, who gave her a nervous smile and a "V for victory" sign. Her parents' friend, Senator Mary Dennison of Maine, would chair the proceedings, and as they made eye contact there was a bright smile of encouragement. And also there were Garlin and her supporters sitting in the back of the room. These were the final hours of the hearings.

There were the usual preliminaries, the polite introductions, even a statement of condolence from Senator Proxley about the loss of Dr. Gary Morgan, which she and her mother graciously accepted with thanks.

It was like all the rituals between two gentlemen of the eighteenth century who a few minutes later would do everything possible to rip or blast each other's guts out in a duel to the death.

And then it started.

There were the usual opening statements by each member of the senatorial committee, the usual platitudes and niceties, especially when they sensed the C-SPAN camera was on them. The committee basically fell along party lines, although Victoria sensed several were crossing over in support of the president, whose party held a majority in the House by a few votes but was in the minority in the Senate. But those few who were wavering, she watched carefully. One was from a state where the slashing of NASA's budget had hit deeply, and a major influx would be a coup. Another, who was actually an idealist, was crossing party lines even though it would not mean a cent of profit for his state. He was that rare kind of man who truly voted his conscience and what he felt was best not just for his constituents but for his nation.

Was he the swing vote?

The grilling at last started, led by Proxley, to whom several on his side had ceded their time for questioning. It was absolutely brutal.

"And how much did this failed venture cost your investors?" Proxley asked.

"It was not a failure," Franklin retorted. "It was never intended to be the primary tower but instead a means to haul aloft to geosynch, at a fraction of the cost of traditional launch vehicles, the means to build the second tower."

"I asked how much."

"Seventy-seven billion dollars," Franklin replied, then paused, his old charismatic combativeness in his expression, "give or take a few hundred million. But when it comes to some government programs, what's a few hundred million or even billions, more or less?"

"Stick to answering the question, sir," Proxley snapped back.

"But of course, sir," and he could not resist throwing in an ever-so-slight inflection on the last word, an echo of another time when African-Americans had to address white men with subservience.

Proxley caught the veiled insult and did not comment for a moment.

"And of your personal assets that survived this disaster?" Proxley asked.

"I have submitted my tax returns to this committee as ordered," Franklin replied. "Personal, corporate, and for the variety of entities in which I have financial interests—my personal taxes for the last seven years as well."

He paused and was truly his old self again.

"Even for the years while Kiribati was my place of residence, I still paid my taxes as an American citizen. You already know, as you have it in front of you."

Proxley nodded, making a show of shifting through some of the papers on the table before him, then turning back to an aide sitting behind him, who shuffled through her briefcase and produced a folder. Proxley opened the folder, scanning through the first few pages.

"And I see that while others lost billions on your scheme, you seem to hold well over a billion dollars still in personal assets."

"My net assets prior to the creation of Pillar Inc. were just over sixty-two billion, sir," Franklin retorted. "It is down to less than a billion now. I do not see this line of questioning, sir, as an exploration of how I profited from what has transpired."

"And yet you still retain more than a billion dollars while others who believed in you are filing bankruptcy. I do think that when these hearings are done that the IRS should look into this."

"Be my guest, sir," Franklin shot back. "And note as well then where that final billion goes. Yes, my friends and backers—for example, those in New Mexico whose financial records I expect you have as well—have lost well nigh on to every dime they put into this. Dr. Fuchida, who is not even a citizen of our country, is sitting on a stockpile of manufactured ribbon that he could sell on the open market for billions, but for some interesting reason—dare I call it patriotism?—is refusing to do so and is giving it to Pillar Inc. on credit with no payment date defined. And need I remind you that I own 20 percent of his company?"

"That is not the point here, sir. I am pointing out that you get others to invest in this scheme of yours and yet you still walk away with more than a billion. Is that ethical?"

Franklin stood up.

"Senator Proxley," Franklin snapped. "I started with nothing and built company after company in what used to be called 'the American Way.' I ventured all on a dream inspired by the woman sitting next to me, her husband, their daughter, and an old friend now long gone. I lost nearly everything I have in it but I have no remorse as an American other than the loss of the life of a trusted friend, the loss of others by this accident, and the financial ruin of those who trusted me. Is that not enough of a burden without you accusing me of far worse?"

Proxley sensed the kill and moved in on it.

"Yes, sir, it does require more."

With that, Victoria stood up.

"How dare you," she snapped, and the room fell quiet, all cameras shifting to her. Even Proxley was caught off-balance by this sudden display of anger.

"Young lady, I ask that you resume your seat or I shall ask the sergeant at arms—"

"Go ahead and tell your sergeant of arms to haul me out of here," she shouted back, "and let the whole world see your tactics! How dare you attack this decent man, who gave all he had for a dream for our entire world—a dream for which my father gave his life. And if my family had it to do over again, we would tell him to go forth and do it, because dreams involve risks and indeed the sacrifice of lives, even that of my father."

There were no tears, only cold rage.

Proxley, for once, was absolutely flustered. To order Victoria's forceful eviction from the hearing would make him look like a domineering fascist. But to allow her to continue . . . how would that look on camera?

"I understand you are emotionally distraught, young la—"

"Do not call me 'young lady,'" she said, cutting him off. "I am *Doctor* Morgan, a title earned by me the same as my parents before me, and you shall address me by that title in the same way I shall address you as 'Senator.' As to emotionally distraught, do not dare to cast me into some sexist stereotype of the hysterical young woman."

Proxley's face reddened.

"Do we understand each other"—she paused—"*Senator* Proxley?"

Another pause.

"Yes . . ." and now it seemed as if the words would not come. "Yes, Dr. Morgan."

She turned away from him and faced the chair of the committee.

"I understand under the rules of this meeting I may request, as an American citizen, time to speak, and I request a vote on that now if Mr. Franklin Smith will cede what he sees as his time as well."

Proxley started to object, but the chairperson, Senator Dennison, reached over, put a hand on his forearm, leaned in, and whispered something. Proxley reddened again.

"The chair moves . . ." Mary Dennison, who had most likely waited years for this moment, paused. ". . . that Dr. Morgan be given the time remaining that had been allotted to Mr. Franklin Smith, to address this committee if Mr. Smith so agrees."

Senator Dennison looked around at the other committee members to count hands. None dared to vote against her, not even Proxley, and she nodded.

"Dr. Morgan, you may proceed."

Victoria threw a quick glance over at Franklin, who had already sat down and was actually smiling at her as if saying, *OK, kid, go for it.*

Dear God, she thought, *what have I gotten myself into?* She hesitated.

"Dr. Morgan, your time has started.

And then she thought of her father, and his final words to her: *When I am afraid, then it is OK for you to be afraid.*

She was not afraid.

"Members of this committee . . . humanity is at a dead end."

She paused, her attention no longer fixed on Proxley but on all the others, including the woman from Maine who she recalled long ago had been supportive of her father and was now smiling, as if with pride.

"We cannot deny it. We've had a gut sense of it for at least a generation or more. That two lines on a graph, if you will, were converging. One line is the ever-increasing population around the world, with each of us—whether born in America, Nigeria, India, or even Kiribati—desiring a better life, a safer life, a life free of the fear, war, pestilence, and starvation that has haunted humanity for millennia. That line is going upward.

"And the other line on the graph: the means to provide such things for our planet, the precious resources of our earth—the soil to grow our food, clean water for all, the minerals to be transformed into everything from structures to live within to miracles of science and medicine, and above all else the energy to power that—that line is moving downward.

"They are crossing now, in our generations. Perhaps it happened a decade ago, perhaps not for a few decades hence but they have crossed and the time of reckoning is indeed upon us. Drill deeper, farm more and more marginal land, dig and claw, but there is only so much that can be taken from this cradle, this earth, until at last we turn upon each other to fight over what is left, and that fight will make the conflicts of the previous century pale in comparison."

Now she looked sidelong at Garlin.

"In the early 1970s a work came out titled *The Limits to Growth*. It postulated that humanity had reached its maximum growth potential, given the resources of this planet, and there were but three alternatives. The first: cut back on all demands for resources to stretch them out. The second: force a decline in human population, though the authors were vague on how to do that other than by the most draconian and fascist and eventually racist of means. The third, the natural outcome if we do not rein ourselves in: war and plagues would settle it.

"Their predictions, as with nearly all such predictions, were off by many decades. Their prophecies, which shaped many of the generation of the 1970s and '80s"—again a sharp look over at Garlin and Proxley—"caused the emergence of the green movement, which I applaud to a certain degree, but conservation alone only postponed for a few generations the eventual paradigm of that work. Their thesis is that ultimately for those of us on earth it is a zero-sum game and then someone loses.

"But there was another answer all along and my father quoted it. It came from Tsiolkovsky."

She now looked to her mother. Though Ukrainian and not Russian she still took deep pride in the fact that the first "dreamer" had come from her part of the world, his statue dominating the landscape in front of the university where she had studied.

"Earth is our cradle. We have grown past our infancy with the industrial revolution that started more than two hundred years ago. And now it is time to decide our future, and that deciding starts today, here and now, with this committee and its decision whether to resume support for the one agency above all others that can see the potential of a positive future ahead . . . and that is NASA."

She paused to scan each of them with her gaze.

"In your hands, ladies and gentlemen, senators all, representatives of our blessed free republic, now rests that future if you have the guts to transcend the politics of the moment and reach for what is not just a dream but a reality that my father died for.

"Transform your thinking. Would you want the railroads of 1850 to be as far as we have advanced and how we live; or have the airplanes of 1927, when Lindbergh was hailed as a hero for daring to cross the Atlantic alone, but have us go no further; or trust in what today seems like the medieval torture of the open-heart surgery of the 1960s in contrast to what is now a one-day outpatient procedure without even a scalpel, and that grants decades more to our lives?

"I think not.

"The math of orbital mechanics is as immutable now as it was 2,000 years ago when Aristotle tried to make sense of it all, when Hypatia of Alexandria was tortured to death for daring to try to explain how the universe worked, Galileo locked away, and then men like Newton, Huygens, and Kepler, followed by Tsiolkovsky, Goddard, and Von Braun, found the means to at least begin to touch the universe.

"But the laws of orbital dynamics remained, and ever since the 1950s we have been locked into believing that rocket ships, though dramatic and awe-inspiring as was *Apollo 11* on the day it left for the moon, carrying the dreams of humanity with it, were the only way to reach the heavens."

Again she paused.

"At a cost of hundreds of thousands of dollars per pound. It is a logic that imagines that we build an entire 747, with airports in New York and London, fly the plane but once, then throw the entire aircraft aside and build another.

"I present to you a new paradigm this day, first conceived by Tsiolkovsky of Russia; then, I must say, with humbleness and pride, in the immediate days after the Cold War it was a thesis worked on by my beloved mother and father, who, at the Goddard Space Center, as part of the NASA team, found a guide in a German who had been forced to flee the land of his birth because he was Jewish. That dream was denied funding . . ."

She paused and could not resist it, having waited years for this moment:

"Denied funding by some in this very room, who scoffed at it," and she stared directly at Proxley as she spoke.

"But then this noble man by my side, Franklin Smith, born into segregation and poverty and who transcended that to dream of a future, not of closing off and ending dreams, but of opening up to limitless growth, and put all he had on the line for that. He put together a team that built the first tower. My father died trying to save that tower. I now challenge this committee to pick up the task, to provide for NASA what it needs to again take us to the 'high frontier,' as President Kennedy once called it, and see it to completion. And that, Senator Proxley, is why I object to your line of questioning and your tone of questioning this day to my noble friend and mentor Franklin Smith and feel compelled to speak up in reply."

She fell silent. The room was silent as well.

"Dr. Morgan, your time is up," the chair of the committee announced, then looked at the other committee members arrayed to either side of her.

"I move to offer to Dr. Morgan an additional five minutes to express her conclusion. Are there any who oppose?"

There was no formal vote, only a nodding of heads. Proxley said nothing.

"Thank you, Madam Chairman," Victoria said with a smile.

"Dare I say this?" she said softly, looking at Franklin, for now she was venturing into something they had talked about obliquely but never directly, firmly, with the usual lawyers present and contracts as thick as an old-fashioned phone book on the table.

He looked up at her and smiled.

"Go ahead, I'm all ears," he said softly. "You got the floor."

"Pillar Inc. is near bankruptcy. Even if my friend Franklin Smith still holds some personal assets, he has, to date, lost over 98 percent of all that he owns, yet he gladly placed that on the line for what he believed in.

"How dare you, Senator Proxley, not reveal the full truth: that in his will Smith leaves all his assets"—she paused, fearful of emotion taking hold—"to create a foundation for my mother's continued work in both the sciences and arts to the sum of $100 million, and the rest to a foundation which I have been asked to head, to work on the development of a means to harvest solar energy from space for use on earth as described in my dissertation."

She paused for a moment, because she did have to struggle for emotional control after all.

Whispered comments now flooded the gallery. Franklin looked at Victoria; he was visibly angry that she had broken a confidence.

"Apologies," she whispered to him.

"I just might write you and your children out," he whispered back.

"It will be worth it," she replied, leaning over to embrace him.

"Can I speak now for Pillar Inc.?" she asked.

He gazed at her and smiled.

"What the hell, you've come this far."

She looked straight at Proxley now.

"For nearly fifty years NASA has paved the way to the future, and we all believed in that dream. My parents—even my mother, who was on the other side of the Iron Curtain on that fateful day—spoke with tears in their eyes of the dream as they watched *Apollo 11* climb to the heavens, the moon the first stepping-stone to the stars.

"NASA fueled their dreams throughout the years of the shuttle, in spite of the tragedies of *Challenger* and *Columbia*. NASA enthralled the world when it turned *Hubble* from a source of mockery because of a misground mirror to an elegant capturer of beauty, bringing images of the distant reaches of the galaxies to us. It was NASA that gave us two rovers, little bigger than toy cars, that first scraped back the soil of Mars and told us that water, that bringer of life, existed elsewhere, and then the stunning triumph of *Curiosity*. And what an honor when the NASA staff elected to name the *Curiosity* landing site after that dreamer of dreams, Ray Bradbury.

"I know my time before this committee is running down."

She looked up at Senator Dennison, who smiled and just nodded to her to continue, then gave Proxley a warning glance that if he dared to interrupt Victoria there would be hell to pay.

"I am not directly authorized to speak for Pillar Inc. but I believe I know what Franklin Smith and the thousands who worked alongside him, including my parents, felt when funding for space exploration was almost completely cut off—when Constellation and Aries were canceled; when the parking lot of Goddard was nearly empty, overgrown with weeds, when thousands had once come daily to help pursue those dreams."

She looked at Franklin who nodded for her to go ahead.

"A bill is in Congress to nearly quadruple NASA's budget this year, with the bulk of those funds going to building the Pillar. And Pillar Inc. responds to that with this pledge: you senators provide that budget, as was once done in the long-ago days of President Kennedy. Reignite the dream that limitless growth awaits us; that our answers for our problems here on earth can now be found in space . . . .

"You make that commitment, and Pillar Inc. will turn over to NASA, to the American people—the people of our entire world—free and clear, all technology it has created to build a pathway to the stars, to be supervised by NASA and the American government and the nation of Kiribati, which has so nobly sacrificed so much of their land and way of life in support of this effort. You do that, and we can work together . . .

"We can work together so that, long after we are gone, it will be said that the twenty-first century was the century that NASA, working for the benefit of all humanity, did indeed open the gateway to the stars."

She fell silent, looked about the room, and then sat down.

Franklin leaned over, pressing his lips to her ear so that no one could record it or guess what he was saying.

"You did give away a lot—never a wise move in the opening of negotiations."

She smiled and leaned back.

"It was go-for-broke time, sir," she replied. "Will you agree to the terms?"

"You're right, young Victoria. Go for broke. Carnegie, Morgan, and Gates would have been proud of you."

"What about the Wrights, Lindbergh, McAuliffe, and Armstrong?"

He squeezed her arm even though seconds before she had put a couple of hundred patents and the prior investments of tens of billions on the line.

The motion to thus increase NASA's budget for that year with the agreement to assume control of the Pillar passed seven to one. Two weeks later it was on the floor of the Senate, where it passed by an overwhelming majority; the identical bill swept through the House and then, three days after that, was on the desk of the president, who signed and proclaimed jokingly with Victoria, her mother, and Franklin by her side that she wanted a ticket on the first ride up.

They were back in business, and that night, alone, Victoria wept with gratitude . . . and remorse that her father was not there to share the moment.

21

Though still in an EVA suit she took a deep breath before opening the airlock door. It held for a second, resisting her grasp, for it had seemed like an eternity since this hatchway had been opened. There was always the chance the seals had atrophied, and before the door was opened, those on the other side had been ordered to don EVA gear as well.

A slight rush of air—outward, actually—as the hatch popped open. She floated "down" through the opening, gazing about, trying to focus her attention on the three who awaited her, almost drawn up in a formal line, floating in the middle of the station.

She extended her hand.

"Commander Singh, it is an honor to meet you," she said, avoiding the line her father had used more than two and a half years ago. "Permission to come aboard."

Singh extended her hand, grasping it.

"Permission granted, Dr. Morgan, welcome aboard."

She next grasped the hands of Philips and Malady which quickly turned into hugs.

"It's been more than two years since we've seen another person," Philips offered, almost as an apology.

Victoria was nearly overcome with emotion, but on the day her father died she had learned to transcend that kind of display. Never show fear unless the one you trust is afraid, and never show open emotion if they were to get this job done, led by a woman barely in her mid twenties.

The fact that she was even on this flight, the first manned mission back to the station since the collapse, was a testament to her inner fire and determination. Though easy on the surface, the agreement that NASA would take over control of Pillar Inc.—but, at the same time, Pillar Inc. would operate as a private firm and, upon completion of the tower, run it—had been complex. Exactly where were the management dividing lines between operations, design, deployments, launches, crews, and who owned what could have proven to be a nightmare. For a while it looked as if the open offer Victoria had made in Franklin's name was turning into a lawyer's dream: hundreds of lawyers arrayed on both sides, with enough paperwork that if loaded into a resupply ship would have grounded it.

Fortunately there was a forceful president who cut through most of it with the sharp demand to get the job done, and quoting one of her old favorite miniseries—a western, also a favorite of Franklin's—declared, "We make a deal fair to us and fair to you. Now everyone shut the hell up: we have a handshake with a man I trust. Now let's get back into space."

Nearly all of the R & D team were shifted from the all-but-bankrupt Seattle firm, back under the aegis of NASA at Goddard, which had the most open space of any with their semi-deserted labs. NASA in no way could meet the payrolls some of them had been garnering in the private sector after going into exile from that beloved lab during the lean years. Many took the cut to see the project through, and for those who had legitimate financial issues, like four kids in college and grad school, "someone" would come through with a scholarship to help balance things out.

Some would continue to work for a scaled-back Pillar, the way contractors from Boeing, Lockheed Martin, Marietta, and other firms once filled the halls of Goddard as well. Launch costs would go fully to NASA and nearly overnight the Brit and his partner felt overwhelmed by the personnel coming in to their bases in New Mexico and their island in Kiribati, going over every inch of the launch vehicles that had been completed but waiting to go since the disaster and wanting to install additional backups and redundancies that would have added tons to the vehicles and required a year or more of downtime.

The president, in an "informal" visit to the facility, talked about the risks Americans once took, including an ancestor of hers who had gone west in a covered wagon in a very different time when such risks were part of life and part of being an American. The message was clear: *We will take risks to get the job done that we once accepted in the early days of* NASA *and must do so again if the dream is ever to be achieved.* The video of the teams who were scheduled to go aloft, arrayed around Victoria, had carried the message home. They were volunteers ready to put their lives on the line. It was time to start flying again. The president closed her interview just before the mission lift-off by invoking Amelia Earhart: "In the days after her flight disappeared, did we ground all aviation? Did we shrink back and say we must rethink all this and not fly again until surely it was safe? Of course not: we forged ahead. And I ask you, what would she have told us to do?"

It resonated, and since Kiribati was relatively close to where Earhart's plane disappeared, Franklin had seized on the moment, and days later the main airport at Tarawa was renamed "Amelia Earhart International."

Not since the 1960s had there been such a flood of effort to rapidly assemble launch systems to haul up crews, supplies, and ribbon. There was, as well, out at Edwards Air Force Base, a new complex—for the time being kept classified—to test out another component of the system. This was where Victoria spent most of her time before launch. She was grateful when specialists were added to their team who had designed similar systems for the International Space Station twenty years earlier.

And as for Victoria, her life had literally turned upside down. Franklin had moved her into the slot of vice president of Pillar Inc., which put her on the cover of nearly every magazine, on the Internet and in print, as one of the youngest top execs of the century—to which she replied that those before her, including Jobs, Gates, and Franklin himself, had achieved far more and started with much less when they were younger than she was now.

With that behind her, she had bullied her way aboard the return launch to the station. It was not just a joyride, as critics screamed; it was management from above, and the term caught on. She needed a firsthand evaluation of what was already in place, what progress had been made during the lonely exile of the three, and when all would be in ready to resume construction. It was one thing to get a report; it was another thing to see it in person.

"And besides," Franklin whispered with a grin even while her mother objected, "it is the stuff of publicity, which we need."

Victoria temporarily shifted out of her position at Edwards, delighted to hand all the technical aspects over to an old NASA hand who was considered the real wizard of such systems and how to package them inside a standard loft vehicle, then get them up to geosynch as the first test models. She spent the following month at Langley, that old training center for Apollo and shuttle astronauts, an intense month of training, then out to New Mexico for more training, including several rides on the dreaded "vomit comet," the aircraft designed to simulate zero gravity, at least for thirty seconds or so per parabolic curving flight at 30,000 feet. She actually held it together this time, with eight hundred hours of flight time under her belt and a commercial flight rating—not much compared to the real pros around her, but it was still enough to at least gain a tad of respect. It was a lot of sixteen- to eighteen-hour days. In a sense it was also a joyful release after so many years of academic discipline and increasingly complex business management decisions. The only thing she truly dreaded was the 7K conditioning run at dawn. Only someone who was truly perverted and a masochist could enjoy such a thing, she muttered every morning at six a.m. as she staggered to keep up with the pack of astronauts, who seemed to actually take pleasure in it all, her pale face lagging behind at times, pride demanding that she sprint to catch up at the end.

She realized, though, that with NASA now fully on board in a team effort, she had to struggle to meet their traditional standards as well for this to go smoothly and for her to be accepted as more than just a mere "tourist."

As for Jason? She had called off the wedding. That had broken her heart and his. It was not that she did not love him; she did. It was just that too much had happened too quickly: the collapse, the death of her father, the mourning, the defense of her dissertation, and then the months of preparation for the few minutes before the Senate that had changed everything.

She had made a promise—"When everything settles down, *we'll* settle down," she told him—but for now . . .

She knew that it hurt Jason more than it hurt her, and with all the transfers of personnel back and forth between Pillar Inc., NASA, and others, she found it interesting that Franklin had personally retained Jason as his "historical consultant."

The usual cheap gossip rags tried to make a play on the whole story with their tawdry headlines that someone else was in the picture with the rising young executive and, it seemed, the eventual heir to Pillar Inc. She could hardly walk down the street with a male colleague, regardless of age, without their grainy photos being spread about! When a Hollywood star, a longtime supporter of the space program, who had starred in a film about one of the most fabled moments in NASA history, came to New Mexico to "check it out," took a ride on the Brit's suborbital craft *Spaceship One*, and pronounced his wholehearted support for the program, the paparazzi truly swarmed, much to Franklin's delight and her frustration. The tabloids plastered a photo of the actor giving Victoria an enthusiastic hug after the flight—which she had gone along on—even though the star was a happily married man and very much a "straight arrow" . . . and more than twice her age.

"Why do you think I became so secretive?" Franklin said with a chuckle when she came into his office to vent, showing him the latest breathless broadcast on her iPad. He just smiled and said, "Welcome to fame."

And she was indeed famous. The young woman who had confronted a senator who had once defeated her father—and publicly brought the politician down—now was cited as one of the most influential executives of this renaissance of the space program. The senator had announced his retirement at the end of the year and there was already a scramble afoot for the special election to replace him, the front-runner an aggressive young man, the nephew of an astronaut of the Gemini days.

They were riding a wave at this moment, but like Apollo, Jason had so rightly warned her, it could also be a bubble, with public attention popping in a day, racing to some other cause, and a year later the budget would be slashed again for some more pressing need "down here on earth." Especially if another disaster hit like the last one. This time they had to do it right—there would be not third chance if this time they failed—and Victoria felt the entire weight of that on her shoulders and understood now why Franklin had seemed to age ten years in the last two, and her mother, back at Goddard, heading up the entire R & D team there on ribbon design, had appeared to drift as well. Still elegant, in the way that Ukrainian women seemed to manage well into their fifties and sixties, nonetheless the trauma of losing the one true love of her life had left its mark. Eva was still as dedicated a scientist as ever, but she had taken a much more mystical turn, speaking increasingly of how the Pillar would be not just a technological achievement to define the twenty-first century, but a renewed spiritual achievement as well, an act of faith that the future was boundless and would transform us.

All of these factors had contributed to Victoria's successful argument that she should occupy the fourth seat for the first manned return to the station in two years. Someone had, of course, pointed out the cost per pound of her estimated weight of 125 pounds, to which she retorted that if she could save the taxpayers a hundred million by what she learned and bring the Pillar in even a week ahead of schedule, that was the payback, and if not, she would personally find a way to pay back every dime of her trip. Her newfound friend in Hollywood announced he'd pay for half of her ticket if that day ever came, then slyly added that if that did not occur, he hoped for one of the first rides aloft on the ribbon.

And now she had ridden the "throne of fire" into the heavens, launched from Kiribati.

The ride up had been everything she dreamed it would be: the drama of the countdown, the kick in the butt of lift-off, the buildup of g's, the momentary near-heart-stopping moment of first-stage separation and second-stage ignition, and what would perhaps forever be a haunting announcement: "You are go at throttle up." Once in low earth orbit they aligned, made their next burn, and spiraled up to geosynch at 23,000 miles over the next day and a half. And if all went as planned, such manned flights would be as obsolete as steam trains and sailing ships, which, long after their useful passage, still held something of a spiritual place in the souls of so many.

She floated in the middle of the station, looking about. It certainly had a worn and battered look about it, unlike the popular image of space stations with gleaming interiors of polished metal and white paint. It almost looked like the interior of a dingy warehouse, except for the startlingly brilliant shafts of sunlight pouring in through the portholes. To conserve on energy, the crew had long ago shut down the usual lighting system; besides, more than half the bulbs had burned out long ago.

"OK to open faceplates?" she asked of Singh, and again flashed on a memory of her father.

"Pressure is equalized," Singh announced, looking back at her control station monitor, then opened her own faceplate and took off her helmet.

Victoria did the same, and it was a tough struggle not to gag. The station reeked of more than two years of human habitation, which in the last months had been reduced to showers just twice a month to conserve water; and while one worked, the other two had to go to their bunks and remain motionless to conserve oxygen. The scrubbers and filters had long ago gone far beyond 150 percentage of usage and over the last month it had been a near-run thing. One scrubber unit had failed months ago. If a second went down after all this time aloft, they would have to abandon the station. In talking with Singh on the climb up, the commander of the station had dwelled on that more than anything else: get the new oxygen scrubbers and filters running before anything else!

She looked at the three. Kevin had given up shaving and just trimmed his beard so that a stray hair did not somehow jam his helmet lock. He could easily have played the role of his fictional role model, the fictional Conan the Barbarian. Both Jenna and Singh had dropped a lot of weight and cut their hair short so as to not be troubled by washing it more than twice a month. Their uniforms were worn, faded, and loose-fitting as they began to take off their bulky EVA suits. Though less than ten years older than Victoria, Singh had streaks of gray in her hair.

And yet . . . the three who floated about her were filled with delight, to a certain degree, although she could also sense a touch of defiance. They had come to work as such a perfect team, and they were not sure how to react to a "stranger" in their midst after their initial joy.

She smiled, extending her hand to each, and instantly noted a certain deference—and knew why. She was the daughter of a former shipmate who had given his life.

She figured it was best to start on a light note.

"The resupply ship that has just docked has on board, compliments of NASA, a dozen pizzas from Luigi's of Little Italy and something called cannolis, compliments of their chef; a dozen barbecue sandwiches from Phil's Bar-B-Que Pit of Black Mountain, North Carolina; and a dozen various curry dishes. And yes, first priority: get a new oxygen scrubber online."

"Thank you, Doctor," Singh replied, and for a brief instant Victoria was almost disappointed by the reaction. "Did you bring along water for showers? Even two gallons a person would be heaven."

"Ten gallons each just for today," Victoria replied, "and a better recycling system to be installed so you can use it again and again."

"Oh, thank God," Kevin of all people sighed.

The argument about the crew transfers was something Victoria had anticipated but not to this intensity. She assumed that, after two-plus years aboard the station, all three would be clawing at the airlock hatch to get the hell out of there in spite of their public statements about staying on no matter what. It was, in fact, the exact opposite of what the experts, newly rehired at Goddard, Langley, and JPL, and who had once managed crews aboard the space station, had predicted.

Rather than being "spacey" they had, instead, become so accustomed to their lives in space, and especially the freedom of microgravity, that a return to earth, with its dreadful gravity, its bustling crowds, and the feared flood of media had in fact become terrifying to them. Nor were there the traditional family ties that tended to bond crews back to earth. Two were single, one divorced, and none had children. The parents of all three were still alive; two sets of parents were ex-military who praised the ideal of service; the third, doctors who did missionary work in Mongolia of all places, went along with that ideal as well. The tragic bond of their fourth crew member whose wife and children had died in an auto accident did not compel them to look earthward with longing, desire, or even much nostalgia.

They had bonded as a team, for a while not sure if they would even survive to the next day, especially when four months back a micrometeor less than half an inch across had blown clean through the main cabin, missing Singh by only several inches, while Kevin was out on an EVA. It was only Jenna's instant reaction, slapping emergency patches on the entry and exit damage, that had saved them. And that "night," with all comm links shut off, they had held Singh as she cried, admitting she had been so terrified that she had frozen in fear. The following day, comm links back open, scant mention was made of the incident, and her two comrades—her two friends—thought nothing less of her reaction and still clearly deferred to her as "the skipper," as they had come to call her.

They were bonded. In private they jokingly referred to themselves as "the monastery." That, like the ancient monasteries of Ireland during the Dark Ages, they had continued to believe in the future and kept ancient and new knowledge alive. And like a monastery they had worked their way around what more than a few on earth, mostly the tabloids, did speculate about in terms of one man and two women floating about alone in space for more than two years. They had long ago reached a very clear understanding that such an issue could tear their unity apart and they were indeed a monastery on board their ship. The one interviewer who had, with a bit of a sarcastic smile, tried to raise that question nearly had his head ripped off by all three when he raised the issue in a live broadcast and they had refused any more interviews from that media outlet, or any other that treaded into that territory.

Now four strangers were coming into their isolated but splendid universe. They were welcomed but also a threat, upsetting the delicate balance of their comfortable arrangement.

Victoria had taken the lead and boarded first; the other three new crew members, waiting in their launch vehicle, expected to be allowed to come aboard, but she had wisely counseled that they stay in their vehicle until she had smoothed the way for these three who had kept lonely watch for such a long time while those down on earth debated the future of this station and their dreams and for a while had even seemed ready to abandon the dream.

It struck her as strange, nearly moving her to tears, which she had long ago conditioned herself to contain, when she looked at one of the private bunks and saw the nameplate of her father. Singh came to her side as if to offer condolences. She forced a smile as she accepted her words about his bravery and inspiration, but said nothing in reply, which she hoped Singh would understand. They had preserved her father's bunk as if it were a shrine to his memory.

"We've not entered it since he left. We really did hope that one day you would come up to join us and . . ." Singh's voice trailed off. So curious, Victoria thought as she gazed at the closed curtains of the bunk. She had long ago come to terms with her father's death. For these three, he had become iconic and what was unfolding now was a ritual they had long contemplated. She must now play her part.

The three floated beside her as she slowly pulled the curtain back and gazed within its narrow confines.

"We haven't touched it since he went on his mission," Kevin said. "We'd be honored if you would go in and check it out."

The gesture struck her as far too sentimental, but she could see that to these three, who just might indeed be a bit "spacey" after all, it was a ritual they had anticipated ever since word had been sent up that she was part of the ascent crew.

They withdrew to the far side of the station by the control center as Victoria pulled herself into the bunk and then closed the curtain. It was a bit like a sarcophagus, a museum, a memorial to her father. Still secured to the wall were half a dozen old photographs, somewhat faded now from the unfiltered light of the sun. Her mother and father with their mentor, Erich, when they first met at Goddard and obviously had yet to realize, let alone admit, that they were falling in love. The standard formal photo, the two standing stiffly to either side of the elderly gentleman, looking at the camera and not at each other. *My God, they looked so young! Dad had not yet been bowed and twisted by the ravages of Parkinson's*, she thought.

A photo of the two of them, now publicly in love, looking up from the desk in Erich's office, papers scattered about, her father gazing at her mother while she faced at the camera; beneath the table it was obvious they were holding hands. Another of their wedding, then one of her mother holding her as a newborn, her father joyfully hovering in the background, slightly out of focus; then a photo of Victoria disembarking from the Brit's *Spaceship One* with a childlike grin after their flight; another of Jason and her smiling, holding hands on a beach; which did give her pause to reflect. And then the one that moved her to tears: her father holding her; she was about four or so, the two of them looking at the camera held by her mother, both of them laughing about some long-forgotten joke.

It spoke much of her father, of what he held to be important in his life, that these were the images he had carried aloft. His personal pad was secured in a holding bin; that was his. It was almost like invading his privacy, and she left it alone. There were changes of clothes, an old faded "Goddard" T-shirt, the usual odds and ends, and then something caught her eye. A hint of gold, his wedding ring with a string looped through it, holding it in place as it floated away from the bulkhead, a slip of paper attached. She took the paper, turned it over. It was his handwriting.

If I don't come back from this mission, give this to my beloved wife as a keepsake of our eternal love. Tell her that one day we will dance amongst the stars off the "shoulder of Orion." Victoria, if you are reading this, as I pray you shall, know how much we both love you.

And now she did cry, a real, deep-in-the-soul cry, actually the first since the day her father died and she had been forced to turn a public face to the world. Up here she was alone, with his things, she did not have to be strong for her mother now, and was thankful the rest of the crew had so discreetly withdrawn. She wondered if they had seen the ring and the attached note, and that was why they had withdrawn to the far end of the station. But her heart told her no. They respected her father far too much to invade his privacy, even in death.

"I miss you so much, Daddy," she whispered over and over as she gazed out the window to the heavens, but that sight gave her comfort as well: it was "his" universe, and somehow she felt he was actually still nearby, smiling his indulgent, loving grin for his little angel, who had given him so much joy in life and so much pride as she matured into who she was this day.

She would leave the ring and note in place until it was time for her to return to earth, when she would return it to her mother. She took several moments for a few deep breaths, gazed out the small bunk area's porthole—she knew her father had spent hours with his nose pressed to the window—then eased herself out of the bunk and floated over to where the other three waited, seated around the "kitchen table" of the station . . . their station.

No one spoke for several minutes. It was obvious Victoria had been crying: in zero gravity the moisture still clung around her eyes. Singh was at the microwave and produced four sealed containers of hot tea, offering one to each, and settled into the seat across from Victoria.

"I have a replacement crew waiting on board the docked vehicle," Victoria announced, wishing to move straight to the harder issues at hand. "You know that."

None of the three who had maintained such a long and lonely vigil spoke.

"We have NASA backing now, more than we ever dreamed of three years ago. The government is putting forty billion into this in the next year, other nations ten billion more. It's stunning what is going on back down there, thanks to you guys. Goddard, JPL, Langley, Kennedy, are again beehives packed with some of the best brains in the world. Even some of the old-timers going back as far as Apollo are pitching in."

She laughed.

"I had one of the original Apollo guys actually all but cussing me out that he was still fit enough to get up here and lend a hand and would pay for the flight if need be!

"We have the same amount next year as well if they see progress. You kept the long vigil, my friends. The whole world knows that—is proud of you—and I think for the first time in a couple of generations a ticker tape parade is waiting."

"So now we are to leave it?" Singh asked. "Is that it?"

Victoria did not reply, just nodded her head, and learned as her father had that such a simple gesture in microgravity required hanging on to the table.

"We took a vote, Dr. Morgan, before you got here. Who better to man this station than us? We are not leaving!" Kevin said angrily, such a sudden shift from but minutes before, when he was all but tearful as he helped guide her to her father's sacred bunk.

"Which, by the way, we are naming *Morgan Station*," Jenna added.

"Those so-called astronauts you just brought up with you, tucked in like Spam in a can: Who selected them?" Kevin asked sharply.

"It was a combined decision of NASA and Pillar."

Jenna snorted disdainfully.

"I looked at their profiles. Never heard of even one of them," Jenna said.

"Two were training for the Aries project," Victoria replied, immediately realizing that Jenna and Kevin had already put her on the defensive, justifying rather than directing. "The oldest, Captain Sanders, flew one of the last shuttle missions, so he's proven his stuff. I can assure you, they *all* know their stuff. The third, she flew with the *Saturn Six* project until that went down."

"Yeah, went down in a flaming wreck. Damn near put the private space industry out of business," Jenna pointed out.

Victoria said nothing, understanding how they felt. She did wonder at that instant if Defoe should have written an addendum to his book, noting that a week after being "rescued," Robinson Crusoe and Friday demanded that the ship turn around and take them back to their island, where in reality they were perfectly happy.

She suddenly realized she had a real "personnel management" problem on her hands and wondered if her mentor, Franklin Smith, had agreed to her going up on this launch for precisely this reason and was now down there on Kiribati, quietly laughing his butt off.

She looked from one to the other.

"They've been well trained. I think you know the change in my role in this entire project." She regretted saying that the moment the words slipped out of her; it implied a threat that she was now "the boss," like it or not. She fumbled for a moment, then continued. "I would not have gone along with their coming up here if I didn't think they were the best. All have a thorough briefing on ribbon deployment."

"Bull," Kevin sneered. "Two years of working up here versus some simulation training? No way! I've racked up over two hundred EVAs, out there damn nearly every day, looking at every angle of how to deploy the ribbon. I'm the only one in the entire universe who has actually stitched two ribbons together while in space and not in some damn simulator. I should ask for a damn raise rather than agree to being sent back down."

"Besides," Singh said, her voice soft, appealing. "We are no longer part of earth. We are the next generation. Live or die, we are part of the stars, the way your father was . . ."

She paused.

". . . and still is."

Victoria stared intently at Singh.

"Would you mind saying that again, please?" Victoria asked, voice choking.

"Your parents and Franklin gave us the shot at a dream when most had turned their backs on the potentials of that dream. As kids we worshipped NASA, dreamed of working for it, saw it as the gateway to the future. At a time when the dream flickered and nearly died—while politicians like Proxley fought against it and demagogues like Garlin denounced it but offered nothing as a realistic alternative—we still believed."

She paused, looking into Victoria's eyes.

"And then we three, out of all humanity we three were given a chance to help fulfill the dream. Hell, you can tell Franklin he is a lousy negotiator. Rather than pay us, we'd've paid him for the chance to do this."

Singh looked at her two comrades, who nodded.

"Though I do wonder what my 401(k) looks like now," Jenna said with a smile, "and my savings? I haven't spent a dime the entire time I've been up here other than to send flowers to my mom and dad each month."

Victoria could not help but smile at that.

"We no longer belong below on earth," Singh announced, and there was a forcefulness to her voice.

"Don't you miss it at all?" Victoria asked.

Singh smiled.

"Sure, I miss the green; and remember, I am from India, and we have the most lush variations of green on the face of that good earth below us—though some Irish I know might argue with me," she replied, with a smiling glance at Kevin.

"I miss my parents, and there was once a young man I still think of at times who I learned recently married someone else," she added.

Another moment of silence.

Victoria did not say anything, though she did feel a bit of a stab.

"Long ago—a long, long time ago—adventurers, explorers from your Europe, set sail around the world on a journey that would take years. I know your closeness to a historian who is an adviser to this project," Singh said. "I remember him from the day we first flew together."

Victoria nodded, struggling to show no emotion, this time holding on to the edge of the table.

"He'll tell you that for each who did return, a score, all but forgotten by history, did not. But they went, many for a journey of years, knowing that it might be for years—perhaps forever—and welcomed the challenge. Some came up on distant shores half a world away and decided, 'Here is my place; here I shall stay.' Some with self-serving, even evil intent, others for the most part idealistic. I want you to realize, Dr. Morgan, that we are the latter.

"We originally came up here on a mission of but six months. That was over two years ago. But in that time we have changed. We talked night after night—if you can define our time up here as night and day—about what we would do when you and this crew arrived.

"And we made our decision together."

She looked at Kevin and Jenna, who were smiling—Kevin, of all people, with tears in his eyes, nodding.

"We no longer belong on earth. This is our place. This is our dream. This is our life's work. We hoped it would be you personally who would come up so we could discuss it as we now do, and we are grateful that you have done so."

She paused, then looked back at Victoria.

"We are staying here to see the job done, and, once done, we are staying anyhow. We are the first of a new generation of spacefarers, thanks to Pillar and now, with blessed gratitude, thanks to NASA, and here we shall stay."

A half hour later Victoria finally opened the private comm link down to Kiribati, Houston, and Goddard. She was actually tempted to use the line "Houston, we have a problem here." But in reality they didn't. She forced a smile as she simply said, "Ground, this is *Station One*."

She hesitated for a moment and then said it.

"Correction. Ground, this is *Morgan Station*. We have an interesting situation to discuss."

The "other three" were finally welcomed aboard with a formal, slightly forced, but nevertheless semi-friendly greeting ceremony. Given the naval background of two of the seven, they observed the old ritual of first saluting an American flag decal applied to the aft bulkhead, then saluted "Commander Singh" and said, "Request permission to come aboard, sir."

There had actually been no tension whatsoever on the part of what was supposed to be the replacement crew. Prior to launch, the flight psychologists at Houston had even anticipated this scenario, at least to a certain degree, and discussed how to handle it. For that, Victoria was indeed grateful to NASA.

The living arrangements were that the three "space settlers," as one media source had already branded them, would continue to occupy their old bunks. Victoria would have the fourth, which had belonged to her father, and the other three, when not on duty rotation, would retire to their docked module and maintain their personal possessions there.

In a gesture of compromise, Kevin even offered two of his precious pizzas as the evening meal with half of his cannolis as dessert, and Captain Hurt, an ex–British Harrier pilot, provided a certain liquid "refreshment" that was absolutely against regulations but which Victoria thanked God he had smuggled aboard in his personal gear bag, even though he might have lost his flight slot if it had been discovered.

"A traditional gift of my Scot ancestors on my mother's side," he said with a smile when he opened the flight bag and pulled out its contents. It did more to "smooth the waters" between the two teams than any speeches or appeals, and by the end of the evening Kevin was embracing the Brit-Scot as a long-lost comrade and explaining the complexities of stitching ribbon together in zero g without cutting yourself in half.

Kevin was now eager to see the "stitching machine" the team had brought up in their cargo compartment and then trying it out on the next day's EVA. They started unpacking gear. One of the precious oxygen scrubbers that had been stowed for quick access in the crew cabin of their ship was soon installed to handle the extra load of four more on board, and within the hour the original three were exclaiming how wonderful it was, while the four "newbies" were gasping, with watering eyes, and wondering how these three "old-timers" had stood it for so long. The place really did stink and would take some getting used to.

As Victoria settled herself into what had once been her father's bunk, she smiled. It was obvious it was time for "the boss" to "take a hike" and leave the crews to get to know each other and merge into a single team. In a sense she would always be the "outsider," but she had no regrets about that. Franklin in his mentoring had told her so often that she would have to take that role, almost like a monk or a nun, in much the same way that the original three in this station had done in order to survive.

The gift of Maury Hurt, the Brit-Scot, had done much to help in the bonding. Amazing, the human bonding rituals, she thought. Surely her beloved and much-missed Jason could give her scores of such examples from the past, of Irish and Chinese working side by side on the transcontinental railroad, perhaps ready to kill each other at first, but then most likely bonded by some of the same rituals, thanks to a hidden still using either rice or potatoes, and in short order willing to risk their lives for each other.

While they had celebrated, she wandered off on her own to examine the station, going over a detailed checklist given to her by a team at NASA. *Morgan Station* been aloft for over three years; it had been built around designs dating back to the 1970s. It was now fraught with perils. As for her "settlers," they had been exposed to radiation from the sun for an extended period. By all rights and responsibilities she should order the three off the station and send them back down the next day while advising the three replacements to keep their EVA suits close at hand and, when not on duty, to spend every minute possible in their own ascent and descent ship.

But she could not. They, far better than she, knew the risks they were taking and had made clear their decision. They had no cause for complaint. She thought of how Robert Falcon Scott, the Antarctic explorer, had written those lines in his final diary entry. He had embarked on an adventure, things had played out against him, but his final words were for others to continue the dream. Such had been the spirit of the age of polar exploration, which preceded that of the sky above, and she prayed that the spirit of this age, which her father, mother, and Franklin had struggled to open up, was renewed again now.

There would be risks aplenty in the years to come as the ribbon became the first truly viable means to reach the heavens and at the same time a way to solve some of the environmental problems on an overcrowded and polluted earth. Her comrades aboard this smelly, aging craft, laughing one moment, talking serious business the next, were the forerunners of a new generation that would lead the way.

And she understood yet again that there were things in this life worth putting your life on the line for.

She gazed at the earth below.

This was no longer about just building a tower to get to geosynch, as her parents had dreamed. This was about saving the world below.

Content, she drifted off to sleep, barely hearing the laughing and singing just beyond her curtain, nor worried about the arguments she would have to counter from the people down below come dawn, explaining that now the station had seven on board and they damn well had to figure out how to double the shipment of supplies to keep them alive while the tower was being built.

22

The Ribbon Goes Down

In the four months since Victoria and the other three crew members had docked, so much had changed, in space and on earth. The team had merged together somewhat well, though when on the following day she had passed the word back to the mission controls in Kiribati and Houston that all seven were staying up for the time being, there had been howls of protest. The schedule was for the three veterans to undock and head back "for home" the day after the new team arrived.

It was a historic moment. The first mutiny in space! And inwardly Victoria rather enjoyed it, as Singh and Kevin articulated their position to the world in such a forceful manner that even the president, the head of NASA, and Franklin were forced to concede, even though it meant a doubling of resupply launches—at no small expense—with the caveat that there would be no more pizzas and they would be lucky to be eating Spam out of squeeze tubes, with showers rationed to one quart of water per week.

The delicate balance of personal relationships also went on edge. Kevin and Hurt bonded wonderfully. Hurt was the crew's new expert on ribbon design, which had evolved significantly in the two years that the station had been cut off, while Kevin walked him through his own thoughts on deployment and stitching. The newer design did bear striking resemblance to old-fashioned movie film, with perforated edges to facilitate a stitching thread bonding them together, either side by side, or laminated one atop the other. Each thread carried a conductivity fiber to provide energy—not enough to fully power, but at least to augment spinners and the ascent or descent of a pod.

All was moving into place for renewed deployment after a delay of over two and a half years to make the second try, this time with the full backing of NASA.

But much was transpiring on earth as well. Oil was peaking at over $225 a barrel now, and there was the usual threat of war in the entire Middle Eastern region as the oil-producing nations scrambled to milk the last of the reserves. With global demand increasing at more than 10 percent a year even as production peaked, some were saying that—rather than fund yet another mad scheme in space—the money could be better spent on R & D for better oil extraction, the cleaner burning of coal, or even fusion power.

The economic crisis in America and the European Union in the second decade of the twenty-first century was coming home to roost in the third decade, taxes to handle the debt loads were spiraling, and many were arguing that the investment over four years of at least $180 billion of taxpayers' money on top of what Pillar Inc. had sunk in and pretty well lost was absurd. Garlin and others like her were readily available on the Internet casts to bitterly denounce the entire project as the greatest boondoggle of the century, out of which somehow the wily Franklin Smith and his cohort, who was simply cast as a sentimental crowd pleaser, along with Victoria Morgan, would find a way to walk away with what was left when the entire project failed as the previous one had.

Perhaps it is best I'm up here, Victoria thought even though she finally agreed to a televised "discussion" with Garlin that swiftly broke down, with Garlin attempting to lecture her as if she were dressing down a recalcitrant undergraduate; Victoria deeply resented it but did not let her temper show, until Garlin mentioned that Victoria's father had once been a student of hers as well and she regretted he had not paid closer attention in her class, a veiled implication that he would still be alive if he had.

"Mention of my father is beyond the scope of this discussion," Victoria shot back, now angry.

Garlin, sputtering, prepared to strike back but Victoria shot first, "When you are ready to debate the merits of what the Pillar will accomplish rather than act in such a disdainful manner let me know, until then I have far more important things to attend to," and she switched the screen off.

Her response was greeted with applause from her comrades on board the station, and from around the world.

The final supply vehicle launched from Kiribati, hurriedly prepared ahead of schedule in order to support the crew of seven, had been a near-run thing, as one of the five thrusters was lost shortly after lift-off. If it had gone down, they would have been delayed nearly a year, since along with additional food, water, and oxygen, the rest of the hull was packed with Fuchida's ribbon, as yet unpaid for. It carried as well the newly designed drop stage, a generation ahead of the one that had carried down the first wire. If the launch had failed, the station would have been abandoned, its reserve supplies consumed by the near doubling of the crew size.

With the supply run docked, the air far more breathable (and someone had smuggled aboard a sandwich, a pizza, and some contraband for the Brit), it was time to truly begin their task. That had darn near triggered a true fistfight. Kevin had demanded the right to direct the EVA as the ribbon was deployed, while Sanders, the actual commander of the second crew to join them, argued he was the one trained for that. Victoria, management skills to the fore, pointed out that it would have to be Hurt, with Kevin—their EVA expert with more hours "out there" than all other astronauts combined—ensuring the safe and continuous deployment of the ribbon out of the four reels, with 23,000 miles of ribbon for the drop, while several reels of the retrieved wire from the earlier effort would be sent out with counterweights attached to balance the load.

With the ever-improving technology of ribbon spinning, the designs had changed, but fortunately the integration of the older ribbon design with the new had been kept in mind.

The descent stage would start the long fall back to earth, while Malady and Hurt, rotating shifts with Jenna as backup and safety control, would supervise the stapling together of the end of one ribbon on a reel to the next one in line. The reels' unique design left the last hundred meters of ribbon exposed, and while only a dozen meters away a reel played out the ribbon to the descent stage—which, once started, could not easily be stopped—the EVA team would hurriedly staple the next reel of nearly 8,000 miles of ribbon to the previous one. When each reel was empty of its cargo, it would break apart, making room for the next reel to start spinning out its load. Once the ribbon was locked in place on earth, its upper end would be attached to the still-intact upper wire of the tower, which stretched upward for thousands of miles, counterweighted by discarded upper stages and empty reels, providing a nearly rock-solid attachment for the reels of ribbon lined up and ready to go. The thousands upon thousands of miles of the old wire now continued to serve the mission, providing the extension for the counterweight that would eventually extend outward 17,000 miles, thus sustaining tension on the ribbon below.

It would be a highly dangerous operation. The deployment of the first wire was a strand only two millimeters in diameter, all on one reel. This was magnitudes greater, a ribbon, with almost fifty times the tensile and compression strengths, requiring four reels, their size limited by the third-stage vehicles that sent them aloft over the last year, the single most expensive line item of the entire budget now under NASA's control.

Once in place and securely locked, within days the ribbon could withstand stress loads twenty times greater than the first wire. Additional ribbon would then be run up from earth, a ton or more at a time, the first load going up to geosynch, then the second one laminating a layer on top of the first one from ground level up to a thousand miles. One more supply run via rocket would carry up additional ribbon, supplies for the team on board, and an extension unit for the station to eventually support additional workers. If the drop was successful, the program would truly shift into high gear; if it failed, chances were there would not be another chance, for surely political will would turn against the program yet again. Though Proxley had announced his resignation, he would surely leap back in if he saw the chance.

And thus it would go with each additional reel of ribbon, most to be stitched on to broaden the width of the ribbon and its carrying capacity. A ribbon a couple of meters wide could have easily endured the hit by the errant Soviet satellite and kept right on functioning, with a repair unit running down on the side of the ribbon not damaged, patching the cut, and then returning.

Each ribbon now had fibers that could conduct electricity to provide supplemental power to a "stitcher," as the units were now called, rather than "spinners." Eventually, some of the ribbons would be almost entirely made of conductive fibers; then Victoria could reach for her particular dream: to use the tower for transmitting absolutely limitless solar energy back to earth.

The day at last arrived, and Sanders, Hurt, and Kevin were all EVA. Someone in Houston casually mentioned that they had just achieved another first—three outside a station at the same time—while Jenna, a bit frustrated that she always had to play backup, remained in the upper hatchway, ready to go if there was a problem. Victoria and the other two astronauts were suited up as well, for safety and in the event of an emergency.

"Let's make a pillar!" Victoria announced joyfully, and NASA broadcast her words to the entire world.

The descent unit fired its reverse thrusters, the reel holding the ribbon, anchored to the wire—the remnant of the first tower—several hundred meters below the station. The immutable law of action and reaction was, of course, at play as the ribbon started to spin off of the reel. Part of the downward thrust was counteracted by its attachment to the counterweighted upper tower and achievement of the first "construction tower," which had stood firm and was now an essential component of this second effort.

It was nearly all automated; much was happening too quickly for human reaction, especially in these first minutes as the ribbon spun out. Though in the silent vacuum of space, Kevin swore he heard a spinning sound, like that of his grandmother's old sewing machine at work. Brushing against the side of the ribbon as it spun out would be like touching a diamond-tipped saw: it would slice right through an EVA suit and the person inside in a heartbeat.

Malady and Hurt worked perfectly as a team, already positioning the second reel behind the first, ever so carefully handling the ribbon. Though it was more than a day before the second reel would begin deployment, they were already at work matching it up with the hundred-meter strand extending from the end of the first reel while Sanders, operating the handheld automated unit, much like an actual sewing machine of old, "stapled" the perforated edges together along the length of that hundred meters.

That took the better part of an hour to complete at which point more than five hundred miles of ribbon from the first reel had been played out, the downward thruster long gone from view except for occasional flickers of light from its thrusters. In space one could indeed see a long way.

Sanders went back into the station to recycle his air supply and rest. They were now on a four-hours-on/two-hours-off rotation for the next six exhausting days until touchdown of the ribbon on Kiribati.

While Sanders recycled his air, took a bite to eat, and hydrated up inside the station—it was indeed strenuous work that had at times nearly fogged up his faceplate—Hurt and Malady floated a safe distance from the first reel, watching it spin out, ready to react in an instant if something jammed up.

All the experience gained in deploying the first wire was now coming to the fore and it was indeed a handsome payoff, in the same way Gemini had once been for Apollo, training and preparing all involved for the "real mission."

A day and a half later the moment came when both of them held their breath. The first reel was just about played out, running out the last few miles of ribbon. It was designed to actually break apart in the middle and separate, small thrusters pushing the two halves a safe distance away, to be retrieved later when time permitted them to be added to the counterweight and sent up the side, but the priority of the moment was giving free play to the ribbon attached to the next strand.

"Ten seconds to second strand," Singh announced, Houston and Kiribati echoing her words a split second later, and it went as designed. The second reel, attached to the old upper part of the tower, flexed down several dozen meters until its own built-in thrusters counteracted the force of the downward pull. The surge was even felt inside the space station, but no one spoke or outwardly reacted, even though it was a bit startling.

"Kevin, this is Sanders. Time for rotation."

Kevin was reluctant to go off duty. He silently looked at Bill Sanders, who grinned and gave him a thumbs-up. Bill effortlessly pushed off and floated directly to the open airlock hatch, where Jenna helped to pull him in. He headed out to replace Kevin in overseeing the second reel playing out and stapling the end of the second strand of ribbon to the beginning of the third.

And thus it went, exhausting but exhilarating as the second reel played out, while far below the thruster unit moved toward the threshold where the gravitational influence of the earth would exceed the upward drag of the ribbon. It extended far down in a long curving loop, which, as it was gently maneuvered into position, with Kiribati Tower Control in command and Houston as backup for this final maneuver, would eventually lock into the same position where the first tower had once connected.

The only partially constructed platform that would have received the second tower was already beginning to rust. Few recalled now that a couple of decades earlier a second launch site for the shuttle had been built, out at Vandenberg Air Force Base in California, to put shuttles into polar trajectories for military missions. After *Challenger* it had been abandoned. The history of space flight had more than one such half-constructed dream, abandoned and rusting away.

But the experience and training gained in building Pillar One was now applied to the far more sturdy and complex second attempt. However, this attempt, particularly at this stage was as fraught with peril as the first.

But this time NASA was behind the effort.

All of its tracking facilities, augmented by military tracking, were now at work, along with the cooperation of the EU space program and even the Russians and Chinese. A few phone calls from the president of the United States could indeed work wonders at times, and she had made it forcefully clear that their help now would be a debt that NASA and America would long remember.

And there went by other channels another clear message as well.

Two American Aegis-class ships now cruised off of Kiribati along with the new British ship *Diamond*, which boasted the most sophisticated antimissile systems in the world. If any state, real or underground, tried another attack, the warning was clear: the missile would be taken down and whoever had launched it hunted down with complete annihilation of the port facilities that sent out the attacking ship. There would be no repeat of the last incident, not with the whole world watching.

And so the second reel of ribbon became the third, gravity now increasingly influencing the flight of the descent stage, ribbon spinning out at a constant rate. When not actually connecting reels together, the three space walkers remained "outside," monitoring the paying out of ribbon in case a reel jammed.

They had a backup plan in the event a reel did jam up without hope of freeing it. They would quickly shift into place the one reserve reel, staple it to the deploying unit, and cut the jammed reel free of the sequence, then sort out the jam later without the pressure that Singh and Kevin had faced with the first such attempt.

They would only have minutes to do so, because with a jam, the tensile stress would build up quickly to the snapping point.

As they floated hour after hour outside the hatchway, watching the reels deploying ribbon, Kevin made more than a few private comments on the comm link about their sanitary state after days in EVA suits. At one point he even threatened to go to the public link on that issue, but of course did not do so.

And then, as the third reel played out, that old law that if anything can go wrong it will go wrong at last came into play.

Kevin and Sanders were inside, changing out and getting a bite to eat while Hurt monitored the deployment and Jenna kept watch from the upper-level open hatchway, when it hit.

They could feel the lurch as the reel silently screeched to a stop, a kink in the ribbon or overlap jamming it up. The sudden stop jarred the entire station, knocking Victoria out of a half sleep, Kevin already reacting, shouting for Jenna to help him and Sanders to get their helmets on.

The entire crew did have upper and lower EVA suits on as a safety precaution in case of some catastrophic event, and Singh shouted for the rest of them to be ready to head to the emergency escape capsules. Victoria ignored her orders, bringing Singh's helmet over, offering to help her put it back on, but Singh shook her head.

"I need to see clearly," she snapped. Victoria floated behind her, watching the cam link. Reel number three had completely seized up. Data readouts were showing there was still slack in the ribbon, as had been programmed in—another lesson based on the first wire deployment—but it would start to tense up within the hour as the downward pull of the thruster continued. A few hurried words with Kiribati and Houston. They vetoed shutting down the downward thruster: the complexity of the calculations regarding its final descent were based upon regular burns, and it would be a nightmare to try to recalculate it all if deployment stopped at this crucial stage, and might even throw the entire mission off. If their team could cut reel three free and replace it with the backup reel, they could continue as planned.

Sanders and Malady were already out the upper hatch, and Jenna, disobeying procedures, went out as well. Hurt was already on the emergency backup reel, struggling to maneuver it into position, hook it to the wire that secured the station and the entire upper half of what had been the old tower in place, shouting for Sanders to be ready to cut reel three free and just push the damn thing out of the way while he and Malady stapled the backup reel into place and started it spinning.

They were five minutes into the crisis when Sanders announced that the third reel was free.

It was proof yet again that no matter how many billions might be spent on robotics, when a crisis came, nothing counted more than an astronaut on hand to take control of the situation and see it through when quite literally seconds counted.

Victoria struggled with two entirely contradictory thoughts, wanting to cry out to the three of them that their safety came first, but knowing enough to leave this to Singh and the team outside. If reel three was cut away but the backup reel of ribbon was not securely stapled onto what had already been deployed, the entire mission would be a failure. If that happened, how could she ever go back down to earth and appeal for another year of mission time, tens of billions of dollars for replacement ribbon, and tens of billions more for future launches at a quarter of a million dollars per kilo to haul it all up to try again? The dream would die, and not even the political power of a pro-space president could overcome such a disaster when the likes of Garlin and even the lame duck Proxley were in the wings.

And yet she wanted to scream for them to know that the clock was running and tens of billions—in fact, the entire dream for the future—was at stake. She raged inwardly that she was not out there, properly trained to put her life on the line, rather than just be in the way. Part of the ribbon could lash back, the reel itself could tear apart, and after months aloft with them, they were as dear to her as any friends she had ever had in her life.

"God be with you and be careful," she finally whispered over the chatter of voices as the three, with Jenna floating half inside the airlock as backup, struggled with the problem.

"OK. I got the first staple from the backup secured," Hurt announced, breathing hard. "Sanders, give me that damn machine. Kevin, I need a little more slack on the backup line."

"Rog that," both said, and she saw on the cam unit that Sanders was handing over the automated stapler, Malady working frantically to laminate the backup reel onto the ribbon that had been deployed out.

There was one more crew member on board, Fredericks, but within days of their arrival he had indeed gone "spacey," and she looked over at him angrily. He was supposed to be the system maintenance expert for the station, a communications and computer expert, and a backup medic. He could be out there as well lending a hand, but instead he had just been told to stay out of the way. How he had ever become a finalist for this mission was beyond her. When he did speak to the rest of the crew prior to this crisis, it was about how many days left before he could go home.

She wanted to shout at him get out there and help, but knew his presence would be far more of a hindrance than a help, and turned her attention away from where he simply floated near Singh, trying to look as if he were somehow helping her.

"Getting it," Malady announced. "Getting it. OK, cut the dead reel free. We're getting a good connection. Hurt, just keep it steady. I need clean openings between the perforations."

"Doing the best I can," Hurt gasped. "Fogging up a bit here."

"Just get it done."

"*Station One*"—it was Kiribati—"we're getting a fairly good radar read. You got a bit of a backlash, a mild harmonic coming up the line from the sudden stop of deployment. Be ready for it."

"How we doing, Sanders?" Malady cried.

"Ready to cut free when you are."

"Cut it!"

Sanders was using nanotube-coated clippers—the sharpest tool to be found on earth or in space—and began snipping through the jammed ribbon. After several seconds of struggling, he clipped it free.

Only seconds later the harmonic wave from the jam hit, a whiplike movement racing up the ribbon.

The shifting ribbon just severed by Sanders cut across Hurt's leg and, with the ever-so-dangerous ease of a filament of carbon nanotubing shifting sideways, easily slipped through his EVA suit at mid-thigh, laying it wide open, then cutting clean across the even more fragile flesh of his leg, amputating it just above the knee, then across the rest of the suit. He looked down at his severed leg tumbling off with absolute disbelief. He felt no real pain, which in those last few seconds actually surprised him. There had been gallows humor among those training to work the tower that to be cut in half by a fiber, a thousand times sharper than a razor, there would be no real pain for a moment, and by the time it did start to register you would be spaced anyhow.

He tumbled free from the ribbon, a moment of watching in fascination as the blood pulsing from his femoral artery hit the vacuum and temperature of space, appeared to freeze into globules of red, and then "boiled" away into mist. The air of his suit rushed out—the cut was above the knee pressure cuff that had purchased precious seconds for Singh—as he drifted farther away from the ribbon, the moisture that had started to coat his faceplate freezing, then evaporating, then the air within his lungs being sucked out. There was barely time for him to gasp out, "Hey, Dad, got higher than you"—his father had been a Royal Air Force pilot—and then unconsciousness mercifully hit.

He never saw Sanders falling away from the ribbon as well, hand gone, sliced clean away as Hurt's leg had been. Sanders at least had enough time for a few less eloquent and far more graphic expletives.

Between the two of them, the reel was spinning clear and free. Jenna floated up, nearly getting caught by the separated ribbon, missing it by just inches, Singh screaming a warning to her. She grabbed hold of Sanders, emergency patch already out. In those few seconds she had been forced to make a terrible decision: even though Hurt was closer, when it came to deciding whether to slam a patch onto a torn suit the diameter at mid-thigh versus Sanders losing a hand, she knew where she had some hope of doing something right.

The patch over Sanders's suit mushroomed outward from the pressure within. She kept a hand over it.

"Kevin, get us the hell in!"

Kevin carefully maneuvered, avoiding the ribbon from the replacement reel, which was spinning outward in a blur, grabbed Jenna by a leg, and pulled her across. Singh shouted another warning, but they were clear of the ribbon.

Victoria, fully suited up, had broken the hatch open to the upper level the moment Singh announced depressurization was complete and had her own helmet on; Fredericks, stirring from his lethargy, following her.

She wasn't sure what to do next; she had never trained for this but knew enough to reach up and hold on to Sanders's legs as he drifted down to the airlock opening, pulling him in before guiding in Jenna and then Malady.

"Hatch closed!" Victoria shouted. "Give us pressure!"

"Where's Hurt?" Singh cried.

"He's gone" was all Jenna could say. "Now give us pressure, damn it!"

Victoria could feel the rush of air flooding the upper deck, Jenna hovering over Sanders, who was cursing at just how damn stupid he was. Once near equalized, Victoria helped Jenna pull off Sanders's helmet, then the mangled upper half of his EVA suit. Blood spilled out in a torrent, floating about. Jenna snatched an emergency first aid kit from the wall near the hatchway.

She wrapped a tourniquet around the lower arm, clamping it down, then checked a vial of morphine. The first aid kit was designed to always be sealed and pressurized, but after more than three years, were the medications within still viable? She didn't waste time debating, jamming the syrette into Sanders's upper arm. Seconds later he started to relax, thank God.

"Stupid damn mistake" was all he could say; then he looked around and asked, "Where's Maury?"

No one spoke, and as the morphine and shock hit, he began to drift.

"Get him down to the lower bay," Jenna said. "Singh is trained in this; she should be able to get the artery tied off."

She didn't even bother to mention Fredericks. Singh knew what to do.

Then she lowered her voice.

"I pray he didn't rupture his lungs with the rapid depressurization. We got to get him below now."

Checking that the lower bay was again pressurized, they gently guided him through the now open airlock, Singh angling him over to her bunk. Victoria following.

"We got to get him back down to earth now," Jenna said.

"Even at maximum trajectory, that is still more than a day off," Singh replied, not even bothering to look up at Victoria as she opened up the full emergency surgical pack and asked Victoria to hold Sanders's arm steady, whispering reassurances to him as he floated in and out of consciousness.

She leaned close to his face, running a finger into his mouth, asking him to breathe deeply, a look of relief, no blood indicating a rupture of his lungs . . . so far.

"We get him down as quick as possible," Victoria repeated.

Singh looked up at Victoria.

"And?"

"And what?"

A moment of silence.

"We still need to lock that fourth reel in place."

My God, Victoria thought. *They are looking at me to give the order to keep this mission going after what just happened.* To add to the horror of it all, as she looked past Singh to the porthole in her bunk, she caught a glimpse of Hurt—fortunately for him, now dead—slowly tumbling away, end over end. She prayed that no cam unit about the ship was recording that, and if so, for the sake of common decency to his family, that someone on the ground was erasing the feed.

No one spoke, but all eyes were on her except Singh's; she was hunched over Sanders, trying with shaky hands to reach for the severed main artery in order to clamp it off.

Victoria, wide-eyed, watched her at work, spared a quick glance at the partial boot that covered Singh's foot, a victim as well of this same tower. And yet here she was still.

"Suit up," Malady said, breaking the silence. "Look, Victoria, I like you; you're a helluva leader. All I ask up here, though, is that we get along, and right now you listen damn carefully to me. Singh is in command here now and I'm taking charge of the EVA. We're hooking up the next reel, then we can stand down."

Fredericks, after totally freezing up on his first EVA and having to be nearly carried in by Kevin, had become increasingly withdrawn. The death of Hurt and the near death of Sanders had totally unnerved him, and Singh ordered him off the deck and back into the capsule that had brought them aloft, but even as he went up and into that unit, she carefully punched in overrides to prevent him from doing anything stupid, such as just unlatching the capsule and heading back down to earth on his own.

Singh had to resume her post after performing emergency surgery that successfully clamped off the main and secondary arteries, and all agreed that Jenna should stay with Sanders.

And so, under Kevin's direction, Victoria—while her mother, Franklin, and hundreds of millions of others on the ground who looked at her more as the CEO or scientist type held their breath—was walked through the paces of becoming an EVA astronaut on the most dangerous mission ever attempted in space.

Without a three-man team, there was no room for rotation or the least bit of rest.

Victoria learned a surprising truth in the hours ahead. Working in zero gravity—as in the famous mission where a lone astronaut had manhandled the massive bulk of the entire Hubble Space Telescope about as if it was a toy—had looked all so easy, but it was not. Though objects might appear weightless in space, they still had mass which resisted movement. It was hard and laborious to find a stable platform to anchor oneself to while trying to staple a ribbon from one reel onto the ribbon of another. And all the while, all she had to do was look to one side and see the body of a friend slowly drifting off and Malady would openly curse at her to stay focused and get this job done.

The first time Malady left her alone to go in and resupply on air, fuel for his small backpack, and water to keep hydrated, she did have a moment of terror. Only a few meters away, the reel was spinning out ribbon at blinding speed. The background chatter of Kiribati Control, which had taken over primary command of the final descent, kept running off the figures of descent rate and deviation from target, then suddenly, in a heart-skipping moment, reported that some space debris of unknown origin had passed within twenty meters of the ribbon.

She cautiously held the two ribbons together as Malady stapled them. It was all strange; she had a flashback memory to the day her father was humiliated by Proxley, calling it all an absurd dream; then, only days later, they were off to Kiribati: *Did I actually get airsick on a lousy helicopter ride?* she wondered. She tried to force the thoughts away, to stay focused on the mission. Hours passed, the only breaks the rotations when one went back inside to replenish oxygen, get more water for hydration, eat a tasteless energy bar for food, then come back out again. The recycling and climate control unit of her EVA suit had long since overloaded; she was drenched with sweat one moment, but then if she stayed in the shadow of the space station for too long, she felt a shivering chill.

The dreams of her parents; the years in which it was an abstraction; as she matured, went to college, learned to fly; the first internship with Franklin, which had firmly hooked her into the dream; the final words her father said to her, and then his last words to the world far below, stayed with her, and pushed her on, in spite of exhaustion beyond anything she had known before, while Kevin, indeed now a superman in her eyes, ordered her about like a roustabout on a construction crew, and she never once objected. The wisdom of keeping him up here aloft was now so clearly evident.

And now it was coming down to this. Stapling together strips of ribbon made of carbon-60 nanotubing, then securing the other end of that last reel of ribbon to the remnants of the first tower, the long strand of wire and discarded equipment which would act as a counterweight as the ribbon, moving with the earth in its orbit, would become a rigid pathway to the stars.

"Hold it steady, damn it," Malady whispered, and she obeyed without question, but she did smile at such a total reversal of roles between the two of them, and respected and loved him for it.

"Last stitch," he finally announced. "That's done. Now we secure the other end of the ribbon to the old wire."

She floated nearby, a few meters away, as he sharply cautioned her to stay well clear of the wire, which was a damn sight more dangerous. He was the one who had devised the scheme of actually weaving the wire through the perforations on the last strand of the ribbon, crosshatching it back and forth for a dozen meters, muttering to himself about his grandmother and how he never dreamed he would become a seamstress, while in the next breath explaining to Victoria what he was doing in case something went wrong as he worked the stitching—meaning that if he punctured his EVA suit, she was to take over while he made it back to the airlock because there wasn't time to screw around with taking care of him while the ribbon was still spinning out.

He finally reached the last stitching, taking the handheld unit from Victoria to "staple" a final seal across the ribbon.

It was amazing to her even now. They were working with what her parents first dreamed of before this project existed and even now, on earth, would fetch thousands of dollars per pound, a fraction of the weight of tungsten steel or titanium alloys, and yet magnitudes stronger. The very tools they used to manipulate it had to be of the same material, otherwise it would be like trying to use a knife made of butter to cut a wire of steel. Without her father and mother, Erich and the team at NASA that nurtured them and then Franklin, would any of this exist now? She knew the answer, and knew her life was on the line at this moment if she made a mistake. And even if she did make a mistake that cost her her life, as long as the ribbon kept spinning out to its final destination . . . it was worth it.

She thanked God for all of them, and for NASA as well, that in the end, resurgent, had come through for this moment, at times her comm channel whispering with some sage advice from an old astronaut, one who had worked on Hubble, of simple reassurance that she was doing just fine and to keep at it. His words were like a dream, a generation of former dreams encouraging the next, and she thanked God for it. She hoped that someday she would have the chance to shake his hand and thank him for his calming words at a moment when she did have to struggle not to panic.

"That does it," Kevin finally said, and then carefully reached across to grasp her hand.

"Time to head in?" she gasped, hovering on the true edge of exhaustion.

"Not yet. Your oxygen supply?"

She looked at the heads-up display projected onto her faceplate.

"Two hours ten minutes."

"OK, with reserve time, that still gives us an hour and forty minutes. Hand off the stapler to Jenna."

They drifted back to the station, where Jenna stood in the open hatchway, and she did as ordered.

"Now hold my hand tight."

Again she did as ordered as he gave a gentle push to his EVA backpack—not much acceleration, just several meters a second, but enough to move them away from the security of the tower and the station module.

"Switch to private comm channel," he said, as he reached over with his free hand and punched the frequency into the link mounted to her forearm.

"You reading me?" he asked.

"On line with you, Kevin."

"Just stay with me for this," Kevin said.

"I'm with you."

Somehow, in this last day of EVA, she had learned a sense of security by being only meters away from the space station. But now? Kevin seemed to just be heading off into deep space, and for a moment it was disorienting, frightful. Earth was "below," or was it above? The sun to "one side," or was it the other? The moon? She decided for the sake of her sense of equilibrium that it was overhead.

And they floated on. Ahead, a small dot of light was resolving itself. It was Maury.

She took a deep breath. She had thought across the hours what to do for him. She had decided he should be returned to earth for a fitting burial. His family would want that.

His slowly tumbling form drew closer. Kevin fired a retro thrust to slow, the last few meters barely closing on him as he finally reached out and took hold of Maury's backpack, joining the three together.

He did not turn him around, and Victoria was grateful for that; she did not want to see his face. Maury . . . the one who had broken the ice between the two crews with his smuggled offering; who had bonded with Kevin; who had the respect of all; who could outswagger Kevin one minute but be as quiet, introspective, even poetic, as Jenna the next as he gazed out at the universe . . .

"Would you join me, Victoria? We're switching to comm link 122.9."

She did as requested; a moment of static.

"Commander Hurt, are you with me?" Kevin asked.

"With you, son."

My God, Victoria realized, *it's Maury's father.*

"And his mother is with me as well."

No one spoke for a moment.

"And your request stands, sir?" Kevin asked.

"That it does, son, and thank you."

Whatever had been agreed to had transpired without Victoria's knowledge.

"Sir, you'll have to help me. Do you have someone who can read the service?"

"We have our minister Father Thomas Allen here, son, he'll help us."

Victoria took a deep breath, punching the keypad on her arm to block off her own voice while still listening as the minister far, so very far below read the traditional Anglican service for burial at sea, but changing the last words to "commend his mortal remains to the universe above . . ."

"Rest with God my good friend," Kevin whispered, and, powering up his backpack thrust, he pushed forward; then, while holding tightly to Victoria's hand, he let go of Maury and reversed his thrust.

She was glad her comm link was silenced.

They watched for a moment as Maury drifted away.

"Son, thank you." It was Maury's mother. "Miss Morgan, God be with you and your venture, and thank you as well. Now, return safely to us."

That hit her far too deeply, and she clicked open her comm link only long enough to offer her condolences.

"Commander Hurt, Mrs. Hurt, your son will forever journey to the stars. I hope when my time comes I have such a fate. My condolences, for he was my friend." Her voice was breaking as she clicked off. Kevin held her hand as she broke down in sobs; then, finally drawing a deep breath, she switched back over to their private comm channel.

"OK, my friend," she whispered, "take us back."

Kevin turned the two about, and started back to the station a kilometer away. It could be recorded that the two had just embarked on the longest space walk ever, but she would cut dead with an icy glare any who would ever dare to mention that.

Not a word was spoken between the two as they ventured back, Victoria at least gaining some orientation and even a touch of the old wonder as she floated across the heavens between earth, moon, sun, and stars, the future her father had dreamed of and which she now lived. *Was this your final glimpse, Daddy?* she wondered, and knew that it was.

Jenna helped to guide them back through the airlock, and Victoria was so grateful to get the EVA suit off. A brief argument ensued between her and Kevin, who had been in his suit without relief for nearly three days, and he had finally conceded that he would shower first while Victoria just floated in silence in the station, looking over at Jenna from time to time, Jenna giving her a thumbs-up and whispering that Sanders was stable and resting comfortably.

And for a moment she did wonder. Was this really worth the price? Haunted by the last words of her father, the stoicism of Maury's parents, the moving words of the burial service, the pale features of Sanders, in drugged sleep while Jenna floated beside him—even the nervous glances of Fredericks, who, once everything was sealed up and repressurized, had finally come out of the replacement crew's capsule, but it was obvious he utterly cracked under the strain and would now have to live with that.

Was it really worth it?

What would my father say of all this sacrifice? she wondered.

But as soon as she asked that question of herself, she already knew the answer.

Perhaps the fate of the entire world in the not-too-distant future would rest on what they did here this day. Was that not worth it? All that they took for granted, especially in flight and then space flight, had been paid for by the lives of others or by the actions of those such as Glenn, Leonov, and Armstrong, who came back, but also the crews of the lost Soviet missions, of *Challenger* and *Columbia*, and others who knew the risks but took those risks. For those who lived, and those who gave their lives for what they believed in, would any complain of their fate or demand a retreat from what they had accomplished?

That was what gave Maury's parents strength, what had given her father strength, and what now must give her strength.

"The descent ribbon is 1,000 meters from docking," Singh announced, but she barely looked over; instead, her gaze focused on the large porthole and the distant earth below.

"All systems nominal. This one is going smoothly: fuel still at 6 percent, more than enough reserve. Two hundred meters, five meters down per second, four meters off target at 322 degrees but adjusting.

"On target, fifty meters . . . forty meters, retro fire decreasing descent rate. Ten meters . . . Five . . .

"We got dock and latch secure! Pillar Two is secured!" Singh cried, actually rising up out of her chair, looking back at Victoria.

And at nearly the same moment her friend Kevin unlatched the door to the shower and floated out, smiling, at least wearing shorts to be decent, his beard shaved off.

"The shower is all yours, Miss Victoria," he said softly.

"Thank you, Kevin."

23

Twelve hours later they had Sanders strapped into the capsule along with Fredericks, who seemed to stir enough to understand Singh's briefing on what to do. As the capsule pilot they hoped at least those instincts would kick in correctly. Singh had reviewed with Dr. Bock on the ground what she had done, and there were a few suggestions about ensuring the artery clamps were well secured and Fredericks briefed on what to do if bleeding resumed. On a private channel Franklin had flat-out ordered Victoria to come down, an order she refused, with Franklin muttering about mutinies and perhaps even firings but she did have a trump argument that she was now thoroughly trained in stitching ribbon, that without her Kevin was the only one with experience and there would be zero backup if Jenna was pressed into that service instead.

"Besides, I want to be up here for the first test run of my project," she said, and felt she had trumped Franklin with that one. Thus she stayed on.

Sanders made it down safely, with Fredericks all but silent throughout the descent, yet another drama that held the world's attention.

Even as his module descended, the ground team at Kiribati carefully adjusted the tension on the tower, ran through the calculations yet again with regard to potential impacts—there would not be a major threat for another four months—and the following day hooked on the first stitcher, which would double the width of the Pillar up five hundred miles from the surface. Another two stitchers would then laminate additional ribbons on top of the first two, doubling the thickness, and then the process would gradually work its way up the pillar. Kevin and Victoria began stitching ribbon from the top down. With only one more expensive rocket-powered supply launch to go, additional supplies after that could go up the Pillar.

They had a highly stable ribbon in place; now it was just a question of strengthening it to handle the first loads that would go up and down its entire length. The next challenge then: to try the experiment that Victoria had designed and insisted must go forward, and she would stay aloft until that was accomplished.

It all settled into a routine in which time seemed to just float for Victoria: a daily EVA to load on the next reel and send it on its way; some hours on her iPad talking with her mother, Franklin, and her various team leaders who were keying up for their test; and, like her father, hours at the large porthole, just looking out in wonder, and dreaming of all that now could be.

NASA's resurgence had been a source of joy. She was given a video tour of Goddard by her mother, introducing old friends who had been called back, and scores upon scores of new young faces who had grown up believing that space was indeed the future of humanity, while so many others became mired in dystopian nightmares. Now, thanks to the Pillar, dreams not believed in since the 1960s were alive again.

Her mother's video tour included a stop at Erich's old office, preserved as if he had just stepped out of it but a moment before. It was now something of a museum for the entire facility, and she smiled at the sight of it, remembering playing under the table as a child of four when her parents held conferences with "Uncle Erich," who always had a small toy or some such thing hidden in his filing cabinet if she was a good girl while he met with her parents.

How she wished he had lived long enough to now see what was transpiring. But, like her father, she had mystical sense that he was still part of the effort and enjoying every minute.

NASA was again the place of the can-do spirit, the dream factory, the inspiration broadcast daily to a hundred thousand schools in America and yet more around the world. Victoria was pleased with the new role she had assumed, of educator. She finally took on a ten-minute spot each day called "News from Space with Dr. Victoria," in which she went over the previous day's events. She turned her imagination to it, stepping way past the routines of showing how a "ball" of water behaved in zero g or doing gymnastics in the station. Instead she would strap a cam unit to her helmet and venture outside so all could see what she could see, leaving time at the end of each session for questions and answers and contests for students who could win a slot in NASA's summer education program, with an ultimate prize, funded directly by Franklin, for a dozen high school students to achieve a flight out to Kiribati and a chance to intern for a month on the base.

Jason had even raised the prospect of a climb aloft on the Pillar, citing how in the late 1920s the Boy Scouts of America held a competition in which the winner, Eagle Scout Paul Siple, went to Antarctica with the legendary explorer Admiral Byrd. Memories of the tragedy of the Teacher in Space Program lingered, but a new spirit of adventure was arising, and several youth organizations around the world indicated they would join in if such an ultimate adventure was offered . . . with which Victoria and Franklin readily concurred.

And, of course, some giggly fifth grader finally did ask the ultimate question while schoolkids around the world were listening in.

She did hesitate for a second when he asked her to show them how they "did it" up there. She finally replied she'd get back to him the next day. Down on earth, the media was quickly abuzz with anticipation about how she would handle it. She spent a day getting ready for that one, a show that she was told hit the top of the ratings with the school crowd. While discussing what to do the evening before that broadcast, Kevin, with a smile, offered to show how the "guy side of things" worked, which she and the other two women on board shut down without discussion.

The show the next day, with a rather clinical discussion of the plumbing aboard the station, was capped with Jenna taking a shower—fully clothed, of course—and it was a hit.

Kevin had grown far more quiet and introspective since Maury's death, and for a while Victoria wondered if he was starting to go spacey, and if so, how to talk him into rotating back down when the next crew came up with the module addition. She finally decided against it. He and Singh would stay on: they had found their lives up there and "there" they would stay. Jenna, however, finally announced one day she was ready to rotate off. It took some prodding but then the real truth came out. It was Sanders. There had been a sense that something was developing between them while he was still on board. He had proposed after returning to earth, and since for the time being he was grounded she finally announced that she would return to earth as well.

The weeks slipped by, the stitchers making the work seem almost routine, especially in contrast to the far more harrowing spinners working off the initial two-millimeter-wide thread. Meanwhile, preparations rapidly continued for Victoria's "grand experiment."

Her proposal had met with some serious resistance yet again: besides putting additional stress loads on the Pillar, it presented more concerns about orbital impacts. But she had argued that even if they lost the link she dreamed of after even but a few days of operation—if it worked only briefly—it showed the way to the future that the Pillar ultimately offered.

The next launch mission up was already being discussed in the media as perhaps truly the end of an era going back to the beginning of the 1960s—the drama of a manned launch into space. Certainly for some time to come the commercial suborbital and now orbital private launches would continue, but even those would die off as the Pillar was eventually opened to commercial traffic and the five-hundred- and thousand-mile stations opened for business. Granted, for decades to come, there would still be thrill seekers who wished to ride a rocket to space, in the same way some still restored and ran old steam locomotives or antique aircraft with just stick and rudder and "seat of the pants" flying rather than autopilot, but the days of rocket flight were indeed coming to an end.

But a heavy-lift vehicle with the power of an *Apollo* or a shuttle lifting off from Kennedy, with all its might and splendor? Garlin was there, of course, to lament that the Pillar now threatened the existence of this very facility that had at its peak employed tens of thousands. She neglected to mention that for some time to come low-earth-orbit launches would still be very much the norm; a new generation of sats would go up, however, with enough maneuvering capacity to avoid the Pillar and booster stages that, after achieving orbital velocity, were designed for safe reentry over the Pacific or Indian Ocean.

This last expensive launch would be for an additional manned module, to double the workspace and crew capacity. The station currently aloft definitely had gone beyond its intended lifespan, and everyone would breathe a bit easier when the team aloft had a fallback position. Packed in as well were the materials and drop units for Victoria's grand experiment.

For in her heart and mind, after all, that was the Pillar's ultimate purpose.

Gone, then, after this would be the days of ascent upon thrones of fire, and Victoria could understand how those of what one pundit now called "the First Space Age"—that of rocketed flight to space—would indeed miss those moments of high drama, in the same way some in the aviation community lovingly preserved and flew aircraft of a long-ago war and the "barnstorming" days of the 1920s and '30s, when they took off from grass airstrips in underpowered "tail draggers," while most others simply sat back and let their iPads guide them through all but the final seconds of landing on modern, paved landing strips.

The launch went without a hitch.

After docking, for the new team there was the ritual greeting of saluting the faded decal of the American and Kiribati flags, now joined by flags of NASA, India, the United Kingdom, and others, the request for "permission to come aboard" from Singh, who greeted them with a touch of reserve. Victoria most definitely felt that reserve as well after so many months aloft with her coworkers, her comrades, her friends.

They looked different somehow, a little too fresh, clean, even tanned, and she wondered how they must look in turn. Spending extended time in zero gravity, even when slavishly devoting two hours a day to the exercise torture machine, made one assume a slightly hunched-over posture, using hands as much as feet to move around, mastering how to glide effortlessly the length of the station by a mere push of a finger without bumping into others, and each instinctively understanding the habits and idiosyncrasies of the others. It must be, the four had discussed more than once, how it had been aboard the sailing ships of the age of exploration, with several hundred crowded together in a living area not much bigger than their ship, on journeys of years, but in their case totally cut off from any word of home, and how when they returned to land it would often take weeks, even months, to learn how to live and move about with the unmoving earth under your feet.

The new team, based on the experience of the last attempt at a crew transfer, and well briefed by Victoria, observed the rituals, one of them, of course, "secretly" breaking the rules with a smuggled-aboard gift, but strangely, this time Kevin did not join in other than a polite sip of the eighteen-year-old Scotch; if anything it seemed to trigger depression on his part. The new crew already had their bunk spaces aboard the new module, and there was a sense of remoteness between the two teams except when directly working together.

With the arrival of the new team and all that was packed aboard their ship it was time to test run her own dream of the future.

The test run required two distinct elements, one of which was in the payload bay of this final launch, the other which would be sent up from Kiribati and anchored at the thousand-mile point. There had been general agreement on the design of the first, upper-level deployment. But the second? What appeared to be the simpler, more logical solution had created howls of protest that Victoria's scheme multiplied the hazards it created.

But on her side it was suddenly quite helpful indeed to have three governors, one of them most influential indeed, from the most populous state in the Union, along with their bevy of congressional and senatorial representatives on board as well supporting the experiment.

In the weeks leading up to the test, an all-out effort was made to build up the lower part of the tower to handle the stress loads.

When she went out on the EVA to observe the unpacking of the equipment, she was a bit overawed. Kevin floated beside her, muttering, "Isn't this a bit much?"

In what were now the "old days" of the wire, it would have indeed been a bit too much; but after months of building up the strength of the ribbon tower, the stress load both for the lower package and upper pack she was now staring at had been reviewed again and again. It was, for her, the ultimate reason of the tower anyhow, and time to test it out for real and to do so quickly before the various protest groups—and there were many—were able to ram through some injunction.

The new crew member supervising the unpacking, Andy Metziger, one of the new crew members selected by Victoria to oversee the transition of this project from design to deployment, now chuckled as he maneuvered the "experiment" over to the ribbon.

"Doc, you ain't gonna believe what happens next," he said on a private comm channel.

Though they had gone over it a score of times in teleconferencing, he explained yet again that the next step, which was to maneuver the "box" (about the size of a small SUV) to the side of the ribbon opposite that to which the station was anchored. The two clamps extending from the box almost looked like jumper cables, with Andy taking over strapping them onto the Ribbon, then stitching them in place. Kevin, who rightly saw himself as the only true master working on stitching, floated a few feet away, watching and saying nothing, but ready to push in if he felt Metzger was doing something wrong. Additional straps, to secure the "box" to the ribbon, were now anchored in. They were down to a safety margin for their EVA suits of only an hour by the time this was done and Andy suggested they go back inside, rest a bit, recharge their suits, then come back out.

"Like hell," Victoria replied. "We got two hours, actually; the safety margin allows for an hour of additional air, I want to see this deployed."

"Your command, then," Andy replied, carefully moving to the far side of the box and releasing several latches. A panel on the side of the box lit up, looking almost like an iPad touch screen.

"Doc, just push the button," Andy said with a flourish.

There was a moment of polite arguing with Andy and Kevin, but this was indeed something she really did want and in fact had devoted her dissertation to, so she did not argue too long. Some wag had programmed onto the screen: *it's all yours, Dr. Morgan, now push the red button!*

Was it time for a speech, a comment? There was a comm link feed showing the operation, beaming it down to earth, and without doubt many were watching.

No, just go ahead and do it.

She pressed a gloved finger against the button, then floated back and away several meters, Metziger and Malady by her side.

After a few minutes Kevin actually chuckled. "Like watching a dozen clowns climb out of a miniature car!"

Not the most poetic description, Victoria thought, *but certainly apt.* What was deploying out of the box was a solar panel, folded over again and again. The mounting system was ingenious, flexible nanotubing that, once deployed out, would lock the flexible units together into a rigid whole. Stretched between each row of tubing, solar panels mounted on a wafer-thin Mylar sheet. In fifteen minutes, deployment was complete: more than five acres in area, a built-in guidance system slowly turned it so that it faced the sun directly. As the upper end of the Pillar did its once-a-day orbit around the earth, it would constantly track on the sun to capture the maximum amount of energy, except in the rare moments when the earth eclipsed the sun; there would be constant energy, no night, no clouds, no atmosphere to block the limitless stream of energy that had been shooting past earth since the beginning of time.

She looked at the monitor on the side of the box and gasped. It was already soaking up nearly 100 kilowatts of power.

Now would come seven days of fretful waiting. Once the "clear and operational" signal was announced from above, Tower Control gave permission to loft up from the ground the second component, which took half a day to climb out to its semi-permanent position at the 1000-mile mark, followed up a few hours later by the first two-man pod of astronauts to oversee deployment. The package locked into place; the drop thrusters were eased out and positioned.

But this was not the go-for-broke 23,000 miles of wire dropping down from geosynch; each reel was holding only 1,700 miles of wire. After all the years of planning, practice, and work in space, it almost looked routine, except for one factor: these beefed-up thrusters were deploying out not to do a direct descent but instead a lateral drop back down to the earth's surface, the wire they were carrying configured for superconductivity capability.

Once well clear of the tower, the thrusters ignited, spinning out their payload behind them, heading in nearly direct opposite directions from each other, one to the southwest, the other to the northeast, arcing away. The two astronauts in the pod watched, monitoring, and if one unit should jam and they could not free it in a matter of minutes, orders were to cut both units loose and return to earth, the test a failure.

For Victoria, observing tensely from over 22,000 miles above, it was nail-biting time. She had been there during ribbon deployment, and in spite of tragedy was directly part of the effort. This time? Well, Franklin had warned her that the toughest part of the job was not actually doing it yourself but sitting back and letting others do it who you had planned with, trained with, and now trusted to see the job through.

Touchdowns from the descent stages were timed within minutes of each other, both splashing down within a mile of their targets, where they were quickly snatched by waiting crews aboard tow ships, hauled to their offshore platforms, and firmly locked in place, the slack in the wires then gradually, ever so carefully brought in. The stress on the Pillar was clearly noticeable; Victoria swore she could feel it in the soles of her feet even as the tower ever so gently swayed in support of the five tons of wire, the load sustained not vertically by the centrifugal force of the earth's rotation but instead borne by the tower itself.

The anchoring of the northern strand to its offshore platform had nearly been halted by several protest groups that tried to maneuver boatloads of protesters in front of the retrieval ship towing it to the platform a dozen miles off the coast. It had been a close-run game of bluff and counterbluff, while overhead a pilot of a small plane announced he was going to ram the wire, until at last talked out of it by a protest leader who finally concurred that he would only succeed in cutting his plane in half, with the added threat of a Black Hawk flying alongside him making it clear it would shoot out his engine if he got any closer.

There was another day of calibrating, of testing, and without public knowledge a sneak test just to make sure the entire venture did not turn into a public relations laughingstock that would far outshine the legend of Al Capone's safe that had humiliated a then famous broadcaster a few decades earlier.

The moment had come.

The video links were hooked in . . . Victoria up at *Station One*—or as it was now called, *Morgan Station*. Franklin was not in Kiribati for this, having instead winged northward to Hawaii, where he was joined by Eva, Senator Dennison, and the governors of Hawaii and California, while in the other direction the president of Kiribati and the Brit and his partner now stood with the governor of American Samoa.

Now was indeed the crucial first test.

There were the usual speeches, all promising to take only a minute, but the governor of California waxing on for ten; many could forgive that, however. His lifelong support of space exploration was crucial when it came to the senators and congressmen of his state.

Then at last the moment had come. The solar panels aloft were properly arrayed and now pushing out over 120 kilowatts of electricity. In the long debates about how to send it down, the choices had ranged from laser relays, to fiber-optic relay, to superconductive carbon nanotubing. That had won out, for the moment, because of the weight factor. As the tower continued to be strengthened, eventually with hundreds of ribbons stitched together, far heavier equipment could be deployed for the laser transfer from middle and high levels.

There had been serious debate about whether to go conservative with this first test, and it would have been far easier to just spread out an acre or so of solar panels down at the 1000-mile position, but Victoria successfully argued to go all the way from the top of the tower and thus prove up front its viability along its entire length even though the bulk of the energy would be lost to resistance on the way down.

The trick was this actual first test of her "wagon spokes" thesis. For this first run, two wires, like wagon spokes or support wires for a 1,000-foot-high radio antenna, sloped down from the 1000-mile transfer point, spreading out 1400 miles in opposite directions, one northward to the Hawaiian Islands, the other in the near opposite direction to American Samoa.

For the first time in history, the world was about to receive its first "taste" of clean, limitless electricity "wired" down from space.

Though they had secretly tested it the evening before, there was now a moment of tension and then playful banter as a friendly argument ensued about who had the honor of "throwing the switch." The president of the United States, patched in as well, was offered the chance but she most graciously deferred, saying, "There is only one person truly deserving of this moment, and that is Dr. Eva Petrenko Morgan. And I know beside her with her heart will be her daughter, Victoria, and in spirit her husband. It is yours, Eva, and God bless you."

With tears in her eyes, Eva threw an old-style electrical switch, and an instant later the semi-darkened room in the governor's mansion in Honolulu burst forth with light, the same phenomena occurring simultaneously in the governor's office of American Samoa.

Electricity, only a century and a half earlier, hailed as the liberator of humanity from drudgery, had in turn all but come to enslave with the demands for more and yet more—which had, for nearly all alive on the planet, become a routine background of life, even as its production was increasingly threatened now blazed forth from a truly limitless source, solar energy harvested in spree . . . At that moment, all in the those two rooms looked about them in wonder.

"Is it really coming from space?" the governor of Hawaii whispered in awe.

"It is indeed," his counterpart from California whispered, tears in his eyes . . . and then he chuckled. “And by the way, since it’s an import, I think, my friend, with the minimal tax you can put on it, you’ve just balanced your budget. And I want a cable too.”

He looked straight over at Franklin and took his hand.

“How soon can you string a wire to California so I can tax it and balance my own budget, sir?” he said with a grin.

And for once, perhaps in decades, someone could speak of creating a tax that could come to generate trillions, and all were in agreement and laughed.

Even while those down below celebrated, Victoria, eyes fixed on the readouts, was already evaluating the energy lost due to resistance, an inescapable fact of any long-distance electrical transfer. She was a bit disappointed with output up at geosynch compared to delivery on earth, but still, it was sufficient for this first test run. Someday soon, the square miles of solar panels deployed farther down “the line,” transferring primarily with laser via improved carbon nanotube superconductive material or enhanced fiber optics, would radiate out from transfer stations set high enough that the “wagon spokes” could literally span the Pacific Ocean from coast to coast. And with this now proven, towers would begin to spring up around the world.

There would be problems aplenty: orbital debris impacts had become infinitely more complex, although to Victoria’s delight the Swiss had recently stepped forward with a plan for an orbital unit, armed with lasers, to start systematically cleaning up the space junk. If any other nation had proposed it, there would have been howls about it also being a militarization of space . . . but the Swiss? Of course they would charge a handsome fee for the service, along with a tax-free share of electricity as well.

And she knew as well that the full realization of what the tower was now achieving was truly setting in. Already political and economic commentators were chattering away about a third wave of the Industrial Revolution: first steam, then internal combustion, and now space energy. Over a hundred years of economic infrastructure built around oil was signaled this day to be at an end. With literally trillions of dollars at stake, even if it was the first step in a true proactive global attempt to control global warming, those whose economies had been built on oil, and with near limitless financial resources behind them, would not just sit back and let this revolution happen without a fight.

The Pillar, even as it was hailed as the gateway into the twenty-first century, had opened up a whole new series of questions and threats as well . . . but as a consultant to Franklin Smith prompted him to declare, thus it had always been since the beginning of history.

"Now, Dr. Victoria Morgan, don't you think it is time you came home?"

The oh-so-familiar voice interrupted her thoughts. It was Franklin.

"I *am* home," she said softly, "but yes, it's time at least for a visit back down there."

24

Sixteen Months Later

So much had transpired in the months after her return to earth. She had forbidden any hoopla with parades and such, insisting that her first duty was to visit the parents of Maury Hurt and then to attend the wedding of her friends Jenna and Bill Sanders, who had declared they would wait until she came back down.

As the tower continued to be strengthened, two more wires went out, these testing the absolute limits, one to Auckland, the other to San Diego. The Auckland wire had failed on deployment, thus necessitating the cutting away of the San Diego line to maintain balance with the tower. The new governor of California was unfazed by the temporary delay, given that with each passing month what went from test runs to true hard deployments with ever-increasing energy loads leapt from computer designs to realities. For those living within the Pacific basin, there were new stars in the heavens, now half a dozen square miles of solar arrays that, when the angle was just right, shimmered as bright as Venus with reflected light.

Upon her return, it had taken Victoria long weeks to adjust to gravity; even months later, if she awoke in the middle of the night, at times she actually fell out of her bed when, without thinking, she simply pushed off with her hands, expecting to float to where she wished to go.

Of course she was happy to be back on earth. There was Franklin to work with, time to spend with her mother, who had resigned from actual design work and now headed up a nonprofit affiliated to Pillar Inc. that was promoting artists and spiritual leaders to use the tower as a means of finding new expressions for their talents and insights. And then there was Jason.

That had been heartbreak, and she wondered if perhaps she was destined to be like one of the monks and nuns of old, her cloister a module up in geosynch. Jason admitted finally that he was perhaps one of those creatures destined to be earthbound and how could they even consider a normal married life aboard a module in space? Her heart, it was clear, was in the heavens.

She wept bitterly the night she returned his ring. At the beginning, when she was up there, her thoughts were so often drawn down to earth. But once back on earth, increasingly her thoughts were drawn skyward, and she finally came to understand that although she loved him, something beyond him called, at least for now.

In her work in the ensuing months, once she had regained her "earth legs," they crossed paths often. There would be an exchange of glances, at times a hurtful turning away by one or the other, but she knew the distance of the heart, which could be even vaster than the distance of space itself, was gradually pulling them away from each other.

Several crews had rotated up; there were now ten on board, devoting their efforts to deploying more and yet more solar panels, which were finally being carried up aboard the ribbon from earth, overseeing the ever-widening expansion of additional ribbon on top of and alongside existing ribbon and even adroitly handling the next impact; this one, by a micrometeor that was indeed fist-size, had punctured clean through two ribbons in the center of the array, shutting down all operations for two days until a team descended and in a little more than three hours had stapled on a patch. They almost made it look routine, and Kevin, one of the two team members, was, as usual, nonchalant about his effort, other than to use it as a continued argument for he and Singh mutinously remaining aloft.

And then the day that Victoria had dreamed about came at last.

Of course there was an air of celebration about the event, though for once Franklin tried to actually make it seem low-key. She wondered if after all that had transpired he just might be a bit nervous.

This day was to be the day of the official opening of the Pillar, its formal transfer from a work in progress to an open commercial venture.

NASA's role was transitioning now into a full-blown R & D effort to take the vast body of knowledge generated by this endeavor, work on it, improve it, and provide seeding efforts for additional towers around the world. The Chinese had at last achieved their goal in Indonesia, but were troubled now by an unstable government that on a regular basis threatened to nationalize the project. But in Africa and South America other firms, with advice from NASA—which was gaining prestige and respect around the world for its openhanded efforts—were getting set for development.

At Howland and Jarvis Islands, both American possessions, NASA was now preparing to make its own efforts at Pillar development, not for direct commercial use (though Victoria was quick to point out that a tower at Howland could act as a support relay, just like a very high "pole" to link to brace an electrical line over to California). With these sites further advances could be tested in structure design and the now very hot topic indeed of deployment of energy from space. The parking lots of Goddard and Langley were again full to overflowing.

The strengthening as well was for the lofting of the long-anticipated "Five Hundred Mile Hotel," Franklin accepting that the public relations value of such a facility would help continue support. Though NASA was less than amused, Franklin had even agreed to the first "space diver," at a cost of an even one million, taking the jump from that small hotel at five hundred miles, capable of housing but a dozen couples at ten thousand dollars a night.

Without NASA it would have, of course, been impossible. But on the other hand, the understanding of commercial usage was an interesting hybrid in which both sides were learning to work together. The famous actor and his buddy, an equally famous director, had the first reservations at the hotel once it was in place, and from there the actor had played his trump card, reminding Victoria he had once promised to pay for her ticket up to the module as long as he got first dibs as a visitor afterward. The actor and director had their slots for a trip all the way to film a documentary.

Going up as well to the five-hundred-mile mark would be her father's favorite composer, Constance Demby; she and Franklin asking only in return that it might inspire her to compose yet more dreams in music, perhaps in honor of all those who gave their lives since the 1960s to reach the heavenly heights.

The Pillar's potential was about to start growing at a near exponential rate. The critical steps of just getting it in place, keeping it aloft, and in a situation in which it could be saved even from a near total catastrophic collision with objects in orbit had been achieved. The Pillar was also guarded by a rotation of ships of the United States Navy and the Australian and New Zealand navies, and surprisingly, in a curious gesture, the Chinese had offered to help, as long as there was a clear understanding that their tower would be safeguarded as well.

As the day approached for her to return to space, she indeed felt torn.

She cherished every moment spent with her mother and working with Franklin. But the crowds, the media, the demand, which she reluctantly agreed to, to tour the States, and appear before yet another Senatorial hearing, were diverting her from the work that she wished to continue in the still-monastic-like conditions at the top of the Pillar. The comm links, the environment, the hands-on experience of being up there, she felt, made her a far better manager of Franklin's vast efforts than constantly being in the spotlight on earth. She could now understand how the likes of Gates, Jobs, and others cherished seclusion so they could continue to work. Jason had shared with her a quote from one of their favorite authors, J. R. R. Tolkien, who, after his epic work gained global recognition, had lamented, "It is not the interruptions that bother me, it is the fear of interruptions that are such a distraction."

The week before she was slated to go back up, there was a dinner at the White House, which was indeed an honor. She sat at the head table with the president, her husband, and their two wide-eyed teenage daughters, who said that meeting her was far more cool than some egotistical Grammy winners the week before. Often during the meal her hand would brush against her mother's beneath the table and they would hold tight, especially when the president spoke of her father and then her mother who had started the dream while still in graduate school and let their example and courage be a light to the current generation.

It was a confusing sea of faces. Heads of various divisions of NASA who grasped her hand warmly, the honor she then felt when introduced to the few elderly Apollo crewmen, one of them tearfully telling her "You've taken us back up, a dream I've harbored for fifty years." And then he embraced her.

And finally she saw Jason, standing near Franklin, and her heart did skip a beat, eyes going damp. There was a young woman at Jason's side, looking properly elegant for such a function, and she saw their hands brushing together. It was Gretchen, the young lady who had guided the first wire down from space. Victoria's and Jason's eyes met briefly; he tried to smile and she turned away to hide her feelings of confusion and loss, even though she knew the decision to break up was much more hers than his.

There were more ceremonies in that final week before heading back up, one that was particularly joyful: her mother was asked to be a keynote speaker at Goddard, to share the story not only of the Tower but of her personal life—how she had come to Goddard, what it meant to her now. Goddard was thriving, and as they pulled into the parking lot, Eva nervously laughed that it was like the days she had heard about, when finding a parking spot was a real pain. But not today, as they were waved through the gate and guided to the main lecture hall, though she did insist on first stopping at what had been her building. She asked for some privacy, for only Victoria to come with her. They stepped into the corridor, but news of her arrival had raced ahead, a small crowd gathering, some of them friends of long ago. She shook hands politely, talked briefly, and then asked for a few minutes alone, the crowd understanding and quietly dispersing.

She led Victoria down a corridor that she remembered well, approached an office, and slowed. Someone, guessing her intent, had unlocked the door, and a security guard standing farther up the corridor, blocking off curious onlookers and smiling, nodded for her to go in.

There was a plaque on the door:

The Office of Dr. Erich Rothenberg. Mercury, Gemini, Apollo, and Pillar Programs. Guide and Mentor to so many who were blessed that he came into their lives.

The office was untouched; someone apparently came in every week or so to dust and vacuum, but otherwise everything was in place as she remembered it. The fading photograph of the young German-Jewish soldier, a British commando in front of a hangar at Peenemünde, V-2 rockets behind him. He and Von Braun, shaking hands in front of the first mockup of the Lunar Module. A photo of him and his wife, shading their eyes against the glare, watching as *Apollo 11* rose from the launch tower. And then one that cut so deeply that they both began to cry. A photo of him, standing almost like a proud parent behind Gary and Eva, an infant Victoria in Eva's arms, and on a table before them his silly model of a tower made of straws.

Eva looked out the window; the tree was still there that a young gangly

Victoria had sat under, intent on her old-fashioned laptop on the day she and Gary had come to his office, utterly defeated after the hearing in front of Proxley. And then, just looking at his table that served as a desk, recalling the first less-than-pleasant encounters and arguments with her future husband. Her heart had told her even before he seemed to catch on that there was something between the two of them far more profound, and Erich knew it too.

She put her fingertips to her lips, kissed them, then touched the photo of him standing proudly behind them.

"Thank you for the dreams you gave us. Thank you for the lives you set before us," she whispered in Ukrainian, and looked back at Victoria, who extended her arms and embraced her mother, whispering a quiet thanks to Erich as well. There was a small package on the desk, labeled: "For my beloved friends the Morgans, you know what to do with it." Eva handed it to Victoria with a smile and then, as if remembering something, reached into her purse and drew out another small box, plain, battered, unadorned, and gave it to her daughter.

"I think you know what these are; you know what to do with them."

Victoria opened both, wide-eyed and in tears, closed the boxes, put them in a pocket of her blue NASA flight coveralls, and kissed her mother on the cheek.

"I'll see that it gets done."

Her mother's speech at Goddard stunned Victoria. She had made it something of a humorous talk at the start: memories of arriving there, the Cold War barely over, the hassle one day when an overofficious administrator actually tried to hustle her out as a spy until Erich intervened, exploding with defensive fury for one of his interns so that the administrator actually appeared to crawl away—an image that drew laughter from most of the audience, especially the younger ones. And then she shifted to what Victoria knew was in her mother's heart but had not been so openly articulated until now.

"Do you truly realize what you are doing here at Goddard, Langley, JPL, White Sands, Houston, and Kennedy, my dear friends, as you work? We call it the 'hard science,' the 'real numbers' that transform shapeless pieces of metal, carbon, and human flesh into voyagers to the stars.

"It is not just about going there and then coming back. No, it is about going and staying. But far more than that, it is about going and transforming.

"On the day Columbus sailed, did anyone on the docks of Cádiz say, 'There goes the future hope of humanity'? That a day would come when, rather than three small ships sailing forth, thousands of ships would return, the skies overhead all but darkened by thousands of planes to save the Old World from true darkness bred in the heart of our Europe? On the day Columbus sailed from Cádiz, did a single person in my home country of Ukraine declare, 'Ah, someday they will come back to help save us, to help us become free, and then together we shall work to go to the stars'?

"But it was far more than that—far, far more. It was to open a world; and, yes, at times the cost was tragic, and that must be remembered as well. But to open a world where any could speak to God as they pleased, and know they were free to do so . . . To believe that, though born in poverty, even born in slavery or the dark legacy after slavery ended, that their children might rise to dreams as yet undreamed of . . . That the grand experiment, never before attempted successfully, that people of all races, creeds, and religions could live together as one . . .

"And think of our creative spirits unleashed in this new world. The arts, the music ranging from the likes of Copland and my husband's favorite, Demby, to jazz, rock, and, all right, whatever noise it is that some of you listen to today with those silly pod headphones permanently stuck in your ears."

That did gain some laughter, more than a few who had kept one earphone in while listening with the other feeling embarrassed for a moment.

"Think of art and painting. The freed grandeur of the artists who captured the landscapes of the Great West, and then to film which at times could so enlighten and change us with classics that showed us the best of what we could be, or just entertain, or to serve as a warning, and, yes, some of them even inspired us to keep reaching for the dream of flight and to journey to space. I daresay many of you are here because of a novel you read as a kid by the likes of Clarke, Heinlein, Asimov, and the beloved Bradbury, or movies of starships traversing the universe that you saw as teenagers and dreamed you could be part of that.

"I am giving to you now, as one of my favorite creators of such shows used to say, 'presented for your consideration' "—and there was a chuckle as she lowered her voice, trying to imitate Rod Sterling—" 'what is ahead for all of us.'

"Therefore, my friends, 'presented for your consideration,' the challenge ahead for the Goddard team. As you do the hard numbers, as you work the science and math, take time to look out the window now and again, to dream, and to consider how all this will change humanity fifty, a hundred years hence. The depressing decades of a belief that we are in a downward spiral, of limits to growth, of eventual collapse, are over at last! My daughter's test of beaming electricity straight from space to earth has proven a success. Soon, rather than megawatts, it will be gigawatts and then hundreds of gigawatts. The old paradigms are at an end, as surely as wood gave way to coal, coal to oil, and now, oil to solar energy—limitless clean energy to fuel the development of the twenty-first century and know that it all started here.

" 'Presented for your consideration.' Dream now of how your hard work shall, for the better of all humanity, give us a twenty-first century that shall far transcend any century before us.

"I thank God for you, my fellow dreamers at Goddard. But I ask you at times to pause, to gaze out the window, and to realize just how wondrous it is what you are creating.

"Take a moment to look and to dream and to think of how different all our lives shall now be, thanks to your work. The dream is still alive and together we shall set the pathway to save this planet—our cradle, as Tsiolkovsky put it—and"—she paused and for a moment appeared to tear up—"who my husband quoted in his final moments, 'and let us reach for the stars.' "

The standing ovation echoed in Victoria's heart long after they had left Goddard.

Her mother then returned to her office in Seattle—to take care of a few things, as she put it—while Victoria finished out a whirlwind tour. She had forgotten how many promises she had made to visit various schools while doing her daily broadcasts, and was delighted with the way she was mobbed, and took a secret delight in embarrassing the brazen young man who had asked "how it was done" up there, reaching into her satchel and pulling out a roll of toilet paper and tossing it to him. He did get back at her though, by asking her to autograph it and then saying he would never use it.

Always her message was the same, be it wide-eyed fourth graders or AP science high school students. Dream big. The field was as wide-open to women as to men—she was living proof of that, as was Singh, still in command of the station above—and regardless of the world one was born into, the model of Franklin Smith. With the Pillar soon to be open with functional paying traffic, plans were already afoot for launches to the moon and the building of a tower there, to Mars, and some at Langley were pushing for more research on plasma and ion drive engines that could cut the transit time from launch atop the tower, without having to haul hundreds of tons of equipment upward at a quarter of a million dollars a kilo to what was now costing less than five hundred a kilo and was expected to eventually drop to ten dollars a kilo in the years to come, when the tremendous cost of this first functional tower was paid off.

With the high-energy drives, journeys to Mars, once projected as three years round trip, could now be done in less than four months, and there was now even serious talk about building a tower on Mars. The first expedition there had ended in tragic failure, a pathetic melodrama exploited by the media, but was not the first English attempt to settle North America on the coast of North Carolina a failure as well? With the building of the Pillar, transportation to and from Mars would be but a fraction of the cost envisioned but a decade earlier, and soon thousands could make the journey if they were willing to take the hard risks of the life that would face them there.

Even the moons of Jupiter were now within reach. But that excited her far less than the impacts right here.

The energy transmission from a solar panel the size of Manhattan, no longer as far-fetched as it once sounded, when hauled a ton at a time up the Pillar, could supply nearly all the energy needs of America. She already had some ideas for overcoming the final barriers to transmitting down such huge amounts of electricity.

The Pillar was just the start, not the end, and she envisioned hundreds of transmission lines from a score of towers. Jason, still in support, even had a popular publication pointing out how America, in little more than seventy years, had gone from but a few miles of rail track to over 200,000, and in little more than fifty years had gone from a flight of but a few hundred feet to jets crisscrossing the world, and so it would soon be with power transmissions from space.

On the day of the first test of the first electrical transmission from space, within hours the long-term futures market in oil out of the Middle East had dropped nearly ten dollars. It had been dropping ever since, even though for the moment demand was as high as ever and the race was truly on as well, with NASA studies in the forefront to come up with a comprehensive global plan to address CO_2 emissions . . . and the world was starting to see that there was only one logical answer, regardless of the arguments still put forth by some of the dislocation of "disruptive technologies." An argument to which Franklin sharply replied, "Do we dislocate now, or do we doom our grandchildren to extinction?"

She finally finished up on her publicity tour, going down to New Mexico for a few days to visit "her" research lab, where she met a delighted Jenna and Bill Sanders, fully recovered and with a prosthetic hand, working on packaging up the next delivery of panels that would now ascend the Pillar in a cargo pod. Both were on the rotation list to go back up within the year.

She spent her last day "down" on earth in an electric-powered SUV, just wandering out into the desert to be alone, camping under the stars, barely able to sleep. Torn now as to where she actually belonged. That night in a half dream state, she did it again, but at least there was no fall as she tried to float out of her sleeping bag to fetch a sandwich and bottle of water from a cooler. The sandwich. Jenna had hooked her on the darn things and her friend at Phil's Bar-B-Que Pit would ship her some from time to time, packed in dry ice. She warmed it in the microwave in the SUV, then just sat and stared at the heavens majestically wheeling overhead.

25

And so the day had come at last. It seemed almost everything needed a ceremony at this time. The NASA publicity team was delighted with the feeds that were being picked up. Unlike the days after *Apollo 11*, when the three old networks could barely give scant coverage, interest in the Pillar remained high, especially after the news of ten days past that an Australian frigate had picked up an unidentified sub moving toward Kiribati from out of the northwest, had aggressively tracked and hounded it, and, on orders of their prime minister, had sent a low frequency signal that the sub either turn about in five minutes or it would be destroyed. Fingers were on buttons in the event that the sub tried to launch torpedoes or anything else. It had turned tail and the Australian vessel, with American support, hounded it for three days as it tracked northwest toward North Korea before diving deep, then going silent. Declassified speculation was that an American attack sub was sitting within easy kill range if it should even twitch the wrong way.

Long-term passive sonar buoys, the first to be deployed in years, now ringed Kiribati a thousand miles out and only aircraft with special clearance after first landing at Fiji or Honolulu—both of which were transforming into major international hubs undreamed of only ten years ago—were allowed to proceed anywhere within five hundred miles of the Pillar. A fair number of people and nations around the world were starting to wake up to the fact that this was indeed their possession as well and a vision of the future.

As for the investors of Pillar Inc., more than a few were less than happy when Victoria, with Franklin's nod of approval, essentially gave it back to NASA to run in a cooperative venture. Arrangements were made that they would break even, but the Pillar no longer belonged to just Pillar Inc., which in the years to come would indeed run the actual day-to-day operation . . . Via NASA, it now belonged to America and Kiribati and, with those two nations working side by side, to the entire world.

Franklin's favorite quote, attributed to Carnegie, which first expressed joy at acquiring wealth, concluded with "A man who dies wealthy dies poor."

He had even sold off his collection of private jets, except for one long-range plane to get back and forth from Kiribati. And it was that plane in a service hangar that Victoria spotted as she disembarked in the stifling heat of Amelia Earhart International Airport in Tarawa.

Nearly the entire island had, of course, been transformed. Its now 12,000-foot runway jutted far out to sea off both ends of the island. Much of what had been one of the most bitterly contested islands of the Second World War was paved over with runways, roads, high-rise apartments, recreation areas, and a bustling prosperity. She had heard there had been some signs of societal dislocation, with some of the inhabitants finally denouncing the destruction of their way of life and moving to the northern islands of the nation, hoping to continue a traditional way of life. To Franklin's credit, with his dwindling resources he had tried to help with that, harkening back to his own childhood of being born into the segregated South and what life would have been like if someone had suddenly plopped down a space port in the fields his father and grandfather had worked as sharecroppers and his great-grandfathers as slaves.

The anticipated maglev that would take travelers and cargo from the main airport at Tarawa the short journey south to Aranuka was only half built, and NASA's budget was focused on the Pillar, not on any amenities on earth for future travelers. That would have to come from some other source; interestingly, a Japanese company was offering to finish that job—at a price and a cut of the transportation profits.

So it was a "puddle jumper" helicopter flight for Victoria and her mother to Aranuka, her mother holding her hand tight, Victoria without doubt remembering how this journey had once made her terribly sick. By the time they landed, she feared for a moment that the midday turbulence would hit her mother instead.

The chopper touched down on Aranuka, another island paved nearly end to end. The grandiose Gothic-cathedral-like terminal that Franklin dreamed of was not much more than a foundation, some walls reaching up a hundred feet or more over the main terminal hall, several complete with classic Gothic arches. It had an almost romantic look to it, more a ruined cathedral painted by an eighteenth-century artist rather than a structure that would still hopefully take shape. Work, though, was continuing, something that Franklin said, like the cathedrals of old, might take decades to truly complete, but once completed would stand for ages to come.

The dozen launch tracks had actually been laid out, and crews were even at work on two of them, a track for ascent and one for receiving descent. The maglev tracks from the island to the platform nine hundred meters offshore had been laid out but were not yet functional. Again, work years ahead. For now, it was boarding a traditional boat at a pier, flooding them with diesel fumes—she hoped the scent of another century soon—as it turned about and took the distinguished passengers out to the platform where, a bit to her embarrassment but also delight, there was actually someone with a boatswain's pipe who piped them aboard. She, of course, saluted the American flag, and then the flags flying next to it—those of Kiribati, NASA, and the Pillar, the bottom the curve of a blue-green earth, the center the blackness of space studded with stars and, bisecting it, the Pillar which looked as if it had been embroidered out of diamonds soaring straight up to the heavens, with the golden rim of the sun at the top.

And there waiting for them was Franklin.

"Request permission to come aboard," Victoria said with a smile, and, grinning, he embraced her.

"Permission granted."

A polite kiss and an embrace then between Franklin and Eva. Several dozen were gathered round. Protocol demanded that she first be introduced to the president of Kiribati, who embraced her warmly and actually draped over her a garland of flowers.

"Blessings for you, miss," he said, his voice husky, "and thank you on behalf of my nation. I believe that in the end you shall save my nation from disappearing. Thank you."

And there were genuine tears in his eyes.

The husband of the president of the United States was there with their two daughters, as wide-eyed and excited as ever—so much so that they actually embraced Victoria and laughed while their father expressed regret that "The President truly wishes she could be here, but other duties call, though she does expect to see you soon enough."

"I will be honored, sir, when I do see her again," and then with a smile added, "atop our Pillar."

Standing to one side was George, now chief of all ground engineering projects for his country and his even more rotund and always beloved doctor wife who had once taken care of an airsick sixteen-year-old girl. Victoria rushed over to them, hugging both, thanking them for taking the time to be with the group this day. Even as they spoke, the doctor ordered her to open her mouth and popped in two ginger root tablets "to make sure our favorite miss does not embarrass herself!"

She gratefully kissed them both.

The Brit and his American partner . . . they certainly had aged these last few years. They, too, had lost billions in the venture with the first tower, but were always easygoing about it all; it was, as the Brit said, worth every shilling if in the end someone did make it.

Then the other protocols of various officials, NASA reps, even the actor who had portrayed a famous astronaut along with his friend the film director, who both insisted she hold to her promise that they would go all the way up within the week. If two giants of an industry could have been captured beaming like children, this would have been the moment, but for now the comm links had been shut down for the sake of privacy, and even for security reasons.

She trusted these two, a rare thing when dealing with most of the Hollywood crowd, because their hearts, be it regarding films about space or the heroism of our military in a long-ago war, were good as their word, and she agreed to the project with one clear understanding. Any dime of profit—she was savvy enough to say—"gross profit"—would go to a scholarship foundation for the children of Kiribati and for high school students wishing to pursue studies in physics, chemistry, and aeronautics. It was a deal they happily agreed to, much to their credit, and in that agreement she had pushed along her endorsement that they deserved a trip up, which the director said he looked forward to filming as background material and even a documentary with the favorite actor providing narrative.

"Shall we get started?" Franklin announced.

She looked over at him and smiled.

Now here was about to begin the real acid test of their Pillar. Over the last year dozens of ascent stages had gone up, all of them cargo-carrying. This would be the first ascent in what in NASAspeak was called PAP2, (Pillar Ascent Pod Two).

She did not know it yet, but Franklin had stenciled across the bottom of it *Gary Morgan Two*.

It was a far cry from the desperate measure of her father on the first Pillar and was in fact the prototype that Pillar Inc. had been working on prior to the loss of the first tower. Two stories high, it was entirely enclosed. The upper level was fitted out with comfortable recliner-like chairs that could be extended into sleeping bunks, lifted almost exactly from upscale first-class on trans-Pacific flights. The lower deck had bathroom facilities and a small galley area. The traction unit was hooked to one edge of a ribbon, and would draw power from the megawatts of energy now coursing down the tower. No more jet packs and rocket thrusts to get started. For these test runs, it even had a very small third deck, just enough room for the occupants to cram in, break free of the ascent stage, and fall back to earth if there was an emergency.

Once additional pods were in place, even that would be done away with; if a pod ever jammed, another one would rendezvous. Future designs even allowed for hard docking so that in a shirtsleeve environment the stranded travelers could transfer while techs would take over and solve the problem.

Franklin, all grins, motioned for Eva to board through the hatchway, and she did so, smiling, followed by the Brit and his partner. Fuchida had even been offered this ride, but he flatly refused, declaring that even flying inside the atmosphere was unnerving for him.

Franklin stood behind her. She was about to step up the rampway into the pod and hesitated. Turning to look back, she breathed in deeply. The air was rich with the scent of the sea. She thought of a favorite play, *Our*

Town, and how at the end the character of Emily spoke of the simplest pleasures of life, the feel of flannel sheets on a cold winter day, the crystal purity of the air, the smell of breakfast cooking, the sound of her father's voice.

Her eyes clouded over as she stood silently, breathing in deeply, soaking in this memory of earth, which she indeed loved and was the reason she had devoted herself to what she now did. *Ultimately, even as we leave the cradle*, she thought, *we shall always remember it.*

She wiped the tears from her eyes.

"Are you OK, young lady?" Franklin asked.

She nodded but said nothing, composing herself as she boarded then ascended the eight steps of the ladder to the second deck, where her mother was already strapped in.

"I could see that," her mother said reassuringly.

"Strange, isn't it?" Victoria sighed. "A time when it was wives and sweethearts standing on docks while their men went down to the sea, knowing they would barely look back when they felt the wind on their cheek and looked up to see canvas billowing out that would take them to distant isles. And now it is us."

Franklin settled down into a chair behind the two, and there was a mild shudder as the ground crew latched the seals on the pod. Comm links flickered to life. For commercial flights, at least for the start, there would be a "pilot" on board, even though that was rather redundant; but it was something that would reassure the nervous. But for this flight, Victoria, the Brit, and his partner sitting farther aft were more than qualified to handle anything.

The screen on the panel in front of her flickered into sharp clarity with a smiling face. She almost wanted to groan; it was an actual recording of a smiling flight attendant running down the old-fashioned safety procedures routine, but this one took three times as long.

"Who the hell made this one?" Victoria sighed.

"NASA and FAA regulations as long as we are inside the atmosphere. Yeah, I know," Franklin chuckled.

Safety briefing done, they waited, the screen flickering for a moment and then a familiar face coming on, one of the Kiribati Tower Control personnel, a smile creasing her soft Asiatic features.

"PAP2, you are first in line for ascent. Cleared for take off. Have a great flight!"

They could feel a vibration as the pod was shifted around from its docking position and then a slight hissing of hydraulics as the ascent wheels locked onto either side of the ribbon, a gauge in a corner of the screen showing power up.

"You are go for lift-off, full power for ascent at five, four . . ."

There was no kick to it as expected. It was actually slow, stately, in the first seconds barely a few meters a second. She looked out to her left; it felt as if they were just gently floating up, like a bubble on an errant breeze.

Gone indeed were the thunder of rockets, the kick in the stomach and butt; a moment's nostalgia for that, until she looked at her mother, who was happily waving to those looking up and waving back. It was almost like a train of long ago, ever so majestically pulling out of the station, well-wishers waving a fare-thee-well . . . except this train was going straight up.

No difference in g's, and for a moment she felt the tug of the earth resisting their climb. She wondered if after being back down on earth she would miss it. Was she actually doomed between these two realities, never to know which was truly hers?

They cleared a thousand feet, ever so smoothly accelerating, again like a streamlined train of long ago that would ease its passengers from a standstill to a near undreamed of 120 miles per hour on the run up the Hudson Valley.

They passed a hundred miles an hour, barely a sensation of movement, but the already annoying computerized safety program stated they should remained buckled in until acceleration was complete.

A few minutes later, through 10,000 feet, now climbing at over two hundred miles an hour, there was a slight ripple as they shot through a tropical cloud layer.

Victoria just relaxed, taking it all in, looking straight up, knowing what would happen and eager for it.

Three hundred and fifty miles an hour at 20,000 feet, faint wisps of cirrus ahead, passed through in a second.

And as the atmosphere thinned, the acceleration picked up. There was no longer that heart-stopping moment of the call for "maximum dynamic pressure" and then "Go at throttle up." Just a steady, smooth climb upward, the ribbon straight above them a blur. A brief glimpse of a round object on the other side of the pillar.

"What was that, Victoria?" her mother asked.

"Just a stitcher unit on its way down on the other side of the tower, Mom."

"Good design," she replied after a moment. "Never could have gotten around that just using a strand."

Victoria laughed softly.

Now 50,000 feet at six hundred miles an hour. In a minute they would be at 80,000 feet, another minute beyond the edge of any winged-jet-powered flight at 100 and 10,000 feet.

"Mom, take a look to your left," Victoria said. "Franklin, you try the right side."

"The curvature of the earth?" Franklin whispered.

"Exactly."

He looked back at her and his grin was a delight.

"Now, my beloved companions, just look straight up and hang on. Mom, you saw it before when you, Dad, and I went up, but Mr. Smith"—for one of the rare times in their long years of friendship she addressed him by his last name—"this is a moment you will never forget."

Franklin nodded, reclining farther back in his seat, no longer even sparing a glance at the monitor with all its technical readouts, and turned down the volume of the annoying recording of the attendant admonishing them again to stay in their seats.

The sky above was shifting in hues. The eternal, wonderful pale blue of a summer afternoon, the darker crisp blue of fall and winter, now shifting through an ever-deepening violet, darker and yet darker . . . and then . . .

"My God," Franklin gasped. "Stars! I see stars!"

Victoria said nothing, just stared straight up, reveling in the moment, a sense of their velocity steadying; it would then gradually ease off as they finally slowed to dock at the Five Hundred Mile Station.

And then the timing of this liftoff truly took effect as the earth, in its magnificent and near eternal journey, rotated eastward at a thousand miles an hour, taking the Pillar with it, the centrifugal force imparted keeping it rigid as they rode upward. The horizon to the east, the demarcation line of sunlight, twilight, and night ever moving, as if coming toward them.

Far beneath them the demarcation line of light and dark moved all so silently as they climbed. Released at last by the authoritative voice of the computerized flight attendant, they unbuckled, walked about with ease, both Franklin and Eva laughing that they were feeling "lighter," and actually programmed in a Strauss waltz, to which they danced about for several minutes, laughing.

And then the demarcation of day and night swept over Kiribati, now over a hundred miles below, and suddenly the cabin was plunged into darkness, the earth below them eclipsing the sun, which disappeared behind the western horizon.

"My God," Eva whispered, looking about in wonder as thousands of stars just seemed to magically appear. "Is this what your father saw?"

Victoria smiled, no tears this time.

"Yes, Mother, this is what he saw."

She looked back at Franklin and stepped over to him.

She leaned upward and kissed him on the cheek.

"Thank you, dear friend, for believing in my parents, in Erich, in me, and for making this dream real."

He smiled, looking down at her with that same gaze her father often had.

"Everything we've been through was worth it for this moment. And especially now your thanks. I know your father is proud of you."

"He is proud of all of us."

She reached into her flight coveralls and drew out the two small boxes her mother had given her at Goddard and opened them up. In one was Erich's Victoria Cross, in the other her own great-grandfather's Order of Lenin. Franklin just gazed at them in silence, her mother coming over to her side, smiling.

"After we stop at the Five Hundred Mile Station," she whispered, voice choked, "I will continue on up as planned. I'll make sure these are placed where they belong . . . up there at the top of our dreams."

The three were silent as she tucked the medals away.

"Pillar Ascent Pod, this is *Morgan Station*."

Victoria looked over to the monitor screen, Singh and Kevin by her side, smiling.

"Good to see you, my friends."

"Welcome home, Victoria," both of them said.

She smiled and her eyes clouded over.

They were right. She was indeed coming home. This was indeed where she belonged now.

"Your father was right," Franklin whispered, looking straight up. "My God. What a heavenly view."